To MAR...

WITH B...

CW00422056

THE
LIFE MACHINE

DAVE PITT

TIME WILL RUN LIKE BLOOD

For Nan and Grandad.

With special thanks to Rosaline for helping me with every step of this journey.

Preface

The spider awoke to the movement of the fly, senses sharpening to focus on its helpless prey, pleasured in knowing it would feed again. With blinding speed it covered the space between, piercing its fangs into the soft body of its captive, as long strong legs seized the fly to spin it round for perfect purchase. If spiders smiled then it was smiling now, if spiders could see the bigger picture however, it would be aware this murder was being watched by a larger predator, but of course it's impossible to know what's going on in another dimension. Isn't it?

1

Alex lay on the white bunk watching the death of the fly, even considering the spider to be a fortunate soul, able to live its life in a web of its own design with no interruptions but for feeding. Nobody ever questioned its reasons for being; it didn't have to care for anything else, and as it returned to its corner with the corpse Alex presumed it also didn't have a memory so couldn't suffer from the past.

'Ahhhhhh...!' He sighed heavily in frustrated boredom because there was nothing else to do here; no way to measure time in this place, no beginning and no end, no alpha and no omega, just endless white light. The window frame the spider lived in was washed over with a brilliant white sheen, the spider was white, the fly was white, the room was white and there was nothing to see through the clear glass panes but a plain white vista.

He had 'maybe died' on the 11th of August, because he could recollect all of his life up to that point, quite positive that thirty one years of it were passed before he found himself here. It was odd that of all the beautiful memories he could have recalled there was only one replayed over and over, that argument. It had been festering for weeks as his jealousy began to rise and rage. Linda had come home late from her shift again, two hours this time, what the hell had his wife been doing for two hours on her own? Unless, well, obviously! This was most likely the millionth time he'd repeated the scene in his head, always hoping it would change, that it would alter slightly as he recalled some forgotten meaning, a softer look or a shouted word that could have been misconstrued or misjudged. Yes it had had been wrong to raise his voice, maybe a gentler approach would have yielded a different outcome, given them a moment of reason that could have saved the love they'd built, but instead they both stood by and watched it crumble. These same thoughts and hopes surfaced each time he replayed his marriage break up, but the truth remained that in the end there was only one way it happened. Feeling sick within this loop of frustration he sat up on the bunk and lifted his knees to his chest, he rocked slowly like the crazy man in an asylum, except he wasn't crazy and this wasn't an asylum.

'What the hell is happening…?' Alex whispered to himself in a voice he knew should be rasping and dry as he hadn't had a drink for hours. Immediately he countered himself for still thinking in hours and days, it was a total waste of the concept of time and really didn't matter anymore. In this place there was nothing but light and the questioning sessions with the Angel. He remembered those talks clearly enough because they had been long and exasperating, and well, when all is said and done you don't tend to forget a conversation with a real live Angel.

'Obviously…!' He stated under his breath then suddenly the door to his cell appeared on the blank white wall, opening outwards allowing him to leave. He knew the routine well enough and walked to the opening supposing there would be no surprises. There it was just as always, the familiar white corridor leading to the still brighter light at the end of it, and Alex knew inside that luminosity was an office without walls, just a white wooden chair he would sit in when signalled to, and in front of him a large white wooden desk which the Angel sat behind. It struck him as he shuffled along the corridor that he'd never actually seen the chair his host sat upon so decided he would make an attempt to try and get a look this time, although he'd hazard a guess it was wooden and most certainly quite perfectly white.

Alex stepped through the light into the office to find the Angel sitting in its usual position. It gestured for him to take a seat before slowly placing its hand down on the desk. It stared across with a look that Alex often perceived as a little fearful, almost as if the Angel were under pressure, perhaps on a deadline to get some conundrum solved. Alex had no such worries, in truth he was beginning to enjoy the joust and parry of their repetitive sessions, after all it was the only entertainment available apart from watching that spider catch flies.

A thousand times already he'd told the Angel the same story and it never deviated because it was the truth. How could you lie to an Angel really? It's just wasn't the 'done' thing, but then again maybe no one had ever spoken to an Angel before. Who knows? Alex certainly didn't as he waited for his beautiful interrogators opening gambit, and when it finally came it was hauntingly familiar.

'Alex, Alex, Alex. What is to be done with you?' The Angel spoke with a soft voice, its long white robe shimmering brighter than the light surrounding it, and full body length wings folded perfectly onto its spine, peaking gracefully up behind its head. Alex had seen them fully open a few times; he believed unfurled was the correct description, usually happening when the Angel was trying to exert dominance over the conversation. There was no doubt it was always an extraordinary sight, one that increased its already otherworldly stature, even though Alex now thought of it as more beautiful than perturbing with his initial fears slowly disappearing through repetition.

'I don't know what's to be done with me, Mr Angel' Alex was answering his hosts question with a hint of familiarity which he hoped they were attaining through these meetings.

The Angels face was gentle as it spoke, its eyes not so much.

'This ongoing situation is not a humorous one Alex so please refrain from attempting to title me...!' Though its voice remained indulgent a little coldness could be perceived when it looked down at the empty desk. As its head slowly raised those eyes had a colour more vibrant than Alex had ever noticed before, a sharp emerald green standing out in the whiteness of their surroundings, rising up to meet Alex's gaze and confirm its reasoning. '...I would suggest what we are trying to achieve here is quite the contrary to humorous.'

'I'm not laughing.' Alex replied with a straighter face than the one he'd previously worn.

'I should hope not. Now listen very carefully Alex. I have been as forgiving and compassionate as I'm able to under such extraordinary circumstances. I have given you the gift of patience and grace to help you find the reason for the true purpose of your being here.'

'...And I have tried to t...' The man started to say.

'Be quiet!' The Angel snapped firmly.

Alex felt rebuked and a little nervous for the first time since his...his what, his arrival, his death, his ascension?

Placing its ageless unblemished hands on the desk it leaned its whole body forward so the space between their faces shortened to about a breath away and thus the Angel spake, and thus Alex listened.

'Our moments together are perilously close to conclusion. You have given no satisfactory answer in response to my question. In fact troublingly you seem to have accepted this rather unnatural situation with contemptable ease. So I have to ask once more...what is to be done with you?'

Alex tried to look anywhere but into those piercing green eyes, yet no matter where he turned they were still before him probing into his soul, questioning his beliefs over and over, touching his sanity, but if this was to be their last meeting Alex at least wanted to clear the air. 'You need to know something...I'm really not religious...not at all.'

The Angel didn't flinch at that admission, no shock or disappointment appeared at the words; instead it reached its hand over and for the first time touched Alex gently on the face, causing a feeling both electric and warm on his cheek.

'Religious, what do you mean by that Alex?'

'Well...okay...I mean I don't believe in religion as a concept. There's no Heaven and Hell, I don't believe there's a God or a Devil and odd as this may sound given our current circumstances I have always seriously doubted the existence of Angels...' Alex pulled his head back slightly letting the Angels touch fall away '...I'm an atheist!'

'An Atheist...? Meaning one without god...a strange way to conduct your life and death wouldn't you agree?' The Angel stood up from its seat. 'It seems you have no faith in any religion or deity driven construct, to you science has all the answers, and I can see you really believe that, yet you've never been concerned enough to study it for yourself, simply basing your unyielding beliefs on...on what...a blind faith in others writings upon discoveries from Petri dishes and telescopes?'

'I...' He stammered.

'...Alex! I cannot waste any more of our existence together with your tiny minded ideas. I have no interest in what you accept or deny, just answer the question I have asked a thousand fold...' Opening its wings soundlessly Alex guessed they were easily ten feet across each perfect arch, with not one silvery white feather out of place. What could he say to such a beautiful creature who demanded only one thing, the answer to the question? 'Why?'

'I've told you I don't know why I'm here. The last thing I remember I jumped off a window ledge to end it all, forty feet straight down on to hard cobbles. I wanted to die, expected to die, I wanted to be free.'

'Free...? The Angel laughed haughtily. '...such an all-encompassing yet nonspecific desire isn't it? Do you feel free now?'

'No.' He replied.

The Angel turned away in clear disappointment allowing Alex to see the beautiful wings in their true glory from behind. Damn he craved to touch them, to stroke downwards on their silken barbs, however he countered that action by considering it could be unwise, perhaps even dangerous, to invade an Angel's personal space. 'Don't give up on me...!' Alex begged, sitting up straighter as it dawned on him this minute could be their last. '...If you say I know the answer then I must somewhere. Don't you have any special powers or magic that could help you find it within me...?'

It turned then glided round the table as its wings slid back into closure. 'How old are you Alex?'

'I'm thirty one, I was thirty one. I think I'm thirty one...yeah!'

'Yet still you believe in magic?' This Angel was getting annoyed. '...I will explain the question to you one last time. Why are you here? Not how did you get here or where is here, nor what am I or why is everything you perceive here white...?' It placed its perfect hands back on the desktop and leaned forward only this time with a tremor of menace. '...It's very simple...tell me!'

At that outburst Alex felt tears building behind his eyes, hot tears, those fattened tears that can bring you to your knees. The breathless kind from childhood when waking from nightmares or being caught out doing wrong and having no excuse, He fought them back with a determined will while holding on tight to his splintering nerve. 'I don't know why I'm here...' He gasped. '...I've told you the truth. I fell from a window ledge expecting to die. All I remember is the shock, like that jerking motion you get when you dream you're falling, you are about to hit the ground and your body shocks itself awake...that's what I felt...only I didn't wake up where I expected. Can you do that... just send me back...?' He asked frantically.

'...Yes of course I could, in a heartbeat...' It replied after a timely pause. '...but sending you back wouldn't answer the question.'

Alex knew he needed to strike before this hope of iron went cold. 'Yeah but that question will probably answer itself in time. Won't it? I mean I've told you everything. Just send me back and it will work itself out...I'm sure.'

'Oh you're sure are you?' The Angel spoke with a hint of mocking.

Alex had nothing left to give; the tears began to roll again as he accepted the Angel's premise, his vision blurring up as his eyes became glassy and warm, all of his weak reasoning and hope disappearing down his face, before being wiped on to the back of his hands.

The Angel looked closely at the mortal interloper's condition resigning itself to feel some pity; clearly this poor soul was lost and lonely, so through the gentle mist covering the ground it drifted over to the man's side placing its arm around his shoulder.

So it was that Alex Walter Webb found himself being comforted by his interrogator, calmed by his only hope of life or death, held by an Angel, causing his breathing to slow and the tears to stop as its touch on his back permeated through to his bones, filling his veins with hope, and his very essence with its light.

'Very well…I will send you back.' The Angel said with a tender whisper.

'Will you…really?'

'I'm afraid it is the only way we will reach a better understanding. So the next time you sleep you will awake where you should be.'

'You're saying I just have to fall asleep and I'll be home?' As Alex asked for confirmation he couldn't help but think of Dorothy returning from Oz.

The Angel smiled down before moving its arm away.

2

11th August

A misshapen yellow moon shone brightly over green grass where parents without faces watched children run on stick legs. To their left an orange dog started to chase an oversized stick that its one armed owner was in the process of throwing. To the right slats of a broken brown fence skewed this way and that like broken teeth, while halfway up a large black tree a blue kite appeared snagged, its white string hanging down, but with no one holding the other end. Standing in the shadow of a nearby house two policemen watched a small figure, it was stood on top of a children's slide and pointing up at the cylindrical spaceship hovering above them. A white and blue craft tilted forward in aggressive attack position, firing daggers down at the park scene, and three sharpened blades were frozen in mid-air about to pierce and impale.

The small man in his orange overalls hated this picture but no matter how hard he'd held the crayons or tried to draw something nicer, a friendlier scene, it always ended up looking like this, a slaughter from the sky.

'So Oscar, could you please tell me what this drawing is about?' A woman's voice gently asked. 'Do you know this place? Is it somewhere you've been, did you go on that slide as a child perhaps?'

Oscar Downes slowly focused on her voice before noticing the picture she'd slid in front of him. His mind flipped sideways and suddenly he couldn't remember doing the drawing. All he knew was there was nothing he needed in those wax scribbles so he looked up past her to the window beyond. No sound left his lips, to do so would bring heavy castigation; instead he counted the bars over the window frame. Eight again, always eight bars in the Doctor's office, almost more bars than pane.

'Would you like to talk to me today, Oscar?' Asked the woman wearing her name badge that read Dr Katherine Kelly, and directly underneath it in slightly smaller font, Senior Clinical Psychologist.

The Doctors patient manner in dealing with his never ending silence was impressive to Oscar. Every day but one, he presumed that must be when a Sunday came round, she had him shuffled into this office where she asked, cajoled, and endeavoured in her practiced way to make him speak. A hard and fruitless task seeing as there were no physical or mental issues they could find to explain his lack of speech, and it was now being professionally perceived that he was just playing dumb. Oscar knew different however, there was no playing involved; his ongoing muteness was born from the fear of devilish punishment if he uttered a word.

Not so long ago the Doctor had given him crayons and paper, told him to make a picture, nothing in particular she'd advised, just let yourself draw whatever you want, why don't we see what's in your dreams? That's what she'd requested so that's what he'd done but he always doubted she was overly enamoured with his work.

'Will you please tell me about this picture Oscar?'

Once more he considered answering, he always had an answer ready, but he wasn't stupid enough to upset the thing he feared so instead counted the bars while answering her questions silently in his head. Hopeful he would be allowed to speak to her one day, and then he could explain...

Suddenly from the darkness of his mind it crawled into the light, the voice in his head, and when it spoke Oscar replied immediately using his silent thoughts, as this menacing abomination needed no sound to communicate.

'It's important that you try to speak to me Oscar...' The Doctor suggested, completely unaware of the man's inner turmoil as the voice screamed in his skull.

Why is it important? He did you a fucking drawing didn't he!

Please don't. She isn't the one you should be angry with.

I know who I should be angry with you little freak.

The Doctor looked closely at Oscar's unmoving expression, fixed like this for so long now, six months since his arrest and not a word had left those lips. She'd been so optimistic when he produced the first drawing, fair enough he hadn't actually spoken but it was still a breakthrough, and although his face remained motionless those murdering hands had gripped crayons and created fourteen pictures so far. Admittedly yes over half of them were scribbles and indecipherable but at least six of them were actual drawings, images from within his locked mind, memories perhaps, dreams, aspirations, but most importantly to Dr Kelly, an open line of communication to the man trapped within. Those childish scrawls convinced her she was on the right path because it was progress, and all progress is good progress when your job is trying to understand a violent psychopath.

'I like the colours you've used, Oscar. I love the blue of the spaceship, very vibrant. Is that your favourite colour...?'

There was really no point in her pausing for him to reply while the voice was around; it would never allow him to speak, though Oscar wished he could at least explain that situation to her. Although his eyes didn't move he sensed the Doctor move around the desk, her face appearing right in front of him, and her warm breath made his cheek tickle but he didn't react to the stimulus.

In that moment Doctor Kelly suddenly noticed where she was and being this close to any patient was definitely not in the training manual. This was far from safe positioning when faced with a serial killer but the Doctor wanted to look deep into his eyes so he wouldn't be able to stare out the window, so all he would be able to see was her, and by blocking out all other visual distraction force him to focus, but this manoeuvre was high risk.

Oscar stopped counting the bars on the window before noticing from the Doctor's unexpected proximity how her eyebrows weren't positioned exactly where they should be. The lines she'd drawn on were in a nice position for her face but the top of the eye sockets where they should naturally sit looked empty and abandoned, like an old path becoming lost at the side of a newly built road. He took note of her light brown eyes and the differences between them, the tiny flecks of gold, and the blackness of her pupils taking in his reflected image

The Doctor studied Oscars face in return, only inches from her own, the small face of an infamous man, one who had graced front page headlines and filled the TV news every day for weeks on end last autumn. This local taxi driver had even spawned a documentary series on his crimes "The Edinburgh Serial Killer" and he was a cannibal, a maniac, or even a demon depending on which news outlet you followed; but no matter who described him it was universally agreed that Oscar Downes was an extremely dangerous individual. Yet here she was leaning into him with no restraints to bind his hands, and that was also her doing because during these one to one sessions she believed, rightly or wrongly, that he would be more relaxed without them. So here he sat free to move, to do as he pleased, or was commanded to at this moment

And then…

'Bip be Bip be Bip!'

Katherine jumped back almost startled to death, before shakily moving round the table to take the ringing phone from her handbag. After reading the caller ID she declined the call and would message her boss back later; she was a little busy right now.

Looking over at Oscar from the much safer position of four feet away felt a lot more prudent. Although being so close she had noticed that he didn't flinch when that ring tone filled the room and her heart with panic. This lack of reaction giving some weight to the theory that the condition he was displaying certainly wasn't an act; this man was definitely 'locked in' in every sense of the diagnosis. Yet strangely he would draw when alone in his cell, this picture of the figure on the slide being attacked by a UFO showing a little of what was going on inside his head, but she needed more.

Oscar was counting eight bars on the window again when he suddenly began to think of Dr Katherine Kelly in a new harsh way. The confidence and ignorance she'd shown by invading his personal space was irritating a part of him that really didn't need to be wound up.

Just strangle her Oscar!

No I won't.

Do it, she's nothing to you.

She's trying to help me.

By making you draw with crayons?

It's a medical technique.

It's a nursery technique!

The Doctor checked her watch as she put the drawings back into the A4 folder before nodding to the large guard who had been watching through a small window in the door, never taking his eyes from Oscar, not for a second. He entered the room as requested and swiftly reattached the cuffs, locking them tightly to the murderer's wrist bones, perhaps a little too tightly for some but Oscar never complained. Then in a secured silence the two men left the office.

Officer Allan Kosminsky, a six foot four unit of Polish Jewish descent who towered over Oscar as he pointed him down the corridor. This lump of a man was twenty two years into his service and had seen them all in that time, the psychos, the cold hard killers, the clever, the sly, and of course the simply bat-shit crazy.

Kosminsky had always suspected Oscar was faking this silent act, convinced that given the slightest chance he could turn, try to kill him and escape. With this suspicion set in stone he knew he couldn't be too careful, one lazy search, one unchecked pocket, a missing item from the cell meant that all of his painstaking duties had to be done correctly and risk free. He unlocked the heavy steel door and began his checks while Oscar moved over to the barred window. When the guard was completely satisfied he left then waited outside, the prisoner knew the drill well enough by now so when the six inch opening halfway down the door was lowered he put his hands through for the guard to undo the cuffs. There was blood on the prisoner's wrists from the tightness of the steel bands, but better safe than sorry…or dead, thought the guard.

3

Alex felt himself reawaken almost as instantly as he'd fallen asleep. His eyes widening as he took in the dizzying view, discovering the answer to a question he perhaps should have asked the Angel; exactly where and when in his original life would he return to? Well here was the terrifying answer standing back on the narrow ledge of the building in Dalmeny Street midway through his attempted suicide. He was forty feet above the cobbles, legs trembling, and his heart pumping pure adrenaline with a decision to be made; a simple choice now firmly back within his grasp...stick or twist?

He could recall his toppling from this narrow ledge, but now he was back he began to remember something else, a suppressed memory hidden away, a sickening emotion starting to twist him up inside. The truth of why he'd fallen was coming back into sharp focus, knowing that any second he would hear someone speak and that it was inevitable. Alex had no choice but to let his body become part of this reality once more, accept this fatalistic piece of human theatre would replay, but then it all became very real. '...Oh my God...!' The words were spat out and the rest of Alex's body began to tremble when the wind blew suspiciously around him, the fear almost overwhelming as he fought hard to stay still.

It was all coming back into perspective in ghoulish technicolour, his horrors resuscitated, and taking over to the point where only this moment mattered. Even his trip to meet the Angel, the months or years he believed he'd spent there were fracturing into smaller and smaller pieces, disappearing because maybe they weren't real. Could it be this was his only situation, the one where he stood on a ledge, a ledge he'd never left, because if it were true then clearly the whole Angel business had been nothing more than a coping mechanism for his mind?

Alex had to deal with this all over again, try to reconcile that one part of his mind was claiming he hadn't fallen yet while the other screamed furiously he had. If that was the case and he'd been here before then perhaps he could do it differently this time? Maybe this was the reason he'd been sent back, if indeed he'd ever left this ledge, or if there was even an Angel? God damn it he was struggling to keep any comprehensible thought on track, his immediate focus being all too real and far below him. Perhaps he could save himself this time if he eased sideways inch by crumbling inch back to the open window, to safety. Do it, do it now, he told himself, but even the idea of moving that first muscle became so frightening his body refused to budge.

'What are you doing...?' A boy's voice suddenly asked.

The sound made Alex freeze in terror and sickening acceptance that he had done this before. That was the exact voice he'd expected to hear, the boy was back, or maybe he was just still here. What the hell's happening to me? Don't panic, keep control, don't look at him, do things differently, don't even talk to him, and he might go away...this time.

'I asked you what the fuck you're doing!' It was delivered with a vicious snarl because this boy hated to be blanked.

Alex pressed his back hard against the wall of the building, the whole structure felt heavy and vast with solid weight seeming to push against his hopes, almost as if it wanted this human limpet off its brickwork.

'Are you fucking deaf or stupid? Which one is it man...?' The boy demanded to know.

Carefully, incrementally, he turned his head to face the boy. 'Help...me!' He asked through tightened lips that were speaking for his tensed and tiring body. The three inch ledge his unsuitable leather shoes were on became his world again as a gust of cold wind moved him, only slightly, but enough to remind him he was barely in control of his circumstance. He pressed his left cheek against the unforgiving stone while trying for his life to keep some centre of gravity.

'Help you...why?' The boy in the blue tracksuit and black baseball cap asked.

'Because I don't want to fall...' Alex tried to catch the boys stare but his teenage eyes were looking down to the street.

'Right, so let me get this...you wanted to die but now you've changed your mind. Is that it?'

'...Yes, I don't know what I want anymore...' The wind gusted again and Alex released a frightened whimper.

'Ha ha...I know what I want.' The boy replied coldly.

Alex looked at the familiar face two metres away in the safety of the open knowing if they could reach some mutual understanding then between them they could save a life, his life. So he tried to choose his words carefully to appeal to any semblance of humanity in the teenager. 'What do you want...err...what's your name?' But Alex's ham-fisted attempt to make a hurried connection was so shallow and obvious that the boy's mood didn't lighten.

15

'Fuck you...I'm not gonna interfere with another man's business and change anything. You gotta do what you gotta do.'

'What's your name?' Alex asked again before suddenly wondering why the boy had said 'change anything?' Did the boy know, was he part of this?

'Robbie!' The boy replied.

'Is that the truth? Is that your real name?' Alex asked hopefully, almost ecstatically for a man on the precipice of death because this was different to before. They hadn't spoken these exact words, the boy had never told him his name; did that mean things could change, that everything wasn't on repeat?

'Your name's Robbie?'

'No of course it's not you fucking idiot. I ain't telling you shit!' The boy smiled his yellowed broken tooth grin.

Alex hated that face. 'Why? Why are you doing this to me? You could stop it and save my life, all this can be over with. Just help me back inside...'

The boy 'Robbie' raised his hand to pull the frayed peak of his baseball cap down onto his shaven head, with the faded blue lettering on the back of his fingers spelling out his beliefs in love and hate. Alex mentally questioned the kid's commitment to one of those messages while wondering how he wore faded tattoos when he couldn't have been much over sixteen.

The true reasons behind his ink were really no great mystery; this 'Robbie' was part of the next generation, one raised on harsh social media and super strong cannabis, porn and UFC, ketamine and kicks. This kid was all about the visuals, the highs, the respect, and obsessed with the video games he played, relentlessly blasting his way through frightening levels of gore while crushing hordes of enemy scum underfoot. Hours into days he would sit around getting stoned while killing anything in his path for a better score or a faster time. So to this boy stumbling on a real life suicide situation was fucking epic, this was virtual reality come to life and giving him an ace story to tell his mates later. He could picture them sitting around skinning up while listening to his tale of how much blood there had been, how the sound of this guy's head hitting the cobbles made 'like a pop', but most importantly for his reputation, they would hear how he didn't help when asked. No sir because he was a fucking bad boy. Yeah in his dirty blue tracksuit and scuffed trainers he would jump straight up the rankings on the streets he slouched through. Those nasty girls would look at him with growing interest because he'd be the genuine deal, a cold hearted fucking legend, and one who they wanted to have filthy sex with whenever he looked their way. For real he could rule his circle of 'bruvs' and 'bitches' by undertaking one simple act, by doing what he was most experienced at, by doing absolutely nothing at all.

'Oh my god, please help me!' Alex begged feeling the tears building up again. So many tears just lately for someone who didn't know if they would live or die, or even if they were alive or dead, then he saw the daydreaming boy snap back into reality and watched his face harden.

'No! Shut up whingeing I'm not going to help you!' The boy smirked.

'So you just want to watch me die?'

'Yeah...yeah I do.'

'Why would you want to do that...?' Alex knew he was seconds from toppling.

'Don't start asking me shit. I'm not the one who climbed out of a fucking window this fucking high up to kill themselves am I...?' The boy was reasoning correctly and loudly as he took a cigarette out.

'I'll give you money. I've got err, err, fifty quid in my wallet.'

'Give it to me then!'

Alex felt it happening all over again, his knees locking up, his balance shifting towards the head, the break point from where he would initially begin the tip forwards. 'I can't reach it...it's in my pocket...but it's yours if you...'

'...Nah, you're alright man, I'll just take it off you when you're on the road.' Then the boy laughed at some personal recognition he'd just thought of before trying to explain himself '...Ha this is weird man...you know what this is like...it's like that foreign shit you know...when you think like you did something before?'

Here Alex was seconds from falling to the road but even now he still couldn't resist helping the boy out. '...Déjà vu!'

The boy smiled. 'That's it...yeah, something like that...'

Alex was losing his battle to stay in control as the first tear fell, skipping down his cheek like a tiny stone across a glass pond, and dropped out of sight. Savagely he remembered this exact moment from before and knew he would begin to follow it immediately. 'You could have helped!' He cried.

'Nahhhh...' The boy breathed the word as he lit the cigarette.

Then Alex's knees buckled sharply as he lost contact with the ledge and all control over his life.

<u>4</u>

Oscar Downes had never suffered from the quandary of loneliness having lived and pretty much worked alone his whole adult life, his hours of solitude were by choice and a pleasure, as he never struggled to keep himself occupied. Even during this current incarceration he could be observed day after day padding slowly around his cell, his prison overalls hanging off his shrunken frame, as he walked to the window then back to his bed, or to his latrine or even as he was doing now, to his only other piece of furniture. On this scratched and bolted down steel desk were blank pieces of paper and a plastic cup full of wax crayons. It was quite a long lean forward for a short man but he found he could perch on the end of his bunk and still stretch out to reach the desk for drawing time. He fumbled for a crayon and paused as he decided what colour to begin with, finally choosing the red one, maybe that was his favourite colour, he didn't really know, and any decision would have to wait as he began to copy down what he'd seen in his mind. If the evil voice remained quiet and allowed him he believed he could finish this quickly. Line by waxy line he drew freely and confidently, swapping colours without looking up, and he would use them all before this work was completed. The image he was creating came from somewhere that wasn't in his own memory, it wasn't of people he knew, and was of some place he'd never been. Throughout this artistic process of pressing down hard with wax crayons he was constantly aware of the guard observing him. He imagined this huge jailer gazing down through the camera set high on the ceiling, watching the screen every second of every hour; and who knew, maybe one day someone would play them back and notice something that Kosminsky was missing, how this emotionally 'locked in' Oscar, with his head down almost level with his drawing hand was smiling broadly as he worked.

This latest piece was completed thankfully without interruption from the voice in just less than an hour. With the crayons now safely put back in the jar and the smile disappeared from Oscar's face he pushed the picture away. It contained no details of his own life so he was done with it. He then walked over and resumed staring at the window, counting six bars on this one, there were eight in the Doctor's office but only six bars here, Oscar automatically and repetitively thought. This was his relaxing time because that other voice mostly remained quiet when he was alone in his cell. During the early years of its tenure locked in his mind it had been considerably more talkative. Those days seemed a long time ago now, over five years if accuracy actually mattered, and familiarity between the two of them had bred such evil contempt that Oscar was thankful when he could enjoy its silence. The voice only spoke loudly or screamed crazily, working itself up into a murderous frenzy, when he was near others. Even after all this time Oscar didn't really know what it was, or how it had come to exist, he had however come to the harsh understanding that the voice in his head didn't like other people very much.

The big guard sat playing solitaire on the computer in his tiny office, which in reality was nothing more than an old storage cupboard, a fact proven by the shoddily filled in holes spaced along the walls where some long discarded racking would have hung. Allan Kosminsky didn't mind, he'd worked in worse places, and he was used to it now after a couple of years employment. He particularly enjoyed the silence and privacy it provided, locked down deep in the heart of the facility as he was. In twenty two years of prison/psychiatric security work he'd been moved around the city a few times and thought at least here it felt something like a private refuge, a secure base for his many duties which for the most part he enjoyed. One of the duties he didn't enjoy however was escorting Oscar to his daily sessions with Dr Katherine Kelly, though ironically it wasn't the proven serial killer that concerned him.

Now Kosminsky had always got along with work colleagues over his many years of service, not buddy friendly with anyone just respectful, but he certainly hadn't warmed to this new doctor. A problem stemming from the fact he was annoyingly aware she saw him as just a big dumb guard whose purpose was to do her bidding. Yeah right! I'm a big dumb guard until you need me to save your life, he thought, picturing the potential horror show of earlier when he'd watched her lean right into Oscars face. For crying out loud the prisoner was a multiple murderer of women, he hadn't been restrained at the time and worst of all he was already in custody, so let's face facts he wouldn't have much to lose if he'd chosen to kill her there and then.

He tried his best to forget about the Doctor and sat back in his chair. Looking down he noticed his rounding paunch, caused mostly because the strict fitness regime he used to follow was now deceased as middle age marched over the horizon. Back in the day he would be four times a week in the gym pushing his body to its limits with a determined obsession, all that sweating toil giving him arms, shoulders and neck the size and girth that would take a long time to return to normal. He'd also dallied briefly with steroids when they'd been in vogue but soon realised they were making him tense at work. It caused a growing concern that punching walls could soon become punching inmates which was always a sure fire way to shorten a career and lose a pension. So with everything quit it transpired that Allan Kosminsky now resembled a mean looking retired weightlifter, which was perfect for the job, but not so great in the dating world.

He'd been single going on eight years, ever since Chrissi had moved to the USA rather than commit to a future with a big dumb steroid swallowing prick. The shock of that rejection causing him to immediately change his ways, the drugs went out of the window and he calmed down his work outs because he wanted it to work out for them, but it was too late. No matter how many promises were offered he was unable to tempt her back from Florida. She'd settled there and began dating a gym instructor, an irony unneeded, and the heartbreak had hurt deeply at the time, but he recovered from its symptoms slowly and carried on by himself. His single life had become one long routine of sitting; sitting around his flat until he went to work, where he spent a vast majority of time sitting down in his office, before jumping on his motorbike to sit down some more and ride home. He thought maybe next week he would sign back up at the gym and sort his life out.

Allan often fantasised that one day he would return to his flat and find Chrissi on the front doorstep, sitting on her suitcase, and telling him she'd been so wrong to give up on their love, like that ever happened in the real world but this fantasy was his and he enjoyed sharing its company from time to time. Allowing the image of a fantastical reconciliation to disappear he went back to concentrating on his important job, securing the safety of human life by making sure his charge stayed locked up in his cell. Using the mouse he clicked enlarge image on the computer screen to try and get a look at Oscars drawing. Then zooming out to view the whole cell from the camera above the doorway he found Oscar standing totally still and staring up at the window.

With nothing new happening it was time for Kosminsky to write his daily report, a demeaning chore that annoyed him because it concerned her; where everything and anything Oscar did or didn't do on a daily basis had to be recorded accurately and emailed to Doctor Katherine Kelly, she was strict about it as well, if his email was one minute late she'd harshly remind him with an instant message that read something like...

Mr Kosminsky,

I have failed to receive my daily report of Oscar Downes behaviour on time. Please resolve this immediately and be reminded I need it sent to me by 7pm EVERY evening.

...and Allan really wasn't in the mood for another one of those.

It frustrated him to think that if she was so bloody interested in finding the answer to Oscar's locked in syndrome then why didn't she come down here and watch him for hours on end. Oh no she left all the hard work to him. Finally after he cracked his fingers like a concert pianist to release the tension, and with a deep calming breath, he began another reluctant report.

FAO. Dr Katherine Kelly.

Daily report of the subject. OSCAR DOWNES.

Following his session with you this morning Oscar returned to his cell in an orderly fashion and lay on his bed.

He used the bucket once. Solid and Urine (4.06pm)

From then onwards he was in the window staring position he favours until around 4.55pm when he sat on his bed and drew a picture. It appears to be a different picture to the previous ones. I shall bring it to your office tomorrow with Oscar at 10am.

At the time of this email he has returned to the window staring position.

Regards

Officer A. Kosminsky.

I hope that puts a smile on your sour face; look Doctor he's done another crayon drawing that you won't understand, then with a flourished wave of his heavy finger he pressed the send button. He pictured her receiving it in her wood panelled office at home surrounded by thick leather bound books that contained all the studies of the human mind, and a resentful hairless cat asleep on her lap. That scenario caused him to smile because he wasn't sure why he'd added the cat to tonight's image, but hey it might be a venomous snake he imagined tomorrow, oh the limitless mysteries of a vengeful mind.

Glancing down at the live feed of Oscar's cell he saw him still standing at the window. The 'subject', as the doctor referred to him, hadn't moved an inch and Kosminsky wondered again what the hell Oscar was thinking about. On the screen underneath that image was the clock telling him it was 7.06pm, so another fifty four minutes and he could go home, but he might go to the shops on the way back and get a few beers; they helped him to sleep being his justification, so yeah a four pack and some braindead TV then to bed on his own. These familiar thoughts simply meant another shift would soon be over, another day done when nobody escaped, no problems, then suddenly with a loud BING the computer cried for his attention.

'What now?' He cried back on seeing his inbox alert flashing which unsurprisingly, but very annoyingly, was from Doctor Kelly. He considered making the self-satisfying decision to not open it tonight, to make her wait; however he was always a lot crueller in thought than deed, so being a considerate professional he clicked on it.

FAO Officer Kosminky.

Why has she spelt my bloody name wrong, are you deliberately winding me up woman? Kosminsky was enraged by the message already and it was only the opening line, thinking maybe he should press close and save himself more stress.

Would you please describe the picture the subject has drawn, as best you can, I need this information ASAP.

Yeah there it is! He knew he should have closed it because now he was stuck here feeling more aggravated. '...As best I can...what the hell does that mean? Is she worried I might struggle to find words to fully describe a drawing that resembles a child's attempt at best. Oh my god! This woman is doing my head in...!' His fists clenched as he looked at the wall. '...ASAP, A...S...A... fucking P...!' Seriously every single character she'd typed twisted him up but he wasn't going to lash out. No sir those days were gone, he was calm, he was in control, and he could do this. '...Okay I'll do exactly what you want and describe it...as best I can ...ASAP!' He began typing with heavy stabbing prods.

FAO Doctor Bitchface

Yes he liked it, definitely a strong opening that conveyed his message, and to be fair he was only following her request to describe things as best he could, then with his finger hovering above the send key and a smile breaking out on his large face he forced himself to reconsider the decision. Yes it was perfect but he'd best not if he wanted to keep working here.

Delete.

FAO Doctor Katherine Kelly.

Kosminsky paused. 'Shit what was it Oscar drew again...?' He clicked on the mouse until he was zoomed back in on the sheet of A4 paper.

> The subject has drawn a large building with many windows. There is a blue figure in the fourth floor window wearing a hat. He appears to be watching another man who is falling to the ground from an adjacent ledge. The falling man has two words coming out of him. The words are 'Help!'... Twice! To clarify that is two separate helps. Also in the sky above the building is what appears to be a white angel looking down.
>
> I shall bring it to your office tomorrow as agreed.

Now leave me alone and let me finish my shift in peace!

For the best part of an hour he was expecting for his inbox to 'bing' again, but quite surprisingly it didn't and soon enough he was finishing his shift by taking one final look at Oscar staring out of his cell window. Kosminsky turned the lights off in his office and remotely the ones inside Oscar's cell before he set the night vision mode to begin its recording. Night shift security would take over now but they were just goons when compared to Kosminsky, in fact if any complications did arise during the night their first line of duty was to call him at home.

<u>5</u>

Back on Dalmeny Street 'Robbie', as he'd temporarily called himself, had watched the man fall to the road where his twisted body lay still, unmoving and apparently dead. There had been no popping sound of skull on cobbles but he could always add that into his own version of events. Some blood had come out though because the boy could see it moving in zig zags along the channels of the stones, it was making little red squares. So the curious and excited teenager raced down the four flights of the stairwell before bursting through the front door onto the street. The body was still there crumpled on the road although the boy couldn't imagine for the life of him why it wouldn't be, thinking maybe his addiction to video games had convinced him bodies just disappear when you lose sight of them for a second; life imitating art or whatever that saying was. The boy was trying to remember the exact words as he approached the body, there was no movement from it as he looked up and down the street which was unusually, but fortunately for him, empty of witnesses. It was all too perfect he could grab the money and leave without being witnessed. Then drop in on his dealer get a decent score, pop round a mate's house to enjoy it, play some console, and tell them his new tale.

As he reached the head of the man he saw on closer inspection how his left arm was twisted underneath the torso. 'Like totally fucked the wrong way round...Proper dead...Blood everywhere...!' All these quotes were being stored away for his reputation story. Some people may never understand but in this boys world it was all about how others see you, actual truth being rarely important, and now he had a top story with an opportunity to make up more details for his fable. He would fill in the gaps with shocking descriptions to gain all the good stuff, the respect, the ass, the status he desired, to become that guy you never messed with because he was the business. I mean come on he'd caused a man to kill himself then robbed him of his wallet, what a total fucking legend, but he was getting ahead of himself because he hadn't got away with anything yet. It was time to stop gloating and get busy; someone could come down the street any minute with it being the middle of the day. With this in mind he grabbed the wallet out of Alex's pocket and smuggled it away in his underwear, concealing it deep down next to his own valuables, knowing it would be safer there and this wise decision proved its worth when suddenly a large golden Labrador on a chain lead, immediately followed by an old man holding the other end, came striding round the corner.

 The old man looked straight at the boy then noticed the bundle on the floor, one that his dog was sniffing, before registering it was a person in a bad way. 'Oh bloody hell…!' He exclaimed, but before he even had chance to ask what happened, the boy was readying his defence.

'Robbie' felt both frightened and buzzing, scared and excited by this whole event but knew all he had to do was stay calm, use his head, chill this wrinkly out, then simply walk away to hometown glory. '…He just jumped out of that window the crazy bastard. He was committing suicide I reckon. I think he's dead…!' The boy lied so easily, being in the moment, loving it and who knows this could add an extra layer to his story, making him into an even bigger legend. The motherfucker who could talk his way out of the tightest situations, yeah he'd got the brains as well as the balls, now none of the girls would be able to resist that.

His mind continued with the fantasy because this bolshie kid could do this shit all day. That old man hadn't seen anything; nobody had seen anything so at worst he was a witness to a suicide.

'That's four floors…I reckon. 'I didn't see it happe…' Jay managed before the old man cut him off.

'Have you got a phone…?'

'Err…yeah!'

'Call an ambulance then!' The old man demanded pulling hard on the chain to hold his curious excited Labrador at bay.

The boy instinctively pulled out his phone then stopped himself from going any further, whoa that was nearly totally stupid! I can't do that, what if the law get my number and wanted to talk to me about it. Nah fuck that, I don't want the cops asking me stuff, forget that shit. This old guy can talk to the ambulance on his own phone, I ain't being any witness.

The old man watched the boy do nothing with his mobile. 'What are you doing…call the ambulance!'

'Err…I…err haven't got any credit.' He lied, believing as always that the deceitful path would get him away from any problem.

'You don't need any credit to make an emergency call…just ring the bloody number…!' The old man insisted while struggling to keep the Labrador away from the body.

Well that's just great he thought, a fucking wrinkly who knows how mobiles work, that's all I need. Think man, think. Running away was out of the question because that ship had sailed and…oh yeah, of course, problem solved. '…Ah yeah man I know but it's got no charge.' He then put the phone back in his pocket as a finishing act to the confrontation.

'What are you talking about…?' The old man said, '…Get down Goldie!'

'No charge man…out of battery…fucking nightmare!' The boy's acting skills were over the top, edging towards outrageously dramatic for even the kindest of critiques.

'I can see it in your pocket…it's lit up. It's clearly got charge, now stop pissing about young man and call the emergency services!'

Now this 'young man' was sixteen years of age but emotionally he was much, much younger. To an expert on all things behavioural such as stress reactions in six year olds, toddler tantrums even, they would recognise this boy's textbook immature traits. Mostly being that he was fine while all things were going his way or he still had options to follow, but if he felt trapped, or worst still had surprisingly lost at something, then let's just agree he could have serious trouble handling feelings like that. Most times in his everyday interactions with pressure or perceived injustice his usual response was to throw the game controller down in temper, stamp on it in worse case scenarios, and then have to find another one, because he was sick and tired of video games and stupid people cheating him out of his successes.

'Shut up you fucking old idiot. You don't know how my phone works. Fucking telling me what to do! You don't even know me, I'll fucking kill ya!'

The old man stared incredulously at the foulmouthed boy who was unwilling to make a call to help a man in distress, why? Then the old man put it together…ohhh!

'Did you have something to do with this?' He asked the skinny youth, albeit a skinny youth who was now starting to tremble with rage.

How had this all gone so wrong in the space of a minute? Everything was going to be easy then this old prick starts messing with his head. The boy could feel the fallen man's wallet against his groin and for some reason it fuelled his fury even more. '…You're not listening to me! I'll kill you and ya fucking dog…' He screamed, spittle coming from his lips. '…So shut ya mouth and I'll go get somebody then I'll come back, alright, just leave me alone!'

The old man looked around him for something to tie the dogs lead to. Walking back two paces he lashed the lead to handle of a front door. Because yes he was sixty three years young but more than capable, he assumed, of controlling this skinny runt. 'Stay there Goldie I'll let you off in a minute…' The dog looked confused and wary. I just have to teach this cheeky brat a few home truths first he thought then turned to face the boy, who was a lot closer than he'd been a moment ago. '...Now listen here you young...Arghhhh!'

A six inch steel blade slid into his stomach smoothly encountering minimum resistance. For a second the old man could feel it move inside him before the pain struck swiftly followed by trauma and panic. Fire and lightning scorched through his pain receptors as the blood increased to his heart for survival, causing him to feel light headed. He'd never experienced pain like it but thought if he could just...Arghhhh...then he felt it again, and then once more. Each stab of the blade slightly less painful than the first but he understood it was all relative as he fell to the floor, and his last feeling was of the knife being pulled out, his last vision was of Goldie staring with the sideways look that confused dogs do, and the last sound he heard was training shoes slapping away down the street. Then there was silence before everything became dark, then cold, then nothing more.

The boy was trying his best to run without drawing any unwanted attention but it wasn't easy with the wallet slapping against his genitals, so without breaking stride he reached in and retrieved it then ran faster still as he left the immediate area. Surely this was the best thing to do; it was just like a hyper realistic part of a videogame when getting away from the kill-zone was the obvious survival move. On reaching Leith Walk and thinking sensibly he should have headed up the hill towards the city, more places to hide that way, but instead he ran downhill towards the docks. In his mind which was being controlled by pure instinct he concluded downhill was faster and easier, even though it was taking him further away from the safety of numbers in the city.

Stopping briefly in an old ruined phone box he pulled out his mobile and quickly scrolled down his contacts before choosing one. It wasn't a completely random choice but it also wouldn't have been his first option. The boy had a few places left where he could stay at the drop of a baseball cap, but not all of them were nearby or could pick him up in their car, and not all of them had a sweet game console set up, so it was Scott Hutchinson who got his undeserved vote. Angrily he forced the phone back in his pocket after leaving a message for Scott who had either missed his call or ignored it. God help him if this boy ever found out he'd blanked him, fair enough they weren't the closest friends but he'd crashed round at Scott's before and once a bro always a bro, so you'd better call me back man. Fuck! He continued to sprint down towards the docks.

At the bottom of the hill he stopped in a bus shelter, breathing as heavy as he could ever remember. Smoking and intense fear tended to do that to teenagers who hadn't eaten properly in weeks. He fell to the bench and tried to sit up straight, but two attempts at this proved futile against the breathless exhaustion that was quickly becoming cramps. He'd try again in a minute but for the good of his ailing health he kept his head down near his knees and talked to his body with a repeating mantra of 'Calm the fuck down...!' This wasn't easy, inside his exploding mind were a million thoughts, all of them screaming to be heard but he was only able to focus on one; he'd stabbed a man with the knife he carried for 'protection', for 'reputation', the knife that he kept in his possession for 'looking hard'. Trembling again with equal excitement and fear he began whispering to himself in breathless gasps. 'What the hell just happened? That didn't happen. No way man! No that did not fucking happen...!' This spiralling loop of denial was strangely calming as he held out the black leather wallet and looked at the initials printed on it.

'A. W...' The boy mouthed, barely a whisper, only sixteen years old but his already damaged lungs were at full capacity and trying to keep up. He looked at the image and pictured the guys face looking sideward at him, that arm twisted grotesquely underneath his body, the same arm that had reached out to him for help. He counted the money in the wallet because right now it was truly all he had in the world to make him feel better, but then annoyingly he spotted another savage injustice. Fuck me there's £140 in here! £140...? Hang on that means the fucking prick was trying to buy his life back on the cheap. He said he would give me £50...the cheeky twat! Looking at the photo on the driving licence he put his finger on the man's face. 'You...are a cheeky twat. Yes you.' He read the name next to the picture and although his reading skills weren't great, he could manage short names like this. 'Fucking...fucking Alex Webb! Huh...tried to do me out of £90? Ha, ha well shit on you, I got the lot and guess what man? Guess what? I'm getting away with it!'

All of his worries were suddenly exploding with positivity because he had money for drugs; drugs would help, help him to forget anyway. Ah the simple things he thought before spotting something else, faded white in a back section of the wallet, and carefully he pulled out a folded photograph of a woman smiling. She was sort of pretty, nice smile and handwritten on the back was an address, and on seeing that this stressed youth nodded in acceptance. Of course it had a fucking address on the back! None of this was real it was a game he was in now, and this was most likely a profitable side mission.

The boy's phone vibrated in his pocket, tugging him away from a burgeoning rape fantasy that was beginning to take a hardening shape. He snatched his phone up and answered it. '...Yeah you better be sorry. I called you like ten minutes ago...have you been wanking or something...what? I need picking up. I was over at my Aunties yeah...no not 'what the fuck'...families are important man...whatever I'm down on the road to the docks bro...in a bus stop by that pub. I ain't got time now it's a fucking long story but I'm here and I need picking up...I couldn't give a fuck get em out the dryer...put anything on and come and get me! Hurry the fuck up Scott! I'm in the bus stop by...err by...hang on...the Lifeboat pub...you know the one...the prozzy one...fucking google it then!' The boy demanded through his snarling, broken and gritted teeth before ending the call. Yes he was happier now; his demands sounded hard and serious because he had to admit he was a bad man now. Just at the moment of this proud realisation he looked down and noticed his blood spattered tracksuit bottoms and then his sleeves. Fucking hell I'm covered!

Fifteen long and deeply paranoid minutes later, after the boy had changed his mind a dozen times on what to do with the knife, a blacked out VW Golf slid in to the bus lane, stopped sharply, and in less than five seconds with a heavy door slam pulled away again.

<u>6</u>

Oscar Downes was seated back in Doctor Kelly's office feeling tired and weak. Last night's sleep had been almost non-existent with the callous nightmares the voice cruelly curated within his subconscious. In all honesty it had been years since he'd slept well but last night had been one of the worst. As soon as he began to drift off the voice had started talking to him, blaming him for their being locked up, and leaving him in no doubt it wanted to kill again, soon.

Now somewhere in the distance ,maybe even in another world Oscar could hear the Doctor talking, asking muffled questions even though she was stood right next to him, and he genuinely wanted to listen but the only voice he could hear was playing its sick games.

Hey Oscar

Go away…please.

Oh yes I'll just go away shall I?

I don't want to talk to you.

That's okay Oscar you don't have to talk to me, you can just listen. Blah, Blah, Blah, Blah…are you enjoying yourself you insane psychopath.

Be quiet…I beg you…!

It was only with some immense effort that he focused on the Doctor who was pointing at the top of a drawing. Slowly her voice came into range with clarity.

'Why have you drawn this Angel Oscar?' She asked for the third time.

Oscar would have answered if he'd known but these drawings weren't his, they were images given to him from somewhere else, so how would he know why. In the end he relented by looking at the picture in front of him, expecting to feel nothing as always, but when he saw the Angel his blood ran cold. He could actually remember drawing that and knew the Angel was important. With his heart racing fast this was the closest he'd been to speaking out loud since his incarceration and his breathing became instantly tight and audible.

Katherine Kelly's heart also began to drum as she noticed the slight change in his demeanour and jumped on it in an instant. Finally a response!

'Come on Oscar. I can see you reacting to this. Speak to me Oscar…!' Her hands went on his shoulders gently shaking them as if trying to physically force the words out. '…Come on tell me about the Angel…you want to speak….show me…you want to speak to me don't you?'

He truly did want to but he wasn't allowed.

Oscar?

What?

You know what will happen...if you speak one word then we will have to kill her, strangle her with your bare hands. Is that what you want?

You wouldn't do that. What about the guard outside?

More than enough time to break this woman's windpipe!

Doctor Kelly was unaware of his inner discourse and demanded more while continuing to shake his narrow shoulders. 'Please help me to help you. I can see you want to speak. Open your mouth...!' She watched the flicker of light in his eyes fade back into a dull blue, the tension in his jaw relaxed, his breathing once more soft and perfunctory. 'Please...?' She appealed one last time before returning to her chair defeated, the moment had passed he'd returned to his usual self, something no better than a mannequin.

Oscar could perceive her retreat and shared the frustration keenly. She'd tried so hard but never stood a chance of winning, when stuck in a struggle between a Doctor and a Demon he'd chose the only real option, the one that would give him a few minutes of respite, the one that wouldn't end up in a murder. Eight bars here, six in there, eight bars here; he counted on repeat while staring at the window behind her.

Half an hour later the guard Kosminsky had safely returned Oscar to his cell, while Doctor Kelly sat in her office looking at all the pictures he'd drawn and re-reading his reports, damn it she'd been close, really close, and she knew that for certain. There had been a definite and defined moment of perception in him but all too soon it was gone, like the brief signal received from outer space that a radio telescope once picked up but never came again.

She thought back to a time when she'd read things other than files and emails about Oscar Downes. There had been a normal life before this, before being assigned the task of understanding a killer's inner workings, and back then she'd enjoyed her job without feeling such an increasing pressure. Just lately, every waking minute it seemed, she played through the milestones reached in her search and found that so far there had only been one, the crayons and paper. Most of the time Katherine couldn't decide if the pressure intensified because she was very thorough at her job or clinically obsessed, and she really didn't know the answer to that either, but suspected it was a very fine line most long days and late nights.

Being a professional expert on all cerebral functions, and following lessons learned at university, she placed herself back in the present by pressing the green button blinking on her desk phone. With that simple gesture she opened her thoughts up to the real world again to find three messages awaiting her attention. Two of them were general enquiries to which she'd reply later by email because surprisingly given her vocation talking on the phone wasn't something she particularly enjoyed. The third message however was from Professor Caroline Wesson, her boss to simplify matters, the woman who watched over Katherine's work on this case. Her voice mail was of no great surprise, just a typically blunt request for an update on her progress with Oscar, but highlighting the chain of command that bound this Doctor tightly. It was one that began with Oscar doing or not doing things, then led to Katherine badgering Kosminsky for information, and always ended up with Professor Wesson pressuring Katherine for her reports. It was a choking chain, forged with links of annoyance and distrust because whether it was liked or not they all had a job to do, someone higher to answer to.

The Doctor began to type her response then stopped herself. No, Katherine thought, I'm not going to tell you that I almost broke through today then lost him. Sod off Professor Wesson! You can just wait with your 'time is of the essence' crap, asking me for intimate details of my work with a subject you have never even bothered to visit. I'm sick of you comparing this assignment to 'the many cases I have studied over the years' bullshit. I'll crack his condition in my own way Professor and I will get Oscar to talk, no, in fact I will get Oscar to sing, and then I'll write an amazing research paper about it and you can kiss my arse Caroline with your three houses and your cars and your horses and your shitty medal from the Queen. Katherine was well aware her anger, though she thought it thoroughly justified, would be ultimately futile because nothing was going to change until Oscar talked.

Considering her current mood she correctly diagnosed that she needed a break from all this right now. A walk outside, perhaps after a crafty cigarette in the underground carpark would be perfect she thought, but before rewarding herself with that moment of pastoral clemency she sent an emailed report to the Professor. In it she stated quite dishonestly that no significant changes in Oscar's condition had occurred, and that more time would be needed to complete her studies. Lying to the Caroline made her feel in control again, go hard or go home was becoming her new motto, in fact she felt rejuvenated so the walk and the cigarette could wait as they wouldn't help her to solve anything. No way Jose, it was time to prove her worth to the Professor, to use all that knowledge from the hundreds of books she'd studied, all the hours she'd put in, and work out once and for all this man's meanings. So pulling out a black plastic folder she opened it up on page one and reread the information on Oscar Downes, before going back to basics with a yellow notepad where she scribbled bullet points of everything she felt to be relevant.

Oscar Downes, Serial killer, 48 years old, No formal education to speak of.

Taxi driver for 22 years in the Edinburgh area, Both parents now deceased, Father suicide and Mother breast cancer, Never married, no prior criminal record, no serious underlying medical issues, attacked by taxi customers five years ago resulting in fractured skull but recovered well and able to continue job, Hobbies, golf occasionally and hiking. Lived alone. (Obviously...!) Big reader predominantly biographies of great leaders, hundreds of books found in his flat. Work colleagues described him as pleasant enough but kept himself to himself. Not affiliated with any groups or sects nationally or online. No serious porn addiction or any deviancy found on his online history.

The bodies of five (5) missing women discovered in his lock up (Garage) all reported missing over the previous 3 months. Women were dismembered. Victim's ages ranged from 17 to 46. ???

My age!

Body parts kept in sealed plastic barrels. Neighbours/witnesses believed he visited the lock up 2 to 3 times a week. Police suspected him after random DNA cross referencing (Yeah go science!) and arrested him after car chase (Televised.). Oscar hasn't denied the charges of murder against him because he hasn't spoken a word since the arrest. No connection between the victims!

Simply appears to be random opportunism. Evidence points to the women being strangled first then throat cut before he committed dismemberment in the lockup. No evidence of drugs in women (Or Oscar). Need him to talk for criminal conviction otherwise a plea of diminished responsibility due to mental issues will be declared. At the moment I am undecided on his motives and mental condition both during and after...then and now.

Katherine closed the folder while thinking of just how many weeks she'd been on this project. Let's see it started in...no way...really...I got my first err...Oh my god nine weeks; Over two months of getting absolutely nowhere in finding out anything of the motives or mental condition of Oscar Downes, not even a bloody hello, she was realising she needed to try harder for everyone's sake. That everyone in this instance was the police who wanted answers, which they required them for the prosecutors who in turn wanted evidence for the courts and well everybody in the media wanted something, anything from Oscar. Only he wasn't speaking, wasn't playing 'bawl', not with her or them and certainly not with the victim's families who desperately wanted some information. It was hard to accept that all they really knew about their girls was they were dead. Even more painful to think that prior to that whilst the women were still missing, those innocent relatives had lived with a brief hope they could be found alive and well, but when that candle of hope had been extinguished and the bodies discovered, the least they could have hoped for was some kind of closure. Oscar's refusal to communicate meant there were only questions, no answers, and all they lived was a sickening perpetual wheel of grinding grief, one where they could never think of their girls without crashing their heads into the brick wall of why? It was up to Katherine Kelly to break through that wall and find a way in so she spread the crayon pictures across her desk and studied them once more. Whatever these drawings portrayed from inside Oscars mind was a tantalising clue, the answer somewhere right in front of her scrawled in all the colours of the rainbow, only she had no idea how close she was, but then again it's impossible to know what's going on in another dimension. Isn't it?

Meanwhile deep in the underbelly of Blackford Facility a vivid new insight into Oscar's condition was about to be discovered. Kosminsky had requested another camera be placed in the cell, the work being completed safely during Oscar's meeting with the doctor, and now the guard was watching the subject stood in his usual window staring position but from a completely fresh viewpoint. This new camera had been fitted to the top of the window frame, facing down at a shallow angle to watch him even closer, close enough to detect what was going on behind those eyes. Kosminsky was captivated by the vibrant pictures from his new high definition toy. It allowed him to zoom in on Oscar's unflinching face and see the tiny veins and pores on his cheek; he could focus right into Oscar's eyes and note the pattern and flecks hidden in them. They were soft eyes, not the ones you would normally associate with a murderer but perhaps that was too cliché. Turning to check on the time Kosminsky startled himself when realising he'd been staring into those eyes for a full ten minutes, during which they blinked occasionally with a rudimentary function because after all the man's body wasn't lost, just his ability to speak it seemed. Now though Kosminsky felt he could look straight into this murderer and if Oscar was acting about any of this 'illness', or if his mask slipped for even a second, the guard would know, and then there would be nowhere to hide for you, my little friend.

After he'd reluctantly wrenched his scrutiny away he began to write his report for the doctor. Following the rules she laid down he explained the extra camera and its purpose and believed surely she wouldn't find a problem in him doing that. He pressed send on the email hoping she would understand and shut the hell up. Then immediately, almost subconsciously, he reengaged with Oscars piercing blue eyes.

7

Every city by simple geographical design must have outskirts of sorts, the little villages that grow up nearby and over time get swallowed up by the hungry black hole that is a growing metropolis, finding themselves daily incrementally devoured and assimilated into the larger system where they will inevitably become part of it but never absorbed completely, always maintaining some smidgeon of their own personality. Under this criterion the big money stays in the centre while the outskirts remain the same but suddenly find themselves having to pay for the privilege of being so close to the rich and glowing, ever expanding beast. These outskirts will most often become overcrowded and underdeveloped, a harsh environment to try and live a life, with some places downright lawless while others, such as the one the blacked out Golf had raced back to, are constantly teetering on the rocking scales of total injustice.

Scott Hutchinson had picked up Jay 'Robbie' Cleaver from the bus stop and regretted it ever since. Mostly because his 'friend' was splattered in blood and stonewall refused to tell him why that was the case on the journey back. Any questions to that effect got the same repeated response, a loud impolite order telling him to shut up and just drive the fucking car!

Now two hours later and with no further information imparted Scott was sitting on the torn sofa in his tiny rented flat listening to this friend of a friend using all the hot water in the shower. Jay had been in there a long time now, forty odd minutes at least, and Scott really wanted to say something but decided it might be better to let the clearly troubled boy calm down first. So seeking a distraction he went to the back door to check on the progress of the fire that Jay's tracksuit was burning in. He used some rusted barbeque tongs to lift a fallen stained sleeve back into the heart of the flame. The smell it created wasn't great but he'd agreed silently with Jay that any outfit covered in mysterious blood was always better after it was thoroughly disposed of.

Scott left it smouldering away and went back inside where he'd sorted out some old work clothes for his guest. This had been a problem as Jay wasn't the kind of friend you would give any of your good stuff to, they were friends only because they knew each other's names and that was about as deep as it went. Scott was two years older and at various times through high school, but mainly out of it when they should have been in it, they'd hung out together, sharing a common interest in video games and cannabis. He knew Jay's family by reputation and in confidence would tell you they were the kind of parental unit that repelled rather than attracted. Scott knew for a fact that for the last two years Jay had been basically homeless, not legally of course, but returning home was really not a safe option, giving him more of self-preservation, self-induced transient life choice. Now at least once a fortnight Jay would come round with some weed he'd gotten from somewhere and stay a couple of days until it was smoked. They would crash out on the sofa for countless hours running around killing aliens, passing, and shooting, driving tanks and wielding swords with their thumbs concentrated hard on the controllers. Jay Cleaver wasn't a bad friend, they had a laugh sometimes, but if you took away the weed, the cider and the games console they really had nothing else to talk about...until now, Scott worryingly thought.

Jay Cleaver stood under the steaming spray, forehead pressed to the tiles, his wiry body scrubbed clean and what little hair he had shampooed to within an inch of its life. It was so much better being here under the water where there no questions, no people in his face, no outside world to add pressure or make him feel cheated. He tried to imagine this was where he'd been all along and the events of earlier were just a story he made up, nothing more than a vivid dream or an extremely immersive boss level that he'd completed, but the shit truth was that he knew better, he'd never forget those graphics; Dalmeny Street had been all too real. Glancing across to the narrow window ledge he could see his worldly possessions laid out, a crappy mobile phone, a scratched and dented tin of tobacco and papers, an orange lighter, a small half empty bag of skunk and the wallet of a more than likely dead guy. Fuck my life!

In the tiny kitchen Scott filled the kettle and flicked the switch on. The plastic lid didn't fit perfectly flush but if you pushed and twisted it just right it would gain enough seal and eventually boil. He searched the cupboard for sugar but came up frustratingly short, albeit there was no real surprise in that, he knew before he started looking he'd been out of sugar for two days. Then a moment of inspiration hit him, the coat he'd worn last week, where was it? Scott located the fake leather jacket half stuffed behind the sofa and searched the inside pockets. Result! Smiling like a world champion he pulled out six sachets of sugar taken from a motorway café. He strolled back to the kitchen with his prize and shouted through to Jay. 'Hey man I'm making coffee...do you want one?' The bathroom door opened and Jay, because this habitat was designed for a signal occupant, stepped straight out into the living room. Scott looked at him from the kitchen and Jay stared back in silence. They were only four feet apart but Scott had never seen his friend dressed in just a towel, his attention caught by the tattoos snaked around both arms from shoulder to wrist, before noticing with a little surprise that he was as slim as an undernourished rake. They held this position perhaps a moment too long before the kettle boiled and Scott turned sharply to find mugs.

Jay sniffed before moving over to the window for a peek through the curtains. There was nothing to see which meant he could keep up his hopeful version of events, the ones where nothing bad had actually happened.

'So you wanna coffee?' Scott asked.

'Yeah...' Jay answered with nowhere near a please or thank you. '...Four sugars!'

Scott looked down at the six sachets and nodded okay, clearly his plan to keep Jay calm and get him the hell out of his house as soon as possible was going to take some sacrifices. In the end he emptied four sachets into Jay's mug before stirring it with a stained teaspoon, then thought for a second and put the last two in as well. '...There you go.' Scott said handed him a mug which was a green and white football with a handle.

Jay's eyes followed Scott until he sat down on the sofa, and when he was done double checking the street he sat next to him. They weren't sitting close together but both would have felt more comfortable if they'd been facing each other, however a sofa can only look one way and this one faced the TV and the games console. It was who Jay broke the awkward silence when he looked over and noticed the jeans and sweatshirt on the kitchen worktop. 'Are they for me?'

'Yeah, you can have em. Keep em I mean. They're all yours...' Scott said as his unwanted houseguest got up and walked over to the bundle, before quickly turning his head away when Jay dropped the towel. The kid looked down at the ridiculously baggy jeans and the green sweatshirt displaying in fluorescent blue *Sneakers Bowling Alley*. It was emblazoned on the front, also on the back and down both sleeves, he eyed Scott with a look that heavily implied *, really I can keep these, Thank you, you shouldn't have, I couldn't possibly,* but to summarise it all in a word he simply said 'Twat!'

'What? To be fair I don't think I'm in your debt...' Scott braved saying this comment because he was genuinely upset at being called a twat when he was clearly trying to help, however half-heartedly.

'What you talking about, debt? I thought we were bloods man!'

'We are Jay...man'

'Well I would've given you better shit than this to wear if it was me helping you out.'

Jay paused to see if Scott would stand down, maybe go fetch him some better attire, but Scott sat his ground taking a swig from his unsweetened mug before speaking. 'Look man…you want to tell me what happened today?'

'What do you wanna know?'

'Are you for fucking real…?' Scott laughed uncomfortably then paused but couldn't wait any longer for a response. '…Okay, I want to know why I had to come pick you up from that bus stop and why you were covered in blood.'

'Uhuh…have you burned the tracksuit?' Jay asked in an immature attempt at changing the subject.

'Yes I have…and that's another question! What the hell happened that you couldn't just wash em…you gotta burn em…?' Scott was feeling a little braver now the boy was looking ridiculous in his old work clothes.

Jay looked down at his bare feet whilst noticeably chewing on his bottom lip. Here was another decision for him to make, tell Scott everything about stabbing the old man or just lie again? 'Scott…man…blood?'

'What Jay…? You might as well tell me. See if I can help.' Scott took another sip.

Jay laughed suddenly and this outburst surprised Scott because the sound was not joyful to listen to, coming over as rather harsh and a touch manic. Then the moment the laugh stopped Jays face dropped back into its surly scruff state. 'This ain't anything you can help with unless you can turn clocks back!'

'Christ man what happened, you said you went to see your Auntie, I've never met her but what's the worst that can happen?'

'I did see my Auntie that's why I was there. We were sitting talking and I wanted a cig…she's not for smoking cigs in the house, anything else yeah no problem but not cigs you know. So I went out into the hallway and opened the window and fuck me there was only a guy standing on the ledge outside the building man…suicidal.'

'Well go on don't stop now…so there's a guy on the ledge?'

'Yeah it was a suicide. He was trying to top himself!'

'I know what suicide is.'

'I just wanted a ciggy in peace…I didn't want to be part of his shit. You get what I'm saying?'

Scott nodded but was nowhere near certain of what Jay was saying. So a man was stood on the outside of a building committing suicide. If that was the truth then what else occurred, where did all the blood come from? Did the guy explode on impact like a water balloon? 'So then what happened?'

'Well I'm looking at him and then he looks at me...' Jay continued explaining still totally unsure of what route to take...truth or dare? The boy thought about his options, if I tell Scott the truth we're bonded forever with a serious secret, but if I don't...then I'm on my own. Fucking hell! He chose to stumble on blindly for now. '...Then he asks me to help him...you know...to grab his hand and pull him back in through the window.'

'Right'

'But I told him no...I wouldn't! He said what? I said nah I wanna watch you fall.' Jay felt little relief from his admission but at least he hadn't lied and that was extremely unusual for his personality.

Scott raised his hands to stop Jay right there. He looked at the boy and faced his palms outwards. 'Why...?'

'Why what...?' Jay replied innocently enough.

'...The fuck did you want to watch him fall?'

'I don't know...I just did yeah, suppose so I could tell everybody about it.' Jay was certainly going all in on the truth now and having to trust that his friend would understand.

Scott however was confused. 'But you could have just helped him...you would probably have been a hero then. You could have told everybody about that.' Scott paused before asking for final confirmation. 'Let me get this straight...you let him die?

'You're making it sound like I killed him. He was jumping anyway. I didn't stick him out there. He made the choice to climb out...then he fell off.'

Scott was getting more confused with each and every sentence he heard. 'He fell off?'

'Yeah man...like dush, dunk...thwump...I can't do it like the way it sounded but it was a fucking weird noise man!'

Scott had to close his wide open mouth before asking. 'Was he dead then...when he hit the road?'

'My Aunty lives on the 4th floor you prick...so yeah I reckon he was dead. Anyway I went down the stairs to see, you know....' Jay realised he was at another fork in the story that could change his path, maybe save his reputation a little, but he wasn't a young man for turning. If he was telling the truth then that was the choice he'd made. Everyone who ever met him or read about him would vouch for that. '...but his arm man, it was like it had gone into his body the way it was twisted back and stuff.'

'Okay you think he was dead...what about the blood...? Scott asked curiously.

'...Oh nah man the blood wasn't his. That happened after when everything got like proper tense and weird.'

Without realising Scott had both hands covering his mouth now, utterly speechless as Jay voiced his story, hoping it wouldn't take long because he felt like throwing up. In the end he was genuinely surprised and grateful how short the story was.

'Right so then this old bloke walks up to me with his dog and starts giving me shit, saying I'd done it and everything, but I hadn't, talking to me like I was some kind of murderer or something. So I told him to stop saying that and he wouldn't stop saying it, so I said shut up man but he wouldn't, he kept on going giving me shit about my phone and stuff...so I stuck him.'

Scott's mouth opened to speak but no words came out. It was more of a staccato Morse code from the back of his throat before he realised he was forgetting to breathe. 'You stuck him...what like with a blade?'

'Yeah of course with a blade, I always carry my shank man for protection...there are some bad people on the streets and he was kicking off you know, in my face? You would have done the same!'

'I fucking seriously doubt that Jay!'

'He was right in my grill you know! You weren't there bro it was getting out of control.'

'Clearly...!'

'...Fuck you!' Jay bit back at the sarcasm.

So Scott paused and spoke his next words gently but seriously. 'You've gotta go to the police.'

Jay's expression remained neutral as he paused then replayed that last request over in his mind. It was either a really funny ill-timed joke or Scott had suddenly turned from an old helpful friend into a new unneeded enemy. The boy thought to himself these very words, nah man he's a blood he wouldn't do that, Scott's just a bit shocked by my epic story. 'He probably ain't even dead you know...!'

Scott was thinking about what to do now all the details were out in the open but couldn't come up with anything better than. 'We need to put the news on man. See if there's anything about it!' Then he reached over for the remote on the arm of the sofa.

'Don't...fucking...touch it!' Jay spoke deliberately slow and mean, heavy with serious threat.

Scott stopped his hand just short of the remote. 'Why?'

'Because I fucking said so...! I get it Scotty you're a bit freaked out. Now fucking sit still and let it sink in. I reckon if we both do that we'll be able to work this shit out...' Jay sat back down next to him in his oversized trousers and ridiculous sweatshirt and looked up to the ceiling before adding. '...Okay?'

Scott sat back on the sofa and with every breath he calmed himself down before a problematic personal realisation hit. 'Oh for fucks sake...somebody might have seen my car!'

'So what, you were nowhere near, you was a mile and a half away from that street?'

'Oh yeah I know! I was a mile and a half away from that street picking up a kid covered in blood. If somebody saw that and then tells the police, I'm immediately an accessory. Oh for fucks sake Jay...!' Scott was starting to shout but he should have known better with his friend's current mental state.

Jay exploded to drown him out. 'Shut up! Shut up...!' He then jumped to his feet and towered over the visibly shocked Scott. '...You are going to shut that mouth and sit quiet, you got that...shut up until me and you have got a plan.'

8

Sometimes in the dead of night when dreams battle with nightmares we can find ourselves in no man's land. With the body at rest one's mind will compose and create all by itself, jumbling up and throwing memories around like the hyperactive toddler it used to be. This occurs because the brain has pathways that it follows when you are awake, habitual routes based on your personality and choices, but when you switch off to go to sleep it starts to make new pathways, searching out areas less trodden, trying to understand itself. Never forget you aren't nearby to keep an eye on it in slumber, you have no control while at the mercy of its curiosity, meaning all you can ever do is hope...hope that it plays nicely.

Oscar Downes lay motionless in the darkness of his cell counting the bars on the faintly lit window, one to six over and over through habit, but a repetitive behaviour with a purpose, to stay in control. Even after five years of intrusion, of sharing his mind with another, he refused to accept defeat to the mental chaos. This war in which he served was completely silent to the outside world but within him it raged constantly with images of bloodied death and destruction. He didn't want to sleep, never wanted to again, so with his eyes becoming heavier he continued the count to stave off the dreaded moment. Oscar fought hard but inevitably his body failed him as his eyes closed leaving no choice but to enter the breach once more, into the swirling bedlam of dreams, where anything and everything could happen.

At the same time some five miles away, in a bathroom that needed a good clean, the large guard Kosminsky brushed his teeth. His reflection in the stained mirror was hinting that perhaps he didn't look his best, overtired maybe, his eyes seemed bright enough but only because the dark patches below accentuated them. All he needed was a full night's sleep, that's the answer he thought a good seven hours and I'll be fine as he spat out the toothpaste and wiped his face with a damp crumpled towel.

A minute later he lowered his bulk onto the bed checking to make sure the alarm was set for 6.45AM, but of course it was, a routine set in stone for 22 years and counting. Generally speaking he was doing okay with a healthy pension awaiting him, all he had to do was keep getting up, keep being professional and not let silly thoughts worry him. The kind of silly thoughts he had about Oscar bloody Downes for a start. What was it with that little psycho that kept getting under his skin? There hadn't been a spoken word between them since he came under his watch, not even a hint of trouble from silent Oscar, yet Kosminsky was still more wary of him than any prisoner he'd ever met. It wasn't the man's silence that worried him; not really, he'd seen other 'subjects' do this kind of stuff before. Hell he'd even had one guy starve himself to death which had been unpleasant, especially when no matter what they did he made zero effort to survive, and no food no water meant little chance. It hadn't been this guards fault of course; he wasn't in charge of their health or dietary intake that was the medics' role. Kosminsky's duties, his job description in fact, were in the field of observation and movement, the risky business that presented the most danger, and it was why he was trusted at least twice a day to be walking side by side with a man who had butchered five women. Step by step with a seemingly insignificant man who somehow managed to convince women to go with him, to trust him, to have faith in their hearts that his intentions were pure and there was no way he would possibly rip their bodies into pieces and stuff them in a plastic barrel.

Why did you do it Oscar? Kosminsky had openly asked him that question a few times now, mostly in hope that Oscar might trust his jailer and that said jailer could get a big one over on Dr Katherine Kelly. Oh he would love it just too much if he was the one who could make a breakthrough, imagine walking into her office one morning with Oscar, the two of them laughing and joking together seeing her face crumble. Hey whoever's in charge up there in heaven do me a favour and let that happen.

Although Oscar was physically asleep in his bunk his mind was walking down a dark and wet cobbled street. His cold bare feet kicked into a bundle on the ground and he wanted it to just be material, a mound of clothes perhaps, but he knew better. This was another lifeless body, almost certainly one of his old victims popping back into his head to revisit while he slept, as he became once more imprisoned in this medium of madness, with the voice doing its worst, taking control again, making him suffer.   He tried to fight back by remembering moments of what his life had been like before it happened, back in the days when he'd been quiet, gentle Oscar Downes.

Experiencing this defensive recall raised a question in his divided psyche; how am I on a cobbled street in a dream and at the same time I can step out into another? It doesn't make sense that I'm trying to remember a different time altogether. How deep does this go? Just how crazy am I? The questions were left hanging on moonbeams as Oscar pictured himself back in his taxi cab, in the centre of the city picking up a fare, just doing his job some five and half years ago. It was one that had started out very much like every other. 'It's been steady away, not too busy, you know.' He replied to the young ladies query, trotting out the same line he must have said twenty times that weekend to various fares.

'So where are we off to then? 'Oscar enquired of the two women estimating they were in their mid-twenties, and whose clothes were almost conservative in comparison to some of the undressed states he got at this time of night. He couldn't quite see the blonde ones face without adjusting his rear-view mirror but that could have looked creepy, and for sure one thing Oscar Downes was not, was creepy. You were always safe with this cabbie; he even had a little motto, a mantra he lived by, and one he proclaimed quietly every time he dropped a young lady, or ladies off safely. 'Not to the door, through the door!' Most cabbies drove off straightaway when they reached their get out point, not Oscar, he always waited until they were putting the keys in, or ringing the bell, and that door was opened and closed. Of course what happened to them after that was none of his business but getting them there safely was. Oscar was simply a nice guy, cheery, small in stature, some would describe him as efficient and honest but not all cabbies were like him. He knew first hand that some of the other drivers in this firm sold drugs from under their driving seat, and others who would just drive prostitutes around in their back seat looking for clients. Of course he appreciated it was easy money but the whole scene didn't hang ethically right with Oscar. He was a taxi driver through and through, picking up souls and dropping them off safely was all he did, and he could prove it. For instance there'd been numerous occasions when a particularly drunken soul, believing they were reasonably sober tried to give him a tip that was disproportionally large, and he would always turn it down flat. Oscar liked the tips of course, if it wasn't for them he'd most probably struggle but he would never take advantage of anyone in an inebriated state. Not good old Oscar the quiet guy who kept himself to his self, that's probably what his workmates would say about him, but they would only be guessing because they didn't really know him. Back then no one knew of his simple interests such as spending hours listening to classical music stations or reading biographies of the famous, but in the end his real passion was driving people about. He delighted in doing his job so much even the heavy traffic that built up in the city centre could be fun. The years and miles had taught him all the shortcuts, all the backstreets and alleys, and it was the thrill of the chase to him. Every fare was a question to be answered and a problem to be solved, to the point where if his car could fit through a gap then it was fair game. He would do whatever it took, legally of course, to get his temporary acquaintance sat in the back seat to where they desired.

'46 Marlborough Drive mate, over the old bridge by the new estate, do you know it?' The frizzy haired brunette girl asked.

Of course Oscar knew it, they may as well of asked him if he knew his own name. His inner roadmap clicked on and he saw the route in his mind, every junction, every traffic light, over the bridge, the other temporary traffic lights for the building work, he'd nearly forgotten about those, down past the hill that led to the docks, back across the estate then a mile and a half more and voila. Fifteen minutes at the most he estimated before looking at the clock so he could check it again when he got there; personal bests are always cherished by professional drivers. Then there were his personal rules of engagement in the driver/passenger relationship. For starters he never opened a conversation with the customers, he always let them talk first, if they wanted to know any more about his boring life apart from whether he'd been busy or not then they would ask. He wasn't about to start giving them his social and political sermons like some cabbies did.

'...Do you know how much it will be, Mister Driver...?' Frizzy brunette asked in a giggly fashion.

'It's on the meter, love, but I'd say around fifteen pounds.'

'Fifteen...?' Frizzy asked.

'...In that ballpark.' He said.

'...The what?' A now confused Frizzy asked with a distasteful look.

'About fifteen pounds...' Oscar confirmed to allay her puzzlement. It was only then he noticed both women were appreciably drunker than he'd first thought. He turned his head to look right as he approached a junction and used the opportunity to catch a glimpse of the blonde one digging untidily in her handbag.

'You gotta tenner...?' Blonde asked Frizzy while continuing her search.

'I ain't got any money left, I told ya.' Frizzy replied. 'I had to pay for the other stuff.'

Just after this Oscar heard bottles clinking behind his seat before Blonde looked up from her fruitless search and spoke directly to him.

'Have you been busy mate...?'

'Oh my god I've already asked him that ya div!' Frizzy was overdramatising her rebuke due to alcohol and whatever else was starting to kick in to her system.

So now what Oscar thought would be routine job ended up being quite possibly the longest fourteen and a half minutes of his working life. It was with genuine relief when he finally pulled the cab up outside 46 Marlborough Drive, but it if he thought things couldn't get any worse, he was tragically mistaken. The women had become gradually louder and more erratic during the ride and now he was being asked, no scratch that, he was being screamed at to let them out of his car.

The whole situation had spiralled terribly as soon as he pulled over to the kerb. Frizzy began stuttering they didn't have any money but it wasn't her fault. Blonde said they were broke at the minute then dropped a small plastic bag with white powder inside. She grabbed it up and shoved it down the front of her blue dress, most probably into her bra, but Oscar didn't look because he didn't want to know. All he wanted was his money and politely enquired whether they had another way of paying,

That was the second it all kicked off and everything about Oscar's life began to change.

'You're a fucking sex pest!' Blonde screamed.

'I'll call the police on you! Where's my phone...?' Frizzy threatened.

Oscar tried to regain some semblance of rationality to the conversation. 'I was only asking if perhaps you had a friend or family member in the house that could cover the cost.'

'Let me out of this car now!' Blonde demanded as if her life were in danger. Drunkenly fumbling with the handle but pushing instead of pulling.

'It's not locked...' Oscar told her but he was struggling to be heard in the melee and that was when he felt the first sharp slap to the back of his head. '...What was that for?' He asked raising his right arm to cover himself from another stinging attack while his left hand attempted to grab Frizzy's wrist to stop her from hitting him. Unbelievably Blonde saw his attempt at self-preservation as a sure sign of sexual assault and leaning forward grabbed his hand and bit down hard. With some serious effort Oscar yanked it free of her bloodied teeth then ordered both of them to get out of his car. Those words were the last thing he remembered of that day, of his true former self. He spent the next two weeks in hospital while his fractured skull was treated; the nurses telling him daily how lucky he'd been, although it began to sound like a common quote wheeled out in those situations, *'Another inch and you'd have been dead or brain damaged.'* Dead or brain damaged? He should have been so lucky. When he was finally released his condition was far worse than either of those options.

It was the thought of his current disorder that brought him out of his memory and back to the dream; he looked down again at the bundle on the cobbled street before turning away , forcing his mind to awaken. Sometimes in the past five years this method had worked. He could get out of the nightmares if he tried, or more truthfully, if the voice was finished with him.

<u>9</u>

At the very same hospital A&E department where a seriously wounded taxi cab driver had been wheeled in five years previously, his injuries consistent with being beaten around the head with a wine bottle and a stiletto heel, a Police Inspector was sat attempting to find solutions to some new pressing problems, but the sister in charge of the ward was being evasive and Inspector Harvey Cooper didn't much care for her officious answers.

'Madam I've showed you my identification would you please let me go through?'

'I can't let you see anyone until I'm given permission to do so by the Doctor in charge.' Ward Sister Tracy Hodgson informed the Inspector calmly but firmly.

It was with a tiresome sigh he accepted she was just doing her job and stood down. Deciding it was better to yield for now he found a waiting room chair and sat quietly assembling his thoughts, but knowing that he needed more information to explain this extraordinary mystery. Seriously, the bodies of two men found on a busy road in the middle of the day with no witnesses, how the hell is that even possible?

Inspector Harvey Cooper was a middle aged, he classed fifty three as still middle aged, happily married policeman without a drink or drug problem and who had no lingering issues with authority. In fact this profession albeit long hours and harrowing at times was his perfect vocation, and for quite a while now harrowing to Harvey had been looking at photos and reading reports from crimes, because actual fieldwork was becoming less and less. There was no need to beat the streets these days, that was for the younger legs, years of experience in using the old grey matter was his form of crime fighting; finding out what happened, who did it, and making sure they were apprehended. That was as deep as he went in this day and age. Harvey had recently joked to his wife that his memoirs would be called 'At my desk and other meetings', and she'd laughed because that was just how she liked it. Her 'Harveypud' doing his work from a safe distance, no chasing baddies in cars or clambering over chain link fences through back alleys in pursuit of justice. Florence 'Flo' Cooper much preferred her husband's Sherlock Holmes approach.

Today however he'd ventured out of the office to the hospital to check on a suspicious event. There were two good reasons for that; it was a sunny afternoon so it was a pleasure to get out of his stuffy office, plus the details coming in of the two men found on the road were far from straightforward. It was the type of mystery the great detective himself may have been interested in, and Harvey could well imagine Holmes demanding Doctor Watson to grab his hat and coat, for the game was afoot. Harvey pulled out his phone while he waited for the Ward Sister and rang his office. It was answered by the station secretary who immediately put him through his superior.

'Right then Harvey what's going on down there?' The voice of Superintendent Jeff Shilling demanded.

'Nothing much here at the hospital Sir...I've got to wait until they've done their preliminaries. It's a strange one though.'

'It sounds it.' Shilling continued. 'I've got it reported that two males were found in Dalmeny Street by a postman at around 1.30pm. The older of the two had been stabbed at least three times and next to him was the body of a man who appears to have been crushed. For god's sake tell me you've got more on this?'

'The older man is Brian Downing, sixty three, a resident in the street. He was stabbed with what appears to be a short blade just six feet from his own front door.' Harvey was reading the details from his small notebook.

'Robbery...?' Shilling asked.

'It doesn't appear he's had anything taken. His wallet was in his pocket.'

'And the other man...?'

'No wallet or identification on him. I had a quick word with the ambulance crew and his injuries are consistent with either a hit and run...or a fall from a considerable height. Forensics is still there now and the area was sealed off just after Constable Hughes called it in. I'm sure they'll come up with something soon.'

Harvey glanced up at the Ward Sister but she wasn't looking in his direction so he accepted there was no change yet.

'Double murder then...?' Jeff Shilling asked fully expecting Harvey's response to be leaning towards that confirmation.

'No Sir, only one murder so far. It appears the younger man might pull through. I'll keep you informed.'

'You do that!'

Harvey ended the call and turned sharply towards the Ward Sister who was beckoning him over.

10

Those green eyes locked on to his were unavoidably the same ones as before because Alex had failed in his attempt to leave the white world.

'What happened...?' The Angel asked.

'I died again.' He answered.

'Did you now?' It said with a calming smile and a little tut.

Alex was once more sat at the white desk in the white space answering the Angel he'd tried to leave behind. 'I must have done. It was different this time though.'

'How so...?' It linked its fingers.

'The conversation...'

'...With the boy dressed in blue?'

'Yes the same boy, same situation, but we said different words.'

'But clearly with the same result...you were unable to change anything?'

'No...and to be totally honest it was worse.' Alex confessed before averting his eyes as he remembered again every detail of his fall to the street, the final seconds as the cobbles approached to an inch from his face, and his arm waiting to be crushed underneath his own weight and velocity. Then just as he expected the smash and the pain or whatever was going to happen it flashed white, and he ended up back here, with an irate Angel talking down at him.

'So here we are again. No closer to knowing what's happening.' It proclaimed unhelpfully.

'Not quite...I think I might have discovered something.'

'Do you really? That's good Alex we certainly need to resolve this quandary so please enlighten me.'

'Okay well I think, because I've done this before...I reckon...' He searched for the courage to finish a sentence he never believed he would actually say. '...I'm pretty certain I might be...immortal.'

The Angel's poker face gave nothing away as it simply repeated the word back to the man. 'Immortal'

'Well yeah you know...immortal. I cannot die!'

'Yes I understand what immortality entails.'

'So you must see it then...I can't die. I've tried twice...and if I can't die then I must be immortal...like you...'

At this the Angel opened its wings and the feathers slid effortlessly into place with sparkling tips in perfect alignment. Damn that's impressive thought Alex, while wondering if he may soon get a pair just like those, and when the Angel didn't reply straight away to his last statement the man continued. '…I mean come on you must be immortal…pretty obvious really…being here and being an angel.'

'Oh Alex once more you both surprise and disappoint in equal measure. You don't even know where here is. You don't know why you're here but all the time you attempt to construct definite assumptions created from nothing more than wild guesses.'

'So are you immortal? A simple yes or no will do'

'In that case it's a simple no because immortality is impossible… everything dies Alex.'

'Except me…think about it.' He interjected.

'No Alex you are no exception. You will die like everything else.'

'So why can't I die now then?'

'That's the big question isn't it?' The Angel said and slowly spun round in its chair.

Alex was visibly amazed by this sight, how long had the Angel had a spinning office chair? He'd never noticed it before and now he couldn't resist the urge to chuckle as it did one full revolution before quizzically looking back at the highly amused man grinning away.

'…What…?' The Angel asked.

11

The massive sun was sat high in the right hand corner of the sky, its beams illuminating a hospital bed and the face of a man underneath the straight orange sheets. An alignment of its rays fell through a large square window then merged with the lamp light coming from the bedside table. It was impossible to tell whether the patient was alive or dead. A nurse in her sky blue uniform and another lady in a dark brown coat stood at the bedside, the lady in brown holding six oversized fingers to her face. She may have been crying. There was a box shaped machine on the opposite side of the bed with a green bulb on top, it was easy to imagine it blinking on and off, while above the man's head and floating in thin air, with no visible means of support, was a blood red question mark.

Dr Katherine Kelly was studying Oscar's latest drawing totally lost in its content. Was this some memory of the time he was in hospital after the taxi incident? Of course if she chose to even consider that hunch then she'd have no choice but to ask...who is the lady? Oscar Downes was a confirmed bachelor with no close female friends or acquaintances ever mentioned in his records. So she decided to pour another cup of tea and approach the picture's meaning from a different direction. What if the man in the bed was someone else entirely? What if that man was in hospital somewhere right now? Or what if she was simply tearing her hair out running around Oscar's hamster wheel of riddles again, by trying to make sense and find hidden messages in the childish crayon scribbles of a madman? The teaspoon tinkled on the cup as she stirred.

Oscar himself was back in the cell after another one sided meeting with the Doctor. He was beginning to believe their brunchtime get-togethers weren't doing either of them much good, she spent all their time trying to get him to speak, while he spent it arguing with a monster in his head mostly convincing it to not kill her. Although now back within the privacy of his four walls and locked in securely the voice had fallen silent. With time to think an idea formed as he stared down at his crayons, he wasn't sure if it was his own or not, it was certainly a dark thought, a frightening route to take, but ever desperate times were calling loudly for desperately large measures.

Inside his cupboard office Allan Kosminsky leapt from his chair when he saw Oscar's idea begin to take shape. He automatically slapped his heavy hand on the alarm and sprinted down the red flashing hallway, slamming through double doors, barely touching stairs as he took them in full flight, before eventually sliding to a halt outside the cell. Kosminsky almost broke the keys to get it opened quickly, only to discover he required even swifter action, firstly by putting his fingers into the prisoner's mouth in an attempt to remove the blockages, and after failing to get them all, by having to push his hand even deeper down the man's throat. It was this desperate effort that caused the natural gag reflex to kick in and the small man began to convulse, which brought up the last few stragglers. When Allan was finally sure they were all out he turned Oscar towards him, there was no change of expression on his little face, just a smudgy rainbow of primary colours around his mouth where the crayons had been forced in.

Kosminsky settled Oscar back onto his bunk and sat with him in an almost brotherly fashion while he caught his breath. Then even though he knew it was pointless he asked. 'Are you okay Oscar, did you swallow any?'

'   !' Oscar replied.

'You seem to be breathing okay. I think your airways are clear. Holy shit what the hell were you doing ramming those into your mouth? Were you trying to kill yourself, is that it…?' Kosminsky suddenly realised he was shouting to be heard above the wailing siren so let them know they could switch it off.

Oscar chose to stare dead ahead and didn't try to speak again, it was pointless when nothing came out, so all he could do was hope his bizarre idea had worked.

The alarm fell silent just as Kosminsky took a safety related independent decision, and if Doctor Bitchface didn't approve then that's just tough shit he thought, while quickly gathering them up

With abject terror Oscar and his wax smeared face watched Kosminsky take the crayons and lock the door, only this wasn't supposed to happen, they were his only form of communication.

'…   …!' Oscar screamed at the top of his lungs.

12

Wicked places exist in our world even if we don't always know where they are. Ancient tales will get passed down telling of deep caves, mountain tops, dark forests or still lakes, and unsettling myths can arise from such locations of evil happenings, legends of human sacrifice, hauntings, even gateways to hell. Wise people listen to such hearsay and stay away for fear of seeing evil or being contaminated by such dark forces. However you look at it these places exist though no one would ever suspect such darkness coming from this particular house. From the outside an observer would see a rather run down 1970's building, containing two separate flats, and certainly unfitting of any semblance to a haunted house. It was perfectly in keeping with the rest of the street and 46 Marlborough Drive had no reason to be thought of as evil, unless the story was still being written of what wickedness entered our world through its walls.

The blacked out Golf had been parked outside the house for two days now and no police had come knocking, while inside Jay Cleaver and Scott Hutchinson were sharing an uneasy alliance, but right now the older of the two young men was starting to lose his shit.

'We can't just not talk about it...we've gotta talk about it. How long do you think we can stay locked up in here? I need stuff...you need stuff...for crying out loud man I've got a job and a girlfriend. Jenna's not gonna keep going for this stupid flu story. Two men quarantining! Nah I'm sorry man this is mental...we've got to do something...!'

Jay was getting something from the kitchen with his back turned to Scott's latest outburst. The whole mood in the house had darkened greatly since the cannabis ran out. It had all been going so well, over twenty four hours spent smoking weed and playing video games, getting stoned and belly laughing while speaking of nothing related to the events of the day before. During those fun hours Jay had felt somewhere near contented, even realising why he liked Scott so much in the first place; the guy was funny, skinned up often, and best of all he was slightly less skilled than himself at video games.

However this shouty version of his on/off friend needed to be told.

Scott's mouth fell silent when he saw the knife. On its own it wouldn't be too frightening, just a normal household breadknife, but the tattooed hand gripping it was tense, had wielded a blade recently, and when he added this to the look on Jays face he knew a change of tack was required.

'Hey whoa, what the fuck you doing, man…?' Scott stuttered, hastily finding words.

Jay began to walk slowly and deliberately towards him. Scott could see tiny flecks of bread still stuck to the serrated edge of the blade, and trying to release the growing tension in his body, his mind threw up the line 'Oh crumbs' but fought down the sad chuckle in his stomach. He was frozen to the spot as Jay halved the distance between them and raised the knife. Scott looked into the face he'd cried laughing with in the last twenty four hours, but who now it seemed was quite possibly going to murder him. His mind could only imagine this crumb covered bread knife was going to hurt, a lot, and he would scream loudly when it happened.

Here it was again for Jay Cleaver, decision time, and he hated having to make them as sound reasonable choices were not his forte. Everything Jay chose to do in his life was a flip of a coin in his head, usually followed by ever increasing lies to justify the first bad decision, it was simply how he was put together, some may call him scum for his many cold hearted actions, but he saw himself as canny. So flipping the mental coin once more he watched it spin, looked down at the result, and decided to hold back on viciously stabbing his friend.

'Scott…Scotty Scott!' Jay said in an attempt to let his quarry know everything was going to be okay, most probably, while said quarry was trying to lower his look from petrified to seriously concerned, but horribly aware his bowels may let go any second.

'Fuck me man you look proper fucking scared.' Jay giggled in a childish way.

'Really…?' Scott's breathing barely able to fill a lung let alone two.

'Is that because you thought you were going to die?'

'Highly likely yes…' Scott confirmed with a touch of gallows humour.

'…Listen to you man being funny. That's cool you know. Nah, man that is…what ya call it…impressive! Yeah fucking impressive, that's what you are right now bro!'

Jay was enjoying himself and feeling this part of the game could continue for a while longer, he touched the knife to Scott's throat so he could watch the steel on the thin skin, then pressed a little firmer to see how soft it really was under there. Fuck, it wouldn't take much, barely any pressure at all to shut that mouth forever. Now for this teenage kid who'd never been in trouble for anything more than shoplifting, even he had to admit things had seriously changed in the last few days, so many life and death decisions with a knife in his hand!

His sixteen year old existence up until now had been a smoke-filled haze of fast food and sofa surfing whilst selling a bit of stuff here and there to keep things going. Now look at me, he thought, I'm a god, a top player on a hat trick of terminations, a triple fucking whammy blood on his hands cold stone killer...fuck I love this game!

'You got any last words...' Jay asked feeling entirely comfortable in his new character.

Scott's eyes were scrunched tight as the blade pressed on his throat, he didn't want to die but if he was going to then he certainly didn't want to see it happen, he reckoned feeling it would be quite enough.

'What...?' Scott replied through his quickly drying mouth.

'You know last words stuff. Fucking hell man I can't put it any simpler. Have you got anything to say before I kill ya...?' He then pushed the knife a fraction harder to the throat. '...Well?'

'Tell...tell my Mom I love her.' Scott blurted out as a frightened tear began to fall.

Jay considered Scott's response and watched the falling tear before laughing. 'Ha...tell her yourself you prick.' Placing his other hand on Scott's pale cheek he slapped it playfully before lowering the knife and stepping back.

'Just promise you won't be giving me anymore shit!' Jay demanded.

'I promise. I promise.' Scott conceded gratefully.

'You see Scotto that's all we needed to do...you know...sort the situation out. We just had to reach an understanding. Now go and clean yourself up man you fucking stink of something!'

Scott shuffled quickly to the safety of the bathroom and locked the door.

Jay felt suitably pleased with how that moment had gone as he turned towards the lounge window for his hourly peek though the curtains. It was all clear so he returned to the kitchen to finish off making his toast with the last two slices of bread. While putting the knife down he noticed the small mirror on the windowsill and caught his own reflection, he liked the way he looked today, growing into this unhinged nutter who'd cut ya if he had to. It helped that there'd also been a change of outfit from the rags his friend had offered him. Jay had taken the liberty of picking whatever he wanted out of Scott's wardrobe and this sweat top and tracksuit bottoms were pretty slick, because they were all dark blue, and they matched his eyes.

13

Dr Katherine Kelly was about as furious at this moment as she'd ever been. Driving aggressively through the morning traffic she was a dangerous weapon, with two wheels on the kerb she rounded a white van to make sure she was first to the roundabout, then barely glancing to check she pulled out so other drivers were given no choice but to stop and beep their horns. Their proactive audible frustrations were pointless however because she wasn't stopping for anything, not even to shout a profanity back in their direction, she needed to get to work at the facility and there wasn't a second to be wasted. That interfering idiot of a guard had already ruined her day, how dare he undermine her position, he was nothing more than a glorified lumbering doorman who she'd reminded on numerous occasions how this worked. If anything changes with Oscars condition she was to be notified immediately, not when he gets the opportunity, not when he has a minute, straight away, and he should never for any reason interfere with her process.

With knuckles whitened on the steering wheel she swerved to pass on the inside of the bus, summoning an even louder horn but even that failed to break through her fury. She was willing to go all the way with this; that guard was not only going to be fired, he was going to be charged, disciplined and disgraced, it was all over for Allan Kosminsky now.

Katherine knew the two of them had never found a connection even though they spent hours together in the same building working with the same 'subject'. The root of the problem being she thought he had an attitude that stunk of, 'I've been here longer than you, this facility is my world and you doctors just visit' or 'these prisoners are my responsibility because I spend more time with them', and all that was truly infuriating to her. She was a fully trained and experienced clinical psychologist who worked in a professional manner, while he was a dumb door opener who believed he was untouchable because of years served and his proximity to the subject. Well he was about to find out that you don't fuck around with this Doctor, no sir, he was going to find that right out.

Braking the car sharply at the gatehouse she regained a modicum of control when realising she had no recollection of actually driving there, before flashing her ID so the barrier could be raised, and she sped onto the ramp then down into the underground carpark.

The guard on the gate watched her disappear into the darkness before mouthing sarcastically under his breath. 'Yeah, oh me, I'm fine, Good morning to you to Doctor Kelly…thanks for ignoring me again…moody cow!'

Kosminsky meanwhile was sat watching Oscar on his computer, neither man had moved for hours, their eyes locked throughout, and the guard was beginning to feel their connection growing stronger. To begin with he'd been drawn to Oscars face like a voyeur who knew his subject couldn't see him. The man's blank expression an open invitation to study all you want because there might be something happening there. After a few minutes Kosminsky found he was unable to avert his gaze, to turn away for even a blink, and believing he could understand what was happening in the subjects head.

At times the guard felt he was almost in, he hadn't cracked the puzzle yet but this bond between them meant he could see the maze, the place where Oscar was trapped. To Kosminsky it appeared as a complex labyrinth with a million pathways leading away but only one that reached its very heart. He didn't know if he was getting closer because his visualised version of the maze gave no clues; simply corridor after corridor through the blackness of a night with bright stars glinting above him. Thinking sensibly he'd tried to use their positioning for a clue but when he looked to the stars for guidance they moved, before his very eyes the twinkling lights slid across the sky and dissolved deeming them utterly useless for navigation, but with gritted determination he continued his quest to find the little man. Oscar was somewhere within this dream, this hallucination, maybe even this different dimension, the truth was Kosminsky didn't know how or where he was going, only that it felt real and he had to find Oscar, ASA fucking P.

The Doctor sat in her office tapping her desk, restless for their meeting to begin, knowing a quick call and he would come lumbering out of the cell block, probably still believing he'd done a good thing by taking the crayons off Oscar, but damn she couldn't wait to put him right on that. There had been a brief moment when she'd contemplated bursting into his shitty little security room and having it out with him there and then, but on second thoughts a sliver of common sense had slithered through her anger. Do it by the book Katherine, follow procedure and nothing can go wrong, so after taking some deep breaths she felt her rage was finally controlled enough for her to plan out the most probable eventualities. Step by step was the answer; she knew that, after all this is what she was trained for, to deal with human emotions. Carefully she worked through the scenario where she just kicked his door open and gave him a garbling volcanic rant; it would probably involve smashing things, probably clearing his shelves with the back of her arm; however that situation always ended with him shouting back and their state of affairs growing critical. Another possible scenario was to avoid having a face to face at all which she could achieve by simply calling the Professor who employed them both then explain the situation to her. Basically just tell Caroline Wesson how this man was jeopardising all their good work and have her fire him. In all fairness this would be a prudent choice, a safe option, but it was nowhere near satisfying enough, she wanted the pleasure of telling him herself so there were no doubts, no misunderstandings, just a job well done when she finished his cocksure career.

While sat motionless at his desk Kosminsky wandered the labyrinth, ever onwards through the darkened corridors leading him to Oscar at the centre of it all. This dreamlike state had begun just after he'd confiscated the crayons. Feeling a certain satisfaction in saving a man's life he'd been marching up the stairs back to his office when he heard the sound of Oscar's scream. It was such an extraordinary roar he'd stopped with one hand on the stair rail to listen again, to validate the sound, but his ears found only the distant drums of his own heartbeat. With twinned excitement and fear he rushed back to the cell and put the key smoothly into the lock, pausing to listen for any sound from within he was met with silence, and feared the worst as he opened the door only to find Oscar standing at the window, except this time with one worrying difference, he was staring directly at him.

The Doctor pressed the intercom down with a strong thumb, hoping it would buzz annoyingly in Kosminsky's guard room and when he replied she would calmly summon him to her office for a chat. For starters there had been no seven o'clock report from him last night and that was bad enough, but when she'd found an email this morning stating he'd taken the crayons from Oscar well that was taking his insubordination to a whole new level of wrongdoing, and she had justification for her actions now.

There was no immediate answer from the guard so she pressed the buzzer again and held it down until her thumb turned white.

In the cell the two men had spoken without speaking and Kosminsky caught his first glimpse into Oscar's veiled mind. He could see the little man was trapped and scared, and although he didn't know what could be causing this fear, he truly believed he could help.

Katherine Kelly could feel her rage rising again, rolling out like molten lava deep under an ocean before turning back into solid blackened rock, so taking her finger from the buzzer she slammed her hand down in rage, cracking the plastic casing under her strike, proof she was travelling way beyond furious now. Okay scenario one it is then as she stood up sharply, the office door almost flinching as she grabbed the handle, before storming down towards the cells.

Kosminsky had eventually returned to his office after the shared moment of connection with Oscar and he'd stayed there all night. There had been no end of shift for him, he had work to do, a man lost had to be saved. So through the night, minute after minute, hour after hour he walked the labyrinth, this place of confusion that Oscar had invited him to. At some point he vaguely recollected sending an email to the Doctor, something about taking crayons, but it could wait as right now he was busy trying to find the centre of a maze.

Katherine's stern gaze was fixed on the route ahead, no second thoughts or doubts were crossing her path, none would have dared as she turned the final corner to face Kosminsky's closed guard room door. Inside her was a maelstrom of fury and there was not a chance she was going to knock as she gripped the handle.

Oscars mind was grateful for the company the guard had been giving him. Although they weren't together yet he could hear the man's voice calling his name through the maze. It was so close, he wasn't far away at all, and when they teamed up the two of them would outnumber and defeat the monster in his mind. It was all going to be okay, all going to be fine and when he was free everyone would understand it wasn't his fault and he could go back to his job and drive people around, take them where they wanted to go, because that's what he did, good old reliable Oscar. 'Not to the door, through the door...'

The professionally respected but now wildly manic Katherine Kelly pushed the thick security door of Kosminsky's guard room open sharply, frustratingly it didn't hit anything solid therefore failed to produce the noisy dramatic effect she'd wished for, but it didn't matter because here was Kosminsky sat in front of his computer screen. She stomped across the couple of yards distance to stand next to him but he didn't react. Then she found her words that had been spilling out in preparation all morning had disappeared as she stared at the side of the big guards face. Confusingly he didn't seem to be aware of her presence. '...Officer Kosminsky I need to have a very serious word with you...!' She was shouting directly at him but her voice faded away in volume and strength before she'd gotten to the end of the sentence. Something wasn't right, he wasn't responding to her being in the room and from his profile she could see his eyes were dark and glassy, all recognisable expression lost as every muscle in his face sagged. There was no doubt he wasn't aware of her presence, of anything for that matter, and she'd seen enough of that expression just lately to know whom he most closely resembled.

The Doctor carefully crouched down at the side of Kosminsky's knee to examine his emotionally unadorned façade, her anger now being replaced by something else entirely, a sense of growing unease although at this moment she didn't know why. Confused by the whole situation she looked at his computer and in the corner of the screen was a tiny image of Oscar's cell. When she pressed the key to enlarge it she began to understand exactly what new feeling was replacing her anger, as the screen showed a high definition picture of Oscar's empty cell...with the door wide open.

Now Katherine Kelly was blatantly a clever lady, an intellectual and professional psychologist no less, so her mind followed the clues with impressive speed. Looking back at Kosminsky's face she found he'd turned his head to the side; she followed his eye line back towards the door, the same door that hadn't made a sound when she'd thrust it open, the same door that Oscar had let hit his hands, and now the door he was slowly closing as the voice thundered in his head.

14

Inspector Harvey Cooper was in his office making notes from the initial findings report. They'd taken two days to compile and reach his desk but he'd been busy; forty eight hours in which time he'd finally spoken to the Doctors in the hospital which gave him a more complete picture. As he'd first suspected Mr Downing the elder man had died from his injuries which told of a savage assault, three deep stab wounds to the abdomen. There was no sign of the man putting up a struggle which meant the stabbings were swift and unexpected, an interesting scenario, because as far as he could tell there was no robbery, but occurring so close to the man's front door meant there had to be something the Inspector was missing. He'd entered the deceased's property with two officers yesterday, using the keys found in Mr Downing's jacket, and although the rooms were untidy and cluttered with a desperate need to be cleaned, he found nothing out of the ordinary. He did discover an old rusted tea caddy at the back of a kitchen cupboard which contained £880 in £20 pound notes, perhaps the old man's rainy day money, maybe his life savings, but regardless of that this discovery convinced Harvey any kind of robbery was out of the question. After all it wasn't hidden very well because he'd found it without really trying so surely a conscientious robber with any level of intention would have done the same, and there were other details that troubled him, for instance the old man's Labrador, which was being looked after by a neighbour for now, was uninjured which pointed to the old man having tied the dog up before the attack occurred. Why? His next detecting step would be to see if there were any connections with the other man on the street, the younger victim still in hospital, the one who was about to have his left arm amputated. Harvey knew about this because Ward Sister Hodgson had called to let him know the operation was booked for today. He shivered at the thought they had to operate on the man who had fallen from a window apparently, the man who fell to earth...Yeah right on Harvey's bloody beat.

Flipping the page he found the paragraph in the forensics report, the one he wanted to study further, and as he read it he began to paint a picture.

...next to the younger man's body there was an errant bloodspot. There was no blood or weapon on the younger man apart from some bleeding from the nose and ear due to a heavy fall, on being notified of this Constable Hughes actioned a search of the area for more bloodspots. A second elongated spot was located three feet away in the direction of Leith Walk; Approx four feet further away was another elongated spot also in the direction of Leith Walk. On the corner of the junction with Dalmeny Street one more bloodspot was discovered. After an extensive search no more bloodspots were found in either direction.

Reading this confirmed his nagging suspicion about the bizarre crime scene, because if there was no connection between the two victims, and clearly one hadn't attacked the other, then there had to have been someone else there, a third person who ran away, and one who was more than likely carrying a knife at the time. Okay so let's get working this out, thought Harvey, still excited when the first occasion of a bloodied scent entered his professional nostrils, placing the report down he breathed in deeply to take in the aroma and now he had it there would be no letting go. He drummed his pencil on the desktop as he began his mental pursuit of the truth.

Here goes, the old man George Downing tied up his dog to the door before he was stabbed by an attacker, who made their escape onto Leith Walk before running down the hill towards the docks. All of this was clearly illustrated with the elongated bloodspots showing the assailants direction of travel and probable speed. The fallen man still remained a conundrum, why he would be there, unless, unless the assailant is also a window killer, perhaps one who pushed the man out of the building but the old man saw it, so they killed the only witness and ran away towards the docks.

Harvey was trying with all his deductive experience to determine a more reasonable workable scenario but none fitted using all the material available at this time. In fact with a small leap it may even account for the old man's dog being tied to the door. The old man did that before he went to confront the killer. Why would he? He would do that because he didn't believe he would need the dogs help, after all if someone is knowingly coming at you with a knife surely you would want to keep the dog near as a form of protection, but no, the old man hadn't believed the dog was needed because he didn't perceive the killer as a threat at first. Now this was all well and good but why would the old man not be alarmed when he'd seen a body on the street quickly followed by the perpetrator? Okay this was trickier than he'd first thought and it stopped him in his tracks for now, but he'd crack it because this is what Harvey loved to do.

His phone rang and he looked down to find it was the hospital calling. He answered with a calm 'Hello.' and immediately recognised the dulcet tones of Ward Sister Hodgson.

'Is that Inspector Cooper..?'

'...Yes it is. How are you...?' Harvey spoke pleasantly even though he was close to being annoyed with the interruption. He never enjoyed being knocked off his crime solving perch.

'I have some news.' She sounded nervous and whispery.

'Oh yes and what's this?' Quickly deciding if the news was good enough he may even forgive her intrusion into his deduction work.

'Well you did ask me to call if anyone came to visit the patient in the coma...you know the one without any identification.'

'...Trust me Sister I know exactly who you're talking about.'

'Well his wife's here now!'

Harvey was momentarily stunned by this information. 'His wife you say...?'

'...Arrived about ten minutes ago, she gave us a positive identification, even brought along his passport...the man's name is Alex Walter Webb.'

Harvey said thank you, told her he would be right over, and true to his word with this kind of information forthcoming he forgave the Ward Sister her intrusion. It was an interesting turn of events and even now new questions were beginning to fizz and pop in his head. For a start the man Mr Webb hadn't been reported as wearing a wedding ring and now a wife shows up a full two days after her husband goes missing. Was that suspicious? All he knew for certain was that his own wife Florence would never leave him lost for two days, and with that comforting thought in his head he grabbed his car keys and hastened back to the hospital.

15

Oscar had the freedom of the facility wing now, he guessed no one else would be checking because they'd believe Kosminsky was on duty, so using this time he checked rooms for useful things. He wasn't sure of exactly what he needed but he shuffled on with his small steps regardless opening doors with the keys he'd acquired from the guard's belt. The voice in his head had ordered him to take the keys but for the last few minutes it had gone quiet. He thought perhaps it might be resting, it had been unbelievably loud back in the guard's office, filling his head with horrible profanities and spine chilling screams. They'd been as loud as Oscar could ever remember, especially when he'd closed the door and walked slowly towards the Doctor, but after that moment he couldn't recall anything else.

The little man in his baggy facility issued shirt and trousers found a shower cubicle; it was exactly what he needed because he felt unclean although he couldn't remember why, but he was quite sure the voice would remind him soon enough. As the warm water sprinkled down Oscar stripped off the heavy clothes and cleaned all the uncomfortable stickiness from his body, washing and scrubbing until his skin stung. After twenty minutes he was satisfied, only to then find he had no towel, he looked down at the stained clothes which were the only material to hand but they were far too dirty to be used. So Oscar sat down on a wooden chair next to the shower cubicle and waited for his tiny frame to dry. He was enjoying the feeling of freedom again, and he knew for certain the voice would appreciate it, which was confirmed when it suddenly spoke; more accurately screamed, and told him what it wanted to do next. Thus wet naked Oscar was given no choice but to listen to its plans as he'd done for five torturous years.

16

At 46 Marlborough Drive the two teenagers inside were sleeping in separate rooms. Scott Hutchinson had been relegated to the sofa while his unwanted friend was spreading out starfish style on the double bed. Barely a word had passed between them since the 'new understanding' had been reached, but Jay Cleaver was now totally dominant and even added a few amendments to the original agreement, mainly concerning Scott's role in this friendship and what would happen to his girlfriend or family members if he didn't do as he was told.

Scott lay curled up on the sofa feeling uncomfortable, miserable, and fearful. Imprisoned inside the flat he paid for. He turned over to lie on his back, then staring up at the chipped paint on the yellowing ceiling he tried to imagine if this situation could actually get any worse, having already run out of food when Jay had taken the last box of breakfast cereal to his room and eaten its contents dry. He jumped sharply when the silence was suddenly shattered by the letterbox clattering only two feet from his head.

'Fuck even the house is making me jump!' Scott mumbled to himself as he rolled off the sofa to retrieve the mail. Nothing exciting, a flyer advertising a local window cleaner that would, wait for it, for just a few pounds more clean the guttering as well, he checked the back to see if they offered any other services, such as removing a murdering nutter from your bed.

Listening to the postal workers steps fading away on the street gave him an idea, but really, just how far did he think he'd get if he made a run for it now? Obviously he couldn't use the car because Jay had the keys; one of the amendments added last night along with any sharp knives being put into his possession. Scott reckoned he could probably make it quite far, especially if Jay was sleeping, perhaps he could even get to the police station and hand himself in. After all he hadn't done anything wrong, well not on purpose because surely you can't be jailed for picking up a mate in need of help, and especially if that mate is a sixteen year old murderer who's holding you hostage in your own abode.

'What ya doing…?' Jay's voice split the silence making Scott jump in his skin again.

'Fuck! Nothing I'm just picking up this shit.' He answered crumpling up the flyer which he threw towards the overflowing bin where it bounced off an empty brown plastic cider bottle before settling on the carpet near the TV. How fucking long had Jay been standing there? It was an obvious concern to Scott but not his main worry right now, he had a more pressing matter he'd thought of while lying on the sofa, a question he wanted to ask his captor, but not without good reason he was mortally terrified that Jay would kick off again.

'Get back on your sofa.' Jay snapped at him.

'Like a good dog?' Scott responded.

'What did I tell you about giving me shit?'

'Jay! I'm not giving you shit I'm just joking you know.'

'That's alright then. Listen I need to do something. I mean we have to do something...like now as soon as...!' With that said Jay bent down picked up the cider bottle and emptied the very last of its flat dregs into his mouth. '...We've gotta go see my Auntie....'

Scott stared at his 'mate' and seriously hoped he was joking.

Jay saw that doubt and added. '...Don't worry...It's a really clever plan...if you think about it.'

Well that was precisely what Scott was doing, and the more he thought about it the more he disagreed, silently of course.

'My Auntie will help us out. Look I've got money but I ain't going to any fucking shops and neither are you. I don't want us on camera anywhere. So I'm thinking we go to my Aunties, get fed, maybe buy some food off her or through her yeah...she could go to the shops for us...'

Jay wasn't making much sense to Scott but just lately that really wasn't unusual.

'...She'll probably have some weed as well!'

Scott looked at skinny psycho Jay and conceded at this precise moment he had nothing to offer this exchange, not a damn thing, he was unarmed, undernourished and under stoned, so he lay back down on the sofa like a good dog while trying not to scream out in mental anguish as Jay continued to explain his 'plan'.

'So this is what we are gonna do Scotty dog. Ha ha...in a bit you're going to drive us to my Auntie's house. Like I said she'll feed us and stuff. Now this is the really good part yeah...this is the clever bit. We can find out what's been going on in the street at the same time...' Jay nodded his head slowly at Scott as if he expected him to jump up and declare him a genius. '...Yeah you know it's a good plan...I am all fucking over this. So come on you lazy shit, get ready.'

Scott could see no good coming from this idea, and with obviously nothing much else to hope for, he decided to get brave.

'I need to ask you something Jay!' He spoke warmly, treading carefully.

'Are you gonna drive us over there or do you need convincing…?' Jay countered.

'Yeah of course I'll drive.' Scott knew he may never get Jay any calmer than this so he asked his risky question. '…What did you do with the knife?'

Jay laughed his horrible hacking laugh. 'It's here…!' He rolled up a leg on his jogging pants then pulled the breadknife out from one of Scott's long football socks. '…Happy…?'

'Not that one.' Scott took a long slow breath before continuing. 'The other one, the one you used on the old guy. I don't remember seeing it!'

'You are giving me shit…?' Jay said in a sickeningly condescending fashion.

'…Why the fuck would I do that? You've got a bread knife down your sock and I know you'll use it. I accept you're totally capable of killing me. Okay? You have my utmost respect under these circumstances so the last thing I would ever do is give you shit. I just wanted to know what happened to the other knife.' Scott had spoken then put his head down and held his breath.

There was a long pause before Jay responded. 'I threw it behind the bus shelter!'

'The one I picked you up from?'

'Yeah, I didn't want to get the wet blood on your seat covers man!'

'That's considerate.' Scott replied sarcastically but Jay missed it.

'There was a gap behind the bus stop and the wall. I dropped it down there. It fell straight to the bottom in all the rubbish and stuff. There's nobody gonna find that.'

'Aren't you worried about dogs?' Scott asked.

'…What fucking dogs?'

'Police dogs, sniffer dogs, they have em you know!' He watched his words have a slow dumbing effect on Jay.

A crucifying long pause passed to the point that Scott began to fear the worst but in the end Jay saw sense. '…Okay I get what you mean. We need to sort that as well…so on the way to my Aunties we go to the bus stop. I'll get the knife back and then we go bury it somewhere.'

'If it's still there…?' Scott said worryingly.

'…It will be!' Jay responded with shaky defiance.

It was a quite beautiful sunny lunchtime in the outskirts as the two young men closed the doors of the Golf and prepared for the drive. Jay was now wearing Scott's oversized red hoodie with his whole face hidden from view, unless you were brave enough to put your head on his lap and look up. Pushing the keys in the ignition Scott looked across at his cloaked passenger thinking he looked more suspicious than ever.

'Aren't you a bit warm in that?' He asked with his only personal preference for disguise being a pulled down baseball cap.

'No!' Jay lied aggressively

'Okay I was just asking.'

'Just swing us by the bus stop and shut the fuck up!'

Scott started the car and soon they were driving away from the house into a world they hadn't seen in nearly two whole days. He turned down roads feeling every person they saw was now a potential threat to their freedom. Reaching the temporary traffic lights Scott eased to a halt but after ten seconds of waiting for them to change Jay started to get edgy.

'Just go they're fucked!' He ordered.

'They're on red man. Do you wanna get pulled over by the police?'

'This is too long. I don't want to be sat here like this, just fucking drive...!' When the car didn't move straight away Jay began rolling up his trouser leg to show Scott the knife. '...I said go!'

'Bro I'm waiting and all the cars behind us are waiting. Just chill man...!' He looked up at the red light then back to Jay sliding the weapon out of his sock. '...Change for fuc...' Scott began to say as the lights finally listened and with immense gratification they moved. He'd survived another of Jays growing threats and could only hope to continue this lucky run of avoiding any physical pain, inside though a strong gut feeling told him the chances of that were slim and none of this would end well.

The car turned on to Leith Walk, heading up away from the docks until the bus stop came in to view. There was a small crowd gathered and then they saw the two policemen, one clearly a dog handler, moving the onlookers away.

'Oh my god...!' Scott blurted as he comprehended the scene. '...No fucking way...!' He forced his nerves to drive calmly past the ongoing investigation before looking over at his friend who had slid himself almost all the way down into the foot-well, so all Scott could glimpse was the tip of his nose peeking out from the hood.

'Okay man, it's just a knife...' Jay said. '...Keep driving and don't do anything stupid...go to my Aunties.'

'How about we just go back to the house...?' Scott said trying to turn the tide towards a less rocky shoreline. '...If you've got money Jay, which by the way I didn't know about until this morning, then we can order food in. We'll be safe in the house and we'll be able to work out a better plan…'

In a dull flash of steel Jay reached over and cut Scott across the back of his left hand.

'…Fucking hell Jay…!'

Scott grimaced and looked down at his now non driving hand to see blood appearing on the two inch wound. Fair enough it wasn't deep but it hurt like hell and was beginning to drip a little.

'Drive to my Auntie's house…' Jay said in a manner that somehow made it sound as if all this madness was Scott's doing.

Two minutes later the first thing they noticed as they turned into Dalmeny Street was the complete lack of police here. Everything looked calm and normal, as far as they could tell the only clue that anything had even occurred was a piece of torn blue and white police tape on a street sign just fluttering in the wind. When Scott completed the left turn the murder scene came into view, but again there were no obvious signs that anything had happened here, even Jay pushed himself back into a sitting position to take in this sight of normality. They both acted as fake casual as two scared young guys in a blacked out car could manage. Scott pulled over when he was ordered to, then without another word they got out and entered the building; the place where all of the problems had started. After a lung busting tramp up the stairs Jay paused outside his Auntie's front door summoning up the courage to knock.

'Is that where you were standing when you saw the guy…?' Scott asked indicating the large window at the end of the hallway.

Jay walked back towards him slowly and deliberately, 'Do you want to get cut again…?'

'…What? No…!'

'…Then shut up!' Jay spat.

Scott knew he was on another final warning and waited quietly as his tormentor knocked on the door. It was greeted with immediate loud barking and the scratching of a desperate soul.

'I didn't know your Auntie had a dog…' Scott said innocently.

Jay Cleaver took a single step away from the door '…She doesn't!'

17

Harvey Cooper finally arrived at the hospital, his journey a little slower than expected because a short cut to speed him along had been anything but. The problem was those temporary traffic lights down in Leith; they took an age to get through. He paid at the machine then returned to his car to put the parking ticket in his window; truth was he didn't have to pay being on police duty, but it made him feel better to do so, like he was giving a little back. He jogged almost jauntily to the entrance and swiftly located Ward Sister Hodgson.

'Is the wife still here?'

'Yes she's up there now.'

'Could I possibly go and see them...?' He asked half expecting to be told to wait again.

'I really shouldn't allow that because its family only...but...' She glanced left then right. '...let's say I didn't know you're going there, well I couldn't stop you walking up to the first floor, private room 6C now could I?' She half smiled before turning away to resume her duties.

Harvey was really beginning to warm to her, enjoying that surprised feeling when a first impression gets totally flipped around because that woman was an angel. Smiling at this recognition he set off to begin his hunt for private room 6C. At the top of the stairs he worked out from a dozen different directions pointed out on a signboard where he had to go, and of course it was the last room at the end of the corridor, couldn't be the first, it never was. He politely knocked and the door was opened by a pretty nurse in a sky blue uniform.

'Can I help you?' She smiled.

'Erm yes...could I have a quick word...out here perhaps?' He indicated the corridor.

'I'm afraid I'm very busy at the moment but if you go down to reception...'

Harvey interrupted. 'Just one second of your time, please.'

She paused then turned and addressed the lady in the room but from Harvey's viewpoint all he could see was the back of a long brown coat.

'I'll be back in a minute Linda.' She said gently closing the door.

'Thank you. I'm Inspector Cooper investigating what happened to the man in there. Alex Webb I believe his name is. You see up until this morning I wasn't aware he had a wife.'

'Okay...?' The nurse said still none the wiser on how she could help.

'Well you see I would very much like to talk to her.'

'I understand but why can't you wait until she's finished?

'That is a very good point…' Harvey thought and said.

There followed a brief silence before the nurse spoke again

'Although they aren't married anymore Inspector…they're separated. I wouldn't want you committing the same faux pas I did this morning.'

'Oh god no of course…useful tip…thank you for that…' Harvey was actually being thrown off course by how lovely he found this young nurse. '…I do need to talk to her now to be honest.'

'It can't wait…?' Her hazel eyes held his gaze.

'…It's very important…police business.' Damn he hated pressuring her.

She checked the time on her fob watch attached to her dress. '…Very well but I'm going to have to stay in the room. Alex needs to be constantly monitored.' Now that medical claim wasn't actually true but she didn't want her patient disturbed, of course there wasn't much chance of that with him being in a coma but all the same he was her responsibility.

'That would be just perfect thank you.' His eyes fell to her chest so he could read the badge, Nurse Juliet Moore.

'…That's alright Inspector…follow me.'

As Harvey entered room 6C his inquiring instincts began to take over. The obvious focal point was the bed with the heavily bandaged Alex laid down in a coma, to the left stood a machine that was clearly keeping his condition stable with its lights flashing calmly, and to the right stood a lady in a long brown mac, the ex-Mrs Webb as far as he knew.

'Who is this?' She asked letting go of Alex's good right hand.

'This is Inspector…I'm sorry?' Nurse Juliet clicked her fingers for help.

Really, she'd forgotten his name already? That hurt his male pride a little but he battled through. 'Cooper! And you're Mrs Linda Webb, Alex's wife?

'No we're separated!' She snapped tersely.

Harvey felt like punching himself in the face, but he began again and tried to pull himself together from his pre warned faux pas. When he glanced at Nurse Juliet her incredulous look reminded him of what an idiot he felt. 'My apologies…!' He offered up somewhat sheepishly.

'How can I help you…?' Linda asked, ignoring his regret.

'…Well I need to find out what happened to your…to erm, to Alex…and I was hoping you could help me with that inquiry.' That was better, he felt like a policeman again.

'Which part?' Linda's face was quite hard looking Harvey thought, even glancing across at Nurse Juliet to confirm that not all female faces looked that way. Then taking out his trusted notebook and pencil, because pencils never run out unexpectedly, he prepared to ask his questions.

'All of it.' Harvey responded. '...When for instance...as in how long have you and Alex been separated?'

'About three weeks now.'

'Three weeks?' Harvey repeated it back because he didn't think that was long at all.

'Yes he moved out. We've been in regular contact. By that I mean we talked on the phone every couple of days. We were trying to find a way to make it work.'

'...The marriage..?' ventured Harvey.

'...No...the separation!'

'...Right!' He kicked himself mentally again and pretended to jot something down on his opened notepad before continuing. 'So could you tell me how you found out about his condition?'

Linda looked closely at Harvey before answering, perhaps scrutinising to see if he was an actual policeman, anyway his physical looks alone must have convinced her because eventually she sighed and answered him.

'I hadn't heard from Alex for nearly three days, when I saw the news and read about what happened, and seeing it was on the street where we used to live, well obviously I phoned the hospital to check...?'

'...And how did you confirm that fact if you don't mind me asking? After all, the hospital didn't know who he was.'

'Oh that was me....' Nurse Juliet piped up. '...He's my patient so when I heard there was a lady on the phone enquiring about him I asked to speak to her. We spoke for a while and she asked if he had a tattoo on his calf of a Celtic cross, which he has, so Linda then came to the hospital and brought along his passport.' She then smiled in a fluttery way feeling a little like a detective herself.

Harvey nodded his appreciation. 'It's fine, I'm not questioning your status to your....hmm to Alex...just tidying up loose ends you understand...' Then he was struck by a new concerning query and turned to Nurse Juliet. 'I'm sorry if this is a stupid question but...can he hear us?'

Her response was both professional and to the point which he appreciated greatly. 'It's been known that patients in a coma can still hear the world around them.' As soon as she finished her answer the room went quiet, suddenly no one wanted to speak, and even she felt weird.

'Erm...would either of you two like a coffee...?'

'Yes please.' Harvey answered.

'No thank you!' Linda replied coldly and with a stare that caught the Inspector's eye.

'Actually no leave that. I think I'm fine.' Harvey said and smiled once more at Juliet who, even without a valid reason, excused herself and left the room leaving the two of them to it.

'Would you prefer to come down to the station to make a statement?'

'No, I certainly would not.'

'Oh right okay. I'll err have to ask you my questions here then.' Noticing the look she gave to her phone.

'I only have a couple more minutes, Inspector. Then I have to leave...so if you could make it quick.'

Now Harvey was an experienced policeman yet he was quite befuddled by this woman's ability to control a situation as he found himself doing exactly what she asked.

'Very well, Mrs...err Linda, this flat in Dalmeny Street, was he still occupying it...?'

'No he was staying in a boarding house by the docks. Quayside Lettings I think. They're the ones you need to talk to. I don't know his exact address I haven't been there.'

'You never visited him?'

'No. We're separated. Also I'm in a new relationship now!'

'Very well...that's fine...!' Harvey said without thinking.

'I know it is!' She confirmed without mercy.

'One final question...' He paused in an obvious play for more time. '...I mean we may need to talk again at some point but for now...could you tell me, do you think he could have been involved in something he shouldn't have, maybe someone, or some people may have wanted him to err...fall out of a building...?' As soon as he finished the question he regretted asking it because of the look it created on the estranged wife's face.

'...Suicide!' Linda replied with total conviction.

'You sound very sure of that.' Harvey licked the end of his pencil.

'I am sure of it. He told me was going to do it!'

'What? Could you tell me exactly when he told you?' Harvey suddenly didn't want this conversation to end.

'He said it all the time Inspector. Our last conversation he said he was going to go back to our old flat to do it!'

'And why do you think he'd do that?'

'He told me it was the place we'd had our most amazing times together…so he wanted to ruin those memories for me.'

Harvey ventured another quick question before the time run out. 'Is there perhaps any good reason why you didn't inform the police of this suicide plan?'

'I'm informing you now aren't I?'

'Sorry I don't follow…' Harvey was genuinely puzzled by her blasé attitude.

'…Please understand, Alex was always threatening to end it all. He once told me was going to drown himself at the docks, another time he was going to lay under a tram, but the best one he gave me was a threat to secure a rope at the top of the castle and throw himself over the battlements. Incidentally these were all in the last three weeks, before that when we were still together he had many more, it was his big finish to the fights we had.'

'So you believed he wasn't being serious about this threat?

'Well obviously not based on past experience. Also Inspector he's in a coma so technically he hasn't committed suicide. He even failed at that…in fact all he's done is jump off a building.'

'…From your old bedroom window…?'

'…It was the front room window actually, the bedrooms at the back…'

'…But you do agree he tried to kill himself?'

'I have to go now inspector. I'm sorry to disappoint you but I don't think there is anything mysterious going on with Alex.' Then by way of farewell she squeezed her estranged husband's hand and without once looking at the Inspector calmly strolled out the door.

'Just one final question…?' The look she savagely threw back left him in no doubt that one more was all he was going to get. '…Did either of you know the old man who was murdered?'

'Well I certainly didn't and I don't believe Alex did, but you can ask him yourself when he wakes up, good bye Inspector.' Linda Webb disappeared through the door.

'Wow she's a card!' He'd wanted to say something much worse but with the chance her husband could be listening he thought better of it. The gentle beeping of the machine was strangely hypnotic, calming even, and now with Linda gone and Nurse Julia still absent Harvey found he was alone with Alex Webb. It was strange to think that this man had been his sole obsession for two solid days and yet this was the first time they'd actually met. Then he thought perhaps 'met' was too strong a description for this situation. The bandages covering his one arm, head and chest were solid thick and white. In fact the whole room was white, very sterile, thought Harvey, before noticing the passport on the window sill. Never one to fight his curiosity he went over and opened it to find a typically awful photograph of Alex Webb's pre accident face. Why did everyone's passport photo look as if they'd just finished a ten year stretch in a South American jail?

Harvey read Alex's emergency contact details written on the back page which said he still lived at the flat in Dalmeny Street, but of course obviously it would, mused Harvey, nobody changed their passport details within three weeks of moving out. Needing a new plan he decided with the weather still being pleasant, that his next port of call should be the Webb's old flat, but before leaving the hospital Harvey made a point of tracking down Nurse Juliet to thank her for her assistance.

<u>18</u>

Alex was sat in the white cell again after the Angel had dismissed him earlier, but he was confident he would be summoned again, so waited for that herald call by watching the white spider reconstruct its white web to catch a white fly. What else can a man do with literally nothing to do? Well for this man it was to repeat the same cycle and think about Linda, the estranged wife who he'd loved with all his heart, even though he couldn't fathom out why anymore. They'd been together for seven years and if he were to grade them he would rate the first year as amazing, the next three years occasionally amazing but mainly comfy, the two years after that very argumentative before a final twelve months filled with deceit and spitefulness. Yes, he reckoned that about summed it up and he also knew why. That was easy because it was all her fault of course, every single bit of it; he wouldn't be here going crazy in this frustrating white world having occasional awkward chats with an Angel if it wasn't for her cheating on him. He wouldn't have wanted to jump off a building and kill himself if she'd kept her knickers on, or worst of all...if she hadn't of told him so many lies. That deceit had driven him up the wall and eventually off it; he smiled at the analogy, but soon found himself back on his usual track. Linda hadn't even been clever about it, going to work in ever sexier outfits, hiding her phone screen from him, working late because of a "large workload and then the biggest lie of all, the stinger that hurt the most, to think he actually believed she was going away on a teambuilding weekend.

The white door to his cell silently reappeared and he was grateful for the chance to think of something else for a while. He stepped through the bright portal to meet an Angel again...only this was a real Angel.

19

On the wing of the facility Oscar had found some fresh clothing, it wasn't perfect but it would have to suffice as he put on some strangers gym gear in a side room. Whoever this garb belonged to couldn't have been a large man as the white shorts and green top fitted him pretty well. It was odd but this running vest made even Oscar look svelte and trim rather than pigeon chested and starving, and he wondered how they tailored such items to achieve this real life magic, tricking an observer's eye into believing you were a far better specimen than you actually deserved to appear.

He touched the back of his head feeling the indentation where the stiletto had fractured his skull, it was itching, and now the voice was stirring because Oscar hadn't done what it asked.

What are you doing?

Nothing!

I am well aware of that. We have to get out of here Oscar.

I don't know how.

I told you how.

I tried to do that. I tried to do what you said but I couldn't do it right. I couldn't cut the skin off properly. I only had scissors. I couldn't get it off in one piece. It went all ragged and torn. I got tired from trying...I had to stop.

Well Oscar you have failed again, just as you did when they caught us.

The wheels were stuck in the mud.

Be quiet. Oh and Oscar...

...Yes?

Do not test my patience.

I won't.

Good boy!

20

Methamphetamine use is on the increase in all of our major cities; its popularity due to its intense high, increasing the user's dopamine levels and causing a feeling of euphoria lasting up to twelve hours, while other associations attributed are an increased libido and a more intense sexual pleasure. Perhaps that's how a meth salesman would spin it out but the facts of long term meth abuse are unsurprisingly not so positive, so let's see how a meth salesman wouldn't describe it.

Methamphetamine use is on the increase in all of our major cities; its long term effects are physical, emotional and cognitive disabilities, causing crippling anxiety and violent aggression alongside insomnia, hallucinations and paranoia. It also causes a condition called 'meth mouth', this is where the addicts clench their jaw so tightly they destroy the teeth which rapidly begin to weaken then rot away.

From all this information there was one simple fact that could be qualified. Jay Cleavers Auntie was a certified meth head.

The strange dog barked as two confused boys waited for the door to open Scott even wincing slightly as a horrible dry croak told them to hold on a minute.'...Come here you stupid shitty dog...get in there...get in there...get in...!' From inside a door was slammed shut and that croaky voice came towards them again. 'Who is it?'

'It's me, Auntie. It's Jay.'

Three locks were quickly unbolted and the door opened inwards. Scott couldn't see her immediately being stood to the side and it was only when Auntie came out and hugged her nephew that Scott's natural instinct to run was triggered. He'd heard stories about people like this but it was the first time he'd seen a meth user up close. She was wearing a filthy black jumper stained in colours that could only have come from a violently ill rainbow pallet with blue flowered leggings that hung loose on her disgusting legs. Scabs and blisters some open and weeping covered the skin he could see and he didn't care to imagine what the hidden parts looked like. Her thin greying hair was matted to her skull. She released the hug, looked at her nephew. 'Oh Jay it's so good to see you...' Her voice rasped higher as she turned to face Scott. '...Oooh is this one of your friends?' Bizarrely it seemed she was trying to act and sound like a friendly Auntie, the type you'd enjoy meeting, but all the wholesome physical parts of her were long gone. What remained was a shell of a person with sunken eyes dark and red, her jawline crumpled so her lips were rutted and distorted, but worst of all were the sores, so many all around her mouth up to her ears and down her neck. 'Give me a hug you...!'

Holy fuck Scott thought but what could he really do in this moment?

So with bravery above and beyond the call of duty he hugged Jay's Auntie, mimicking joy in the most credible way possible, while trying to avoid making any actual bodily contact. His eyes were shut tight as she moved in and the scent was incredible, she smelled of halitosis and sweat, but they were just the underlying aromas almost totally masked by the overpowering stench of pus and shit.

'Hello. I'm Scott.' He said pulling away a little too quickly.

'Are you okay?' She asked.

It was then he glimpsed what was left of her teeth. 'I'm fine...just a bit shy.' That wasn't a total lie, especially when it came to hugging strangers, but in this situation admitting his shyness felt like a superpower.

She went inside and her completely unaffected nephew followed, but Scott held back, a couple of seconds passed before Jay popped his scrawny nasty face back round the door 'Come on you prick!' So tentatively he walked down the rubbish cluttered hallway into a living room he imagined even Hell would have to redecorate. In all fairness Scott wasn't new to this, he'd seen his fair share of doss houses and drug dens, but this was way off the chart. There was no way of knowing what the stains and smears on the walls were from but he doubted any were pleasant. She grabbed up clothes and blankets strewn over the sofa throwing them into a corner that already had its fair share of flammable items. '...I'd make you a nice hot drink but they cut my water off yesterday.'

'That's okay Auntie. Are they coming to put it back on soon...?' Jay asked, using what Scott could only describe as his best fake nephew voice.

'I doubt it...the sneaky bastards!'

'They can't leave you without water Auntie.' Jay said with a tone that sounded genuinely concerned, as if there were some real chance an injustice had been served here, when it was blatantly clear this woman never paid bills of any sort.

'That's what I told them but they did it anyway. They snuck in when the policemen were here...used the law to protect themselves they did, the sneaky bastards...' Suddenly she started with a retching cough that Scott was amazed she had any control over, the awful noise only stopping when the dog started barking and she responded. 'Shut up you fucking idiot...!'

Quite unsurprisingly the dog fell quiet.

'When did you get a dog?' Jay asked.

'Do you want to meet it...?'

'...Not really' A truthful response as Jay had no affinity with dogs.

'I would!' Scott said enthusiastically, anything to take his mind off this situation and give it something else to focus on.

With that she went to a door in the hallway and opened it. The sound of frantic dog feet rushed in then a blur of panting yellow fur jumped straight on to Scott's lap. It was licking his face with such fervour it felt like it was trying to burrow into his very soul, most likely to escape this place. Now Scott had met overenthusiastic dogs before but this one was taking the excitable dog biscuit, so he ruffled its fur and gently stroked its ears feeling how soft they were, and found this was a beautiful huggable dog that loved fuss. Scott was feeling bad that this big softy was stuck in this hellhole when all of a sudden the dog turned and saw Jay. Instantly its posture turned rigid as its hackles rose sharply, its weight went back onto its hind legs as it began to snarl aggressively. Instinctively to save what he felt could be the imminent mauling of his friend, Scott grabbed its collar spotting the nametag flash its lettering 'Goldie', and before he knew it he was using all of his strength to hold the dog back.

Jay of course had recognised the animal straight away, staying perfectly still while he watched it bounce over his friend, and that stillness was based on the ridiculous hope of something he'd heard years ago; that dogs had memories like goldfish. Well that theory was bullshit now and could be forgotten because this dog clearly remembered him as the one who'd killed his owner. It followed quite naturally that it would want to kill him back, to tear his throat out, and only Scott's determination to save the dog from itself was preventing that from happening. The struggle with Goldie reopened the cut on Scott's hand, there were red smears getting onto the dogs snarling face, and he seriously doubted the aroma of fresh blood was helping this situation. All through this melee Auntie was losing her shit in the only way a meth head can, by whooping crazily and scratching her scabs. She started screaming at Scott to take the dog back to the bedroom, some of her spittle landed on his cheek, he wanted to retch, so he dragged the stubbornly murderous dog back into the filthy bedroom and shut the door. He listened to it snuffling, its claws under the door trying to scrape its way out and sincerely hoped it would understand he was only trying to help.

A confused Scott came back in and took his place on the filthy sofa, he looked over at Jay who was still sitting with his knees up to his chest like the self-preserving coward he was.

'I'm not keeping that crazy bastard here any longer. I'll phone the police so they can come take it back.' Auntie declared while reaching for her glass smoking pipe, the thick brown stains smeared on the inside standing testimony to its position as her most used and required object.

Scott really didn't want to watch her do meth right now. Change the subject, do something, quickly. What with the dog struggle and the smell of the flat he decided to try and move things along a bit. 'So I heard there was a bit of trouble on your street the other day...?' He even relaxed slightly when he saw her put the pipe down without using it.

'Oh it was a right sight...' Aunty began. '...There were police everywhere and ambulances. First everybody thought there must have been a fight. I looked out and saw two bodies on the street and thought the same, I couldn't see very well because my eyes have been playing up lately, anyway it turns out a man who used to live there...' She pointed at her own front door which Scott took to mean the man who'd lived in the opposite flat on this floor. '...well he came back and jumped out of the building. How silly is that? I'd jump onto the train tracks if it was me trying to kill myself...'

'...Don't say that Aunty!' Jay interjected with what Scott believed to be both untrue and undeserved sincerity.

'Did you know him then...?' Scott asked in an attempt to stick to the plan of why they'd come here in the first place.

'Hey Jay this one sounds like a policemen. Listen to him asking me all his questions. You alright there copper?' She laughed then hacked.

'I'm not a policeman!'

'I know you're not...only pulling your leg...' She managed to say then her horrible laugh came again which bled into another coughing fit. After almost a minute of clearing her throat, which Scott thought pointless because it wasn't going to sound any healthier, she continued. '...Yes I'd seen him and his wife sometimes. I didn't know their names because I like to keep myself to myself...but they weren't quiet neighbours...sometimes they argued day and night, shouting and breaking things, really screaming. I had to put my head under the pillow some nights...then when they finally moved out it was much better for me. I don't like to be disturbed you see.'

'Nobody does...!' Scott said and to which Jay didn't respond, clearly missing the barb directed at him. '...So he jumped out the window then?'

'So they say...but nobody saw it?'

Scott then decided to play dumb in a vague hope he might learn something new. 'Do you think he fell on the other man?'

'Don't you watch the news…?' She cackled again.

'…Not anymore no.' He flicked a look at Jay who was watching him intently.

Auntie began rolling a yellow lighter in her scabby hands as she spoke. 'It was Brian Downing. He lived just down there, he was stabbed by someone and then they ran away. It's becoming a horrible place round here for decent folk to live in.'

'Did anyone see who did it, Auntie…?' Jay popped up with an obvious self-serving question.'

'Oh I don't know about that. Why are you so interested? Here it wasn't you was it young Jay?' She asked then began to cackle and cough again.

'No Auntie why would you think that? I haven't been to see you for a few weeks now…have I?' As Jay asked this he looked confidently over at a slightly confused Scott.

'Oh there's no point asking me is there…' Auntie replied. '…I don't know when you're here and when you're not, my memory isn't what it was. All I know is that you're a good boy and you come visit your favourite Auntie as much as you can.'

'That's right I do.' Jay smiled. Scott felt nauseous again, especially when the two boys stood to say their goodbyes and Auntie insisted on more hugs while her mind counted down the seconds to lighting her glass pipe. In the rumpus of phoney 'take cares, lovely to meet yous and pop round anytimes' nobody heard the car pull up on the cobbles outside.

Inspector Harvey Cooper turned the engine off while taking a call from his office with new information. He was thrilled. '…So they've found the murder weapon?'

'Yes!' His secretary answered 'It was discovered at the bus stop down by the Lifeboat pub. The landlord was checking his CCTV and saw a figure acting suspiciously. The camera angle isn't great but you can clearly see a person drop something behind the bus stop. We sent the dog squad down there an hour ago and they've found the knife…'

'Are we sure it's the same knife…?'

'Not conclusively no, we'll be running it through the tests as soon as possible, but it's a steak knife with a wooden handle and it's covered in blood. The video fits with the day and the time of the murder to within fifteen minutes, and we know from forensics that a suspect ran in that direction.'

'Perfect...so did the CCTV didn't give us a clear image of the suspect?' Harvey wanted more.

'No, the camera's fitted on the roof of the pub to monitor the car park. It looks down on to the area taking in a small bit of the bus stop. You can only see the suspects legs because the shelter's covered in advertising panels and also it's pretty vandalised.'

'Colour or black and white...?' Harvey asked hopefully, though if he were a betting man he'd pick the answer.

'...Black and white I'm afraid.' She said and he won his own bet.

'Of course...right so we have a weapon but it's going to have to be checked in the lab? Okay thank you, that's progress...' He moved his thumb to end the call.

'...Oh there's a bit more inspector. The camera also picked up a car. It's seen pulling into the bus stop then quickly drives off with the suspect.'

'Any information on the car...?' Harvey asked sharply.

'...It can only be seen for a couple of grainy frames. We're trying to locate other images from the area but we think it's a black VW Golf. No decent view of the number plates I'm afraid.'

'Is there anything else...?'

'...That's all, Inspector!

This case was gradually coming into focus with each new puzzle piece, soon he would have the complete picture, and then whoever did this was going to be arrested and sent to prison, simple. There was never any need for kicking down doors and car chases, that was for the TV, all you needed was a little patience and a clear logical mind. In Harvey's vast experience every criminal gives themselves up, usually through sloppiness, and it was beginning to appear this event was no different. He made some notes, his pencil flicking grey lead strokes onto the paper as it recorded evidence, clues, thoughts, and soon, inevitably the answer. With notebook stowed away in his jacket pocket Harvey now had some options, he could return to the station and follow up on the discovery of the knife, or he could stay here a little longer, after all he'd come here to see the scene for himself, hadn't arranged to meet anyone, so was simply detecting alone with what he knew and because it felt like right. Additionally of course it was a beautiful day and he was out of the office, being outdoors on duty was a rare treat for him, but probably not as rare as a sunny hours in this city.

Now his original plan had been to walk down towards the docks to see if he could piece together the route the killer had most likely followed, but there was no need for that now, all the new information told him the suspect had run down Leith Walk to the Lifeboat pub, ditched the knife behind a bus stop then took the opportunity to call an accomplice who picked him up shortly after. Harvey's brain began its calculations and automatically his cognitive cogs clicked round to the word 'Unplanned'. The Inspectors reasoning for this was simple enough, the running away, the ditching of the knife and the delay in getting picked up. It was either the shabbiest, leakiest, ill thought out murder plan in history or an unintentional random act of violence. That troubled him as he fished his notebook and pencil out again, because that common formula was always the hardest form of violence to understand. So he decided to leave the bus stop inspection until later and thought it might not hurt to take a gander down Dalmeny Street. Climbing out of his car he walked fifty yards away from Leith Walk, in the direction that he knew the suspect hadn't taken, there was method to this madness, he was seeking a different viewpoint, another angle to try and answer the question of where the attacker had come from rather than where he went. Looking up then down the street he saw so many apartments in the tenement buildings, they covered both sides of the cobbles four floors high, yet nobody had seen a thing. This troubled Harvey but of course in this area there's every chance that could happen. People who lived on streets like these were mostly renters, the elderly, students, reformed drug addicts, people who didn't like to get involved. If you were lucky enough to find anyone at home in the middle of the day they probably weren't outside sweeping their front step or washing their windows while gossiping to their neighbours. Those times were sadly long gone, changed completely, even in the years since he'd joined the force. He counted thirty two cars parked the length of the street, of which three were black VW Golfs, and he guessed it wouldn't hurt to jot down that trio of number plates.

Scott had never felt such a strong mix of emotions about leaving a place in his life. It was an almost overwhelming rush of relief to be removing himself from the skanky flat with its disgusting tenant; however that feeling was balanced horribly against the sorrow and growing pain at having to leave the dog in there. Scott had worked out why poor Goldie hated Jay during their parting exchange with Auntie; it was the old man's dog, the poor guy who Jay stabbed to death in cold blood and who had watched the whole thing. Goldie was in that horrible flat now because the police had asked her if she could possibly look after the dog so they could get on with their investigations and Auntie, who was no doubt off her face, had agreed to it. He suspected her neighbourly favour certainly hadn't come from compassion, more likely from a desperate need they would go away and leave her alone, but now it appeared she was stuck with the silent witness, and Scott who would have loved to have taken the dog with him was stuck with his guilt.

They reached the bottom of the stairs where Jay suddenly and viciously grabbed Scott pinning him to the wall. '...Don't you ever...ever judge me?' He spat angrily.

'What the fuck Jay!' Scott managed to reply even though his 'friends' hands were pushing his jacket up to his throat and pressing hard on his windpipe.

'I saw what you did...your fucking face...!' Jay pushed up harder. '...I'm warning you don't ever do that again!'

'...Jay...man...what...? The words forced out in tiny gasps.

'...Fucking judge me or my family. Yeah she does a bit of meth, so what...?'

'...Noth...ing...' He was sailing close to passing out.

'...That's right, nothing. Now shut your mouth and drive us back home.' He released Scott and opened the front door before pulling his hood over his shaved head. '...And another thing...'

Scott was straightening his jacket. 'What?'

'We need some weed so you'd better ring somebody to come round to our house. I've got cash so don't worry about it...see if you can get some of that Thai shit yeah!'

Instantly an assortment of new problems assaulted Scott, who the hell was he going to contact to bring round the weed? Why the hell didn't Jay, the biggest pothead he knew, have someone to call for weed? Only these queries were put somewhat in the shade by the realisation that somehow 'his house' had suddenly become '*our* house'? He must have appeared to be daydreaming for a second while he had these thoughts because Jay was talking to him over the roof of the car in a grisly tone.

'Are you gonna fucking open it or what?'

Harvey noticed the two young men leave the tenement, giving them no more than a cursory look, before noticing the car they were getting in to; a black VW golf, tinted windows, so he began a slow jog back up the cobbles.

'Boys...excuse me boys, I was wondering if you could help me...?' He shouted it in a professionally controlled manner, no need to make them jumpy because if he could get them to talk he might find out if they'd seen anything, or better still, discover these were the truly stupid kind of delinquents who might return to a crime scene.

21

Guard Allan Kosminsky began to wake up; he'd been continuing the search for Oscar at the centre of his mental maze, but in the last few seconds the walls of the labyrinth had started to fade. As he regained some focus and faculties he became acutely aware of the small office around him, the overpowering metallic taste in the air, and looking over to the door, what his reality had now become.

The body of Doctor Katherine Kelly lay in the far corner of his guard room, hair pulled forward covering the face, but he could guess by the angle of that neck to those shoulders she was dead, while deep rich bloodstains patched down the front of her blouse and still pooling on the tiles under her legs confirmed it. He caught something silver reflect in the scarlet puddle and on closer inspection saw a pair of scissors. Scattered around her legs were ragged strips of flesh. Was that her nose laying half hidden in the folds of her skirt? Kosminsky accurately surmised without closer inspection that her face had been completely destroyed, around the doctor's corpse were smudged and skidding footprints, as if someone had been working on her and struggled to keep their feet on the slippery tiles while doing so. The door handle was covered in thick globular blood and he didn't want to touch it, which instinctively made him check his own hands only to discover they were clean. Of course they were; he wouldn't have been able to do that to a woman, even one that had made him as angry as she did at times.

There is only a precise type of wickedness that can do things to such a degree and somehow that type of evil had controlled him briefly, through hypnosis, power of suggestion, mind control, whatever the hell it had been. He really didn't know but he did know he'd been duped to take his eye off the job and that made his anger rise. 'Fuck you Oscar you little freak shit!' Throwing his chair across the room he turned to check the camera feeds and found his computer screen blank, the cables severed, the connector leads yanked from the wall sockets, and all of them covered in fingerprints of blood. Oscars fingerprints, the doctors blood. Reaching inside the coat for his mobile phone he sighed angrily, it was gone. 'I swear Oscar you are a dead man!'

Surveying the carnage around him and knowing the little lunatic was out there shuffling around killing again infuriated the guard even more. That bastard had stolen his phone and Kosminsky made the decision there and then he was going to find him and beat the living hell out of him. It didn't matter what he did anymore, his security career was down the toilet anyway with a senior medical professional hacked to pieces in his guard room, and all because he'd let a psychopath trick him. No matter what transpired he was quite sure senior management wouldn't be sympathetic to his pleas, even if he explained he'd been mind-controlled or whatever the hell it was that Oscar had done, and he was damn certain he wouldn't be forgiven for being such a weak minded gullible moron. 'Fine   Oscar...!' Kosminsky screamed '...Lets fucking play!' This big guard wasn't bothered anymore by the gloopy gore on the door handle he just wanted to find him. He even slipped in the thick red stuff as he reached for it and felt the cold fluid touch his palms as he turned it. It was glutinous and he couldn't get a clean purchase so took off his jacket and covered his hand to turn and pull. He realised at that moment, when he'd given all he had and the door didn't budge, exactly what Oscar had done. 'You Bastard...!' Kosminsky retrieved his chair, placed it back at the desk, and then sat down with a frustrating grimace to work out his options. He began by trying to put his situation in some logical order to best make a plan. Oscar has taken my radio, and my mobile phone, he's killed my computer so the cameras are down and to finish it all off in style he's locked me in my own guard room. There was no escape now; the hefty door was there for good reason, made of welded steel strong enough to ensure the guards safety in the instance of a riot. It was beyond durable, designed to withstand an assault by any number of criminally insane patients desperately trying to enter and assail the occupants. In short it was built to last and he was locked in with his only hope being that someone would come to check on him. The main problem with that optimism however was no one ever came to check on the crazy part of the facility, he'd ordered them not to for a start, and because he was big guard Kosminsky doing this job since before they could wipe their arses, they'd listened. Well for sure Allan regretted saying that now, shouting his mouth off to the younger guards, and with each glance over at his mutilated company he felt that regret grow. He was trapped in a real life horror movie, in a ten by eight room with a torn up body, and no one near to help.

Now human fear is one of the strangest emotions, an intensely unpleasant response, and never worse than when it's prolonged. It naturally triggers the fight or flight mechanism and because that's usually a simple on or off reaction people rarely respond differently, but this particular situation meant both of those natural options were off the table so fear began to rise. Gently enough at first, calmly accepting the situation, but slowly as the minutes past by and the doctors body began to ooze more blood he gradually slid into an uncontrollable anxiety. He began screaming at the heavy door but it barely made a whisper out in the empty corridor, so anyone who walked by wouldn't hear him and besides they would more likely be interested in following the bloody footprints that lead away from his door, up towards the doctor's office.

22

Alex and the Angel sat across from each other with the mortal beginning to wonder about the fundamentals of his heavenly host. Did it have to shave or go to the toilet? Was it married to a partner or to God? Were there any baby Angels?

'...None of those!' It said answering questions Alex had only thought of.

'Are you reading my mind...?' He asked a little perturbed.

'Hmm not really, just the material elements, the stuff right at the front.'

'What...?' Alex felt even more uncomfortable.

'I can read your face and aura and through familiarities I have from spent time with you I can quite accurately predict what is on your mind.' The Angel spoke as if this shouldn't be dumbfounding but Alex begged to differ.

'...I see...' He didn't. '...so if you can read my mind then find the answer you want. You insist it's in there then you have my permission to take it out.'

'I have just told you I can't read your mind.' It spoke truthfully then reclined in its spinney chair, still unsure of why Alex had found it so hilarious the first time it spun round.

'Are we just going to sit here again?' Alex enquired.

'I believe that is all we can do.' The Angel calmly retorted.

'Okay...go on then ask your question.' Alex put his palm down on the white desk and waited to give his usual useless answer.

'Very well, why did you laugh when I span around in my chair?'

'Ha ha that's not the question I was expecting but okay Mr Angel...'

'...Not my name...!'

'Okay! I laughed because I didn't know your chair did that and I think it might have something to do with our current dilemma...going round in circles. I don't really remember now but you're an Angel and that's basically a normal office chair. Don't you think that's a bit strange...? '

Alex felt confident that was the best and most honest response he had.

'Would you prefer I had a golden throne?' It asked.

'No not really...this is a tough enough experience as it is. I wouldn't want you getting delusions of grandeur. Changing the subject...I had a thought when I was alone earlier.'

'Did you now? Tell me.' The Angel sounded genuinely intrigued.

'Well I'm here in this place, your place...and my body is elsewhere, back in my place. So...are there limits involved here, boundaries, sell by dates? I suppose I want to know how much time I have before I couldn't go back even if I wanted to.'

The Angel stood and walked away a small distance. Alex had never really seen it do that before, mostly it was in its chair, in his face or just plain gone for a while. 'You need not worry about that.' It replied from fifteen feet away.

Alex disagreed strongly with that answer. 'Oh I think I do. I mean I'm in two places at once. Just give me one understandable reason why I shouldn't worry?'

'Because you are already out of time....' The Angel again answering in a tone that presumed Alex would instantly understand

'So it's too late...?'

'No.' It replied.

'So I can still go back...?'

'...Yes.'

'But you said I was out of time!'

'You are. That's why you can still go back...' The Angel with one flap of its opened wings rose from the ground before silently gliding to his side. '...Listen carefully to me Alex, time exists in your normal state on earth and here it does not. Therefore here you are out of time as you think of it. Your perceived construct and conceptions of time do not exist in this place.'

'Uhuh...I'm still having trouble with that part...so time doesn't exist here? Seriously...how the hell can I even comprehend that? My whole brain works on counting time...it's the only method I know....'   Alex didn't get a quick enough answer so decided to ask another question he'd thought of. '...This place here, this white office, white world setting, is this the only way we can do these meetings? Does it always have to be so blank and uninspiring? I mean can you change it?'

'You wish me to alter the questioning construct scenario...?' The Angel asked this out loud and kept its face straight

'...If you wouldn't mind!' Alex felt he was on to something although he wasn't sure exactly what it was, but in his current disembodied state even a nothing something was better than a something nothing.

'Please explain what you are thinking about now...?' The Angel asked and for the first time it frowned.

'I'm just trying to understand what the hell's going on?' Alex replied in an assured manner.

'Yes but nothing something, something nothing is all I picked up and that's just a mess of a thought.'

'Put us somewhere else.' Alex requested.

'...Somewhere else?'

'Yes a place with stuff to look at, listen to'

'Such as...?'

'...I don't know...let's say...yeah okay a tropical island.'

By the time he'd finished the sentence they were on a beach whose immaculate sands stretched out to the horizon left and right, directly ahead was an astoundingly blue ocean, and behind Alex a jungle forest thick and lush.

'Better...?'

'...Absolutely.'

Alex reached down and picked up a handful of sand feeling the grains fall slowly through his fingers.

23

The two frozen boys slowly reanimated as the stranger approached them. Who the fuck is this...?' Scott asked stylistically through tightened lips.

'...Just shut up! I'll sort it.' Jay side-mouthed in response, the boy's tone and manner also telling Scott to be ready...it could get messy.

'Hi there, good day to you both, my name's Inspector Cooper, Harvey Cooper, I'm investigating the incident that happened here a couple of days ago and I just wondered if I could have a quick word. Would that be okay?'

'Yeah you can but I don't know anything about anything.' Jay said.

'Well I haven't asked you anything about anything yet!' He took out his notebook, more for effect than use. 'Is this your car...?' Harvey wanted to see inside but the blacked out tints were keeping its interior hidden.

'It's mine!' Scott said so suddenly his own voice made him jump and his stomach began flipping in panic.

'Are these tints legal...?' The Inspector asked tapping the back window with his forefinger as he did so. '...They look quite dark.'

'They're only one way. I can see out fine.' Scott replied sliding the car keys back in his pocket. This was all he needed a Police Inspector looking at his car, and the pause as the Inspector studied his face was excruciating, the tension building like some western shoot out, and Jay wasn't helping. In the end Scott chose to release some of the pressure. 'We're visiting his Auntie...she lives up there...' He pointed. '...the one with the moon and stars curtain thing.'

The Inspector glanced up to the dirty flat window for a second before continuing his chat and turning his attention to Jay. '...So you've come to visit your Auntie. I suppose she told you all about the trouble they've had round here...?'

Jay looked at the ground with his face barely in view. '...Yeah, yeah she said it was pretty bad. That's why I came to see her actually...check she was okay.'

'That's thoughtful of you.' Harvey pronounced while trying to get a better look at the hooded boy.

'Yeah well you know she's family and shit...sorry...stuff. What happened here the other day was pretty bad.'

'It was...it certainly was. What's your name...?'

This was the exact moment that Scott realised how this was going to play out.

'My name's...Carl!' Jay said and it stunk of a lie as well. The Inspector nodded then turned to Scott who was praying he wouldn't bring him into it.

'And yours...?'

Fuck! Scott lacked the same get out clause that Jay had used. For god's sake he'd already admitted this was his car, this cop knew exactly what he looked like and now he was writing down the registration. In panic he searched through the filing cabinets of his mind for something remembered from a TV show or story, just one scripted perfect response to satisfy the situation, to make this bastard leave them alone, but he found nothing so was caught out bang to rights on the simplest of requests.

'...I asked you your name' Harvey changed his tone, more business-like with an inflection of threat, a gauntlet thrown down at the young man's feet.

'My name is...err Scott!' What else could he say? He knew they shouldn't have come here even though he hadn't done a thing wrong, his only involvement had been picking up a mate he didn't much care for and then spending time getting stoned and playing video games while fearing for his life.

'Scott...what...?' The Inspector enjoyed this tiny rhyme; it sounded cold and caught their attention, and not without good reason he was growing enormously suspicious of these two. His keen professional eyes spotted that Scott had pulled his sleeve over his hand. He was clearly hiding something though Harvey didn't feel it was a weapon, more likely a drug bag or an injury.

'...Hutchinson. Scott Hutchinson. I'm sorry officer but we have got to go. We'll be late for stuff. It's been nice talking to you...' He paused. '...Can we go?'

Jay watched his friend squirm under the most basic of questions, and perversely enjoyed it, while he was feeling calm and under control. This was just another part of the game, as soon as the Inspector introduced himself he knew the nightmare level they'd been sharing was over. Scott had proved himself to be a true and helpful ally, even though it had taken constant physical threats to achieve it he felt pretty sure this player wouldn't grass him up. Not even now, at this moment when he had an authority saviour right there, because let's face facts there was no reason at all why Scott shouldn't just look at the Inspector and point an accusing finger at his friend. Yeah the chaotic level of the game they'd shared was over and now it was going to become something else, something very different. Jay began slowly moving his feet into position, no more than a centimetre at a time, just a little closer was all he needed, all the time fearfully aware that one mistimed move and his character was going down, but get it right and he might survive. While his friend waited for the Inspector's permission to tell them they could go, Jay took a single player decision and made his move. Scott couldn't believe what he was witnessing and cried out. 'Carl nooo...!'

24

Within the pastel green walls of the late Doctor Kelly's office, Oscar was stood at her desk looking at the drawings, even though he didn't remember making them he did feel they were important, so carefully folded up the three he liked the most, the rest he slid down the back of her desk never to be seen again. Checking the room for other useful stuff he spotted her long coat, a burgundy check type affair, and it looked warm so he picked it up and slipped his pictures into the pocket

It felt so incredible to be free again, just like meeting an old friend, an old friend with whom you'd shared the best of all times. Oscar recognised something of the man he used to be, the man he used to love to be, and the man he was relieved to find still existed, but just as he felt one brief second of accomplishment the demonic voice roared with furious force.

Get us out of here!

I...I don't know how...

DOOOO IIIIT!!!

It receded back into the darkness and Oscar calmed himself down before returning to his memories. It had been five and a half years since he'd lost his 'real' self. It had taken the length of one heartbeat, just after the stiletto heel of a drugged up drunken girl's shoe entered his head. A ridiculous cocaine and alcohol fuelled overreaction causing an entry point through his fractured skull. Yes the medics had arrived and patched his head up, the hospital staff giving him excellent care while plating and stitching it all back together, and yes all those experts had certainly saved this little man's life; but for all their x rays and assurances about his condition improving none of them knew the terrible truth. Something was very wrong, a monster had gotten into his head, it hadn't been there before but it was there now, and he couldn't tell them that tragically all their medical procedures had done...was seal it in.

Every moment since he'd left the hospital it had shared his mind. Even now he didn't fully understand what it was, but the numerous victims understood, for certain they knew what it could do and now Doctor Kelly who'd been trying to help him knew. This voice, monster, demon or whatever he imagined to call it was part of him now, controlling his thoughts and actions whenever it chose, causing him to perform atrocities at will, but now for a few short glorious minutes he was free of its grip, it backed off because it wanted something, something it knew it couldn't gain without his help, a way out of this facility.

With his head clear Oscar was able to come up with a plan of ridiculous simplicity; first of all he used Kosminsky's phone to order something he needed, then he put the Doctors coat on over his vest and shorts, and finally by simply looking through the keyhole of the office door he waited until the young receptionist left her desk. That didn't take too long and when she did he shuffled through the reception, closing the door behind him, and found the stairs down to the underground car park.   When he reached the bottom of the stone steps he stayed hidden in the shadows, things were far from over, if anyone saw him now he'd be caught, or they would be dead. Oscar didn't particularly want either of those outcomes so waited patiently for the something he'd called for.

The gate guard who had been so rudely ignored by Dr Kelly earlier that day observed a car coming up the drive. It stopped when instructed at the lowered main gate and he indicated for the driver to roll his window down.

'What are you looking for…?' The guard asked the cab driver.

'There's a taxi ordered for a…Doctor Kelly?' The driver pointed up at his licence number and then down to the text on his phone, even reading it out in a bored paraphrasing fashion. '…My car won't start. I need a lift to blah blah…I am at work so please pick me up from Blackford Facility…tell the guard on the gate it's for Doctor Kelly and it's an emergency.'

'That's all well and good mate but I'm afraid I can't let you in without some better authority than that.' The guard announced.

The driver held up both hands. 'Hey whatever, no problem, I'll wait here. Are you gonna call her?'

The guard nodded then rang through to the Doctors office where it was picked up by the receptionist, Rebecca, who finished drying her hands by wiping them down her top.

'Hello Dr Kelly's office…?'

'…Yes this is the main gate security. There's a taxi here for Doctor Kelly apparently her car won't start and he's been called to come and collect her. Do you know about this…?' The guard was only doing his job, to the letter, there were genuine crazies kept in this facility meaning you had to double check everything. The big guy Kosminsky had taught him that.

'…The Doctor isn't in her office at the moment.' Rebecca replied after a short delay. 'She may be down in the secure area. I do know she was furious when she got here earlier…'

'…Tell me about it she ignored me completely. So what we doing about this taxi then…?' It was a problem this guard was uncomfortably stuck on.

He knew all about the gate protocols stating that absolutely no unauthorised vehicles were allowed on site, but he also knew the Doctor could get him fired in an instant if he was seen to be deliberately pissing her off.

'I can't get in touch with her right now...' Rebecca said. '...I assume she's visiting the cells. Look just let the taxi in to the car park and I'll sort it.'

This reassured the guard enough that he looked over at the driver.

'...I'm opening the gate alright fella...now straight ahead down that ramp to the car park and wait there. Do not get out of the car and keep your doors locked. Somebody will come see you. Okay...?'

The cabbie acknowledged before rolling his cab down into the darkness.

Oscar heard the taxi first; he'd know that sound anywhere, and then watched excitedly as it came down the ramp towards him. The young man driving wasn't a face he recognised so that would make it easier he guessed. As he waited for the car to stop he felt some pride in seeing his little plan coming together; only this morning he'd been locked in a secure unit under mental observation but now in just a few short hours he'd managed to eliminate his doctor, jail his jailer and manoeuvre himself to within a few feet of freedom with a getaway vehicle in place. The next part could be tricky of course but he had a growing sense that everything would somehow fall into place. He was Oscar Downes, he was good at things he put his mind to, and that's why the voice had gone away and left him to it.

As the driver pulled into a space Oscar didn't waste any time, walking up silently to the driver's side of the cab. Not to the door through the door.

Rebecca was in reception looking at her computer screen which confirmed the location of Doctor Kelly. All the staff wore badges when on site and a simple piece of tech fitted into them allowed her to track them. You couldn't be too careful in a place like this and the system worked, indicating clearly that Doctor Kelly and Allan Kosminsky were in the guard room. Presumably a discussion of some sort was being held, and with the Doctors mood this morning she didn't believe it could possibly be a calm chat. So with that in mind, and with total trust in the technology, she headed down to go see the taxi driver to inform him of the Doctors current situation. The last thing she needed was an impatient cabbie roaming round the place. When she reached the bottom of the steps she looked across at her mountain bike still chained to the railing, before spotting the taxi four bays further on. Approaching the car from the passenger side she couldn't see the driver at first, but as his head came in to view she stopped. There was a blue pen, a biro no less, buried halfway into the drivers head, forced in through his ear, his eyes and mouth were wide open, lifeless. Her expected reaction was to instantly scream, but she found in this moment that time moved very slowly. Rebecca had seen it, acknowledged it and was about to react to it, but he didn't give her the chance. Instantaneously she was grabbed, pushed face down hard onto the concrete, with both hands secured tightly behind her back. A clever employment of the belt from the Doctor's coat, the same place he'd found the biro. With the woman helpless and bound his true voice, Oscar's voice, whispered closely in her ear. 'I could kill you right now! Please don't speak and certainly do not scream. I'm going to turn you over. Forgive me I'm not looking my best...' He hauled her round so she could look up into the eyes of Oscar Downes. '...Now if I ask a question I want you to answer with one blink for yes and two for no...do you understand?'

She blinked once because down here in the darkness of the carpark this was her nightmare come true. Every morning without fail Rebecca's mother told her to be careful at work, always worried about her precious daughter being in the same place as that murdering psychopath 'Downes', and every morning that precious daughter comforted her mother by explaining there was nothing to worry about. The facility was well manned, secure, and she was always careful. Her mother's constant concern did have a genuine basis, one of Oscar's previous victims had worked next to her in the same factory, meaning he'd already tainted their lives once, and now it was happening again.

Rebecca looked up at the man sat across her chest, the same man she'd been talking about with friends and colleagues for months, because this was her bogeyman, the one she'd feared for a long time now, and although her life didn't flash in front of her eyes, the last five years most definitely did. To begin with there had been the warnings, especially for young women to stay safe at night. Always travel in pairs, be alert and keep your phone charged, because there was a serial killer on the streets. She and her group of friends followed that advice to the letter but when her mother's workmate had gone missing, it all moved much closer to home. From that moment she eagerly followed every detail of the case, it was local after all, and when the police had finally caught him, after that televised car chase through a muddy field, she'd cheered with her mother and friends because it was finally over and they could feel safe again.

No one thought for a minute that Oscar wouldn't be jailed immediately and everything could go back to normal, but in hindsight that had been hoping for a little too much. The murdering bastard, as her inner circle liked to refer to him, refused to speak to anyone, causing a criminal delay in the proceedings, and it was this delay that led to the authorities securing him a wing of a psychiatric facility. He would be kept for observation at the place where she worked, bringing him even closer to home. Unsurprisingly and customary in keeping with the sick and shallow society we breed Rebecca found herself super popular for a while, all her friends wanting to know what he was really like, oh come on, surely she had some gossip, working where he was imprisoned. All of that fakery faded quickly when it became abundantly clear that although undoubtedly guilty of such horrendous murders Oscar Downes was in fact extremely dull. Only now as she looked at that face just inches from her own she realised he'd livened back up.

He placed his forefinger on her cheek pressing a slow line down to her chin. 'What is your name?' His plain voice asked steadily. When she didn't answer he nodded an agreement she could speak, for now.

With a breathless whisper she replied. 'Rebecca.'

He seemed to taste the name as it came from her trembling mouth. 'Rebecca, tell me do you know what your name means?'

'What?' She was confused.

'It means captivating beauty. I quite like that...but rather ironically it can also mean to tie or bind. Which I'm sure you would agree is very apt.'

'Yes.' A single word barely audible as she felt the belt on her wrists, it was beginning to slow the blood flow, making her hands numb.

'Hmm I will let you live Rebecca if you do exactly what I ask...I presume you would like to live...?'

'...Yes.' That word was louder, stronger in her throat, when she realised maybe he didn't want to kill her, he needed her.

'Then let us see if you can earn your life by being very, very, good.' With that he slid his hand inside her jacket.

When the phone rang at the gatehouse the guard answered it quickly, he really wasn't comfortable having a vehicle on the premises that hadn't been approved, and now he was being asked to help somewhere else. Stepping out of his gate box he made his way to the receptionist, she'd called to say she was down in the carpark with that stupid bitch of Doctor and needed a hand. He mumbled as he marched towards the entrance. Yeah I'll help move your car...yeah I'll give you a push... then you can sod off and stop giving me shit, and take your unnecessary taxi man with you...the fucking staff in this place, they're more trouble than the patients. He thought all of this as he stomped down the ramp.

Rebecca had been turned on her side to face away but it didn't help particularly with the events that followed. The sound of the guard being choked to death was still sickening to listen to, and when his body fell to the floor next to hers she almost passed out. All of this was followed by the patter of Oscar's bare feet moving to the taxi door and the driver's body being pulled out, the noise of his head hitting the concrete was horrendous. The sound of impacting skull was indescribable, yet unmistakeable, and her panic grew knowing she was the next problem Oscar would have to sort.

His plan was really coming together now, he'd nearly done it, all that remained was to jump in the taxi, operate the gate switch and drive away, but then the voice bellowed and Oscar was shaken from his growing pride.

You killed without my help.

I know...I had to.

I suppose you did. Aren't you forgetting the girl?

Rebecca!

Yes Rebecca.

If you go away again I'll take care of her...on my own.

The voice slunk off back into the shadows of his thoughts, then five minutes later the taxi pulled out through the raised barrier, and Oscar said 'not to the gate through the gate.' Smiling broadly as he reached the end of the driveway, because oh my god he loved driving a taxi.

25

Against the background of waves lapping at the shore Alex imagined, because he knew this wasn't real, that he could feel the heat of the sun warming his skin. He was sat in his chair at the desk on the sand, the other chair, the spinning one, was present but vacant as the Angel stood staring out over the sparkling blue ocean.

'This is much better.' Alex said with a sigh.

The Angel didn't turn when it spoke. 'I would have to concur.'

'So do you want go over everything again...?' Alex asked in his new relaxed state.

'Unnecessary...' It replied. '...I'm satisfied that you have no idea what is happening'

'Good, I don't. Thank you for finally listening to me.'

'It is because of that belief I have taken it upon myself to find the answer to your presence here...' The Angel turned from the ocean to face him. '...so instead of why are you here? I'm asking why is here allowing this to happen. I think it may work.'

'Brilliant! That's right up there with my something nothing, nothing something idea!' Alex replied with a warm smile.

'And I will concede that your pointless thought was the spark for my new approach.'

Then for the first time they smiled together.

26

Inspector Harvey Cooper had watched Jay disappear round the corner but didn't even consider giving chase; he was fifty three years old now and didn't do that sort of thing, so instead with raised eyebrows he'd asked the other young man if he would be so kind as to accompany him to the station. Now precisely one hour after that request they were sat across from one another with a tape recorder between them.

Scott was eighteen and streetwise so Harvey guessed he wasn't the grassing type. None of the youngsters were nowadays, no respect for the law; but this particular Inspector was an experienced and skilled interrogator. So the stage was set for a head to head, a battle royale in a high stakes session, two heavyweights in the world of show and tell going for it without mercy blow for blow, so no matter how you looked at it a furious tear up was on the cards. However what actually happened was not only a little surprising but also a touch disappointing, to the point where the mug of coffee Harvey placed on the desk at the start of the interview hadn't even gone cold by the time he turned the tape recorder off. Because Scott Hutchinson didn't just talk, he sang like a bird, in an aviary, on fire! No detail was missed in his confession and Harvey knew for certain he was getting it gospel. When a man is as scared and tired as this Hutchinson guy was, well it's obvious he would only tell you the truth. So Harvey just sat back and listened on as more puzzle pieces were delivered to him with a big bow around them. Everything Scott knew was given freely, from the suicidal guy that Jay let fall to the murder of the old man, from the phone call at the bus stop, to all the threats over the past two days, and even the cut on the back of his hand. After Scott finished his confession he, for the second time in just a few life changing hours, asked the Inspector a particular question. 'Can I go now...?' Harvey agreed that he could, but advised him to stay at the station for now, just for a little while until they'd caught Jay. Then he left the young man, and his coffee, in the interview room and proceeded to try and get an update on the running boy. Oh excuse me Harvey thought, things had changed so quickly again, the running murderer boy.

At this moment the said same boy was currently sat between some industrial sized wheelie bins behind a mid-range hotel. Jay had run through the back streets that ran parallel to Princes Street until he was exhausted, and a little disappointed because it really hadn't gotten him very far. Over the last hour he'd heard sirens, and not sure if they were for him or not he decided to lay low. If he was to have any chance of beating this tough level, he reckoned it wouldn't hurt to presume the worst case scenario at all times. Hours passed by as he remained hidden in situ, only now he was starting to feel the chill as the longest day of his short life began to darken, but it had given him a lot of thinking time where he'd imagined an inventory in his mind like the ones you have in a video game. Methodically ticking off his haves compared to his have nots he found he needed food first, then a change of outfit; because tired and hungry while running around in a bright red hoodie was certainly not the best blend for someone practising stealth mode. He also wanted someplace warmer to sleep than behind a hotel, but most of all he needed a plan of what he could do going forward, an objective of sorts, but as that chill began to bite he still hadn't formulated one. In the end the hunger pangs got him, so sensibly taking off the recognisable hoodie even though he was cold, he braved a little walk to a takeaway he could smell on the main road. Energy levels were essential for any character to succeed, so with his face exposed he approached the kebab shop.

Unsurprisingly there were cameras behind the counter, he couldn't avoid them so acted and ordered as calmly as possible as they recorded his visit. Then with the astonishingly fast food purchased he returned to sit behind the bins, and after putting the hoodie back on he ate the food while thinking on what happened.

Jay Cleaver was sixteen years old and for the life of him couldn't remember if that meant he'd be sent to big prison or not. At best it would probably be some form of young offenders unit but it didn't make much difference really, after the stuff he'd heard from friends who'd done time, the general consensus was they were both pretty fucking grim. While swallowing a length of deep fried potato he made the decision that no matter what he wasn't going to either of those places like those fallen heroes who'd gone before. Guys he knew who had fathers or brothers in the nick always gave you the feeling that they had lost a little pride in their champions after capture. While the criminals are getting away with it they achieve more and more reputation points and the rewards that go with such success. It seemed to Jay that after heroes were caught and jailed they became something else, something less than what they had been, losing their cool nicknames and all their reputation points.

Finished with his greasy chips he then thought about Scott, guessing his friend was safe, and then using the worst case scenario rule that he was sticking with, that the Inspector knew everything now. It was obvious his friend wouldn't have any need to lie and protect Jay's ass anymore. For Scott Hutchinson the game was over and because he hadn't actually killed anyone, in fact all he was guilty of was being a pussy and letting a younger kid bully him around, he would probably be rewarded with an extra life. Jay thought on that twist of fate as he put the Styrofoam tray in the bin. He felt no regret for his actions, in reality he felt good that he'd run, as by doing so he'd released Scott from the game and most probably saved the poor kid from his self.

Comforted by his reasoning Jay pulled some cardboard boxes from the bins, flattening them down he then pulled them around him, and for one night only became just another homeless statistic. In the fitful sleep that followed he dreamed of making a plan, a strategy to help him win, an endgame to be conquered so he could also be rewarded with an extra life.

At six in the morning, and with any dreams he may have had instantly forgotten, Jay was woken by a large African man with greying hair throwing bundles of laundry into the back of a van. He peeked out from under his hood, shivering in the cold dampness of the morning dew, and realised as his brain slowly warmed up that the man was talking to him.

'You cannot sleep there my friend....' It was a voice as deep as Jay had ever heard. '...This hotel will phone the police if they see you.'

'Okay, okay!' Jay replied through his dry cold lips. 'I'm going.' He attempted to stand up but his muscles were stiff from the cold and damp. The laundry man came over and held out a gloved hand to help him up. Jay looked him in the eyes, unsure of who to trust on this new level of the game, before thoughtlessly but gratefully allowing himself to be lifted.

'Are you in trouble...?' The laundry man asked and Jay immediately thought of a dozen lies to respond with but in the end he decided to avoid the question altogether and hoped the man wouldn't push him on it.

'...I need a change of clothes.' Jay tried to work out whether this man knew about his predicament. Surely the police would be after him so maybe his face would have been on the news by now; after all he was a wanted for stabbing a guy in cold blood and the law didn't allow that kind of thing to just slide. 'Do you know who I am...?' Jay enquired as he stamped to find a little feeling in his freezing feet and regain some suppleness in his arched spine.

'No I have never seen you before. Should I know who you are?'

'Not really man. I'm just a homeless kid.' Jay smiled as best he could. The last time he'd genuinely smiled felt like a long, long, time ago. 'Have you got any clothes in that laundry stuff...or in the van?'

'Just sheets and tablecloths my friend...you don't want to walk around in a sheet. People will think you are pretending to be Jesus...and look what happened to him...!' The laundry man laughed at his own pithy observation. '...Is there anywhere you can go...?'

'Not really' Jay responded, because he was damn sure all of his usual associates wouldn't want him rocking up like this. Suddenly panicked he checked his back pocket see if the money was still there. He pulled out Alex's wallet and feverishly counted the notes, it was all good, and then with a feeling of warm relief he looked at the driving licence of the man he hadn't saved. In the pocket next to it and staring back at him was the photograph of the woman with the different address scribbled on it.

'I must go now!' Laundry man said as he closed the doors of his van.

Jay thought quickly. 'Can you give me a lift...?' He asked wearing the face of a scared sixteen year old rather than a cold hearted killer in a video game.

'...Where do you want to go...?' The man asked in a style suggesting it could be a problem if it wasn't in a convenient direction.

Jay looked at the address on the photograph and repeated it back.

The van driver shrugged. '...Yes I can go that way. That is up in rich houses. I have to collect laundry from the big hotel there.'

Jay didn't care what he did up there he just wanted to move, and he needed to get warm, so thanked him then jumped up the three steps into the van. Instantly he found himself high above the road as the laundry guy began pulling out on to the rapidly filling city streets, feeling the childlike exhilaration of being in a big bouncy vehicle, but also the adult thrill of heading towards some wicked excitement.

The hour was still early on this cold city morning but Harvey Cooper was already at his desk, hands on the back of his head, looking at the reports on his computer. The officers conducting the search had found no sign of the boy and that annoyed him, he didn't like having a teenage tearaway running around his streets, especially one with a dangerous weapon. Then suddenly finding Jay Cleaver, the murdering kid with a knife, paled in to insignificance when he looked at the new report just coming in. 'Oh my God...!' Harvey exclaimed with a rush of equal adrenalin and horror, his hands left his head and went palms down on the desk. After a few moments trying to still his thumping heart he rushed to the next room to see his secretary, freshly arrived, taking off her coat.

'Good Morning Sir.' She cheerily offered.

'Get the team in here now!' He ordered.

'They won't be in until eight Sir...'

'...I don't care...call them, wake them, just get them in here...NOW!'

'Sir...?'

'...Oscar Downes has escaped from the facility!'

27

Rebecca Jones had fallen asleep from exhaustion while curled up in the pitch black. It was a tight space with a heavy aroma of petrol and leather and when raising her head it hit a hard metallic surface. She tried to work out exactly where she was but that proved difficult and it was only when trying to move her hand to scratch an itch on her brow that it all came flooding back. Her hand didn't do as it was bid, it was bound, both hands tied together behind her back, terrified in the dark she cried out but the gag muffled any sound. Rebecca stopped screaming when the truth hit home harsh and hard, she was in the boot of a taxi being driven by Oscar Downes.

The small man wouldn't have heard her cry anyway, he was enjoying himself, having driven around in circles for most of the night with the radio on, before taking a short trip down the motorway and listening for the breaking news that he knew would inevitably come. His only stop came at some services where he vaguely remembered the voice screaming at him to sort out the problem of how he looked. Oscar had to agree that the gym wear and long ladies mac were ridiculous attire for a man escaping a secure psychiatric hospital, so he'd followed the voice on this one and pulled into the rest area, but everything after that was a little blurry.

In truth he'd sat motionless in the services for almost an hour, until eventually a Land Rover pulled in behind him, and then Oscar had watched a young man get out and enter the services building. He wasn't overly tall and his jeans, sweater and shoes were everything Oscar desired. A plan was required so between him and instructions from the voice they moved into position and lay down on the floor directly behind the man's car. Oscar hoped his small frame would perhaps look like a woman in this large coat and bare foot and what type of young man wouldn't offer to help a damsel in distress.

Returning to his car the driver felt relieved the uncomfortable burning sensation was over, that piss had been building rapidly, he'd almost pulled onto the hard shoulder to sort it, but then remembered a reality cop show where a guy got caught doing that and was given an on the spot fine. So he'd held it otherwise he wouldn't even be in the services, but seeing as he was he got himself a coffee to see him through the next three hours of his journey. He really hated driving this late but he'd rather get home to his wife and baby son than spend another night in a shitty hotel.

Oscar lay lifeless on the ground waiting with the patience of a spider, positioned so he could see the man's feet as he approached, then watched silently as those feet broke into a run when spotting the body on the floor. The man had asked Oscar if he was okay and getting no reply put his coffee cup on the roof of his car to crouch down and help. It was what happened next that Oscar was hazy about; he always was when the voice took over completely, but shortly afterwards Oscar remembered that he and the voice stripped the bludgeoned man of his clothes and put the Doctors mac on the corpse. They placed him in the Land Rover sat upright, looking like just another weary traveller having a well-earned rest. Oscar glanced in his mirror as he pulled the cab away, satisfied that the crime scene looked innocent enough with the collar of the mac buttoned up tight. Twenty minutes later he located a quiet layby and pulled the taxi over smoothly. It was the voice that had forced this stoppage, a rasping desperate howl that Oscar couldn't ignore. It was an odd thing but for some reason the voice didn't, or couldn't, travel too far from the city, every time he even thought about driving away to a distance of comparative safety the voice objected strongly, forcing him to go back. Oscar noticed the clock on the taxi's fascia and it glowingly told him it was almost seven AM. There would be another news bulletin soon but so far those radio guys hadn't mentioned anything about his escape, which was a little disappointing, how had nobody noticed in almost fourteen hours that the psychiatric wing was unmanned, the gate to the facility open, and the people who were supposed to be working there were either dead, missing, or trapped? Well while the going was good he thought it might be wise to get a different car. Oscar truly hoped he wouldn't have to kill anyone for it but accepted that may be a by-product of his intention.

The voice interrupted his plotting and what it said surprised Oscar.

We have to go back.

Why? I thought we were escaping.

We have to return to the city.

Rebecca remained silent in the boot, her cramped body screaming to be stretched out flat, her wrists stiff and sore, with her mind trying to fight back a heavy sob. The car coming to a stop had awakened her senses as she listened carefully for a clue to her fate. Maybe Oscar had forgotten she was here? For god's sake she'd already urinated on herself twice and didn't want to imagine what would happen if she stayed here much longer. Should she make a noise and cause a scene as loud as she could manage in the hope someone might hear? It was while fighting that instinct for fear of getting his attention that she listened carefully, someone was talking, she could hear his voice in the car, or was that two voices?

Oscar leaned over and picked up the pictures from the back seat, it was something to do, opening one up he looked at the park scene with the UFO shooting its daggers down and the figure on the slide and...and then the voice came back.

We need another car Oscar.

I know but there's no one else here.

So you are just going to wait and hope...is that you're plan?

I don't know.

Well I know things...I know you didn't kill the girl.   Why?

I didn't want to. She helped us.

She did what you asked because she feared for her life.

Leave me alone...I don't want to hurt her.

Rebecca heard the car door open followed by footsteps on gravel. The catch opened up the boot and she was instantly struck blind, her eyes unable to handle the surge of morning light bursting into her world. She felt hands pull her up before sliding her down gently to the ground where immediately something began tickling her neck, it felt like long grass but was quickly forgotten when, with an incredible and indescribable satisfying effort, she firstly straightened her legs out. Oh god that felt good as every vertebra in her spine found a natural position they had been denied for a whole night. Slowly, carefully, she braved the bright light to open her eyes. A dark shape loomed in from her right and with stop-start focus it slowly came in to view. It was a high hedge stretching away into the distance to where it met another. Starting to gain some clarity she found she was laid down on the inside edge of a ploughed field. This hedge hid her from the main road, the long grass all around her was so soft and welcoming that she didn't even mind the feeling of the rash forming in the crotch area of her earlier accidents.

'Rebecca...?'

For a minute she'd fantasised she was alone, that Oscar had decided to leave her to be found, tied up and hidden from view but free at least. Hearing his voice plunged her back deep into the icy sea of fear once more.

'Rebecca...?' He repeated and pulled the gag down from her mouth

'...Yes...Mr Downes.' Unsure as to why she'd thrown in that respectful title but she had to try something.

112

'I hope you aren't too uncomfortable.' With this sentence of partial empathy he carefully pushed her over so he could see her wrists, they looked raw and bloodied so he undid them, he then noticed the wet patch on her skirt and knew it was time to make the important decision, let her go or kill her? Unfortunately for Rebecca the odds weren't in her favour, the voice wanted her dead and the fugitive side of Oscar wanted her dead, it was only Oscar Downes the taxi driver who wanted her to live. Even trying to avoid those stats he couldn't deny they made it two to one in favour of breaking her neck here and now, after all it was the safe option. He moved to a more comfortable kneeling position over her prone figure, and reaching his hands to her throat, ready to let the voice have its way.

'Who were you talking to?' Rebecca asked unaware she was a second from death, and believing his hands were moving down to help her up.

'...When? Oscar was genuinely curious lowering his hands for a moment.

'Just now in the car...I heard two voices. Who else is in there?'

The voice came hurtling from the shadows at the back of his mind and looked in to her eyes. 'No...not now!' Oscar pleaded but the voice took control and he was thrown back into the middle of the maze, frozen out, muted, totally unaware of what his body was doing.

'Who are you talking to...?' Rebecca asked with heightening fear.

'...*Me*.' Oscar's mouth snarled in a crackling deep voice quite unlike his own.

'Aren't you Oscar...?' She looked up at his face seeing all recognition was gone. He looked the same but if she had to describe it, then quite simply, it was if the lights were on but he wasn't at home.

'*No, no, no, Rebecca I'm not Oscar...he quite likes you, wants to let you go. However I disagree...strongly!*' The last word was snapped off as it left his mouth, like the sound of dry bone breaking,

'Who are you...?' Rebecca rolled over onto her back with her bleeding wrists staining the grass.

This bizarre Oscar's hands reached out to either side of her head and held her just above each ear.

'Who are you...?' She asked with total conviction this was her dying breath.

Those hands stayed in place but no more pressure was exerted.

Rebecca knew she was hanging on by a snapping thread but she at least wanted to know who was taking her life.

'*There is a balance. It is the only way the universe will work. So I am the one who keeps the balance...so it can't go too far either way.*' The voice confusingly explained; all the time its fingers still in contact with the side of her head.

'And you do that by killing innocent people?'

'*None are innocent in these eyes...*'

'...So are you real or just part of Oscar's mental illness...?' She asked this while playing for time and inwardly praying someone would pull into the layby.

'*If it satisfies your hunger for knowledge in your final moment then I am both, I am Oscar's mental illness, but I prefer to be thought of as an enlightened entity. Are we ready to die now...?*'

Rebecca was floundering but felt a lifebelt had just been thrown. '...So you're stuck inside of him...?'

The laugh that came out of Oscar's mouth was hearty and terrifying.

'*Stuck? I can go wherever I choose!*'

That was all she needed to know even if it was dropping her to a new level of desperation, a place where she could die right now, or a place where she picked up her survival dice and threw them one last time.

'Why don't you come and live with me...?'

'*Shush now...*'

'Why not we could escape...they won't be looking to throw me into prison. If you can really go wherever you choose then leave Oscar, let him get caught.' Her words sounded heartfelt but the actual sentiment was unclear due to her having no real idea of what she was doing, but if any explanation was required for her actions, she thought perhaps not dying in a layby was the overriding concern.

'*Why would I want to do that? Oscar and I have an understanding.*' The voice said but tellingly released its grip on her head.

'Because I know Oscar doesn't want you, he was just biding his time in a cell, hoping you'd go away.'

'*You know nothing!*'

'Yes I do...!' Rebecca snapped back. '...I know everything including what the Doctor's plans are. I've seen all the paperwork and requests. Oscar is going to be taken away soon. He's out of time, the board of directors at the facility are ready to try a different method, they're going to operate on him...on his brain, and to cover their actions afterwards he will be debilitated. That will be your life, what will happen to you, but if you move into my head...'

'...*Tiresome lies so I spare you a little longer!*'

'...No it gets better because...I want you to do it. I can go anywhere and do anything. I'm just a young woman in everyone's eyes...I'm not going to prison any time soon. Oscar is a recognised psychopathic serial killer...he won't get far. So you can stay in there and remain faithful to him, a man with no future, or you can join with me...'

'*You would want that...?*'

'...Yes! That is exactly what I want...please...'

The seconds ticked and three cars passed by but nothing changed until the voice finally spoke. '*I will have to pierce the back of your skull, extremely painful, even then it may not work and you could die from the injury...but it's my way to get inside your mind...*'

'Do whatever you have to.' She closed her eyes tight, gambling that if she died now then it at least it wasn't for a lack of trying, but knowing if she survived a new life awaited her, and who knows it could be far greater than the dull one she currently had.

The voice turned her face down; picking a sharp stone up from the dirt it raised Oscar's hands high.

28

Next to the beeping machine at Alex's hospital bed Linda Webb sat quietly, just visiting her comatose soon to be ex-husband but already beginning to feel his helpless condition was dragging on, so to save face she'd tried her best to play the role of the dutiful worrying ex-wife. As she was now discovering being newly separated in a marriage can often be a complicated affair, but this rather unique situation was an exceptional test of anyone's good will. She felt unable to turn her back on him even if she wanted to, not while he was like this, selfishly fearful that to do otherwise would mean he'd win and she'd be portrayed as the bad guy.

One afternoon last week she'd explained all her feelings to him with no idea if he could hear or understand, had confessed and opened up with all her truth on why and how it had all gone wrong for them, but still nothing. There were no clues from his outward appearance to show where he was hiding, perhaps he was just floating around in some blank nothingness waiting to die, but whatever the truth of his condition there was no way she would quit first. All the same todays visit was done as she checked her watch to see forty minutes had past, time to go back to her new home. 'Bye Alex...' She said then tapped the back of his motionless hand and left.

29

The Inspector was doing this job with gusto knowing time was of the essence. His rudely awakened team were scrambled and gathered in the briefing room, with Harvey explaining the astonishing news that Oscar Downes had escaped from the facility, but only after gruesomely killing his doctor, a taxi cab driver, and a gate guard. His rapt audience listened on as he explained how the senior officer on duty, one Allan Kosminsky, had survived the ordeal but wasn't much use to them due to the trauma of being locked in a room with the mutilated doctor for twelve hours. When the door had finally been forced open it became clear to the medics he was in a bad way so he was sent to hospital under sedation. Then there was also the receptionist, Rebecca Jones, twenty four; who was missing, believed kidnapped by the suspect. All of this followed by the suspicious death of a young father at a southbound services, which at the moment was also being linked to Downes escape. Harvey followed this passionate update with a plan of action, the hotspots he thought Oscar may go to and how he wanted to coordinate the search, he'd been missing since late yesterday afternoon, he had a vehicle, a taxi of all things, and the Inspector wanted everyone on this, nothing was to halt their efforts until...

BUZZZZZ!

...Until his phone rang and he was given the news; Oscar had been apprehended only five miles away in a layby. It was suspected he must have dumped the taxi because it wasn't at the scene; but there was also no sign of the Secretary. Apparently he'd given himself up without struggle and was being returned to the station, he was still playing dumb to the arresting officers, just doing exactly as he was told.

After taking a moment to regather his thoughts Harvey promised his assembled dumbstruck team he would speak to Oscar when he arrived, that he would make him talk, and the room relaxed a little because they understood Harvey was on the case, but even before they could enjoy the moment he'd ordered them to resume and redouble their efforts to locate the boy who was still on the run. In the end the general feeling amongst Harvey's team was one of bitter relief, believing that searching for this Jay Cleaver sounded a hell of a lot more appealing than hunting Oscar Downes.

In the middle of a leafy crescent where people's success was displayed on the outside of every house, at the top end of the city, up on a hill affording excellent views of the castle and the sea, a young man in a black puffer jacket and blue jogging bottoms sat on a bench under an oak tree. He'd been there quite a while now smoking roll ups, occasionally glancing over at one particularly swanky house, and it was anyone's guess what he was doing there, but in such an affluent area as this with their stone walls and cameras he really didn't fit in.

Jay Cleaver mumbled vicious spite as he watched another top of the range Mercedes roll out through solid high gates; these rich people off to their ridiculously rewarding jobs were his natural enemy, he could never be like them. All were his nemeses because it was only money, or in his case the lack of it, that made any difference between them in the real world. Only in this instance he knew something they didn't, this wasn't the real world anymore; this was an exuberant new level of the game, the virtual reality he was determined to enjoy to the end.

Guessing it was about half ten he checked his phone which told him two things, it wasn't that early anymore, it was almost 12 o clock lunchtime and he only had 12% battery life left. Well fuck your number 12! This information made him tense up again when only a few hours ago he'd felt blessed.

Jay had been dropped off about half a mile away by his new friend. That African guy in his laundry van, who may have been about fifty by the look of his balding grey hair, had, for no reason, helped this young kid out. Jay really couldn't remember the last time a total stranger had ever done anything for him; the guy's name had been John; his surname was apparently Kenyan and totally unpronounceable to the kid, but this kind man, this legend of a human being had not only given Jay a lift to where he wanted to go, he'd then given him his coat. Who the fuck gives away their warm coat to a stranger? As he looked around the crescent he bet not one of these rich pricks would give him a second look let alone their coat. No, 'African John' had been real while all these wankers were phoney, simulations of human beings and therefore in Jays mind fair game to be despised. Yeah he was going to have some fun at their expense; with John's simple act only strengthening his belief that this wasn't the same world he used to live in, this was a whole new construct, a heightened reality giving him a chance to fight back.

Fishing out the wallet again he checked the photograph of the woman and the address, before looking up at the black gates, this was the place and that expensive pile in there was her house. He felt obliged to double check because that Alex guy on the street hadn't seemed like the sort that mixed with people like this, he didn't look like one of them, and so if this was his girlfriend then he was doing alright for himself, seriously punching above both his weight and bank balance.

This part of the mission was still unclear to Jay so he was being patient and treading carefully, because the only plan he had right now was to wait until he saw her. Obviously she would have to go through those gates at some time and when she did he would make another plan, one where he could see her up close and personal. So he waited and watched imagining what his intentions may be towards this female stranger, in truth he didn't know anything about her, and then wondered if this wasn't a side mission at all, but that she would turn out to be a key character in the game, maybe the one that would help him achieve his victory. Now   Jay   could believe such things because he was a simple kid who had survived his short life using his two natural attributes, pure instinct and selfishness. It wasn't how he wanted things to be but he hadn't lived a life under a loving roof, his emotional education was stunted as it tried to form under various pressures and depths, and it was all because of his parents who hadn't given a shit and disowned him years ago. So he'd been forced to look out for himself and he'd thought, until that day on the window ledge, he'd been doing okay. It was that Alex guy suddenly offering him a life and death choice that changed everything, admittedly yes he'd panicked as he'd never had one before, but his bored mind wanted to see what would happen if he didn't help. Well he was certainly finding out now, on the run which he had to admit it scary but exciting, and a million miles away from the lazy bum life he'd been living.

Since walking out of school three years ago, just after his thirteenth birthday, he'd moved between the different houses of mates, cousins, Aunties and sometimes strangers to help keep himself fed and watered. Regardless of receiving the same advice a hundred times, going home was not an option. To do that would have ended up in nothing less than violence from his Father and earache from his unsympathetic Mother. They were the two reasons he stayed on the move and 'on the rob.' Shoplifting had become his main source of income and he'd found trusted connections for trading his stolen goods, mainly perfumes and razors, for weed and tobacco. Damn it was two days since he'd smoked his last joint and he was beginning to get tetchy for good reasons, he was alone, homeless, and the police were hunting him for murder. Facing these truths together was difficult, increasing the pressure to a level where he was beginning to crack. Fuck it! He didn't want to go back anyway, all he wanted was to carry on playing this game to see this woman and tell her something, although right now he didn't know what that could be, he'd think of things to say and do to her soon enough.

30

Mild mannered receptionist Rebecca Jones had quite unsurprisingly never burned out a car before. The green plastic petrol container in the boot having only an inch or so in it but that had been more than enough. Setting light to the taxi on the waste ground did have a specific purpose; it was a flaming SOS to be spotted by some busybody then emergency services would be called and would arrive to heroically save her. She thought the speed and size of the blaze was impressive as she stumbled away. God she hoped they'd hurry up as she fell first to her knees, then face down onto the dirt, her body trembling in shock. The three inch wound on the back of her head was still bleeding and as Rebecca laid there the fuel tank on the taxi exploded.

Only forty minutes ago after leaving a confused and lost Oscar at the wayside, she'd driven slowly and deliberately for a distance of two miles, her fractured skull aching and pounding with every movement of the steering wheel. Driving slowly because she considered the deal she'd cut with the voice could soon be worthless; after all her actions would be of no use if she was going to die from this injury anyway. These thoughts became major worries as the voice hadn't spoken a word since its inception into her head, and Rebecca was starting to think it was perhaps some trick or a deception on its behalf, the twisted act of a murdering beast doing what it does best, killing people for its own satisfaction, seeking vengeance for some balance or whatever bollocks it had been talking about. Spotting a broken gate to her right she'd stopped sharply to reverse into it, knowing she couldn't drive any further before collapsing on to the steering wheel, blood running out of the wound making the back of her neck sticky and tight.

What are you doing Rebecca?

Her human heart leapt with relief, it was here! She couldn't bring herself to raise her head but she was overjoyed, it had worked, it was in her mind and that was perfect because she needed help, she needed guidance and it was here to tell her what to do.

Destroy the car and we will be saved. They will take us to hospital and seal me in just like they did with Oscar...then we can get to work. Do you want that Rebecca?

Yes I do.

Then lift your head, stand, walk just a few more steps and do as I say.

I will.

Then you can rest. Then we can rest. Then we can play.

Yes, yes we can.

So after obeying and setting fire to the taxi she'd buckled, bleeding from her head and wrists, and looking like the picture-perfect victim of a serial killers kidnap attempt, then just before fading into unconsciousness she made out an approaching siren, and it was quite the most beautiful sound she'd ever heard.

'Inspector Cooper...!' His secretary called out as the greying man left his office for another briefing on Jay Cleaver. '...Inspector!' She repeated.

'Yes?' He replied abruptly.

'They've found the taxi burning in a field!

'Is she dead...?' He guessed at the answer.

'...No!'

'What...?' Harvey was shocked by Oscars new M.O. Had he actually spared her life?

'She's being treated in the ambulance...!'

Everything inside that ambulance was floating in a fuzzy haze of blue and grey with tiny twinkles of red and green. Rebecca could feel the mask over her face and whatever she was breathing was softening all the edges. Slowly she began to drift away, but before losing consciousness she silently prayed they could save her, she didn't want to be denied this fresh start that promised her the whole world, a second chance that she would embrace, to live with strength and vigour...and vengeance on her mind.

31

Alex couldn't deny he was beginning to cultivate strong feelings about never returning to the real world. Why would he? Here he was sitting on a beautiful beach with an Angel where every second, if time existed here which the Angel said it didn't, was as perfect as he could ever dream of, and it was these particular thoughts that eventually led him another other recurring one. Was he dreaming? Was all of this simply a way of his mind coping with his own death, some heavenly vision he'd created to soften the pain of failing so miserably at the life he'd thrown away? Could it be he was struggling to accept the woman he still loved deeply, the friend he'd depended on and his soul mate for life, had fallen out of love with him for her own reasons then given herself to someone else, and not just anybody else, her dickhead of a boss. Alex had disliked the smarmy overconfident rich prick from the moment he first met him, which was unusual because he didn't really have the gene to dislike people on first impressions, usually he was dead against that shallowness of character, but something about that guy had made an immediate imprint he felt uncomfortable with, and sometimes he wondered if that dislike had somehow helped Linda into Gary Swann's bed.

The jealous spark was ignited when she'd returned from her initial job interview glowing about how lovely Mr Swann was, then immediately tried to dampen her words by explaining that everyone there seemed really nice but there'd been something in what she said, enough to force out a tiny pang. Alex had repeatedly tried to extinguish such thoughts but they always seemed to relight, like trick birthday candles, because some sixth sense told him this preening cock would try to lay his hen. Fighting the concern was futile and it gradually reached a point where every time she mentioned Gary's name Alex became defensive, abusive and a total arsehole. They would argue and fight louder and more hurtful, meaning that even if she never had any intention of shagging Gary Swann; well Alex's unreasonable over reactions were always keeping that possibility open.

So there you go, why would he want to leave this peaceful paradise and go back to that life? All the pain he'd felt when she packed her cases, started the car to steer her new course to Gary Swann's big house on the hill with his six bedrooms, and his three cars and his boat and his jet ski and his fucking healthy tan in December? Oh yes he knew all about those things because Linda had told him, cruelly accentuating all the attributes

Gary possessed and he lacked, over and over during the tiresome repetitive verbal battles that he lost. So in the end he'd given in and admitted defeat to her, to saving their marriage, and he would never forget looking into her eyes through his tears to say goodbye, just as she said good riddance.

At that moment a furious Alex had tried to hurt her with one last comment, one hurtful barb that she should now admit that his suspicions had been right all along. Huh how do you like that? To which Linda had simply nodded and said yeah...probably! Fuck it was that 'probably' that hurt him the most, as that 'probably' hinted she may not have gone if Alex had been a better man, but it was a lifeline thrown far too late to save him.

'You look troubled Alex. Are you suffering...?' The beautiful voice asked.

Alex jumped in his thoughts then saw the Angel sat across from him when he lifted his head. '...Oh you know. It's tough being stuck on a beach out of time all of the time. Ha...!' He faked a happy laugh, but of course he should have known better than to try and sell fake to an Angel; they clearly weren't the types for duping.

'...I don't believe you.' Also Angels were nothing if not abrupt and to the point.

'Well okay...I'm thinking I don't want to go back. I want to stay here with you.' There, Alex had admitted it out loud, confessed his true feelings and hoped for a much reaction better than the one he got.

'No!'

'Why?' He turned his face up towards the sun.

'Because if you stay it will mean I have failed. My undertaking is to find out why you are here.'

'But I thought we'd exhausted all lines of investigation? I mean I don't have a clue and you are just sitting around now. You used to question me and leave but since the beach appeared you never go anywhere. I don't see how either of us is finding anything out.'

'Alex answer me a question...if you could go back to that ledge, climb back in the window and carry on with your life, what would you do with it?'

'...Err...erm I don't know.'

'Huh...well think about it and give me your answer.'

'Why? It's pointless...' Alex exclaimed. '...You're asking me to imagine a future that I've already told you I don't want.' Alex didn't like this sudden slide in their conversation, and he really didn't appreciate the Angel telling him he couldn't stay, so he searched deep inside his transitory soul for some truth, or at least an idea, of what he would do if he went back.

'Well...?' The Angel asked.

Alex was suddenly finding its voice irritating, for a while he'd believed they were creating a bond but now the Angel was back to just doing its job, whatever in hell that profession was, but he still tried his best to explain. '...You do understand what suicide is, don't you? It's the final act of someone who doesn't want to be alive anymore, the direct result of a soul having so much pain and confusion and hurt that they can't work it out. It's an end and they chose it, maybe the one aspect of their awful life they can control. Shall I go on...?'

The Angel had listened intently but then misunderstood Alex's final salvo and offered up. '...Please do.'

Alex responded without hesitation. '...It was a rhetorical question, but ironically one a suicidal person may ask. "Shall I go on"? Look can we change the subject? I'm finding this one quite depressing.'

'So have you thought about my actual question?' The Angel asked.

'Fine okay I would climb back in through the window, thank the boy who helped me, and then gone back to my shitty boarding house, run a bath, and probably cut my wrists before the water cooled.'

'Is that a joke?'

'No clearly not...don't you see, just because I didn't want to die when the boy interrupted me, he was making it uncomfortable so yes I chickened out, but that doesn't mean that I didn't want to die...what do you want me to say?'

'The truth...!'

'Well that is the truth. Why are you doing this to me...?' Alex was becoming frustrated as he didn't see the point to it.

'...Because I'm doing my 'Job' as you call it. This is how it works. I have to do all things logically and in order when it comes to operating the machine. We have 'exhausted our lines of investigation' as you put it, in finding out what you know about being here. We have looked in to your past and found nothing that helps to explain this situation. So what does that leave?'

'I don't know what it leaves!' Alex shouted and slammed his head down hard on the table.

'It is perfectly logical...' The Angel suggested.

'...There is nothing fucking logical about any of this!' Alex was shouting even louder but the Angel waited until he finished.

'It leaves...your future!' It said calmly.

'I don't have a future I just told you.'

'...You must have!' The Angel responded sharply catching Alex off guard for a second.

'Why must I...?' Alex's angry blaze was reduced.

'...Because that is where the answer lies...' The Angel looked at the man and chose its next words carefully. '...You will go back and do something in your future life that causes this.'

'Oh please don't, don't say stuff like that, my heads going to burst...'

'...I told you it was logical.' With that the Angel stood and walked elegantly back over to the water's edge. This gave Alex a moment to think, to quantify, to try and accept that maybe it was the answer, but with no frame of reference he couldn't.

'Okay I have a question for you...?' Alex said and walked over to join his host in looking out over the glittering sea. '...If what you're saying is somehow right, that something I do in my future life causes me to be here, then how can we stop it, because quite clearly it has already happened otherwise I wouldn't be here.'

'Oh Alex, Alex, Alex what is to be done with you?' The Angel repeated its earlier triple mantra and smiled alone. Alex didn't respond.   A   few moments of heavenly calm passed as they watched twinkling waves lap the shore, the beauty and rhythm bringing some composure until he was suddenly struck by another important thought.

'What did you mean earlier...?' He asked with his curiosity heightened.

'...When?' The Angel replied, totally unaware of what was about to come of the man's mouth and the effect it would have.

'You said something about...operating the machine!'

'Oh...!' Spake the Angel, then looked at Alex with a pondering stare, before it promptly disappeared, quite literally faded away, leaving the question unanswered on the ocean breeze.

32

As the metallic blue Mercedes pulled up Jay Cleaver watched the gates begin to smoothly open, and it was definitely her, the lady in the photograph. He moved swiftly to close the space between them.

Linda was feeling more relaxed now she was back at Gary's house, still unable to call it her home as she'd only been living there a few weeks, and it would take a lot longer than that to have any claim on this gorgeous property. When the gates reached their optimum position for entry she drove the car, the one that Gary had said she could use, up towards the house whilst carefully avoiding the driveway lights that marked the short but winding route. These three feet high poles were extremely useful at night but a real pain during the day; they made turning this large car a little tight up the gravelled drive, so concentrating hard on not knocking any over she didn't notice the figure slip in through the gates before they closed. Now Linda would normally be at work at this time but Gary had given her two weeks leave from work after hearing of Alex's condition. He was hoping the break would give her the chance to visit the hospital and make things right in her head so she was making the most of it. He wouldn't be home until teatime, five hours away, so on the journey back from the hospital she'd done a little snack shopping and made decisions on what to do with herself for the rest of the day. Those plans mainly involved sunbathing if it stayed fine or watching a box set if it clouded over.

Opening the silently smooth car door she reached over to retrieve her new handbag and climbed out into the warm sunshine, flicking her hair in the reflection of the window and feeling good because the only person who could possibly catch her being so vain would be Estelle, but the housemaid wasn't in view, which made a change because she was usually very keen at keeping a close eye on the new woman. Linda laughed inwardly at the thought of the jealous maid then turned quickly on hearing the gravel crunch behind her.

'Don't scream...!' Jay whispered viciously in her ear as he twisted her handbag free arm high up her back, feeling her panting immediately as his chin sat on her shoulder, before pushing her forward with his free hand. '...Walk with me!' He moved her over in the direction of the tennis court which was surrounded by link fence and high trees. '...Get in there!' He ordered throwing her roughly onto the court where he realised with great satisfaction they couldn't be overlooked by anyone.

Linda was flat on her back, the artificial grass warm to the touch, with her wide fearful eyes looking up to see her assailant.

'What do you want…?' Who was this teenage boy trespassing on her…his…their property? He couldn't be much over seventeen and his black puffer jacket looked way too big for him and far too hot for this weather.

It turned out to be a quite accurate appraisal, as he took it off the very moment she thought of it, dropping it to the floor, as Linda tried to make sure she didn't think about anything else he was wearing.

'What's your name…?' He asked in an unappealing way.

Linda's heart was on double time but it wasn't from abject fear. This young lad wasn't that big, if he tried anything physical she reckoned she could fight him off…at first. '…My name?'

'Yeah…your name…' She saw his teeth weren't in a good state, before noticing his shaven head was growing back in dark uneven patches and looked as if it needed another shave soon, so even in her most generous of judgments he looked a mess. Weirdly she relaxed a little when the young man had asked her name, for some reason forming a strange correlation believing murderers or rapists were rarely so civil.

'Linda…' She said trying to show minimum concern. '…Could you tell me what you're doing here…?' She managed to ask. '…Has this got something to do with Gary? Because if it has then I'm afraid I can't help you.'

Jay didn't have a clear answer for her of why he was here; still thinking this was a new mission in the game, and one that kind of felt completed now. All that time spent waiting on the bench trying to think of what to do with her but now he was here, nothing. Why would he, he didn't know her, didn't particularly want to know her. Surely he'd done enough to finish this bit, he had the lady in the photograph captured on the floor, level complete, auto save, time to move on. The only problem was she'd just gone and thrown in a third wheel by mentioning a Gary. Who the fuck is Gary?

'Who the fuck is Gary…?' Out of his mouth came the precise words he'd thought inwardly, he lacked any natural filtration unit, but she didn't reply straight away and then compounded the problem by trying to sit up straight,

'Stay fucking down…!' Jay raised his voice in complete confidence no one could hear them in a garden this size.

'Okay, okay...Gary is my...' Linda was going to say lover but that sounded way wrong in this situation, lying on her back on a tennis court with an unpredictable teen. 'My boyfriend...Gary's my boyfriend. This is his house...he'll be back any minute...' Linda felt it wouldn't hurt to try the old 'don't get starting anything with me boy he's on his way home routine.'

'...I couldn't give a shit if he turns up...!' He said in a tone both convincing and unnerving. '...So who's Alex then?'

'Alex? You know my Alex...?' Now she was confused but with no little relief that this wasn't some random kid threatening her, they had a connection, he knew Alex.

'...We met briefly.' Jay answered about as honestly as he could.

'Okay so what do you want with me?' She asked.

Jay reached down, pulled up his trouser leg, and removed the breadknife from his sock. It still had a lightning bolt smudge of Scott's blood on the blade. He put it down next to him noticing the healthy colour begin to drain from her cheeks. The rays reflecting off the artificial surface were becoming hotter so he pulled the thick red hoodie off and sat there topless. Linda was close to fainting with the heat, the tension, and now the bizarreness of the moment.

Jay leaned in towards her. 'I need to tell you something about Alex...I think it must be why I'm here...you see some of it was sort of kind of my fault...' He watched her expression change from panic to perturb. '...I was there with Alex at the end and err...I can prove it because I got this...' Pulling the black wallet from his pocket he slid the photograph out.

'...That's you isn't it? I knew when I saw it that it might be important. So I thought I'd come round and return it to you. Try to balance things out you know...so I might feel like I've done a good thing.'

He offered the photo to her and she accepted it with a trembling hand, but before she turned it over she knew exactly what picture it was; Praia da Luz, the Algarve, their first holiday together, ten days of sun, sex and sweat. That's how she remembered it, but again chose not to tell the topless boy about her love life.

'Is that his wallet...?' She asked knowing very well it was. It had been a horrible Christmas present that spoke immeasurable volumes of frustration towards the end of their relationship. It symbolised in cheap leather the drawn out death rattle of their last six months as she headed towards her inevitable decision. He simply wasn't the one anymore; so naturally when it came to present buying she'd been clean out of imagination and extremely thin on thoughtfulness. It could have been worse; it could have just been a pair of socks, but Linda wasn't that type so in the end she'd brought him both, socks and a wallet for Christmas, and he still didn't catch on that things were coming to a head.

'Oh yeah it's his...!' Jay replied then opened it and removed the notes. '...Sorry...I need the money.' He handed the empty wallet to her realising any thoughts of sexual assault were gone, he really didn't want to, and besides it was way too hot. 'I'm going to go.' He said, convinced this level of the game was definitely done with now, surely. Jay stood up wrapping the knife in the bundle of hoodie and jacket.

Linda noticed as he stood above her that his skinny frame barely cast a shadow with the sun directly overhead, and also instinctively felt she was safe from physical attack, then in her eyes he shrank at that moment, even with the knife at his side and those topless tattoos on display he looked more of a young boy than a young man, One with no other intentions but to leave the way he came

'I'm sorry for what happened to Alex...was he an old boyfriend?'

'No...well sort of, used to be...actually he was my husband. We're separated.'

'Ha! Of course that makes sense.' Jay paused. 'Like I said I'm sorry.'

'It's okay...there's no damage done. I won't phone the police on you.' Linda really wanted him to believe that, but at the same time was wondering if perhaps she might be relaxing too soon. She climbed to her feet for a stronger position of equality.

'I could have saved him you know.' Jay said apologetically.

'Sorry?' She queried.

'I could have saved his life...he asked me to.' As those words were admitted out loud Jay became even more convinced that this felt right, that coming here and seeing Linda to return the photograph was the sole reason for this mission. Loads of games have levels that aren't all about blasting and hacking your way through, the old days of button smashing mindlessly on a joypad were disappearing now, in the newer more detailed games you had to learn things about your character, help them to grow to get those extra respect points, and by giving the game more of yourself it would give you more stuff back. Damn Jay Cleaver loved video games. 'But I let him die!'

Linda was suddenly thrust back into surreal confusion. '...What do you mean you let him die...Alex isn't dead!'

Now it was Jays turn to pale in the sun as puzzlement clouded his undeniable perception of what he'd seen. 'No, he is dead. I watched him fall, I saw him hit the ground and he was dead...his body was fucked after...sorry, smashed after...on the road!'

'Yes he fell...but he didn't die. Alex is in a coma, he's going to lose his right arm. That is, as you accurately said, fucked. I've just come back from visiting him in hospital. He's alive...sort of.'

As the boy took in those words she saw his true face appear under the layers of stress and attitude, and her only wish at that moment was to hug him.

'Is he going to come out of it?' Jay asked feeling his jaw tighten and he fought back to relax it. He was neither angry nor relieved on discovering this news; instead he was feeling a sensation rare for him, an emotion he couldn't name, though anyone else would call it compassion.

'He might do, yes. The doctor told me...and it sounds strange saying this...that it's up to Alex if he recovers.'

Then on impulse she opened her arms to offer a hug, he stared sideways at her and stood firm for a moment before moving forward to accept it, and as they hugged, Jay cried, then Linda cried and neither one of them really knew why. It could have been over Alex's plight but perhaps this went deeper, more personal than they realised, just two people struggling to make sense of their lives.

Gently releasing him away so their foreheads were the only part touching she saw a bulbous tear fall from the end of his nose. '...Would you like to come into the house? I can get us a cold drink, something to eat if you want...before you go, huh...?'

By rubbing his forehead slowly up and down on hers Linda perfectly understood an accepting nod when she felt one. They moved apart but she held on to his free hand. 'What's your name by the way...?'

'Jay...Jay Cleaver' He answered. His eyes were red and his shoulders were starting to match.

'Well Jay Cleaver, I'm Linda Webb but you already knew that....'

He lifted his dirty tear smudged face and smiled. This boy was sixteen and still uncomfortable in his own smile but this one felt nice because he really meant it.

'...This way then.' She said with a motherly softness while leading him by the hand to her, his, their front door.

33

Harvey was rapping his fingers lightly on the desk so it sounded like tiny galloping horse hooves, he wasn't really aware of doing this because that was all happening in the real world, and he was currently deep within a state of focused thinking. He looked at his watch for the third time in the same minute almost trembling with excitement about his next meeting. Sometimes he wondered just how many people actually loved their job, truly loved it so much that most days they were would rather be there than anywhere else in the world, well today was certainly going to be one of those days.

The interrogation was about to start and he was desperate to get his teeth into Oscar Downes. Lots of people had tried before, experts in mind coaching nonetheless, all had failed to get him to talk, but none of those had been Harvey Cooper.

Six months ago this serial killer was chased though the city in his taxi by no less than six blaring police cars. People filmed it on their phones, their images put out on the national news, then the international news, and the man Harvey was about to talk to was witnessed in real time driving like a madman out into the hills by millions of people, some wishing for him to be caught, some for him to escape, such was our modern world of social media, always awash with conflicting opinions.

Harvey had served as part of the massive task force assigned to find Oscar Downes, but in the end two 'other' Inspectors were drafted in from 'other' regions and when it was over those ungrateful bastards took the plaudits, then lorded it over the suspects questioning, squeezing Harvey right out of the picture. Blatantly he wasn't pleased with what he believed to be a major injustice in the justice system and complained officially but to no avail. So yes he was secretly delighted when the 'other' Inspectors had tried and failed to break the killer. Oscar wasn't talking to anyone, but even when faced with his wall of silence Harvey was given no opportunity to speak to his adversary. He truly believed Oscar to be his nemesis because of the hundreds of hours he'd put into hunting the man during his known three month killing spree. There was somehow a connection between the two of them, even if they'd never met and regardless that no one else could see it, this Inspector felt it and he was rarely mistaken on such things. He wasn't sure exactly why he felt such a bond, it wasn't as if Harvey had any direct hand in catching Oscar, nobody did really, in the end it had been lady luck that helped catch the man.

Oscar's identity had been discovered by one Henry Hornblower, a teenage kid 'on the rob' who'd broke into his lock up by chance and discovered five large plastic tubs. Forcing one open out of genuine curiosity he found Oscars third victim, well most of her, no one knew to this day where her other body parts had gone. Simultaneously two miles a taxi driver had been stopped by the police and asked to give a random DNA sample, but the little man had panicked, jumping away from the policeman holding the swab and back into his taxi before flooring the accelerator in an attempt to escape. There followed a forty minute live televised chase that began in the city and ended in the hills. The hotly pursuing law enforcement quickly joined by a TV news helicopter who never lost sight of the cab, following it in full focus all the way to its rather undramatic and sticky end. While trying to make a break for it through a farmer's freshly ploughed field his cab had slowly but surely come to a stop, beached on a bank of soil with two wheels off the ground and still spinning as the officers swooped. That was how his murder spree ended, the police had only been fishing, collecting DNA samples at the taxi rank hoping to fall lucky and they certainly did that day. With the discovery made by young Mr Hornblower at Oscars lock up confirming his evil deeds, they had their man and it was over, the media cried!

Harvey had been sat at the station that day watching it all play out, and without any appeals for his input over the following two weeks he was left with little choice but to reluctantly move on to another case. Shortly afterwards the 'other' Inspectors returned to their 'other' forces with gilded decorations but there were no special thanks given by them to him or his team. So it was no surprise that a gnawing frustration and sense of unfinished business had never left him, and was what made today so very special. As his secretary pushed his office door open wide she said the words he had waited so patiently for. 'They are ready for you now Inspector.'

'Thank you' He took a deep breath. 'How do I look...?'

'...You look...ready for business sir...' She smiled broadly then brushed a tiny string of cotton from his jacket while Harvey took another deep breath. He then straightened his posture, gave her a small wink, and took the stairs down to Oscar. Four policemen, appearing militarised and oversized in their body armour, ushered the small man in before attaching him securely to a bolted down chair, cuffing his wrists and ankles, and only when they were sure he wasn't going anywhere did they allow Harvey to enter the interview room to get his first up close and personal moment with Oscar Downes.

The killer chose not to make eye contact with the Inspector; instead he was looking everywhere else, taking in his surroundings, silently understanding his place in the scheme of things. When Harvey was settled he nodded to the officers and they filed out of the room locking the door on the two men. Quite naturally Harvey spoke first. 'Hello Oscar…?' He greeted the man then reached inside his pocket and placed some folded papers on the table. 'Drawings of yours…?'

No reply, no surprise.

'…I'm Inspector Cooper but you can call me Harvey if you wish. Now I don't know how any of your previous interviews, interrogations if you will, were set up. I presume they were recorded and had witnesses on the other side of that two way glass there. But I'm going to tell you this meeting is different; this set up Oscar is more private and personal. There is no recording equipment, no one out there listening in, just the two of us. I promise you that's the truth.'

Oscar gave no hint that he was listening, instead his gaze found a small spider's web in the corner of the ceiling and focused on it, but he found there was no spider near so imagined where the spider could be to distract himself. Perhaps it had other webs to check on, maybe it had been seen and squashed, or it could have gone on its holidays. These innocent thoughts were a gentle distraction, helping him to ignore the policeman because he could hear and understand everything Harvey said, but there was nothing interesting to him so he continued to gaze at the abandoned web.

'I know a lot about you, you might say I know everything there is to know about you, but of course all that's old news isn't Oscar…?' Harvey wasn't surprised or disappointed by this façade of ignorance, it was totally expected. This man hadn't spoken a word that anyone knew of for at least six months, Oscar Downes was a skilled criminal mute, but Harvey was a law enforcing persuader with years of experience in finding the right combination to open silent locks. '…Let's get to know one another shall we? We should perhaps start at the beginning, with your family…' Again no reaction but Harvey had a few initial details he wanted to clear up by using the *how* rather than *what* you ask method of questioning. '…Your mother Cynthia was a strange woman wasn't she Oscar? I've done some research you see; found out she was a prostitute down at the docks before she married your father, Walter. In fact it's highly likely you were

134

conceived in the back of a car during a mutual cash transaction. Certainly makes you special Oscar, because I'm sure good old Walter would have been astonished, as any kerb crawler would, that the particular girl he liked to visit had somehow let herself become pregnant by a client. Thinking surely she would have taken precautions to be careful, after all a pregnant whore isn't of much use to anyone, but how he really felt of course we don't know. What we do know however was he did the right thing and asked her to marry him...' Oscar was still refusing to bite but Harvey didn't mind as he'd more pressing points to make. '...So heavily pregnant she married Walter, one of her clients, and they moved to the outskirts of the city, where they raised you as if you were just a normal planned child. It's unclear if they were accepted by their neighbours as just another family or if people knew their secret and judged them...but let's be clear Oscar, and I only bring this up because any rational man would have wondered the exact same, how could your father have been sure you were even his child? In my research I've found family pictures and your mother, Cynthia Curtis, as she was known before you came along was an attractive slip of girl. I doubt she struggled to pay her rent if you know what I mean...would you like a drink of water, Oscar?'

Up until this morning the small man would have been protected from such pointed comments, the voice would have been there to distract him, screaming inside his head so Oscar remained on an even keel but for the first time in five years the voice was gone. He didn't know why or how or where but he did know that everything inside his mind was pure Oscar, and this purity of understanding was new to him, meaning it wasn't as easy to control his emotions.

Harvey had an inkling his words were having some effect so pressed on. '...No, you're not thirsty? That's fine; don't worry about it we're just talking here. So let's get back on track and assume that against the odds your father...was your actual biological father. Well good old Walter Downes battled on; working hard to look after the woman he'd picked up on a street corner and the child that she bore. Of course the next big marker in your life was their deaths. I can't imagine what that was like for you, nine years old, being left with a young baby sitter and your parents never coming home. That must have been traumatic, almost worried you to death until you found out where they were...do you remember why they didn't come home...?'

All through this talk Harvey was watching, waiting for a response, a small shift in posture or demeanour to let him know his 'facts' weren't falling on deaf ears. Hoping for the tiniest tell and there it was, his heart leapt as Oscar slowly drew his gaze down from the empty cobweb and fixed Harvey with a pure cognitive stare.

Here's here, in the room, in the conversation.

'Hello Oscar...' Harvey smiled. '...How are you feeling?'

The small man looked the Inspector's face up and down then held his stare. 'Mean!' The single word pushed out of a dry throat.

Harvey's pulse pounded at this breakthrough, he'd done it, but now calm down and concentrate, just because he's bitten, he's still on the line, we haven't reeled him in yet.

'...Well thank you for speaking to me...' Harvey paused before announcing rather surprisingly. '...Well that's my job done here. I shall conclude our chat now and go back to my other duties...' Harvey pushed his chair back feeling Oscar's eyes on his back as he turned towards the door.

'...I said 'mean'...!' Oscar emphasised the word and the Inspector stopped his hand just short of pressing the buzzer.

'...I heard what you said. Is there anything else you'd like to add or can I go?' Harvey felt his imaginary fish hook push deeper into Oscar's gaping mouth.

'...I thought you wanted to talk. Here I am...' Oscar's voice was calm and stable but his stare was piercing.

Harvey just had to act reluctant a little longer. '...Yes you are and yes I wanted you to talk...but you've done that now...to be honest that's all I really needed.' He returned to the table to pick up the drawings, they were all part of his elaborate plan to destabilize the prisoner.

'Explain what you meant...?' Oscar demanded delicately and Harvey could have got excited by it, responded quickly to Oscar's question, but this Inspector was proving he still had it and enjoying this joust more than any in his career. This moment was perfect and with growing confidence he knew the more he resisted the more Oscar would push, because as with most things in the universe, it was all a balancing act.

34

Jay was totally buzzing to have completed that nightmare running level, amazed to find himself at this amazing checkpoint, years of practice told him this is how games worked, you achieve a difficult goal then find somewhere to replenish your energy and here it was, sat in a beautiful steel trimmed granite surfaced kitchen with a bowl of hot tomato soup and easily the best bread he'd ever tasted. Everywhere he looked around the whitewashed room he saw magical things, floating shelves and glass cupboards holding items of beautifully organised quality. There were machines and shiny gizmos, he had no idea what they were for, there was a freezer big enough to dance in, and all he could smell was this soup and bread because everything here was just so fucking clean and new.

'Is that okay? Is it too hot?' Linda asked as she placed the soup pan into the dishwasher.

'No, no, it's very nice thank you.' He wiped a tomato dribble off his bum fluffed chin.

'When you're finished I was thinking...I mean it's up to you of course but...you could take a bath if you wanted. Our maid Estelle could have your clothes washed and dried in no time...if you'd like that...?' Linda closed the dishwasher then stood with her hands palms down on the work surface; no defensive posture was needed now because she wanted to help the boy who'd thrown her down on a tennis court less than half an hour ago. In hindsight that had been a misunderstanding, crossed wires between two souls from differing viewpoints, and hey she thought, in this world that happened all the time.

Estelle Christou, the aforementioned maid, was flitting around the place having given a cursory nod when Linda first introduced her to the boy. There was an immediate distrust and she didn't want to get any closer to him. She'd worked for Gary Swann for nearly two years now although she rarely saw her boss. He went to work in the mornings and she came in with her own key during the day. She made the bed, cleaned the bathroom and kitchen, wiped and dusted everywhere, then went home before he returned. This was her job and deep in her heart this was her house, she was paid to take care of it and that dirty boy didn't belong here anymore than that Linda woman, who was already beginning to get on her nerves by asking her to do things. Now Estelle understood clearly her lowly position in the world when it came to her profession, so what and whom her employer introduced her to, was just something she had to work with;

however she hadn't been enamoured with this Linda Webb from day one. In her experience women could 'click' no matter what their differences in status, but if one of them was false and out of their depth, pretending to be better than they were, then difficulties would always arise. That woman had only been here a fortnight and was already in the habit of pointing at things for Estelle to do without using actual words, and now here she was in the freshly cleaned kitchen feeding a criminal stray by the look of things, and expecting Estelle to happily do everything she asked.

'Estelle...?' Linda enquired like it was the most natural thing in the world.

'Yes?' Replied the maid hiding her true feelings as the best staff must do by painting on a professional smile.

'Would you run a bath for Jay please? I also suggested we would wash and dry his clothes before he left. Is that okay...?'

'...Of course.' Estelle replied. She then promptly plumped a cushion a little over firmly, before placing it down and trotting upstairs to the bathroom, all the while trying to work out exactly what the word 'we' meant in Linda's head.

Jay had never been in a place as smart as this where everything looked brand new and expensive, and it got him wondering if this Gary bloke was a drug dealer to have so much money. In his limited experience it was only through illegal business practices that you could afford to live like this.

'What does Gary do?' He asked.

'He's a financial consultant...!' Linda replied then thought it best if she explained it in a little more detail. '...he invests rich people's money.'

Jay reckoned he could do a job like that with a little training, and pondering this rich fantasy he made his way up the stairs feeling the carpet thick and soft under his feet.

'The bathroom's through there...' Linda pointed. '...If you just want to throw your clothes out on the landing and have yourself a good soak I'll make sure they're cleaned...'

'...Thank you.' Jay couldn't help noticing he was saying those two words way too much, but he was in a spin emotionally and mentally so thought it best to try and sound as grateful as he could. After throwing all his clothes on the landing as requested he shut the bathroom door before climbing into the large oyster shell bath. It didn't have ends which was a new experience for Jay, all the baths he'd ever used had a tap end and a not the tap end, but this tub with its almost circular design had no such commonalities. He worked out that hot water poured in through three holes evenly spaced around the sides and when the bath was optimally filled they would sense the depth and change into air jets. All this technology simply meaning that Jay was having his first ever Jacuzzi, and in the bubbles and steam he washed in a rich man's water that never got cold.

The only trouble with having one of those rare moments where you put your head back, let your arms float and try to think about nothing, is that you inevitably, logically, begin to think about everything, and there was only one word jumping out at Jay from his landfill of thoughts...'If'. If he hadn't have gone to his Aunties that day, if he hadn't gone for a cigarette, if he hadn't have been such a prick with Alex then none of the rest would have happened. Like Scott Hutchinson had said he could have been the hero, the young man who saved a life, but no he fucked up. There were no amount of 'Ifs' going to help him now, those 'if's were set as facts in his past, and with a perfectly natural young man's angry reaction he smashed both arms into the foam dispersing water which sloshed out onto the tiled floor. 'Bollocks!'

Looking up at the lit ceiling he let his whole body slide under the water, and it was down there in the shallows of a £3,500 bathtub that the really big 'If' struck home. If he'd saved Alex he wouldn't have gone down to the street to steal the wallet, wouldn't have seen the way the old man looked at him and therefore naturally wouldn't have pulled his knife out and pushed it into the man's gut. Whilst fully submerged he felt his own stomach, pressing the soft skin, as he recollected how easily the knife had pierced the old guy's flesh. So easily in fact Jay actually thought his first lunge must have missed, but became convinced when he found pulling it out wasn't as easy, that and all the blood down the blade. He remembered he'd stabbed the old man three times because he'd heard somewhere on the streets, or a drug fuelled house party, back in his recent past anyway, that three was the number of stabs to ensure, what do you call it, success.

'He didn't have to die. He didn't have to die. Fuck!' He repeated passionately and privately as he slid his tattooed chest back to the surface.

'Are you okay Jay...?' Linda's voice came to him clear as a bell and he nearly jumped out of his skin. Wiping the foam from his face he saw the bathroom was empty, and her voice hadn't come through the closed door either it had come through a small speaker just over his right shoulder. The circular piece of mesh fitting perfectly flush in the middle of a foot square tile with a silver button underneath, that said 'Listen' if turned to the left and 'Speak' if moved to the right. Reaching out his fingers and noticing they were beginning to wrinkle he moved it to speak. '…Yes I am….' Then he paused awkwardly. '…Thank you.' before switching it back to neutral and wondered if intercom shit like this also meant cameras, surely not. Though hey, if she wanted to see his goods they were here and he wasn't ashamed of the package. In fact the only time he'd ever had sex with a girl she'd remarked on how well hung he was for a skinny guy, and Jay had taken that to be a true compliment because he knew for a fact that particular girl had seen loads. Dragging his mind back from filthy sofa memories into the present he thought maybe he was done with the bath, as even a magical jet filled bath that never went cold could lose its novelty after fifty minutes and he reached for the towel placed on a white wooden chair for him. This must be made from the same stuff as the stair carpet he thought as he dried himself in seconds within its absorbent luxury. He liked it so much he decided to forgo the dressing gown option, which to be fair would have looked massive on his slight frame, and attached the towel around his narrow hips. He could get use to this; so much so all the thoughts of guilt and ifs were gone as he resumed the game.

Struggling at first to open the bathroom door he finally found the system, a push down, a twist and there you go, he preferred normal ones. He then popped his head round the wall to take a peek downstairs only to find Linda with her head already popped round peeking up.   '…I'm all done. Thank you!' Jay said and instantly followed it with a thought to stop saying thank you, you prick!' He looked back down at Linda.

'Your clothes aren't quite dry yet, probably another half hour. Hang on…!' Linda bounced up the stairs towards him and he noticed she'd gotten changed into a more comfortable looking blue jumpsuit as she beckoned him to follow her into a bedroom. Even Jay questioned the sense of that move, confirming with utmost certainty it wouldn't look great if this Gary guy came home to find him dressed in his towel being called into the bedroom by Linda. Instead Jay stood in the doorway, unprepared to go any further because he didn't want any misunderstanding; also that Estelle woman had just walked across the hall downstairs and glanced up at him. The look she gave held no other meaning, it was harsh and cutting, and then as he turned back to look at Linda an armful of clothes hit him in the face. He caught them all and held them out to find an expensive looking black Adidas sweat top and bottoms in his hands.

'Put those on for now. Gary won't mind they're his old ones. Get dressed then come down. We'll have a coffee.' She closed the bedroom door and went downstairs as if all of this was perfectly normal. Jay really wasn't certain it was but he did know the saying about gift horse mouths so he returned to the bathroom to put them on. As he closed the bathroom door he heard Linda call along the corridor downstairs 'Estelle would you be a darling and make us some coffee. Thank you...!'

'Woah...!' He said as the full length mirror showed a young man looking proper base in this get up. Base to him was a good thing, a great thing, and this jet black ensemble made him look double base, successfully pulling off the always difficult to nail 'stylish murderer on the run' look. Everything was all too brilliant he thought as he hopped barefoot down the stairs. He took a high backed leather seat at the vast grey granite topped island. Linda was sat at the other end with her coffee as Estelle placed a steaming round mug in front of him but didn't say a word.

'Thank you.' Jay couldn't believe he'd said it again, he'd tried to say something else, but then decided to give up worrying about it. Estelle went upstairs where he presumed she was going to clean up the bathroom.

'You look very smart. ' Linda remarked as he blew on his coffee to cool it.

He nodded his thanks before trying to explain himself.

'I'm sorry about all that before...you know scaring ya, I didn't know what I was doing. I still don't really...but we're kind of friends now...yeah?'

'Strange as it sounds yes we are! Just to let you know I threw your knife away...because that's what friends do. You're a good boy Jay I can tell.'

He accepted the compliment as a green light to open up and tell her the truth before he left, he didn't want there to be any questions hanging over his original intentions, after all they were friends now and in his head friends told each other the truth. '...I was thinking about raping ya, before you turned up. When I saw you I thought no I don't want to...'   Jay paused on noticing Linda's bemused expression, then played the words back in his head, and spoke again quickly to clear things up.   '...I mean...no I don't mean I didn't want to rape you, because of how you looked. I mean I saw you I and thought...I'm not going to because...she's too nice.'

'Nice...?' Linda responded and instantly found herself participating in the strangest conversation of her life.

'Yeah...' Jay knew he had the words in his head to explain himself but his brain kept farting them out in the wrong order. '...I don't know how to explain it.'

141

'So if I hadn't looked nice then you would have raped me...?' She was only teasing but her face gave nothing away.

'..Yeah' He said in a perfect combo of confirmation and question. 'No...I don't know!'

'Let's talk about something else.' She suggested and let him off the hook.

'...Yeah let's do that...thank you...' He truly couldn't stop himself from sounding grateful.

During the next minute a lot of things happened and didn't happen. They didn't change the subject because they were sat in an uncomfortable silence listening to the tumble dryer purring away. This shared moment was then shattered when they both heard a car pull up sharply on the drive, its door slamming, and then gravel crunching under heavy determined feet. The front door flew open. 'Linda!' A man's deep voice bellowed.

'In here darling...!'

'What the hell is going on here...?' Gary Swann demanded to know when his large pin stripe suited frame came round the corner. In the doorway he stopped for a moment taking in the scene before focusing his attention on the teenage boy sat in his kitchen, with his girlfriend, drinking from his mug. '...Who the hell are you?' He asked the boy firmly.

'This is Jay he...' But Linda was cut off immediately.

'...Did I ask you anything Linda? No! I'm asking him...!' He stared at the boy who he noted looked very comfortable in that Adidas gear. Hang on! 'Are those my clothes? Is he wearing my stuff?'

Jay really didn't know what to say but totally understood when someone didn't like him, after years suffering from negative first impressions he was used to it. This man in his striped shirt and red braces didn't like him, that much was clear but Jay somehow fought the urge to react, he just stared at the man's face which he thought looked about ten years older than Linda's.

Gary Swann was used to tough confrontations in a business capacity, he knew all the tricks and moves, about owning the room, dominating your quarry, he knew about cutting a deal and walking out of the room leaving the other poor sucker with nothing, but what he didn't know about was Jay, or how to deal with him.

'Its fine he's a friend I'm helping him out...' Linda spoke to break the tension.

'In my bloody house...!' Gary snapped in her direction and a visibly stung Linda went quiet. '...I was in a meeting, a quite important meeting when I get a phone call from Estelle telling me there's a strange boy in my house taking a bath...'

At that moment Estelle made a noise as if she'd dropped something upstairs, but Linda knew it was just a way of letting her know she was listening and had no regrets.

'...Who's the boy I said, and she said Linda's just brought him home. So you do understand why I would like some answers to my fucking questions...!' Gary rarely swore believing it signified someone who struggled with vocabulary. 'Now be quiet, we'll discuss things later, right now I want to talk to...Jay is it?' He moved in so the boy understood he was big and strong and within in range to punch him at any moment.

'Jay Cleaver...' The boy fearlessly responded.

'And do I know you Jay Cleaver...?'

'...Nah!'

Now apart from swearing, another gear grinder for Gary was smartarses who gave short smartarse answers. 'Nah...?' He mimicked Jay but again the boy fought the urge to make a scene.

'My clothes ready yet?' Jay looked nonchalantly around the man and asked Linda even though he could clearly hear the spinning tumble dryer.

'Are you blanking me? Don't I exist in my own bloody house?' Gary was shifting towards really annoyed now and slapping the boy crossed his mind.

Jay slowly stood up and because Gary was looming over him he bent down a little to duck under his arm and take his mug to the sink. As he placed it on the side he looked at both of them in turn but said nothing. Gary Swann was shocked by this affront and was now rapidly becoming livid.

As Linda watched the standoff she knew this messed up situation was all her doing and would take a lot of sorting, while upstairs the eavesdropping Estelle knew Linda was getting some comeuppance and smiled, while Gary knew that at any minute he was going to grab the little shit and throw him out. However what nobody knew, apart from Jay Cleaver, was that moving over to the sink had been a planned move, a strategy placing him in a fresh position of power, and knowing a boy needed skills and tools to survive in this game Jay had manoeuvred his character right next to the cutlery drawer.

35

Harvey asked the handcuffed prisoner. 'Oh so you really want to talk now...?'

'Explain what you meant...' Oscar repeated while also wanting to know why the Inspector was calling a halt to their meeting, because surely Cooper wanted to learn more about him, this couldn't be it.

Harvey had a few options to choose from now, attack, defend or consolidate, he decided to attack. 'I just needed you to talk...see Oscar the only doubt we had about you has now been answered. We know you killed those five women and we certainly know you killed Doctor Kelly and the gate guard and the cab driver at the secure unit. It also was you at the service station murdering that young father on his way home to his family, just to get his clothes, and you'd have to admit any denial would be weak as you're still wearing them now. So just in case there's any misunderstanding Mr Downes I will clear it up, you are a murdering piece of filth who is clearly a danger to anyone you encounter so the question we had to answer wasn't if, or even how, no, the question the law needed answering was simple...are you sane? Your silent act was skilfully performed and of course hindered our work, I mean the wheels of justice would have taken their turn anyway but it was possible you might have been declared insane and then a secure mental institution would be your home, but I have to tell you that unsurprisingly the victim's families don't want that...I don't want that, better you're sent to the toughest darkest prison we have and rot for the rest of your life. All of that can happen now thanks to your vocal compliance, proof the silence was just an act and you don't have any form of 'locked in syndrome' or 'PTSD' or whatever modern claptrap your defence team may have dreamed up. You are compos mentis, so will be charged and sentenced with the full force of the law.' Harvey then sat back in his chair and folded the pictures together, he hadn't even looked at them, why should he, he had the man now and it didn't matter about the drawings. They'd only been an extra layer of emotional trickery to help knock Oscar off balance, to make the whole experience more immersive and it had worked beautifully, his job was complete.

However Oscar wasn't finished talking yet. 'So that's that...?' He licked his dry lips.

The Inspector nodded yes but of course it wasn't, he wanted to know more, he wanted to know everything, and as he sat across from the small man he knew with total certainty he would never get a better opportunity.

'I'm not insane...' Oscar dry mumbled. '...Could I have that drink now?'

Harvey walked to the door and pressed the buzzer. After a brief wait it opened and he requested the officer to fetch some water. This simple act proved to Oscar that the Inspector had been telling the truth, no one else was listening or watching this conversation. They only came when he buzzed, interesting. Watching him stood by the open door Oscar wondered if Harvey wasn't just baiting him a little, not that he could do anything while hand and leg cuffed to a bolted down chair. The officer returned with a plastic bottle and Harvey made sure the door was locked again before approaching with it.

Oscar leaned forward as much as he was able and watched Harvey messing about with the top, struggling to unscrew it, and he didn't much care for the delay in opening the bottle. 'I'd offer to help.' He said, as Harvey struggled a moment longer before breaking the seal.

'Open your mouth.' Harvey said putting it to Oscar's lips and pouring carefully, he didn't want the man to choke now, not when he was so close, so close to what? Building a trust perhaps, finding out the truth of what made this serial killer tick. Even though he doubted that would even be possible with someone like Oscar while he had his undivided attention he may as well try.

'Thank you...' Oscar said and Harvey wiped a dribble from his chin.

'I'll tell you what Mr Downes I'll stay a little longer with you if we can carry on talking. I might try you with a few more questions, after all it is my job...'

'Well understand then that I'm not insane.' Oscar repeated his earlier claim unsure if Harvey had heard him the first time.

'I never said you were. I said you were a murdering piece of filth...' Harvey took a swig from the same bottle before continuing. '...I've always known you weren't insane Oscar, hence why I have always wanted to speak to you one on one, it's all those pen pushers and box tickers out there who think you're crazy. To those people everything's simple and clean cut when it's plain old insanity at play but prefer to know why you think you did all of your...work!'

'Inspector...Harvey, before all of this...this carnage...before I was a murdering piece of filth...I was a nice man, a good man who went to work every day and drove my taxi taking people wherever they wanted to go; so thoughtful of other people's needs that I wouldn't even consider a personal relationship because I didn't want to burden anyone else with my life. I went home alone after my shifts and read books on composers and authors, artists and generals, all the great minds. I enjoy reading about great people...'

'And did this little man believe he deserved to be great?'

'...Please don't interrupt me with the same hack psychological guesswork you were just slagging off. I'm trying to explain something...' Oscar then sighed before carrying on with his tale. '...I love to read about those creative geniuses and the amazing inventors, the brave explorers who discovered and defined new things, new worlds. That was my joy.'

Harvey was patiently wondering where all this was leading but the cork was certainly out of the bottle, even if its contents were spilling everywhere, as Oscar continued his bizarre defence..

'...It was my day to day back then, working, reading and sleeping. Truthfully I never in my whole life asked a soul for help, never talked behind the back of another person, or picked an argument of any kind. If I ever felt I'd gotten a bad deal or someone had deliberately taken advantage of my good nature, I'd put it down to experience, believing it was just one bad day that would turn out to be good tomorrow. My mother taught me that...' Oscar locked his eyes on Harvey while he said the next part. '...I worked hard for long hours applying myself to becoming the least needy man I could, the least interfering, the type you wouldn't need to worry about because I didn't want plaudits and applause, didn't want to be seen at all. I was honest, hardworking always, and got on with my job to the best of my ability. My father taught me that...' Harvey was listening intently as Oscar continued his tale. '...So like I said before all of this...I was a good man. Then one day something changed and I became part of another world, a place linked to terrible things, but I didn't choose it. So yes physically I killed and dismembered those poor women, and I'm also freely admitting that with no fear of your justice. What I'm trying to say Harvey...is if you ever speak of my parents like that again...I will give myself completely to finding you and satisfying *my* need for justice.'

Harvey understood a threat on his life when he heard one but he wasn't for backing down while he felt on top. '...That was a sinister warning delivered with satisfyingly immaculate menace. I'll take it on board Oscar...now tell me more about this other world, the one with terrible things.' Harvey crossed his legs under the table; after all it appeared he may be here for the long haul.

'We shall get to that but I'm not quite finished with you yet Harvey. What happened to me changed everything, but I do remember the old Oscar Downes, every last detail. For instance I remember all of my fares...' He grinned.

'...Your fares? Harvey's look was puzzled.

'Yes. I can recall all of them if I try, and there were thousands. I suppose when you live alone and don't really socialise you have to put your mind to something.'

'I suppose you do.'

'For example I remember you...Mr Cooper.'

Harvey shuffled in his chair slightly; a gentle shiver rippled his spine, and unhappy with Oscar's demeanour and tone. 'What are you talking about?'

'Let's see now...three years ago, I picked you up from Valentina's Restaurant after what you told me had been your office Christmas meal. You unsurprisingly asked me if I'd been busy that evening, you were wearing a sandy coloured overcoat and your lovely wife was a riot in blue floral, she'd won a raffle prize. You weren't gentlemanly enough to tell me her name but you did seem very happy together.'

Harvey was more than a little disconcerted by Oscar's details but deciding to keep playing it cool, he genuinely didn't remember that particular evening, mostly because the office Christmas party went to Valentina's every year. 'That could be right I don't remember...'

'Oh you can trust that it's right.' Oscar's expression became passive again. 'I dropped you off at number 7 Wilkes Avenue. A lovely house on a very nice street that I presume you and your wife live at.'

Harvey felt another shiver rise up his spine. He'd always thought that common description of fear was just a turn of phrase, but as with most things it must have its roots based in truth. 'Are you still threatening me Oscar?'

'Simply enlightening you on little Oscar the taxi driver, how he remembers everything...in case it may become useful in the future!'

Harvey regained his composure, fighting to keep himself on top in this conversation, Oscar was clearly a clever and dangerous antagonist but what the Inspector wanted to know was just how he'd gone from meek and mild to crazy and killing. 'You keep saying 'before all this' and you 'changed all of a sudden', what does that mean...what happened to you?'

Oscar looked over to see the spider still hadn't returned to its empty web and smiled. Perversely it appeared as a nice smile, Harvey thought so anyway, not the kind that belonged on the face of one who committed murderous acts and kept corpses in plastic tubs. Then as he replied his smile disappeared. '46 Marlborough Drive happened!'

36

Linda Webb was feeling all types of messed up now, after warming to and befriending a boy who'd basically attacked her, and turning that whole situation around, she was now being viciously ordered to keep quiet by her lover, boyfriend and boss Gary Swann. He was angry with her and the boy yet they'd done anything wrong, but it was about to get much worse. She jumped up as he made his move, leaping from her seat she threw herself between boy and man, ending up in Gary's arms and trying to push him away.

Jay stood watching the wrestling couple as they stumbled in a tangle of limbs down to the tiles. This commotion soon caused Estelle to come running down the stairs shouting in her strange accent for them to stop, her face a picture of bewilderment when finding Gary struggling to get Linda's hands out of his hair where they'd apparently taken root.

'He isn't doing any harm!' Linda shouted keeping a tight grip.

'Get off me and get out you stupid slag!' Gary demanded with his squealing tone revealing that the hair pulling was hurting a lot.

'Get off him you bitch!' Estelle threw her comment into the mix of grunting profanities and thuds as feet and hands bounced off surfaces. She tried hard to separate them by fair means, and when that had little effect she went foul, deciding that if hair pulling was the weapon of choice then so be it. Soon Gary was shouting in agony at his hair being pulled by Linda who was screaming as her long brown tresses were yanked hard by Estelle, who was now being dragged on to the floor with the two them.

Unnoticed by the warring factions the boy pulled open the kitchen drawer hoping to find a knife, but he didn't find a knife, no sir, he found a lot of knives. Holy shit is that a fucking machete? Jay inspected the rest of the gleaming culinary armoury while the adults continued their fight, all of them refusing to give an inch but he cared little for their dilemma, he was too busy pulling out the heaviest most dangerous looking cutting tool. He looked at the name of it engraved on the handle, there were a set of six, and they all had their descriptive titles on the handles, but this one had his name on it in every sense. 'Cleaver' etched on a beautiful rectangular hatchet. Jay couldn't believe how much time he had to think about his next move. The three adults on the floor had reached a totally exhausted impasse, a stalemate that left them all in situ at his feet and once more he was being thrown back into making those life and death decisions again.

Fuck why was this always happening to him? Thinking that whoever designed this level of the game was one cruel sadistic bastard.

While waiting for things to calm down he thought back to the start of the game when all he'd done was choose to go for a cigarette, then got involved in an attempted, then aborted, suicide, that led to the old man and what followed and now he travels here and tries to do the right thing by returning a photo and look at it, he's suddenly fucking judge and executioner again. Holding the handle tightly it was thrilling how heavy the knife was, how well designed because it felt so comfortable in his hand, and he knew there would be no doubt at all if this went into a body. Noticing his gaunt face reflected in the large square blade he reckoned he looked good for having that bath even though everything was turning to shit around him. So what did this game want him to do now?   Using his experience in the virtual world he concluded that in all decent video adventure games a player is often given moral choices, these options are available to help or hinder your journey when you got through to the later levels. With different decisions leading to alternate endings players could elect to slash and stab their way forwards, but they can also opt to avoid major confrontations and negotiate, sometimes even try to sneak stealthily around a problem.

At that moment Gary looked up from the bottom of the female pile to see Jay stood over them holding the cleaver. Now he didn't want to unduly alarm anyone but he was snared in a follicle death grip, so made the decision that he could probably improve everyone's situation by shouting.

'Put that knife down Jay!' with the alarm in his voice having an instant effect. Linda quickly let go of his hair and looked up with strands of greying blonde stuck to her fingers before pulling her own hair free from Estelle's bony claws, as all three quit their wrestling and waited to see what Jay would do next.

'You're that man they're looking for on the news...' Estelle suddenly shrieked as she looked at the large knife. '...It was on the radio. You've killed someone...'

Finally some fucking recognition, he'd been seriously beginning to believe the police had forgotten about him.

'That old man they found next to your husband, the one that was stabbed...?' Gary asked Linda but she didn't answer. '...Did you know that's who he was...?

'Yes' Linda answered.

'What the serious hell...!' Gary said loudly realising immediately it was a weird statement but in fairness this whole situation was strange. '...Look Jay we don't want any trouble okay. I'm going to stand up now and...'

'...I don't fucking think so Gary...you're gonna stay sat the fuck down!' Jay raised his voice to the old prick and of course with the added ingredient of a hefty cleaver it worked like magic. The red faced man instantly froze in position being given no choice but to stay sat the fuck down, which he did, on his expensive tiles, in his bespoke kitchen.

'Estelle...?' Jay asked and she looked back nervously. '...I want you to go over to that dryer...' He waved the weapon in the general direction. '...and get my clothes.'

'Yes of course...' She then paused for a moment. '...Now...?' She was unsure about the task because the dryer was still having a little tumble.

'...Right now!' Jay ordered gently and watched the fat arsed maid scuttle across to the machine before turning to his new friend.

'Can you believe that Linda? It was all going so well until billy big bollocks ran in!'

'Get out of my house!' Gary requested firmly. He didn't shout, knowing his position was still too vulnerable for that, he just toned it down a little. '...Please just go and take her with you if you want.'

'You total bastard Gary Swann!' Linda swore in his face and put her hands down to raise herself up.

'Sit fucking down Linda...!' Jay snapped at her. '...unless the man with the big knife says it okay? Can you both understand that simple rule? It's like a game...we'll call it Cleaver says, and if Cleaver says sit down what do you do?' Jay's blue eyes were darkening in the bright sunlit kitchen.

'I sit down!' Linda said accepting the rules of the new game.

'...Do you want them now or shall I put them in a bag...?' Estelle asked with a well-timed interruption. She turned the machine off and began folding his damp clothes then placed them neatly on top of the dryer.

'A bag would be great Estelle. Just don't do anything stupid, okay...?'

'...I won't it's just here.' She pulled out a large green plastic bag for life and gently slid his clothes into it.

'Thank you Estelle. Now come back over here and sit down with the happy couple.'

The maid did as she was told because it was in her nature. It was in her blood. Now the three captives were sat on the floor like a primary school class with Jay stood before them, his eyes flicking their attention from one to the other. There was a fully expected uncomfortable silence before he split it wide. 'How much do you earn Gary...?'

'What...has that got to do with anything?' He answered.

'How much do you fucking earn...a fucking year...? Just tell me the number Gary and don't lie because...well trust me just don't lie...how much?' Jay was playfully swapping the weapon between hands because damn it felt nice.

'Last year he cleared £150,000...after tax.' Linda said helpfully.

'How do you know what I earned...?' Gary barked

'...Because I work in your accounts department you idiot!' Linda snapped back with no quarter given.

Jay considered the amount, confidently working out it was more money than he'd ever seen in his life, then looked around the plush surroundings once more before walking towards the huddle on the floor. Gary closed his eyes, Estelle put her hands on her head and Linda looked up at him appealingly as he closed the gap, before walking calmly past to grab his bag of clothes

'I'm leaving now. I'll be taking these as well...' He pointed down at the borrowed black Adidas outfit and Gary nodded his agreement. '...So okay I don't want to have to say this but I've kind of gotta...don't phone the fucking police! Just sit there until ya big gates shut and then sit there some more and talk about everything that's happened if you want. Because if I find out you phoned the cops on me then I promise that on the day I get out...I'll find ya and kill ya...you got that?'

'Yes!' Gary said a little too enthusiastically.

'I fucking mean it old guy. If any of you grass me up I'll chop your heads clean off!'

'Okay we've got it! None of us are going to phone the police.'

'And what else?' Jay asked stroking the blade.

'Or tell anyone anything...' Gary replied quickly.

'That's right Gary. Nice house by the way. You must be really good at gambling other people's money. To be honest though and based on first impressions I reckon you're a total wanker. Open the gates, Linda.' He helped her up and she nodded before moving to the front door and holding down the button.

Jay paused in the doorway for a moment as he remembered something he'd really meant to say earlier. 'I'm glad Alex didn't die and I'm sorry for what I did to him. Can you tell him that...?'

Linda half smiled and held back a tear as she opened the front door.

'...I mean it, all of it. Alex wasn't a bad guy. That guy sat there though, a total dick, but he's rich so I understand, and Linda if any of them two try and call the police...pull their fucking hair clean off!'

With his valedictory message imparted this psychologically tough level was completed. So Jay dropped the cleaver into his bag and strode confidently down the gravel driveway to see what this game had in store for him next.

<u>37</u>

'Oh right yeah finally, it's about time you showed up! I've been feeling a little neglected here...' Alex shouted those words at the Angel who'd appeared and was now gliding up the beach towards him. '...I know we haven't got time here, as I understand it as such, but whatever we do have here instead of time, that was a long length of it...where in hell have you been?'

There was no emotional reaction from his host as it drew nearer. '...I have been doing my job...and also Alex, please be reminded that I don't have to answer any of your questions.'

'Don't be like that. I really thought we were getting on.' Alex smirked in a friendly conspiratorial fashion but the Angel gave the man's look short shrift. 'Fair enough...where have you been then...?' Alex asked over politely.

'Looking in other places...'

'Right...and...?'

'And I have found nothing useful to help answer our problem. Have you received any enlightenment on why you're here?'

'The best I've got is immortality but you blew that theory out of the water so...no.' Alex looked at his hands noting they hadn't tanned even the slightest under the beautiful sun.

The Angel sat down. 'Tell me while I have been absent, what have you been thinking of...?'

'...Shockingly I've been thinking about where you disappear to. I've also been thinking about my wife and hoping she's okay even though she's with another man and probably having a great time. Most of all though I've been thinking of asking you about 'operating the machine', so would you like to give me a clue about that confession...?' Alex waited in silence for what felt like another age before the Angel replied.

'The machine is what makes everything work.'

'I'm sure it is...but I don't know what that means.'

'It runs all the elements of the universe inside and out, operating smoothly because every part of it reacts and responds to every other part. It is perfect in its function and design. Is that any clearer?'

'Obviously not...!' Alex responded.

'Would you prefer I gave you an example...?'

'...If that's not too much trouble.' Alex felt some of the Angels inspiring glow return. Here he was sat in some bizarre existence 'out of time' with it trying to explain to him, a mortal man, how the universe actually worked. Holy crap!

'Very well Alex, we will take you as an example as a part of the universe...'

'An excellent choice if I do say so myself...' He joked, hoping to get a nod of recognition or a smile but nothing came back. The Angel just circled the desk like a beautiful heavenly tutor delivering a lecture.

'...From the moment of conception you have affected the universe around you. From your birth onwards each and every breath you have taken has caused a reaction on a massive scale and a molecular level. These variances though very small, are just as important as the very large, in fact more so, because there are more of them. Are you following?'

'Not really but carry on it sounds great.' Alex got himself comfortable in his chair and listened on as the Angel told him a wonderful story of life.

'Now with you being an atheist as you proudly told me, and believing the scientific approach above any faith options, I will have to explain it to you leaving out the religious element. So Alex, you have been making slight alterations to the machine every second of your life, therefore it follows that every molecule around you has also made the same amount of changes, and the machine understands how to read those changes, then uses all this information to create new beginnings. It exists by constantly running smoothly and freely because nothing in existence is stationary, all parts are in constant motion moving and colliding with every other part, and through this continuous flow of matter new states are made so the machine can grow and be healthy...' The Angel paused for Alex to catch up, but looking at the man's blank expression it thought that unlikely to be soon, so decided to carry on and hope that eventually some of it may become comprehensible to him. '...The machine is continuous therefore never ending, this is in part to what it's made of, pure matter, and this matter reacts with numerous other universal constants such as gravity and time, when these are mixed up with the rather chaotic quantum ingredients such as wimps, quarks and bosons, all of these things cause it to perpetually run. It cannot be stopped by natural means nor should it ever stop. Of course some of those unruly elements in constant collision can mean that it needs some maintenance, an overseeing eye to be kept on it, in case of an unforeseen problem...' The Angel broke off once more for a response but yet again the face he looked upon was blank. '...I can't really put it any plainer than that Alex, but I can add for transparency that the overseeing eye in this instance is me. That is, as you like to call it…my job.

Listening as hard as he could Alex finally and completely accepted he wasn't dreaming, up until this point being in a deep slumber had remained an option, but it was clearly impossible he could be imagining this moment as there was no way he could have made-up the words the Angel was coming out with. 'Is it question time now…?' He asked with eyes wide, hungry for more knowledge, and positive this information was precious and priceless even though he couldn't get his head around any of it right now.

The Angel shrugged slightly.

'Right okay, so all this stuff happens on a molecular level…?' Alex asked.

'Yes and much smaller and larger levels…'

'So everything you're describing now, the small, medium and large levels all react with each other to keep the machine running…?' Alex was taking a punt on what he thought he knew.

'Simplistic when put in those terms…but yes.'

'Cool!' Alex gave his honest opinion.

'…Cool?' The Angel questioned distastefully.

'Yeah…I think I've got it, just science isn't it? I mean we call it the universe you call it a machine. That's the only difference.'

'Hmmm…' The Angel retook its seat and settled down. '…I shall begin again Alex and let's see if it becomes any clearer. The Life machine is…'

<u>38</u>

'...I took them to 46 Marlborough Drive, where they said they wanted to go, and once there they attacked me for no reason...' Oscar was speaking quite slowly trying his best to help the Inspector understand. '...I hadn't done anything to upset them Harvey, it was a misunderstanding but they began hitting me around the head, then I...'

'...Oscar! I know all about the incident. It's all on record; those young girls accused you of sexual harassment. Their version of events differs quite dramatically from yours...they said you offered them a way to pay for their ride home that involved sexual acts, the types of which you wanted to see and have done to you. Pretty lurid descriptions they gave as well, and to be honest if half of what they said was true you deserved a smack on the head.'

'I didn't ask them for anything!' Oscar said and thumped back in his chair as hard as a cuffed man could manage.

'Look they didn't take kindly to your offer; they signed a statement saying that you wouldn't let them out of the taxi. Let's be straight here Oscar, these were two young women trapped with a sexual predator, I'm not surprised they reacted as they did!' Harvey was all over this interrogation and this fresh denial wasn't helping anything. He was thinking that if all they were going to talk about was where those women attacked him for no good reason, there wasn't much point carrying on; maybe he should even call it a day.

Oscar brought himself back up to his full height and asked the Inspector to listen to him and not interrupt if he wanted to know the truth about everything.

The Inspector nodded, willing to give the infamous Oscar Downes another five minutes, after that he could happily let him go rot in a cell. 'My apologies please continue.'

'Those girls were bait...' Oscar rather surprisingly said.

'...Bait?'

'Yes bait to get me to that house. I promise you on my Mother and Fathers grave I did not approach them with any form of aggressive or sexual behaviour, that is not who I am or have ever been. I have no interest in sex; something I never had a drive for. I knew from a young age I preferred my own company rather than the pitfalls of relationships and after a brief dalliance with masturbation during my hormonal teenage years, I discovered the whole process to be ultimately unsatisfying, pointless and disgustingly messy.'

'...It's an interesting confession but difficult to prove in court.' Harvey couldn't resist the whimsy and fortunately Oscar let it pass unchallenged.

'Inspector, tell me why I wasn't charged with any offence for this so called attack...?' Oscar knew the answer but waited a moment for Harvey to draw a breath and just when he was about to speak, Oscar cut him off and continued. '...I wasn't charged for many reasons; there were no witnesses apart from the two drunken girls, no physical evidence of any sort to incriminate me, while various work colleagues were questioned about my behaviour and character and not one could be found to drop even the merest hint that I would be capable of such a thing. The police investigating the allegations told the girls the case would be difficult to prove and perhaps they should drop their complaint, after all they had fractured my skull with a stiletto and a champagne bottle, and afterwards the police assured them it was probably enough of a lesson to stop me ever trying it on again.'

'I know all of this, Oscar. Do you have anything to tell me I that I don't know? Otherwise I'm afraid my time is precious.'

Oscar leaned forward putting his elbows on the table making his chains rattle. 'After they attacked me, I was unconscious, slumped forward on my steering wheel. They ran off into the house screaming and laughing, a mix of emotions that I couldn't have comprehended, but I can tell you exactly what happened when they got in the house. First of all the frizzy one put the champagne bottle down and it wasn't even cracked, she was very relieved about that. At the same time the blonde one noticed she'd broken the heel of her shoe on my head and she was upset. Then the frizzy one cut up two lines of cocaine and they snorted them away in one go. The blonde one looked out of the window of the house...'

'...46 Marlborough Drive...?' Harvey interjected.

'...Yes...after about ten minutes they started to panic because I think they believed I was going to drive away, but I couldn't could I? I was stuck there, unconscious with a fractured skull and do you know what else Inspector...I heard them call the police. I can tell you word for word exactly what they said, describe to you precisely where they were in the house and everything they did up until the police arrived another fifteen minutes later.'   Oscar was looking at Harvey for his reaction.

'But you weren't in the house you were in the taxi.' Harvey offered up.

'...I was in both.' Oscar stated clearly.

Harvey didn't understand this revelation at all. 'How were you in both?'

'Well I was in the car slumped over the steering wheel unconscious...but I tell you now Harvey I was also in the house watching them...'

'...And you know that's completely ridiculous.'

'Ridiculous or not that's where my mind was. Have you got a recording of the call they made to the police? I can prove it...repeat it exactly to the word...'

'Look I don't know what you're playing at but I'm afraid a ghost story isn't going to wash...' Harvey was close to leaving the room.

'I'm not talking about ghosts...aren't they the spirits of dead people? I can promise you I have never had an interest in, or a visitation from, or witnessed any paranormal activities, but I am telling you what happened and it has nothing to do with a ghost, Inspector.'

'Then what are you talking about Oscar...?' Harvey thought he might soon be making up his own ghost stories to find an excuse to leave this killer to his fantasies.

'...It was a voice.' Oscar said firmly although his eyes looked afraid as if he may have overstepped a mark.

'A voice...very well!' Harvey felt somewhat saddened by Oscar's admission. 'You have about a minute before I carry on with my day. I'm very disappointed in you Oscar, in my mind I imagined today would be different to this, a memorable one we could both look back on, a celebration almost of cop against killer. So unless you can give me any form of proof, even spooky proof that what you are saying isn't just the mumblings of a sad madman then I'm afraid our meeting is over.'

He walked to the door before realising he hadn't picked the drawings up again, as he returned to the table the man spoke.

'Look at the drawings...' Oscar asked with sudden enthusiasm.

'... I don't need to look at them.' Harvey replied sharply.

'...LOOK AT THEM!' Oscar shouted with his loudest and best impression of what the voice had sounded like inside him.

Harvey was momentarily stunned by this angry outburst and stood staring at the little red faced man, until finally and reluctantly he opened up the pictures. The first one was the scene with a figure standing atop a slide with a bright blue and white UFO in the sky shooting daggers down, two policemen were watching, there was also a broken fence and a kite in a tree, its artistic quality similar to something an ungifted child may do.

'I don't have the time for this.' Harvey said.

'Please...look...' Oscar repeated his request indicating the second drawing in the pile.

Harvey sighed, accepting he'd have to play this game with Oscar, having waited so long for the chance to meet the killer he wasn't going to really let it end so quickly. Although he'd admit this part of the meeting was becoming confusing and tedious. Unfolding the corners he opened the next, the wax crayoned image of the man falling from a window with a figure in blue next to him and an Angel looking down from the heavens. Now that's strange. The Inspector felt a sudden temperature drop in his body and even at his most reticent he'd admit that the image in this drawing was something unexpected, after all it was a pretty accurate attempt at recreating the scene from Dalmeny Street, with details clear enough even using basic primary coloured crayons.

'That one now...' The dark artist requested. '...Don't be scared.'

Harvey picked up and opened the last picture; it caused his eyes to widen and twitch slightly in physical confirmation of disbelief, before he stepped back and let the paper drop open on the table. In front of him was an image of Alex Webb in his hospital bed with the machine bleeping next to him, at his bedside was Linda in her long brown coat and there by the door for all to see was Juliet, the pretty nurse in her sky blue uniform.

His mind requested a deep breath then took in all the oxygen it provided before he looked into Oscar's eyes now alert and fully interacting with him, and then back down at the wax crayon drawings, especially the last one. That was definitely the hospital room Harvey had visited, it was exactly the same as he remembered, but Oscar had been locked away when that occurred. All tedium completely gone he was totally intrigued again by his nemesis.

'When did you draw these?

'Over the past three weeks.'

'While locked in the facility...but how on earth could you have imagined this?' He asked.

'...I didn't imagine it...' Oscar smiled with a mixture of relief and confusion as tears welled up. '...We went in my dreams...the voice took me there.'

39

In a hospital bed thirty miles away from its previous host, deep in the darkness of a young lady's sleeping mind, the voice awoke from its slumber. The switch had been successful and the hole in her skull now sealed up with stitches and tape. It was pleased with its decision to trade bodies as it moved down the hallways of her knowledge exploring a whole new universe of female thoughts and memories.

Rebecca Jones tried to open her eyes but the pain was so instant and sharp she gave up. Her breathing was constant and healthy bringing a tiny smile to her lips as she wiggled her fingers and toes, but when connecting that her smile was the cause of the discomfort in her head she reverted back to a straightened face. It didn't matter though because she was alive and she would heal, so her priority now was finding the voice.   Being so new to this she had no idea how to communicate with it unless it spoke first. Frustratingly there was no way of perceiving if the transfer had actually been successful, she'd a vague memory of it talking to her before she collapsed but that could be wrong, after all at the time she'd just received a heavy blow to her head, so she tried to clear her mind of all thoughts and concentrate, in the hope it would help with the connection.

The voice however would communicate when it was ready, for now it was lost in a new world of Rebecca's memories, fascinated by the glimpses and emotional perspectives of family and boyfriends of girlfriends and pets, of cycling and shopping and working and crying. It found a lot of memories of crying, certainly more crying that it had ever seen in Oscar, and putting those pieces together the voice deduced quite correctly that women were far more emotional and complex than men.

Rebecca was upset by the silence and suddenly more than anything else she wanted to go home. Her heavily bandaged skull was banging as if someone were throwing furniture around in her head. Feeling alone and fooled she wanted her own bed, the perfect hiding place for a stupid young woman who'd believed in a happy fairy-tale ending. Even the fact she was alive didn't make up for the disappointment, loneliness and gullibility she felt.

40

'...All I'm saying Sir is that I really don't know what to think at the moment.' Harvey was standing straight backed looking out of Superintendent Jeff Shilling's office window, staring down onto the busy thoroughfare below where hundreds of people made transient patterns on the footpaths of their life's journey. Every single one of them lost in the present, controlled by their past while being led blindly to an unknown future. Of course he wasn't thinking about any of that philosophical claptrap because he was trying to understand something altogether more baffling.

The Superintendent spoke in an attempt to calm Harvey down using common sense. 'Harvey! It's a crayon drawing made by a man we both know is not firing on all cylinders. I understand you're spooked by it and to be honest, just between us two, I share your unease. It's a strange picture and clearly relates to an event that we both now he couldn't have witnessed, but come on now, we've seen magicians and mind readers do dumbfounding tricks like this on TV all the...'

'...Sir! With all due respect this isn't on TV.' Harvey wasn't certain of what he wanted to hear from Superintendent Jeff Shilling but he knew he wanted more than it was just a magic trick from a talent show

'I know it isn't Harvey and like I said I do agree it's a strange picture.'

'What about this one...' Harvey bravely interrupted his superior and rushed to the desk pointing at the picture of the falling man.   '...This is Alex Webb, this is him falling from the window in Dalmeny Street and it's just not possible for Oscar to know about that!'

The Superintendent realised he was going to have to stop this circling and get them both back on a forward facing track. 'Harvey, I understand your obsession with Oscar Downes...'

'...This is nothing like an obsession Sir. I'm just trying to do my job...' Harvey was getting passionate about this but he knew better than most that going toe to toe with this commanding officer wasn't wise and hadn't worked out well in the past.

'...Inspector Cooper! Jeff Shilling slammed his fist on the desk for silence, and then calmed himself before speaking again but Harvey knew the warning signs that demanded him to retreat. '...I'm sure we both have actual things we need to be getting on with, real work based in the real world, so if you wouldn't mind I suggest we do that.'

'Yes Sir I'm sorry I err...' Harvey tried to explain but he was cut off again.

'...It's alright Harvey. You've clearly been working hard on this, and Oscars thrown us a new riddle of sorts but it's over with now; let's deal with more pressing matters. Is there any news on that young man Cleaver?'

Harvey toed the line and accepted the change of subject. '...No Sir, he's proving difficult to locate. We have some footage of him in a fast food shop the night before last but nothing since. I have a four man unit working on it and posters are going out today in the press, shops and online. We'll find him Sir.'

'I certainly hope so...before he stabs anyone else!' A harsh cold comment from the Superintendent fully intended to remind Harvey of his duties and he wasn't finished yet. 'You can leave Oscar Downes alone now. We have him in custody and everything we need to move forward for a conviction. That case is closed...do we understand each other?'

'...Yes sir.' Harvey nodded, a subtle form of salute, then picked up the drawings from the desk and turned to leave.

'Oh and Harvey...?'

Sir...?'

'...Brilliant work getting the bastard to talk...!' Jeff said this sincerely then moved to the window to look out on the same view Harvey had seen, a clear gesture that the conversation was over.

'Thank you, Sir.' Harvey backed his way out of the door before returning to his own smaller office. On the way he tried to align himself with his superiors thinking. He couldn't argue with the actuality of priority, seeing that Oscar was under lock and key while Jay Cleaver was still roaming the streets, but surely those pictures meant something. Sitting back down at his own desk he checked the latest reports but found nothing new on the Jay Cleaver search. The problems he faced with it were a lack of information and funds; it wasn't an official manhunt because there had been only one death. You would need to kill a few more than that for the powers on high to release the money for a full scale search, so he didn't have infinite resources or even a decent description of what the young man was wearing let alone where he might favour to go. At the moment there was an undercover team of two keeping an eye on Scott Hutchinson's house and Jay hadn't returned there as far they knew. Reminding him it was time to let the Hutchinson guy go, they couldn't really hold him at the station any longer, even for his own safety, and let's not forget they had nothing concrete to charge him with.

Harvey buzzed through to his secretary.

'Yes Sir?' She answered promptly and politely.

'...Could you inform the cells they can let Scott Hutchinson go? Tell them to give him a personal alarm and emergency numbers to call. Inform the unit watching the house to continue for now...at least until I say different.'

'Yes Sir! Is that all...'

'Yes...actually no, before he leaves can you get them to bring him up here. I'd like a quick word.' Harvey wasn't exactly sure what about but he'd think of something.

He wasn't in a cell as most would imagine because Scott Hutchinson had unrestricted access to the station kitchen for coffees and biscuits, the bathroom for showering and other ablutions, while also being free to watch TV in the mess room and play on their Xbox. The only titles they had were sports sim games while Scott preferred a good shoot em up, of course he could totally understand his type of gaming experience probably wasn't the best option if you were a copper going out on the beat, it making perfect sense that a nice round of virtual golf or a football game would be much more calming than a zombie holocaust slash fest.

For the last three hours he'd been growing impatient, the novelty of his situation wearing off, and wondering when he'd be allowed to go home. There were a few reasons for this pressing concern, firstly and most importantly he really wanted to smoke a joint, secondly his diet which wasn't great at the best of times had been appalling during his stay at the police station, two meat feast pizzas yesterday and a sausage and egg sandwich this morning, then thirdly and most importantly the sleeping arrangements were meagre and left a lot to be desired. They hadn't been allowed to let him occupy an actual cell because he wasn't an authentic prisoner, this meant his bed had been three chairs lined up in a corridor with a thin sponge mattress on top held down using his own weight.

So it was with great relief that the door to the mess room opened and a policeman entered to tell him he could leave. The officer then gave him a small black device with a red button on it, said button was covered with a quick release top and he was told to activate it if he thought his life was in danger and units nearby would come to his aid. Thanking the policeman for the device, which he was well aware in anyone else's book was a jumped up rape alarm, he collected his things together. He politely asked if he would be getting a lift back to his car in Dalmeny Street and was told yes of course. That's a result, he thought, but first of all Harvey wanted to see him for a quick chat. Scott had no idea what else he could tell the

Inspector, he'd spilled his guts on everything he knew already, but obediently he nodded and followed the cop up the stairs.

Harvey was sat behind his desk and smiled as Scott was brought in. He bid the man to take a seat and began. 'Hello Scott, it seems ages since we had our chat, doesn't it...?' Choosing to open the exchange with familiar niceties was a time wasting exercise; he still wasn't entirely sure why he had the young man in front of him. The Inspector certainly wasn't going to be telling him anything that the officer driving him back to Dalmeny Street couldn't have relayed just as well. '...I just wanted to fill you in on the situation regarding Jay Cleaver. As you may have surmised we haven't found him yet and that's why we've kept you here. However we cannot justify withholding your movements any longer so reluctantly are forced to let you go. Now of course this does carry a level of risk and I believe you've been furnished with a personal attack siren?'

'Right here...' Scott replied tapping the rape alarm in his pocket.

'Excellent and please don't hesitate to use it. Now obviously I believe it would be in our mutual interest for you to let me know if Jay tries to make contact in anyway at all. That can take any form, social media, texts, calls or of course visiting your home. You will you let me know won't you?'

'Yeah of course I will.'

'Good, well then, thank you for your continuing cooperation with this matter. I'll be in touch if I have any further questions.'

Scott stood to leave then noticed the drawings opened up by the window sill. He saw the one of the falling man and remarked. 'I could have drawn it better than that.'

Harvey looked back up. 'I'm sorry?'

'Your crime scene sketches...that one's rubbish if you ask me.'

'Oh they're not important...' Harvey told him.

'Who did it, a witness yeah? Jay said there was nobody was there but I suppose they must have been.'

Suddenly Harvey's instincts prickled. 'Why do you say that...?'

'...Cause that's the same colour tracksuit he was wearing...when I picked him up after the stabbing...the one we had to burn.'

Harvey was astonished by that information but chose not to react in front of the young man. 'That's very interesting...' He said in an unsurprised tone. '...I'll let the artist know how accurate you thought his work was.'

'Don't bother on my behalf it's alright. So can I go now...?' Scott asked that question for what felt like the umpteenth time in the last few days.

'...Yes of course. I'll be in touch. Goodbye Scott...and thanks again.' Harvey rushed the farewell because he wanted him gone. He needed some alone time to reconsider his position on Oscar and his crayon drawings.

<u>41</u>

Gary, Linda, and Estelle had all waited as instructed by Jay Cleaver for the gates to close, there followed a heavy palpable tension when no one had spoken for ten minutes, but in which time Gary had stood up and gone to sit out on the patio after grabbing a bottle of Italian beer from the fridge. Estelle had then apologised to Linda for pulling her hair, explaining she hadn't known what else to do, and then without another word she'd unsurprisingly finished her duties early for the day and gone home, leaving Linda with a serious dilemma. She actually didn't have a clue where to put herself now in this unbelievable mess, Gary was out there in the sunshine but certainly didn't seem to be enjoying it or the beer, so in the end she decided to go to the bedroom and lay down, quite sure he would have something to say soon but also aware he wouldn't speak to her until he was good and ready.

The young man who had unintentionally, and then intentionally, caused all the bother at the house was staying off the main roads as much as possible. He was heading away from the house and up towards the hills, feeling in his bones that the city levels were over now, it was time to roam the open world for new adventures. As he marched on towards his new goal every step caused the knife in his bag to jump, it felt kind of comforting that he was constantly aware of its presence, and setting off he had a lot of time for many thoughts on his way to 'anywhere far away from here'. He was questioning himself deeply about whether he'd done the right thing or not, the weight of the swinging knife demonstrating he could have taken the three of them out easily, and working out the results if he'd decided to go full on maniac. First of all that maid would have caught it right across the back, then he would have dropped it one time straight down from her and into Gary Swann's face. He pictured it all like a cut scene in a video game, the ones where the graphics became so much better than what you were actually playing, but found even in his twisted imagination he still couldn't kill Linda.

Reaching the outskirts of the city he heard his first police siren but it was a long way off, he listened carefully clamping his jaw down tightly without noticing; only relaxing it fully when the sound faded away in the opposite direction. Jay continued to walk as the cooling sun slowly went down. There had been no more sirens so he reckoned the Cleaver game players back at the house had chosen to listen to him if they'd called the cops they would have been up here by now with a brand new description of what he was wearing. Inside the pockets of his new black jogging pants he felt the money, hundred and forty quid after his trip to the kebab shop, a useful amount of cash for a teenage boy, but out here here in the darkening fields totally useless. It was a realisation that caused a new wave of thoughts of what could and should have happened at Gary Swann's house, horrible and obvious thoughts making him feel like an idiot. Why hadn't he asked for anything useful from there, or even just taken whatever he wanted while he had the cleaver in his hand, feeling pretty sure he would have been given anything he requested?

He was still inwardly kicking himself when he spotted a barn over in the field to his right, although on closer inspection it wasn't the kind of barn he would have wanted, being no more than a three sided construction. It was made from corrugated metal sheets with what looked like the rustiest of them dropped on top, but filled with straw bales that looked dry enough for a night's shelter. Reluctantly he accepted it would have to do, as the only other place he knew along this road was a further two miles uphill, and there was no way he was going to try and navigate that in the dark.

Holding his shopping bag to his chest he clambered over the fence, before comically falling over on the other side where he landed with a substantial thump that made him breathless momentarily. '...For fucks sake...!' He swore loudly at his fallen self then looked to his left and realised everything had just gotten so much worse. On impact his bag had been torn open by the blade of the cleaver. He stared at it incredulously; the bag for life was dead, brilliant! Now he had a pile of clothes and a massive fucking knife to conceal with nothing to carry them in. '...Piece of fucking shit...!' He aimed this insult at the remains of the bag on the floor, shivering in the breeze with a hole sliced clean through it. Picking up the knife he carefully wrapped Scott's red hoodie around it before adding his other clothes on top and set off towards the barn, sorry...fucking shed! Furious with the choices he'd made he stamped his way to the entrance. Once inside he began to calm himself as he settled in best he could, by manoeuvring the heavy bales around to make a bed like construct, he then positioned the 'bed' so he was mostly out of sight but still able to see the lane he'd just left.

After another hungry hour had passed and with the light disappearing completely he returned to his bed for the night. He'd been sat outside for one of his last remaining cigarettes, because as dumb as he could be at times, even he knew smoking in a straw barn was questionable.

Back at the warm house Gary Swann was finally good and ready to speak to his girlfriend, and it was a lot sooner than Linda expected, she hadn't even got herself horizontal on the bed after crying for an hour while sitting at the end of it. The bedside lamp revealed his face tight with tension as he entered the bedroom, the red braces he wore, which he didn't need but he honestly believed made him better at business, were off his large shoulders and hanging down. For some reason Linda thought of bloodied entrails, perhaps not appreciating how close that could have been to the truth.

'You're still here...' His voice was gentle and composed for such a usually loud man.

'I'm still pretty shaken up by it all.' Linda hoped to god he wouldn't just say everything was all her fault. He didn't.

'That boy that was here, he killed the old man in Leith...stabbed him to death in the street.' Gary moved closer as he spoke then sat on the bed slightly away from her.

'I know. He said he came here to rape me.'

'Are you being serious...?'

'...Yes, but when he saw me he changed his mind because he thought I looked...like a nice person...' Her voice was breaking slightly and some overdue tears scratching at the back of her eyes. '...I don't think he would have done it anyway. He's just a really confused kid. I thought I could help him feel better about things...' She paused then thought of his face when he'd first tasted the bread. '...He'll never have any of this.' She indicated the whole house. 'I'm sorry Gary...I was just trying to be what he thought I was...a nice person!' The first stray tear rolled down her cheek.

Gary was as confused as he'd ever been, the impact that young man had brought down on his life now causing him to question everything. 'Do you think I should call the police? I mean he's headed off god knows where now with our knife and my clothes...and I don't even want to think what could happen to the next person he meets...' Gary slid his hand across the duvet so it was halfway to hers.

'...We promised we wouldn't. You heard him, he said if we did then he'd come back. Do you want to risk that...?' She noticed his hand; he was looking the other way when she slid hers towards it, their fingers entwined and for the first time in a whole lot of horrible hours they looked at each other properly, clearly, and with meaning.

'Why did he even come here? How did he know...?' Gary asked.

'He stole Alex's wallet and returned a photograph he found of me.'

'I don't get any of this. Why would he stab that old man then steal Alex's wallet…? Gary squeezed her hand in both comfort and hope it may illicit an understandable answer.

'…I don't know.' She said honestly. '…Maybe he's just got something inside him that makes him do bad things…' Her hand responded to his squeeze. '…but underneath he's a good kid who hasn't had many opportunities in life.'

They both sat in long comfortable silence thinking, trying to decide what to do next until Gary looked over and Linda caught his stare. 'How's your hair?'

'Fine, how's yours?' She replied with a little smile. Then slowly they moved closer together until a tiny laugh became a warm embrace.

Estelle had covered the two mile distance back to her home in double quick time, even allowing for the constant stopping and looking behind her for the skinny boys approach. Now walking sharply through her garden gate that wouldn't close properly she fumbled for the keys, firstly dropping them before opening the door to the familiar smell and protection of her own home. She decided to hold off on getting changed straight away and poured herself a medicinal amount of gin which she swallowed in two swigs. Her hands were still stiff and tremoring from the grip she'd held on Linda's hair, an action that had felt good because that 'lady' deserved all she got, and maybe Estelle presumed and hoped this would be the end of Linda's intrusion into her life and she could go back to cleaning Gary's house the way it used to be. There had been some lovely perks to the job before he started courting her; for a start the house was empty during the day and Estelle used to love taking a long leisurely bath then cleaning it all thoroughly before he got back. It was by far the easiest and best paid cleaning job she'd ever had. Pouring another gin the only image that gave her any pleasure involved Linda Webb packing her bags and moving out.

On the big soft bed Gary and Linda's shared embrace reached another level, and they made love like two souls who believed this was their last day on earth.

Much later on that evening, a mile and a half away as the crow flies, a shivering Jay Cleaver lay in his straw manger wearing all the clothes he owned. With his cold hands covered by pulled down sleeve cuffs he dragged another bale across and covered his legs, it was uncomfortable but he felt a little warmer. It was going to be a long night for this ill prepared kid and the final thought he had before exhaustion took him away was vocalised quietly. 'Why didn't I take some food...or a fucking sleeping bag?'

<u>42</u>

'Oh right yeah you come and go as you please now do you? Leave me here alone with all the knowledge of the universe, all the stuff I can't even begin to understand, and then you just bugger off.' Alex was reacting to being left alone again and wasn't particularly happy about it.

The Angel had disappeared in frustration at Alex's lack of learning but now reappeared in the sea, and while everything Alex could see was an illusion, a fact he often forgot about, it appeared to be walking on water as it approached the desk and chairs. 'You will be pleased to know I have worked out what the problem is.' It sat on its chair with more than a hint of smugness. '...I know why you're here.'

Alex hadn't heard words as positive as these in what felt like millennia. '...Holy mother of...err sorry...you do...why then...why am I here?'

'There is a glitch!' The Angel said triumphantly.

Alex was stunned into a bemused silence hoping for more explanation but the Angel wasn't forthcoming. '...A glitch? That's your big news?'

'Yes...you Alex are stuck in a glitch...within the machine.' The mortal man unsurprisingly didn't respond so the Angel attempted to elaborate. 'All the innumerable elements of the machine I told you about, the matter and the forces which move and react with each other, you do remember me teaching you all of that...?'

Alex thought teaching was a little too strong a word as he hadn't grasped any of it, but he definitely recalled being told something similar, so he lied confidently. '...Yes I remember.'

'Well occasionally, very rarely in fact, some of those parts can be forced into such a pattern of links they cause a blockage in the flow...'

'...What?' Alex deeming that the term 'blockage in the flow' didn't sound a pleasant occurrence in any context.

'The molecules and ions, elements, quarks, whatever you wish to call them have stopped moving at a certain point. If we can find out where that is then we can repair it.'

'I see...can't you just send me back?' He couldn't handle any more of this gobbledygook and was discovering his familiarity with an indecipherable Angel, even on such a beautiful heavenly beach, was beginning to breed contempt. Yes his mind was finally made up now he wanted to return to his own time.

'No, that wouldn't work. Even if we tried it would just bump you straight back here.'

'...Obviously! So you said it's rare for this to happen. How rare exactly...?'

'Well it used to occur a great deal in the beginning when the gases were forming, and of course when the solid states such as stars and planets came into being, but such collisions became rarer when all the stuff of the universe found its place, giving us this perfect balance and symmetry where everything has room to move and exchange freely with everything else. It is so very difficult to try and explain this to your mind...'

'...Oh you think?' Alex replied then picked his way through the words the Angel had given him, but he couldn't see the answer to his question anywhere so repeated his first one. 'How rare an occurrence is it?'

'Obviously in your particular galaxy it has never happened.' The Angel sounded, and if Alex wasn't mistaken, looked excited by this universal event.

'I see...but you're the guy that oversees the machine right...?' Alex figured he was making sense. '...so there's a solution?'

'Perhaps, first of all I would need to find out what kind of blockage it is, how big it is, where it is, but of course most importantly from our point of view...when it is.'

'Oh for fu...' Alex stopped short of completing his profanity; even though he was extremely agitated with its vague response he did believe the Angel was trying to help him. '...Okay you said earlier that 'we' can repair it...did you mean that? Can I actually have some input, do anything to help, that would be better than sitting on a fake beach staring at a repeating pattern of waves washing up on the shore...?'

Those green eyes looked at him harshly '...I can assure you Alex that every wave you have observed on that ocean is unique and relevant, touching this shoreline only once before it dissipates and begins a journey elsewhere!'

'Alright...!' Alex wasn't expecting the Angels rebuke about such a tiny detail. '...I suppose waves look the same to most people.'

'I am sure they do but you Alex are clearly, not most people, and to answer your question yes you can help, in fact it is imperative you do, and by that I mean I cannot do it without you.' The Angel walked away down the beach.

Alex shouted after it. 'I know what imperative means!' but when the Angel didn't respond he began to follow. Catching up they walked side by side along the shore until he asked his next question. '...You know how you changed that white space into this beach?'

'Yes…' The Angel shuffled its wings.

'…Can you change it to something else? I'm bored with this now.'

The Angel glanced across at him. 'And what would you choose…?'

Excited Alex mused for a moment before requesting. 'Make   this   place a…'

43

Oscar was sat quietly in a cell again only this time he didn't have the fear the voice used to bring. Those grisly nights when he would feel it savagely grab his mind and take him out into the night to show him things, evil things, horrible imageries, tiny slices of death. The voice had screamed its desire for murder and mutilation until they were finally caught, then it had screamed to be free, and this small man controlled by it for so long had forgotten about his own soul. Only now he was back and the voice was gone, apparently for good, allowing him to think clearly once more and Oscar Downes was an avid thinker. Finding he could enjoy the freedom and time under the police station, take these hours to slowly rebuild the man he used to be, the one who read books of incredible accomplishments by great people. Slowly, little by little, thought by thought, he began to question everything he'd been through. He wanted the voice gone altogether, not just from under its control, that had happened already and he'd survived, he needed it gone from his memory and existence for good because it was still out there somewhere free as an evil bird doing as it pleased, while he was stuck behind bars charged with its crimes for the rest of his life. Oscar used to be an optimist, because a bad thing today could be a good thing tomorrow, but even he looked at the obstacles blocking his voyage of retribution from even beginning and promptly admitted defeat.

Before the light faded completely he looked around his cell reading the graffiti of former 'guests'; the vast majority were drawings of sexual reproductive parts which he hoped weren't accurate otherwise his own innocent idea had been very off the mark. There were names and dates scrawled in pen and scratched into the plaster, and everyone it appeared who had ever been here, was entirely innocent of any crime, and none more so than this man. He closed his eyes and lay back realising he must accept his fate, after all he had physically killed all those people even though he'd been given no option by the voice in his head, and as he waited for the light to totally disappear he knew any form of understanding justice was unthinkable, and all he could hope was that perhaps, somehow, a miracle would occur.

In his darkening office Inspector Harvey Cooper was finding it hard to believe Jay Cleaver was still out there somewhere, his unit having found nothing since the kebab shop. He hadn't turned up as far as they could tell at any of his previous or possible haunts. Officers had called on all the names that Scott Hutchinson had given them then followed those up by visiting a list of new names they'd procured, and still nothing on the boy's whereabouts. It was a mess and a mystery and there weren't many things that Harvey detested more than those two bedfellows. Even the unit he'd put on the job were losing hope and as far as his own investigations were going he was stumped. Without a recent sighting or a decent tip off he felt jammed frustratingly in a blockage, the feeling that he couldn't move on was beginning to stress him out. When noticing it was getting late he called his wife to apologise and explain his absence from another dinner. She understood, Flo always understood, and at the end of the call she asked her 'Harveypud' to send her a message when he finally set off, as there would still be a nice meal and a cold drink waiting for him.

With his secretary gone home if he needed something finding he would have to do it himself, although he wasn't sure what he wanted, well that wasn't exactly true he did know one thing, he wanted to talk to Oscar Downes again. Staring once more at the drawings he added up the risk reward odds of such a decision; well the risk was clear enough, the Superintendent would hit the roof with cries of insubordination after telling him in no uncertain terms that the case was closed. The reward though was tempting; just another ten minutes with the prisoner would satisfy his curiosity and hopefully put to sleep the ridiculous questions these pictures created. Two minutes later without too much of a struggle on his moral compass he walked down to the cell block and into the corridor where Bob Jenkins was on duty.

'Good Evening Bob!' The Inspector said entering the duty room. Harvey's demeanour was good-humoured enough, relaxed even, as if it were just another pop down to the cells for him, but the simple fact was that Harvey never went down to the cell area. Bob was fully aware of that, as he swiftly scrambled to put the mobile phone in his pocket and stand up.

'Oh err alright Inspector, everything okay?' Bob blurted out in a confident tone but underneath he was far from comfortable with Harvey's unexpected visit. It wasn't as if Bob had done anything wrong in his duties, he'd made sure all the prisoners were fed and watered and their lights turned off for the night. No, that wasn't the problem; this Inspector had walked in to find him playing a game on his phone. Even a complete rookie cop, who Bob Jenkins certainly wasn't, knew you weren't supposed to be playing war games at work, and although the Inspector wasn't his immediate boss he was a higher ranked officer which could turn out to be just as problematic.

'...Sorry about that Sir, just err...its quiet this evening...my apologies you caught me red handed ha-ha...!' Bob with no time to think had decided to go for the jovial approach in hope of the best results.

The senior officer's poker face gave nothing away but behind that construct he really couldn't believe his luck. All the way down from his office he'd been trying to concoct some elaborate story to convince Officer Jenkins to do what he asked, he'd even been willing to bribe the man but now he recognized he had the upper hand immediately, and done nothing to gain it. So all he really had to do now was keep his stony face a little while longer and perform the role of a senior ranked Inspector. 'Playing on your phone there Officer Jenkins...?' He asked rhetorically. '...while on duty as well.' before strolling out into the corridor believing the sound of his steps made it a little more menacing as he spoke.

'Yes Sir.' Bob replied and followed the Inspector into the corridor knowing very well he'd been caught bang to rights, but what he didn't know very well was Harvey Cooper, at least not well enough to chat his way out of this.

'Not very professional is it...?' Harvey put his hands behind his back in a pale imitation of a Gestapo officer as he paced. Some may say the pose was unneeded and perhaps a little too dramatic but it seemed to be having the desired effect.

'...No Sir.'

'I mean think about it, can you imagine what would have happened if I had been Superintendent Shilling walking in to see that sort of behaviour? I'm sure you're aware of his feelings about these...what would he call it...breaches in standards. We all have to concentrate on our duties Jenkins however mundane they may be to perform at times. Need I remind you there are prisoners here under your watch relying on you, as we all are, to be alert and aware at all times? You're paid to give your full concentration to the job, to be ready to react immediately in case of an emergency situation. Am I going too far in reminding you of your job?'

Bob Jenkins sheepishly shook his head.

In the space of ten minutes Harvey was back to enjoying his own job again, back in the saddle, and choosing to turn the screw a little further on poor Bob so he could be assured of getting what he wanted.

'Do you enjoy this duty, Officer Jenkins...?' Harvey stopped pacing and his tone held just the merest hint of threat.

'...Yes of course Sir.' Bob was telling the truth but all he wanted was for Harvey to burst out laughing and tell him he was only joking, perhaps a quip like 'Oh Jenkins you should have seen your face', however Inspector Cooper didn't have a reputation for joking in the station and Bob saw no reason why he would be trying to gain one now.

'Have you written up your paperwork for today's shift...?'

Bob so wanted to lie but knew if he did then Harvey would probably ask to see them. 'No sir.'

'...I see. Do you have any completed ones for the week so far...?' Harvey was beginning to feel a little cruel watching Bob squirm as his anxiety grew. You can be too good at your job sometimes, he thought.

'...No sir I'll do them immediately.' Jenkins was becoming quite desperate with his tardiness exposed. He turned towards the filing cabinet to take out the relevant blank paperwork, convinced this to be the only possible course of action to stave off a disciplinary or worse.

'Officer Jenkins...Bob!' Harvey called out to stop him in his tracks.

'Yes Sir?' He looked the Inspector in the eye with his new backup strategy that comprised of chin up and take the punishment.

'I think you and I could reach a satisfactory arrangement about all this...' Harvey said relaxing his dominant pose. '...In fact I know we can. Would you like to hear my proposal?'

'Very well Sir.' Bob was deeply intrigued.

'It involves both of us keeping our mouths shut...' He explained precisely what he wanted and within five minutes and just a little persuasion he followed Bob Jenkins down the darkened corridor before asking him to turn on the light in Oscar's cell.

As they stood at the door Bob felt strongly that he should remind Harvey of what he was about to enter into. 'Sir...the prisoner isn't in restraints and I really don't want to be having any trouble down here.'

Jenkins was unable to think of a more polite way to say it. The truth was startlingly clear; he didn't want the Inspector to be brutally attacked by a serial killer, especially while he was the one on duty. There was getting a disciplinary for playing on your phone but that really paled into insignificance when compared to the culpability of allowing a senior officer who shouldn't be there in the first place to die horribly.

'Don't worry about me Bob. I believe Oscar and I have an understanding.' Harvey said confidently while waiting patiently for Bob to get on with opening the door.

'You believe you have an understanding Sir?'

'If I didn't we wouldn't be having this little chat, now open the door and when I'm inside lock it. I think ten minutes should be enough. Do we understand each other Jenkins...?'

'Yes sir, ten minutes.' He put the key in the lock.

Oscar had jerked awake when the strip light buzzed into a frenetic flickering before settling down to its dimly lit hum. Through his experiences of detainment during the previous six months he knew this was highly unusual, that after light's out you were lights back on within half an hour, no it wasn't right, so tensing for action he listened to the key turn in the lock and watched the door slowly open. In his slumber there'd been men's voices in his head but he hadn't known if they were real or not, now he knew they must have been because they were coming into the cell. His first thought was that finally, after worrying about this exact type of event for months, someone was coming for him, off the record so to speak. So he was more than a little surprised when Harvey entered and again when the door was locked behind him.

'Good evening Oscar...' Harvey spoke clearly in hope his voice would help with instant recognition and avoid the risk of being attacked. There was no doubt the man was a dangerous individual and after their previous encounter in the relative safety of an interrogation room with handcuffs, he was in Oscars domain now, with him unsecured and himself unarmed.

'...I'd like to talk to you about a few things.'

Oscar didn't respond.

'Would that be okay...?' He was as wary and alert as if he were three feet from an alligator, rather than a small unassuming man cowering on a bunk.

Oscar was equally wary but not of attack, simply unsure of the Inspector under these unique conditions, this face to face contact was a rarity in his world and he didn't trust this man enough to relax completely. After all he had shown him the drawings and told him about the voice, truths he'd never shared with anyone but it hadn't made any difference, this policeman had still sent him down here.

Harvey stepped across to the chair under the darkened window. 'I'm going to sit here if that's okay with you...?' Taking the silence to be positive he sat down but didn't turn his back for a second, watching Oscar intently, prepared for any sudden movement, and after taking a few moments to allow both men to relax and feeling his pulse drop to an acceptable level he spoke.

'I've found another mystery in your drawings...' There was still no response from the hunched up prisoner. '...I'd like to talk to you about them. I don't want to talk about the murders, just those drawings. I believe they might be important, and as I'm sure you can tell I'm doing this unofficially, or else I wouldn't be allowed to just walk in here and chat with you unaccompanied and without official permission. So please if you want to talk just call me Harvey and like I said, I only want to talk about your pictures. Will that be okay..?'

Harvey saw Oscar uncurl himself from his foetal positon and slide himself slowly to the end of the bed, his heartbeat rising again as he watched the killer's bare feet reach the stone floor. When he'd settled himself Harvey became aware they were only two feet apart, with Oscar between him and the locked door, now this certainly wasn't, by any stretch of the imagination, going by the book.

'Harvey?' Oscar spoke slowly and softly. 'That isn't a common name is it...?'

'...It's my fathers.' Harvey said feeling relieved Oscar was still in the mood to talk.

'So are you Harvey junior...?' Oscar smiled and showed his teeth which were chipped from five years of night time grinding.

'I suppose I would be in the United States.'

'So true...' Oscar looked down at Harvey's shoes. 'Do you know what your name means...?'

'I think it has something to do with iron.'

Oscar gently chuckled. '...Don't undersell yourself Harvey. It means blazing iron or battle worthy. Nice shoes by the way.'

Harvey nodded his appreciation but still hesitant to just come out and start firing questions at Oscar for two reasons, he didn't want to upset the man and have him clam up again and reason two, simple self-preservation for his own life.

'My wife got them for me...' The Inspector was trying to play it at Oscars speed but was acutely aware he didn't have much time. If Harvey was caught down here talking to this prisoner his job would be in serious jeopardy having given his word to an extremely agitated Superintendent that he was finished with the Oscar Downes case, so if this visit came to light he knew no amount of excuses involving crayon drawings would help his cause. 'Oscar, I don't have a lot of time with you, I wish I did but you're getting transferred tomorrow to Longmarsh and it won't be so easy to see you there.'

'I know I am and I know it won't...' Oscar leaned forward reducing the space between them further. '...Do you know what that makes me think?'

'No I'm sorry I don't.' Harvey said carefully.

'It makes me think that you...just want to use me, ask me your silly questions and after I answer them you'll go home happily to your darling wife while I can go rot in hell.'

Harvey hadn't even considered that Oscar might want to cut some kind of deal for what he knew, but for now decided to ignore it, and if by doing so Oscar clammed up then so be it, he wasn't going to get anywhere if he let him play around.

'The drawing of the man falling in Dalmeny Street, I know for a fact you didn't make that up. The figure in blue is Jay Cleaver, the one in the picture next to the falling man.'

'Who...?' Oscar asked.

'The boy in the window in the blue outfit, he's a suspect we are hunting in connection with the falling man and the stabbing of another shortly afterwards.' Harvey found he was pointing his finger, non-aggressively but he countered it, quickly realising it may come across as aggressive and he was frankly in no position to be that.

'I see...so is the falling man dead?'

'No he isn't, he's been in a coma. They've amputated his right arm because it was snapped completely under the fall. It's the same man you drew in the hospital bed with the nurse and the lady in the brown coat...'

'...Ohhh he's in a coma!' The small man nodded with understanding.

'Yes!' Harvey found he was struggling with this new version of Oscar, at the first meeting he'd appeared a beaten man but now there was an altogether more confident, sinister side, on show.

'Fancy that.' Oscar thought for a moment, appearing to see some deeper connection, before continuing. '...well that explains the question mark I drew above his head.'

'I did wonder about it.' Harvey offered.

'Oh that makes perfect sense. A question mark of whether he'll live or die...is the stabbed man dead?' Oscar asked in the same tone someone may enquire about the weather.

'He died at the scene.' Harvey answered feeling he was doing okay in this game of trust.

'I thought he might have.'

'What do you mean...?'

'...We saw him come round the corner and confront the blue boy, Jay you said, we could tell it wasn't going to end well but we must have missed the actual attack because...because it wanted to go.'

'This is you and the voice...?' Harvey asked briskly.

'Of course it's me and the voice, I couldn't have been there on my own could I?'

Harvey needed to find some solution he could understand, quickly. Oscar appeared to be giving him all the answers but he still couldn't work it out. 'Right I'm going to tell you what I think and feel free to correct me if I go wrong, but please because we are running out of time, indulge me.'

'The cell floor is all yours Harvey.' Oscar sat back on the bunk to listen and crossed his legs.

Harvey began. 'A voice appeared in your head after your altercation with those women five years ago?'

'Correct, outside 46 Marlborough Drive!' Oscar interjected.

'Shortly afterwards it controlled you and forced you to commit murders although we don't know why...'

'...We do know why. It lives to kill!'

'...Okay I've got that it lives to kill. Now you understand Oscar you're not the first serial killer in history to claim they were driven to murder by a voice in their head. Although I have to admit you are the first that has shown some kind of proof concerning that condition. These drawings you have done of moments that you claim the voice showed you they're...very compelling.'

'Of course they are. They're true representations of what was shown to me. I'm just not very good at drawing things.

'Okay so tell me about the other picture, the one with the slide, the policeman and the UFO with the daggers, what is that all about...?'

'...You won't be pleased to hear this Harvey but I don't know what that's about...' Oscar's declaration certainly disappointed and it was about to get worse again '...If you remember I didn't know what the other pictures were about until you told me. I just wanted to show you my drawings...I didn't know why. You put them on the desk so naturally I responded.'

Harvey was falling swiftly from what had been a growing high as he found more frustration and yet another dead end. ''Tell me then how do I know the voice isn't still inside you? That you two aren't just playing me along...?'

'...Because if it were still here Harvey, you'd be dead already!'

That short statement stopped the conversation in its tracks as Harvey and Oscar looked at each other. The foreboding pause was finally broken when the prisoner continued his cautionary tale, and strangely as he detailed what he knew of the murderous voice he began to visibly weaken, bravado failing him as he told the Inspector of its methods. Harvey couldn't help but notice how the voice had caused so much damage inside this man's mind its traces would always be there. 'The voice can make you do anything it wants. It cajoles, it demeans, and it threatens.

'So why do you think it has left you now...?' Harvey wanted an answer, a theory even, just a starting point.

'I have no idea!' The small man looked helpless and about to cry as some ghastly memories and feelings came back.

'Anything at all Oscar, please help me to believe you!' Harvey was trying his best to keep the man focused and in the moment, both for Oscar's sake and because their ten minutes was rapidly coming to an end.

'I can only guess it knew I was going to be caught again and locked up for a long time. Like any other sentient being it doesn't delight in being imprisoned. That's all I can think of.' With this summary over Oscar's tears began to fall.

Harvey moved over to the bed and reached out, humanely pulling the small sobbing man to his chest where he held him for a brief moment.

Suddenly there was a knock on the cell door and Bob Jenkins concerned voice. 'Inspector your times up. We'll both be fired!'

Harvey reluctantly released his hold telling the man he had to leave now. '...but if it counts for anything Oscar, I believe you. I've been doing this job for a good many years and I know, categorically I'd say, when someone is telling me the truth. I just don't know what I can do for you now...' Harvey was holding back his own trembling lip and itchy eyes at the savageness of this injustice, but quickly stood and regained some composure, while Oscar looked up at him with dense tears tumbling to the floor.   Harvey shamefully bowed his head as he turned to leave.

'Inspector..?' Oscar said weakly.

'...Yes Oscar...?' Harvey watched the small man regain a little composure to stand up on weary legs.

'It won't help me I know that...but there are more pictures. I did four more. The Doctor has...well had them. I can't remember exactly what they were of because they weren't the ones I liked the best.'

'More drawings like these...?' Harvey was astounded.

183

'Yes...other things the voice showed me.' Oscar   pulled   himself   up   to stand straight with dignity. 'Goodnight Harvey!'

'Goodnight Oscar.'

The Inspector left and when the door was locked the small man walked to the window and through ingrained habit began to count the bars.

<u>44</u>

The Edinburgh morning sky was clouded over which accompanied a serious drop in temperature. It caused a maid to think that yesterday now seemed a million miles away when the weather had been so hot and she could have been cut to shreds by a young psychopath with a cleaver. It was for that reason she was still being careful and observant while walking back to the large house where she worked. Estelle Christou had chosen to not tell her husband about any of what happened, she knew him too well, he would have overreacted as true Greek men are historically prone to do. She'd intended to tell him, absolutely when he returned from his shift at the kebab shop, and she almost did, on his arrival however she could see he was tired and not in the best of moods so let the idea go, choosing to massage his large shoulders instead before he fell into a heavy snoring sleep. By calming rather than riling she avoided the high probability of him requiring revenge, gathering other men from the shop then leading the hunt for the boy carrying even bigger knives of their own. Strangely Estelle found herself smiling at that image as she pressed her security fob for the gates to open. Crunching up the driveway she wasn't sure what she'd find here after yesterday's terrors, there were no cars out front but they could always be in the locked garage, so she decided to go straight to the kitchen and put on some of that nice expensive coffee.

'Good Morning Estelle! Bit of a change in the weather. How are you feeling…?' Linda's voice enquired, her head popping up from the large sofa. Estelle froze for a second as the woman rose and came over to greet her. '…Gary's still in the Jacuzzi. He's not going in to work today, understandably. To be honest I didn't think you'd be here. You can still change your mind you know, have the day off, it wouldn't be a problem.'

Estelle didn't know what to do or say as Linda walked right up and delivered her a stiff upper hug before continuing the one-sided conversation.

'I just wanted you to know that we are all going to move on from this Estelle, from what happened yesterday, nothing is going to change and we will stick together and get through it.' Linda released her grip and Estelle relaxed slightly. 'Gary and I have talked about our actions yesterday at length and have decided we aren't going to let it fester. I just need you to know that we completely understand why you were grabbing my hair and Gary accepts why I did it to him. So if it's okay with you, Estelle, we will just carry on as if nothing happened…yes?'

Estelle noticed the coffee machine was already on and looked at Linda before nodding her agreement.

'You still look shaken up. Are you sure you're okay?' Linda asked.

'Yes.' Estelle replied with the fakest of smiles then walked through the hall to hang up her outdoor coat. How the bloody hell was that horrible woman still here? Estelle thought savagely then put on her cleaning coat to find yesterday's rubber gloves still in the pocket. 'Where would you like me to start today?' She asked, ever the professional, though it was taking a Herculean effort to keep it that way.

'Oh there's no need to start rushing around just yet, let's have a coffee first.' Linda suggested smiling sweetly.

Estelle thought very seriously about refusing this poisoned chalice but she really did fancy one of those nice coffees, so removing the rubber gloves that were half on she walked into kitchen and sat on a chair, the same one Jay had occupied only the day before.

Linda turned away from the sink area and walked over to the stairs. 'I'm sure Gary will be ready for his now. If you can just bring them up we'll be in the bedroom.'

Up close one would have noticed the sharp twitching in her eyelids as Estelle was ready to explode with rage, but she sat there quietly until Linda had bounced up the stairs. '...Total   bastard   bitch...!'   She   muttered snatching the mugs down.

Inside a three sided shed in the dew covered field Jay had been awake for hours. He guessed probably since about four but he couldn't be sure because his phone had given up the ghost, so all he knew for certain was that morning had broken and morning was fucking freezing. The bales he'd tried to position to get some form of comfortable sleep had slowly collapsed during the night, causing his frozen body to wake up in a weird position with his feet in the air and his neck twisted sharply to the side, resulting in a stiffness that was hurting him a lot.

He looked at his dim reflection in the black mirror of his dead screen before throwing the phone out into the field. At least they wouldn't be able to track him now his location signal, if they could really do that kind of thing, he didn't know, he was a sixteen year old kid.

During the miserly few hours when he'd managed to fall sleep a few savage dreams had come and gone. Mostly they'd disappeared as such fantasies are apt to do but there was one he could still remember clearly. In it he'd been back in the window looking across at Alex on the ledge.

He'd tried to be different this time, to lean out and help him, but the man fell anyway when he couldn't get a firm grip on his hand. So he was forced to watch him fall again, only this time his body didn't hit the cobbles and stop with that horrible noise, this time it just disappeared straight through the road. Jay ran down the stairs but when he reached the street there wasn't a bundle of bones on the ground, no broken body on the street. Then the old man walked round the corner as before, his dog looking at him, panting with the enthusiasm of meeting a stranger. Instinctively he felt for the knife in his pocket and it was still there, the steak knife he'd stolen from his meth head Aunties kitchen a week before, only in this version of events he left it where it was. The old man looked at him and said 'thanks mate and please say thanks to your Auntie for looking after Goldie here.' At that unexpected moment he'd slipped out of the dream, opening his eyes to find he was still in the shitty shed, but with his neck twisted against a straw bale like he'd fallen from a great height.

During the next hour while rubbing the frozen nerves in his neck and shoulder he tried his best to find some meaning to the dream, but Jay really wasn't a descriptive thinker. Instead he just ended up wondering once more where Scott was, he assumed still wrapped up in his duvet, free as a bird and toasty as hell. The idea went through his mind of struggling back to Scott's house, but it was the first place the police would look, besides it was a lot further to return there than it was to carry on with the game, and Jay Cleaver was many things but he was no quitter.

Those thoughts were instantly obliterated when he heard a deep rumbling sound nearby; it was coming from behind the shed. Moving stiffly because of the pain in his neck he stood and found a small gap where the corrugated sheets didn't fit together tightly. He peeked through to see coming from the next field and turning into this one was a large blue tractor now heading his way. 'Shit...!' As always his first instinct was to run but he'd have to be quick over the open field, and obviously if he chose to do that the farmer would see him, but even more obvious, and painfully so, was that running was out of the question with his neck refusing to loosen up. This left him no choice but to use instinct number two, hide. He peeked through the slit again and reckoned if that guy was coming straight to the shed then he had about half a minute. Thinking quickly, but moving slowly, he used the squashed bales of his bed to build a barrier between him and the entrance. This exertion and the pain from his locked neck almost making him weep, but he countered the discomfort with a positive belief that if he kept still and quiet he might be able to dodge this new level boss.

Within that blue tractor a grey haired farmer whistled tunefully as he trundled his way over to the barn. He needed two bales for the animals feed, and thought that by getting them now both he and the animals would be eating at the same time. Pulling up close to the shed he switched the engine off then tutted as he marched to the doorway. The bales were stacked high meaning he'd have to knock the highest two off the top, using his usual trick of raising the tractor bucket up and working them down. Back in the day he would have physically shaken the stack and caught them as they fell, but those moves were thirty years ago, he was a little past that nowadays. To start his plan of action he first had to check the stack on all sides, this included the side where by the look of it some wild animal had destroyed a few of the bales, he thought most probably a badger but either way he was going to have to sort that mess out.

'Bloody hell…!' The farmer groaned as he began the strenuous chore.

'Fuck this…!' Jay shouted. As usual thinking the words first then vocalising them loudly because the farmer, while grabbing up an armful of the disarrayed hay, had put his large gloved hand directly on the boy's calf. This had caused him to jump up from his concealment and then instantly regret it as his stiff neck and shoulder combined to bite back hard. '…Argh!'

'What the bloody hell do you think you're doing sunshine?' The surprised farmer yelled then took a step backwards still holding some of his hay.

'Nothing…!' Jay snapped back like a surly teenager. '…I'm just walking!'

'In my shed…?' The farmer dropped the hay, removed his gloves, and reached to his checked shirt pocket for his phone.

'What the fuck ya doing…?' Jay asked seriously.

'Calm down I'm just calling authorities…' The farmer replied.

'…What? Why? Fuck off!' Jay reached his hand into the support beam where the knife was rested. 'Don't call the police…!'

The farmer looked at the shouting boy with a serious face but a smile in his eyes because he was only joking; he had no intention of phoning the police, rather the number he called was to his wife back in the kitchen to tell her what he'd found, and he knew exactly what she would say as well. In their perfect partnership he let his wife deal with all the people stuff, he was a man of the land for life and only really cared for that and the animals he raised, able to tell you instantly what mood his cattle were in or why the sheep were bleating but whenever there were things involving people he would always call her first. They'd been married for thirty seven years and he didn't doubt for a second she would offer this homeless boy an invite to come back for some breakfast. Mary was as soft as they come and he was about to hand the phone to the boy so she could speak to him.

'Hang on a minute its ringing...speak to my...' He said before rapidly discovering that this one unfinished sentence, spoken during a simple comedic misunderstanding, was the last he would ever utter.

Jay shocked himself with the force of the blow, astounded by the damage it caused, and looking down at the man's injury he fought the urge to laugh, but only because he thought it looked just like his own neck felt.

A female voice broke the silence quickly stopping his inappropriate urge to chuckle. Jay was confused at first before noticing the phone in the farmers twitching hand. As he carefully bent down to check it he imagined the farmer jump scaring him, shooting his arm up and grabbing his throat like they did in movies, or video horror games, picturing the bizarre dance they would perform if they were to grapple each other, the two of them struggling each in their own personal pain, the boy with his stiff neck and the farmer with his head hanging off; man that would just be too mental, he thought.

The woman's voice spoke again so Jay picked up the phone and looked at the name, Mary. '...George...Are you okay...are you hurt? George...George?'

Jay was dumbstruck as an awful realisation hit; had he reacted without thinking again, come on no surely not. If that were true he was feeling sorely cheated by the games twisted plot. This twitching farmer said he was phoning the police, although playing it back in his head Jay did think it was a bit of an overreaction for finding someone in your barn, but fuck this game was clever. How would he know the farmer's sense of humour, there'd been no clues and there were other reasons he responded like he did, mostly he'd panicked to be fair because he was already on the run for murder, and his neck was killing him, and he hadn't slept well. Surely under those circumstances anyone would have acted in the same way, but looking down at the man's condition, his head being held on by only an inch of attached muscle, he couldn't truly convince himself of that.

'...George if you don't speak to me right now I'm phoning the police and an ambulance...!' Her voice had become noticeably higher and more fragile.

Jay had the phone in one hand and her husband's blood on the other trying to make sense of it all. In the end he chose a well-trodden mental route to make it more manageable, blame the game because it was better than real life. In fact the only difference he'd noticed was you couldn't turn the console off and sleep in your own bed, not in this world, here you had to stay in the game all the time, totally immersed and take your time-outs by appreciating the amazing graphics. Desperately trying to refocus his mind on the journey ahead he slid the phone back in the farmers now blood drenched shirt pocket, then he wiped the blood off the weapon and wrapped it in a large piece of oily rag he found under the seat of the tractor, before walking away from the games 'Barn Chapter' as quickly as he could.

'...George...George...!' Mary's voice pleaded on her dead husband's chest.

The boy who was now starving hungry and heavily blood stained, decided to stay on the field side of the fence as much as possible. He reckoned he could do the two miles today, even with his current disability, to reach the last level. It was the only other part of his dreams he could remember, the sharp toothed boss he would have to defeat, to beat the game, to become a legend.

<u>45</u>

Gary came into the bedroom towel drying his hair to find Linda sitting at the mirror putting on her make up. 'Horrible day yesterday, baby, but seriously that was an amazing night! How are you feeling this morning you dirty minx...?'

Her eyes looked over at him nonplussed.

'...I'm joking I'm joking!' He quickly added.

Linda turned from the mirror and smacked his towelled bottom with her bare hand. 'That's the last you're getting for a while with that attitude.' She laughed a little as she spoke and he laughed as he listened.

'...Your coffee...!' Estelle shouted from the landing because she couldn't knock the door with fat mugs in each hand. It was Gary who went over and let her in exclaiming. 'Oh lovely...! Thank you Estelle.'

She handed him his mug before placing Linda's on the window sill furthest away from the mirror she was seated at. 'I'll put yours here Linda I don't want to clutter your table.'

'Oh don't worry about that I'll make room' Linda replied, but by that time the maid was gone and already down the top two steps.

'Gary!'

'What?'

'She really doesn't like me.'

'Yes I know I was there yesterday.' He sipped the froth from the top of his mug.

'It isn't just yesterday, it's all the time. She's very protective of you.'

'Well I do pay her wages.'

'I know but not to act as personal security. Look Gary I don't see her as a threat but she really likes you...'

'...Darling how could you she's a married woman!' He said in mock outrage.

'So am I!' Linda reminded him.

Gary conceded he'd been hoisted by his own petard so moved in close before telling her. 'Yes but you're not my cleaner.'

'You are such a charmer...oops I'm sorry its work hours now, should I call you Mr Swann?'

He gently touched the cheek that she'd just applied blush to and kissed her neck. 'I don't suppose you could take some thing's down for me Linda...' He asked while mimicking a gruff boss voice.

Tempted as she was she had to decline for now. 'Not at the moment boss man. I have to go and see Alex this morning.'

'Why?' He asked massaging her shoulders.

'...Because he's still legally my husband and he's in a coma...also they amputated his arm yesterday for crying out loud. He needs me, he really does...he hasn't got anyone else.'

'Jesus! They really just lopped his arm off?' Gary pulled a nauseous face.

'Yes...I didn't get much chance to tell you yesterday because of...because of what happened.' She studied his face hoping for an honest reaction of concern, sympathy or maybe a little support after their intimacy last night, but it wasn't forthcoming.

'Aren't we spending the day together?' He whined.

'Gary...they had to amputate his arm. It was torn clean out of the socket. Any day now he may choose to come back to us and open his eyes to discover he has one arm missing. If I know Alex he won't take that very well, plus I don't think anyone should have to go through that alone.'

'Of course not, no, you're right. I'm the one being over protective now...' He took a swig of coffee. '...Shall I drive you, I'm not doing anything today?'

'Are you sure?' She asked, even though she wasn't sure herself about his coming along.

'I wouldn't have offered if I didn't mean it. I'll just finish my coffee. Shall I bring yours over...?'

Linda sighed. '...If you wouldn't mind.'

Twenty minutes later, as those big gates closed behind the exiting Mercedes, Estelle watched from the kitchen window considering her options before making a definite decision. She knew if she went through with this it would be based on the fact that her working life was becoming a living misery with that stupid woman here. Things had to change but Estelle was aware she held no sway over her employer's life choices, and it would be ill advised to physically throw the woman out on the street, meaning in reality she had no devious weapons to hurt Linda with. Well maybe not today but there is always the future, so perhaps with a little courage and deceit she could light the fuse on a revenge bomb that would one day blow up in that woman's face.

Estelle put the three dried mugs back in the cupboard, took a deep breath to steady her nerves, and then called the police. The morning news had carried a report the police were appealing for help in the search for one Jay Cleaver. Now she could tell them all about the boy, about his clothes, the weapon he was carrying and of course, where he'd been only yesterday. Surely that would be of some help in catching him, and then maybe one day Jay Cleaver would come back as he threatened to inflict his revenge.

The hotline number was answered promptly. 'Hello... yes I'm phoning you about the boy. I know where he is...Well I know where he was late yesterday...Yes...Jay Cleaver yes...my name...sorry of course, my name is Linda but I'd rather not say any more than...I saw him on the Victoria Gardens estate...the big houses on the hill yes. He was wearing a black training outfit and he had some other clothes with him. Blue bottoms and a red hoodie I think, also he was carrying a large knife in a green bag...if you come up this way towards the fields I'm sure you'll find him...my surname, oh I'm sorry no...I can't tell you anymore...It's just Linda, write that down.' Estelle replaced the house phone with a small glow of satisfaction then continued her chores. Her wait for revenge had begun, and it felt good, because she was prepared to wait for a very long time.

46

Harvey hadn't returned home the previous evening until after ten. Flo had been asleep but he hadn't disturbed her, then after a quick reheated meal and shower he'd slept fitfully before getting up and out of the house by six. Back in his office within half an hour and now three hours later he was still sat there when the secretary walked in to tell him the news.

'There's been a reported sighting of Jay Cleaver sir!'

'Whereabouts…?' He asked sharply.

'…The witness reported that he's almost certainly heading up out of the city towards the hills…' She was reading from her notepad.

'Huh…I wonder what's up there for him…' Harvey said then pondered on his own question. '…There's farmland, woods, the zoo, an old church and the private airport! Get the unit up there and tell them to start scouring.'

The secretary closed the door quietly before quickly re-entering. '…Sorry sir I almost forgot, the tip off also said they believed he was carrying a large knife in a bag.'

'That's not really surprising. Okay inform the unit about that as well. Is that all…?' Harvey was still being sharp with her.

'Yes sir.' As she closed the door again she wondered why the Inspector wasn't his usual self, not knowing that a superior question would have been, how could he be his usual self?

Things had changed; Oscar had altered him to the point where the naturally serious and grounded in reality Harvey Cooper was beginning to believe in stories of spirits, and entities, or whatever the hell was going on. For the last hour he'd been making calls to associates who might have more information, mostly the unit sent to clean up at the facility after Oscar's rampage and escape. It had been a wise and productive move because he'd learned that Doctor Kelly's office was untouched. Nothing had been removed, meaning the other drawings would still be there, and no one else in the world apart from him knew how important they could be. So how do I get them? His first thought would be to take a drive over there, tell them who he was and find them in the office. Then his logical mind kicked in, if I do that and Shilling finds out I'll be in trouble, so another way would be to find out who's working on the facility case and try to call in a favour, but this held the same risk as the first option, because after all, who can you trust? There were other routes he could take that might work but they wouldn't be quick and he wanted those pictures now, he wanted them here in front of him so bad it was breaking down his analytical thought processes, so what the hell, if speed was of the essence then there was only one path to take, he was going over there directly, and once there he'd check the lay of the land and wing it.

Oscar had been dozing lightly before being woken by Bob Jenkins telling him to stand facing the wall and to not try anything stupid. He did as he was told as three officers came in to 'assist' in putting on the cuffs.

'Your carriage waits...' Bob said as the three burly men escorted Oscar to the prison van at the back of the police station. When it came into view Bob stopped the groups march. 'You might need this.' The   small   man turned to see what 'this' was, as the white towel got draped over his head. Now all he could see was the floor, two feet of daylight between the door and the back of the van, and in that small gap he heard the voices of families he'd wronged cry out.

'Die you piece of scum! A widower's voice cried out.

'Murdering swine!' screamed the shrill voice of a lost father.

'Rot in hell Downes!' threatened a priest.

'Hang the bastard!' said the twin who lived her life alone.

With so much hatred pouring down Oscar thought if he tripped and fell now he may be crushed under its weight. It was a painful and passionate crowd although there weren't as many as previously, but the ones here now were the hard core, those who still remembered the atrocities this evil man committed in their city, to their wives, mothers, sisters and partners, and not one of these people had forgotten for a single second who Oscar Downes was, and what they still wished for him.

The policeman to Oscar's right was standing next to the small tinted window taking a look at the two dozen or so people at the gate. In the past this officer had often wondered how these mobs found out so quickly when there was a 'celebrity' in town. Someone must have tipped them off, he thought, and smiled to himself. 'I   think   you're   losing   your   appeal Oscar...' the policemen on his left bellowed as the gates opened, but then the heavy bangs and profanities began to rain down on the vans bodywork. '...There's only about twenty here today mate. There were two hundred when we first caught ya!' Oscar ignored the policeman's jibe by putting his head in his hands, trapped as he felt, within a thundering hail of hate with no one to help. The policeman was correct though it had been much worse and considerably louder during those first times, but back then Oscar had the voice to listen to, the voice always helped with the onslaught of his senses by screaming louder than any anguished horde could manage. This time though he felt every rock of the van, every hand slapped on its side, and could comprehend clearly every horrible word they sent to him.

'Off to Longmarsh for you big man!' The policeman to his left said.

Oscar understood the ironic joke and looked down at the steel cuffs shining on his wrists, and when the van slowly pulled away he felt some relief, as those other voices mercifully disappeared from his mind.

By the time Harvey got down to the yard he'd just missed the unruly circus of Oscar's transit to Longmarsh, and if being honest he was happy about that. The man the dispersing crowd had directed their venom towards would always be guilty in their eyes, and even if Harvey could somehow prove he was under the influence of a demonic voice at the times of the murders, he knew it wouldn't make a bit of difference.

The gates were still open so he jumped in his car and drove straight towards the facility, the place where he hoped the most bizarre legal defence in criminal history would have its origins.

An uneventful journey followed, apart from conflicting thoughts crashing in his mind, questioning his own sanity at times, doubting himself, until the car came to a stop at the lowered security gate. There a newly appointed guard asked him his business so Harvey showed the young man his ID and white lied to get what he wanted.

'...I'm working on the investigation and have just been informed one of our officers left a small but vital piece of evidence in the Doctor's office. I'm here to retrieve it. I shouldn't be long.' Harvey kept the look on his face business like.

This new guard had been told to let no one into the facility, unless they were police investigators and to be fair this guy seemed legit. 'I'll have to get someone to accompany you. It's all on shutdown you understand since that nutter...'

'Yes I understand!' Harvey interrupted because he didn't appreciate the word 'nutter' when describing people with mental health issues.

'Okay then Inspector you can go and park under there and wait until someone comes to get you.'

The guard who believed he was safeguarding nutters then raised the gate and Harvey drove forward down the ramp. As his eyes adjusted to the darkness of the car park they were drawn to some faded chalk marks on the ground where details of the deaths had occurred, and an eerie feeling of after the Lord Mayor's show came over him. He couldn't think of a better analogy as he tried to picture Oscar in this very place killing two men. When he chose his bay and came to a complete stop his phone rang which startled him, now Harvey Cooper wasn't the jumpy kind but was happy to admit that being here and suddenly hearing the noise of computerised bird sound had caught him out.

It was his office. '...Inspector there has been more developments...'

His secretary was full of good news at the moment, he thought, although her timing could do with improving.

'Go on!'

'...The body of a farmer has been discovered, a mister George Jordan, Seventy two, he's been almost decapitated!'

'Where...?'

'...Up in the hills, and it sounds like your boy, a single blow with a heavy sharp instrument.'

The secretary then fell silent and that silence stretched out as Harvey took in the information before slamming both hands down hard on his steering wheel. '...Right okay what's the farm? He got ready to jot it down in his notebook which had been a little neglected lately as what he was focusing on was probably best left unrecorded.

'...It's called Black Sheep farm it's on the North road up by...'

Harvey cut her off. 'The private airport...I'll get up there as soon as I can...!'

'Actually there's another reason for calling sir. The Superintendent wants to see you and he said straight away. I told him you'd popped out and he ordered me to get you back here now. Where are you by the way?'

Her asking annoyed Harvey but she was just doing her job. '...I'm ahh...it's a personal matter but I'm heading back tell him...!' Harvey ended the call then slammed the steering wheel again, three times, hard. What, how and why now? He shouted those questions internally which was just as well because at that moment a small hand reached down tapping at his window.

'Christ Jesus!' He exclaimed after jumping up again before looking out to see a young lady with a clipboard smiling down.

'Inspector Cooper is it...?' She enquired politely as he climbed out the car then offered her handshake.

'...Yes it is, thank you for meeting me.'

'My pleasure...!'

Harvey was still trembling slightly so declined the handshake, he really didn't like how nervous he was becoming lately. '...Could we possibly be quick about this I've just received an urgent call, they need me back at the station.' He breathed in deeply to portray a semblance of calm professionalism.

'Of course Inspector, if you could just fill in this entry form then print and sign your name I will take you straight there...'

Right now he didn't want to sign anything that could be evidence of his visit here, but in the same breath he would have done a handstand in his underwear if he thought it would help hurry things along. He quickly scribbled his name down before she pointed out he had to print it as well, and then he hadn't dated it, and oh of course silly him he needed to write down his number plate. '...It's all part of the new security measures. Since the 'incident' everyone has to fill them in.' She smiled dutifully again as he finished the paperwork. 'Excellent, follow me....'

Harvey fell into step without protest although all he wanted was to give her a kick up the backside to move her a little quicker. As they walked up the stairs Harvey wondered just how effective filling out a form would be if another 'incident' arose. Oh I do apologise Mr serial killer with an evil voice in your head making you commit murders, could you possibly fill this form in before you carry on? It was just ridiculous time consuming health and safety gone mad, and for crying out loud where the hell is this office? I've got to go!

After another three minutes of inane chit chat about the new security upgrades they finally reached the office of the late Doctor Katherine Kelly. He knew that because her name was still on a removable piece of card on the door which he thought a bit uncaring, even a touch callous that it was still there, but respecting the recently deceased wasn't why he was here.

The young lady had been carrying a key and she revealed it with a flourish and another smile as she popped it in the lock. 'Will you please in the name of god hurry up' Harvey thought as the door was pushed slowly open allowing him to rush in and begin his search.

'I could help perhaps, if you let me know what you're looking for...'

The irony for Harvey as he rummaged through folders and files on the desk was that she'd been as smiley and helpful as any person could be, but damn she was stressing him out. Okay fine he thought if it will stop you standing there smiling inanely you can help. '...I'm looking for some drawings, A4 size done with crayons.'

'I haven't seen anything like that but if they're here I'm sure we'll find them...' It was another happy response as she began her search on her side of the office, the one by the desk, the one he'd already glanced over before moving on to the two large filing cabinets rammed with folders.

'Damn this could take hours…!' He moaned out loud and it was genuine disgruntlement because he only had minutes. '…Please I've checked the desk already…' While watching her get down on all fours and look underneath. God bless her she was trying in every sense of the word and his annoyance was becoming very hard to contain.

'Are these what you're looking for…?' She asked and stood up holding four sheets of folded A4. '…They must have slid down by the wall.'

'They could be…' He said in an unemotional tone, although his real feelings were excitement plus extra relief as he took them from her. He flicked through them quickly without noting their content; just that they were drawings, because there was no avoiding the uncomfortable fact he was out of time. Sliding them into his jacket pocket he looked over at the young girl. 'Thank you…erm…?' He faltered with her name.

'Lucy…' She didn't smile this time. '…but you never asked.'

'My apologies Lucy and thank you again. Now if you wouldn't mind jogging back to my car with me, I really have to go.'

<u>47</u>

The lush jungle canopy was all shades of green, alive with the sound of birds and small hidden mammals, with its floor covered in giant ferns pressed against abundant tall grasses. Occasionally the undergrowth would quieten as some larger predators walked by, hunting in its clearings and although Alex knew it wasn't real he bloody loved it. 'This is so much better than the beach, don't you think...?'

'It makes no difference to me.' The Angel replied.

'Well I like it...Dinosaur time!'

'Yes the Jurassic period, as you asked for.'

'Can we change it again in a bit? I've got loads of ideas...'

'...No Alex, we can't keep swapping the scenario. That would be pointless.' This response was the nearest thing to a shout Alex had heard from his host.

'Alright I was only asking.'

'We have things to do, remember? You are going to help me find the problem so we can fix it and return you home.

'Okay let's do it...' He looked over at the angel '...What exactly are we doing again?'

'We are fixing the machine but we need to find where the problem is first.' The Angel repeated exhaustingly.

'Okay I've got that. So what do I do is what I'm trying to get at.' Alex looked around sharply as the sound of nearby undergrowth cracking under a great weight filled his senses. 'Woah what is that...?'

'...A large predator I presume. There were many in the Jurassic age' The Angel informed before removing a small square object from inside its robe. Those breaking sounds in the jungle were getting very close and Alex was looking intently but couldn't see the culprit through the thick undergrowth. It also didn't help that he kept glancing back to see what the Angel was doing and between the two he couldn't decide which was the more pressing. Suddenly the guttural deafening roar of a dinosaur shook the world around them.

'...If that thing attacks me will it hurt or is it not real...?' A deeply concerned Alex asked.

'Did you feel the ocean when you placed your feet in it? The Angel enquired seemingly unconcerned with the oncoming threat.

'Yes of course...!'

'So I think we can safely deduce you would also feel the full effect of everything else you have requested...'

'...Then I don't want to be here...!' Cried Alex, as directly above him the huge head of a roaring T rex appeared over the canopy, bending the trees forward with its great weight, opening its massive jaws to snap them closed over the terrified man. Alex fell helpless to the floor, both hands instinctively coming up to protect his head, with his body scrabbling to escape before opening his eyes to find there was nothing to see, nothing to hear.

'...Calm down Alex!'

He looked around to see his host standing three feet away holding a red leather book. They were back in a world that was once more white and blank. 'Shitting hell...!' He said and his heart started again as he realised he'd never been happier to see nothing at all.

'Don't swear Alex, it is a coarse and horrible waste of vocabulary. There are always better words to use, beautiful ones to explain your feelings.

Alex had always been adept at spotting a rebuke when he saw it and that was definitely one. 'Well I'm sorry but all of that was a bit too real, I was inside its mouth, I could smell and feel its breath!' He was still shaking in the world of white and looked beyond the Angel to where the desk and chairs were situated.

'Which is the precise reason I changed our situation back to one I thought may be more productive. Come this way, our work begins.'

'Is that a bible...?' Alex asked a little worried by the books appearance. '...Because you know, even after all this stuff up here I'm still not interested in any of that '...In the beginning this and that happened and who begat who after begatting somebody else stuff...'

The Angel sat down on its swivel chair. Alex sat where he always sat. '...So is it a bible...?' He asked again hoping his hunch was wrong.

'To some yes.' The Angel answered.

'Nice and cryptic, okay then...is it a bible to me?'

'It is the true book of wisdom, all visions and their possibilities are within its pages. I believe by using it correctly we will be able to find the purpose for our being together and therefore repair the problem.'

'So it is a bible.' Alex moaned.

The Angel scooted its chair round so it was sat next to the crestfallen man; Alex was surprised again because he'd never noticed it had wheels, so many surprises for a single chair, before realising that almost everything the Angel had been doing today was new.

A brief moment passed between them with Alex considering that listening to the bible read by an Angel would most probably be the finest way to ever hear the scriptures, straight from the winged horse's mouth so to speak, so he settled himself comfortably for their look at the 'great' book before saying. '...Come on then let's do it but I tell you now I'm not for converting...' Alex resigned himself to the entire religious bumph he expected to hear as its perfect fingers opened the cover.

The Angel leaned in as Alex looked at the inside of the book, watching the effect it had on the man who was momentarily speechless, his pupils dilating, his heart thumping heavily, as his whole concept of life and its natural laws disappeared instantly. His human eyes were watering with joy as he scanned the pages 'Can I swear now...just once?'

'If you must...but keep it short.'

'...Eh...eh...ah...!'

As the book revealed to him what it could do and what it truly was, so Alex tried, but ultimately failed, to find one single human profanity to justify in any way what he was seeing or feeling.

<u>48</u>

Jay Cleaver, currently the most wanted man in Edinburgh was staying low, flat on his back to be more accurate, down in a shallow gully that bordered the narrow road. They'd nearly caught him a few moments ago while he stumbled along in uncomfortable pain, caused by the still contracted muscle in his shoulder; and almost failing to hear in time the police car speeding up behind him. Only at the last minute did he comprehend the danger to leap off the road landing heavily in the ditch, the impact causing him to squeal in pain as the car skimmed by. When it sped away he cursed himself for being so lax and in doing so discovered his chipped teeth had savagely clenched down on his tongue. '...thor thucks thake...!'

He soon found trying to ignore the pain in his mouth was taking up a lot of energy; sweating profusely he stayed low and guessed correctly the police had a good idea where he was now. Of course they did, either they've found the farmer guy or one of those three liars had called the police. Now for the first reason he could understand the police being called, their logic at the end of the day based on discovering a farmer with his head almost severed off. However the second, where someone from that big house had grassed him up after promising they wouldn't, well that idea just made him angry, in fact there was no denying this whole game was beginning to infuriate him.

Looking at his current predicament, one where he was literally in a hole, he realised this wasn't the best time to be angry, and probably better to just keep moving. I can do this he thought regaining his feet to feel the warmth of excitement running once more in his veins; he was getting closer to the big boss fight to complete the final round of this bizarre game, an ending he truly believed his whole short life had always been heading towards. Jay then messaged the empty air around him as if online players were actually listening in, like the games developers themselves had him on loudspeaker and needed to know his review of their creation. '...I'm gonna win...I ain't finished yet...I don't think it's fair though, I'm playing this game injured, I'm hungry, I've bitten my tongue really hard and I've got loads of cops after me, so it's going to be the toughest level yet but I swear down I'll complete it...you're not gonna beat me..!' This determination came from imagining the satisfaction he would feel if he could get to the end and defeat this insane virtual reality, knowing the prize would be magnificent of course, it was just a question of how many difficult to earn reputation points he would gain. He guessed it would have to be millions for such an awesome victory, probably a life time's worth so he would rocket up the popularity charts, maybe even all the way to legendary status, before he returned triumphantly to see his admiring peers and fawning fans down by the docks.

Suddenly another car sped by in the same direction. Jay didn't react, as he couldn't see the road from within the gulley so it could have been anyone, but his rumbling gut spoke to him of more cops. He knew what was going to happen now because he'd watched their reality TV programmes; soon there would be dogs and helicopters with heat vision cameras, maybe even guns, while all he had was a butcher's utensil and a dream.

Reaching a boundary fence he waited a full five minutes to regain his composure before tearing through the hedgerow to continue on this mission. A morose tiredness caused by the incessant hunger pangs reduced his usual vitality and he cursed himself again for not taking any food when he had the chance. What he wouldn't do now for just one slice of the amazing bread Linda had given him, but instead he swallowed his own saliva hard so at least something would go to his stomach.

Those invisible game designers he believed were observing his progress could be so cruel sometimes, harsh to their own customers for good reason, because they knew better than anyone that any great game is worth the sacrifice. This section however was rapidly becoming excruciating and desperate for Jay as he stumbled on through the thick grass.

On the other side of the city in hospital room 6c, Linda Webb was sitting next to Alex's bed holding his hand. There was no doubting she still cared for him, only wanted the best for him, but goddamn it she wished the lazy sod would wake up already.

Gary Swann was stood by the window looking on watching a wife tending her sick husband. It should have been a beautiful moment but witnessing their intimacy he just felt guilt, something of a spare part, and thoroughly out of his comfort zone. The heavy bandaging over Alex's amputation didn't help the situation, the thought of the wound was particularly uncomfortable to focus on, and because of this Gary tried hard not to look but that was futile. The doctors had chopped the poor sods arm off and he stupidly thought of a hundred reasons why an amputation would be bad and only one where it might be seen as a positive

'Hey he won't weigh as much!' Gary suddenly said with the words reaching Linda over Alex's prone body.

Slowly she raised her head before giving him her greatest ever look of disbelief.' 'Really Gary, you think that comment is useful...?'

'...It came out wrong. All I'm saying is that if he did worry about his weight...I mean I didn't really know...I don't really know him...I just think he probably won't have to now...his weight you see...because he's lost some...' The words trailed off completely as it struck him how inappropriate his statement had been, and how he didn't have the mental capacity or words to fix it because there were no positives he could find about the removed limb, so he made the wise decision to change the subject but only after inadvertently creating an armless elephant in the room. '...Do you want a coffee..?' He didn't want to be there anymore.

'...Yes please...' She lied.

Gary left and closed the door behind him with a fool's relief and truly wishing he'd gone to work instead.

Linda listened to his heavy steps walk away down the corridor before speaking to her husband. It had felt wrong to talk to Alex with Gary looming over them because whatever happened between a man and wife was their business and no one else's. 'Sorry about Gary being here, we're alone now. You won't believe what happened to me yesterday. The boy who was there in the building when you fell came to see me and returned your wallet. He told me he'd stolen it off you and told me to tell you he was sorry. That's crazy isn't it?...there's just no telling with some people...but now the news is starting to report him as some kind of psycho but I believe he has a genuine innocent side...he told me to tell you he was glad you hadn't died...'

'...No thanks to him!' The deep male voice said and she turned to see Gary surprisingly returned to the room and listening to her from the open door.

'I thought you were getting coffees!' Linda felt embarrassed and snapped angrily at the interruption.

'I was then I bumped into that Nurse. She said not to worry she'd go get them. Alex is in good hands with her around...'

'Nurse Juliet, yes she is lovely.' Linda admitted.

'She is that...' Gary concurred while skilfully concealing the merest whiff of lechery.

Meanwhile back up in the killing fields of pain, Jay Cleaver struggled agonisingly on towards his endgame, stopping suddenly to drop and roll in the long grass, hiding from two police cars speeding back towards the city. He presumed they were probably the same two cars and if he was correct in that assumption then he believed he must be doing well at this tricky hide and seek level. All he had to do now was find an energy point or a hidden medikit and he would be well on his way, this player knew how these games worked, there had to be sustenance soon or he wouldn't have the strength to carry out his task. Walking on some twenty yards he had to take another rest, his neck and shoulder were still giving him serious jib. He reckoned he hadn't even travelled a mile yet and it was easily after lunchtime now. Those groaning thoughts were taking over now, shouting at him that he hadn't eaten a thing since the gorgeous bread and soup back at the house yesterday afternoon. You don't have to be a genius to know if you were going on the run there was every chance you would be living rough, that you may need a sleeping bag or even a blanket, just one or two few useful supplies, after all that house had been massive, it would have contained loads of the treasures he required right now, basic food being the main one.

As in all video games Jay knew there would be health boosts and food caches hidden away close by. All he had to do was find one and for that desperate reason alone he would continue his search. There'd be no more rest until the game played fair and gave him an opportunity to restore his health. So Jay raised this failing body with its aching stomach, its painful neck and its sore bleeding tongue, accepting the challenge before once more shakily moving on towards his goal.

49

Alex asked with widest eyed look he had ever worn. 'What is it?'

'Think of it as the manual for the machine. We are going to need it.'

Alex didn't care at all for the Angel's answer he was far too busy, fixatedly captivated by the images he witnessed within its pages, and he defied anyone to describe what he was experiencing? This was perfectly beautiful insanity as whatever he thought of appeared in the book, his life played back to him in a cascade of colours and imagery, first watching himself as a chubby baby being cradled by his mother, then as a toddler running with a bloodied knee. There were triumphs, tears and moments he'd thought forgotten, gone forever, and every one of those moments instantly sparked another memory that bled through on every second of his life, and soon he found he could jump forward and leap back at will. His heart nearly burst when he saw his first love in the school playground, Penny…Penny…something or other…but before he even had time to think of her surname the memory changed to a drunken teen party where he witnessed his naïve younger self crying, those tears caused by the pain of losing Penny to another boy, and this in turn flowed into images from other parties, other girls he'd loved, the good the bad and the surprisingly ugly. Even thinking of love by itself caused the images to change again, showing a multitude of moments he'd shared with everyone he'd ever loved, and without knowing how or where the time had gone he finally reached the part with him falling from the window ledge. Of course he knew the story of Alex Webb should end there but the images kept coming and continued on beyond that moment, unlived memories in places he'd never been, where everything was still about him but all brand new and fresh, like watching himself in an amazing movie that he didn't remember filming.

'Seriously what in god's name is this?

'I have told you, it's the manual. All the answers to help us fix the machine are within it. You just have to find the right section, the exact chapter, only then will we know what's gone wrong.' The Angel was explaining as best it could to the heavily distracted man who was finding it impossible to break his gaze from the pages.

'Everything about me is in here exactly as it happened. I can see it like I was back there again but watching from the outside. This is an overwhelming incredible visual compendium of my life…' Alex tried hard to vocalise what he was experiencing and felt that blocky wordy description summed it up best.

'Not just yours Alex…everyone's.' The Angel said.

Alex was struggling to listen while spinning by every possible means, his mind from the visual, his stomach from the relived moments and his heart from the emotions, all of them swirling in a vortex of every single thing he'd ever been and everything he would go on to be. He tried to force his eyes from the book but even that request made a connection, bringing into view memories of a hundred times he'd refused to look at something, Every thought he had opened up pathways to new ones and it was available and replayable, all of his existence inside and out shone brightly then melted away as another memory appeared and disappeared and he continued to spin through all of his time, until finally with a leather bound thud it stopped.

The Angel had slammed the book shut and at that precise moment Alex thought he might actually die from the shock. '…Do you see now? How we can do this…?' It asked gently, unaware of precisely what the book might have done to its human observer.

Alex's stretched out mortal mind began to slow down like a carousel when it's time to get off. It relaxed in stepped stages before finally coming to a complete halt, and immediately all he wanted to do was go round again. There were so many things he desired to see but hadn't the time or the control to focus on. 'Why did you do that?' Alex asked breathlessly.

'Because we have to find out what's happening. All the answers are in the book.'

'No shit they are! I think I get that now. Sorry, excuse me, I'm trying to focus but did you say something about everyone's life is in there…?' Alex asked even though he was pretty sure he knew the answer, he'd felt the other lives and their memories, but still waited for its confirmation.

'…Yes, as I said everyone and everything is in there. It's the manual for the machine, the instructions, the information it feeds upon so every working component large and small can be found, seen, and studied…'

'…That's crazy…its insanity!'

'To you perhaps…but what did you learn?' It asked.

'Well I learned I have a future after the suicide. That's a big weight off my mind. I saw some of it happening so at least I know now that I don't die. I'll go back to earth and carry on.' Alex remained ecstatically relieved by this news right up to the moment his host spoke again.

'That may happen, yes...' The Angel said stretching it wings so wide the left one fell across Alex's back.

'No it does happen. I saw it!' Alex snapped sharply.

Hmm'...what you saw were all the particles in the machine reacting with each other in the past and the future. However there is one simple rule in the universe that you have to understand Alex. The past has happened and cannot be changed but the future hasn't...so it can. You saw a probability and believe me when I tell you there are billions of those...'

'...I want you to open the book again!' Alex was hungry for another spin.

'Of course you do.'

'Now...!'

'...Please Alex be calm. The problem we face is that you are not actually dead and not officially alive so this rather risky viewing has to have a purpose, and I believe that purpose it not for you to just look back over your life, but to find out where the problem is within the machine. So if I let you back in, you will have to concentrate, observe my instructions to only visit specific times and places.'

'Not a problem.' Alex nodded keenly while looking into the eyes of the Angel, knowing he would agree to anything just to see inside the book again.

'I don't expect you to master it straight away but trust me, try and go only where I say. Understood...?' It asked holding his stare

'...Absolutely!' Alex replied while sat unflinchingly at the Angel's side like a dog waiting for the ball to be thrown.

<u>50</u>

Harvey Cooper knocked the door of Superintendent Jeff Shilling's office with even more trepidation than he'd felt upon entering Oscar's cell. The new drawings were still folded inside his jacket pocket and the minute this rollicking was over he would have a proper look. Clicking his neck to relieve some tension he entered when the Superintendent bellowed him in.

'You wanted to see me sir?' Harvey found himself standing to attention as if he were back at training college.

'No! I wanted to see you an hour ago but you were clearly too busy to give me any of your valuable time then!' Jeff Shilling was annoyed and there was no way his position or personality could ever hide it.

'I'm sorry about that sir I was...' Harvey said still trying to think of a decent excuse but found himself instantly cut off.

'...I couldn't give a shit what you are! That bastard Cleaver has virtually chopped a man's head off and the most experienced Inspector I have in my station, the one I selected to be put in charge of finding that lunatic just pisses off out the station...' Shilling didn't like to swear but it felt right because Harvey had seriously aggravated him.

'I sent the unit up there before the attack happened, as soon as I knew about the sighting...' It was a flimsy defence but Harvey was putting up a fight.

'...Well done Cooper but regardless of your tame effort another innocent person has died, because of your inability to locate Jay Cleaver, and I'm not just talking about this morning, I'm talking about yesterday and the day before when, and I have to say this, you've been doing a pretty shit job so far...'

'I arranged a four man unit to search the area.' Harvey bleated but he was hurt by the truth in Jeff's words, fully aware and rudely reminded he hadn't been giving the Cleaver hunt his full attention.

The Superintendent continued with his uncomfortable dressing down. '...I gave you this remit because I know how you work. I need you to understand Harvey that the man I trusted to sort this Cleaver business out, well that man would have hunted and investigated, cross referenced, and absolutely made every other officers working time a living misery until the boy was found, but I'm afraid on this occasion I have seen none of that same tenacity and professionalism, and because of that I can only surmise your focus is elsewhere.'

'Sir I can...'

'...I haven't finished yet Cooper! Believe me when I'm done talking to you man you'll know about it. There will be a very definite ending to this meeting, now be quiet...!'

Harvey had fully expected he was going to be in for a hard time but this appeared to be getting far more serious. Had he really screwed things up this badly? Still standing to attention all through this angry diatribe he'd had no moment to relax as Jeff continued.

'...You see I know the reason why you have let me and that farmer down, why you've failed in your duties, and that reason has a name, Oscar Downes. A serial killer who has already been found and arrested and is currently sitting in a cell in Longmarsh prison. Now I fully appreciate that we may have different techniques in our policing habits, so call me naïve in the ways of modern methods if you will, but I would have thought the criminal still loose on the streets with a knife would be your bloody priority...!' The Superintendent's face flushed but he wasn't finished yet.

'...and I know where you went this morning Harvey!'

'Sorry?'

'Your covert visit to the Doctors office to pick up some mislaid evidence.' Shilling resisted the urge to smile. This wasn't about gloating.

'Yes sir I did...but how...?'

...'For Christ's sake you're not the only policeman in the room. I've got thirty eight years' experience under my belt, during which time I've been on all the rungs of the ladder, including the one you're hanging on so desperately to now. I'm sure you think that my only high ranking purpose is to allocate cases to real policemen like you or shake hands with the Lord Provost occasionally!'

At this juncture Harvey tried but couldn't avoid seeing the photograph of Jeff and the Lord Provost greeting each other on the wall behind his desk.

'I'm still a working investigator just like you Harvey, so when I get a hunch, when I get the slightest whiff that somethings not right, and especially when I suspect a trusted colleague, a valuable part of my team is taking his eye off the game, then I will act and make calls.'

'Sir, fair enough I admit I've been preoccupied with Downes but something isn't right.'

'I don't want to hear about bloody drawings and psychic abilities Harvey...!'

'..But it's why I went to the Doctor's office. Oscar told me there were more pictures and after the strangeness of the earlier ones I needed to see them...' Harvey pulled the papers out and held them tightly.

'...So I suppose that's them is it...and they're going to help us are they Cooper...how?

The Superintendent was right of course, in truth all Harvey had were wax crayon scribbles of events Oscar couldn't have seen, so really apart from their oddness, what were they worth? Opening up the pages to take his first look he found a jungle scene with a badly drawn dinosaur biting down on a screaming man, the next revealed a blue tractor by a barn full of hay and on the ground a body with no head. 'Jesus Sir, look...'

He offered the drawing to Shilling.

'...Harvey I don't care for this rubbish!' But even on saying this he took the drawing then sat down to look at it. Shilling accepted on seeing the originals that Oscar's pictures were something special that he couldn't explain, he didn't doubt the strange allure they held, but he did fail to see any practical use they may offer. This one however made him shiver to the core because of its prophetic image, yet he still maintained they weren't useful to their cause. He reasoned that he found them interesting in the way a half decent video of Bigfoot was intriguing, you watch the footage and see the evidence clear as day then you convince yourself it must be real, later you move on to something else and the thought of a giant hominid creature walking the woods just becomes a maybe. '...Like I said before what's the point...?'

Harvey couldn't answer because he was entranced by the third drawing. In this particular picture Oscar had given them much more than a party trick, this time he may have just handed them living proof. Harvey's eyes widened as he slowly turned to Shilling.

'...Sir I believe we know where Cleaver is heading...!'

Shilling didn't wait to be handed the drawing instead he moved round to Harvey and they studied it together. There was a figure in black holding a large bloodied knife on top of a small hill, it was surrounded by a moat, here and there some orange blob animals with stick legs were standing around, and behind them a narrow road snaked away with blue lights dotted along it. The knife was being held aloft in some form of victory salute and the mouth was open wide, coming out from it was the single word 'Completed!'

'He's going to the zoo?' Shilling ventured.

'Or he's at the zoo already!' Harvey said pulling out his phone and calling for the unit to meet him there. He then refolded and pocketed the drawings before seconds later, without having asked permission to leave the Superintendent's office; he jumped in his car and raced towards the zoo.

Now Jeff Shilling wasn't upset by Harvey's sudden exit, in fact he felt surprisingly delighted, because after all he once again had his best man on the case.

<u>51</u>

Gary and Linda finished had their coffees and Nurse Juliet entered the room to take the cups away. Neither of them had spoken for a good ten minutes, instead they'd slurped and sipped, listening only to the gentle but persistent beep of Alex's bedside life support machine.

'Are you done with those...?' Juliet enquired. The coarse material of her nurse uniform making a distinctive shushing sound as she moved.

'Absolutely...that was lovely thank you.' Gary said while displaying his most attractive smile, not too big or cheesy, just enough to exude confidence and display a smidgeon of interest onto its recipient.

Being an attractive young nurse Juliet knew the games of older men and smiled back politely before she picked up the cups and left.

After a brief pause in which time Gary looked at his Rolex twice he decided he had to say something. 'You think we're making much difference here baby? We could go do something else, a bit of lunch, somewhere nice? Hey we could go to Valentina's we haven't been there for ages. I miss old Paolo. What do you think...?' He took her free hand in his and for a brief moment all three souls were connected.

'...I suppose we could.' Linda had acceded to his request because in truth she was hungry, and Alex wasn't giving her anything back, so maybe a spot of lunch would be a lovely option. It was certain she'd come back again tomorrow to hold his hand and watch him sleep some more.

'...Great stuff...!' Gary said a little too enthusiastically, but it was difficult to hide how much he wanted to get out of the room, watching his girlfriend's estranged husband do nothing for an hour and a half was bloody hard work. Feeling relieved he walked over to the chair and picked up their coats, putting his jacket on and holding hers up so she could slip into it. There were some moments when he wasn't just a cocky epicurean lecherous boss, on rare occasions he could be a gentleman with manners, when he remembered to, and of course most tellingly when he was getting what he wanted.

Over in a white world as far, far, away from the hospital room as you could possibly imagine, an Angel was telling Alex off but finding its words having little impact. '...You are not even trying. Why won't you adhere to the simple instructions...?' This annoyed Angel was sat at his side with its perfect hands upon the closed book.

Alex slowly refocused on the present, feeling dizzy once more as the roller coaster ride of seeing his particles dance their way through his years slowly came to a stuttering halt. With his vision back online he lifted his gaze to look the Angel straight in the face. '...Wow...huh...that was incredible! It just gets better and better every time! I can control it more now. I've just watched and felt and experienced all over again every minute of my wedding day. Only this time I was everyone at the wedding. I could see and understand what they saw and when you put it all together you feel...!'

'...I am well aware of how it works...!' The Angel interrupted with a hint of a sharpened edge. '...but I didn't ask you to do that, I requested you try and find a moment where you believed time may have stopped...!'

'...Don't you see that's what I did...it felt like that exact thing happened on my wedding day. It was perfect, the sun shone and we were in love surrounded by family and friends and we partied until the early hours, the rest of the world didn't matter at all that day, time had stopped for us.'

Alex felt he had explained what he meant beautifully, finding his capacity for learning increasing, both his vocabulary and understanding to describe his thoughts were growing because of the book. It was as if having these experiences over for a second time brought more clarity. The lessons he'd learned throughout his life were being taught afresh and educating him down to a deeper level of comprehension. He was burning again to be allowed back into the book, and thinking that this was what Gollum must have felt in his need to possess the ring, to have just one more chance to feel its power. This book was becoming his whole world, and unlike any bible he'd ever heard of, was causing him to unconsciously rub his hands over and over with avarice.

'I think you should have a rest for a while Alex!' The Angel lifted the book to conceal it within its robe.

'No...!' Alex barked. '...Just give me one more chance, just one, I can do it. I promise. Tell me where you want me to go. Please!'

The Angel considered its options and what choice did it really have? To stop the work they were doing and leave Alex as lost as ever in this place, or allow him to continue on, to find the answer whatever the cost. It placed the closed book back down on the desk and made Alex look into its eyes by putting its heavenly hands on his cheeks and lifting his mortal head.

Alex felt the warmth and compassion melting over his face as the Angel's fingers made contact. There was nothing he wouldn't do to please his host as long as the book was opened again.

'Very well, but this time Alex, I want you to go to where you are now, exactly where you are in your world at this very second, can you do that...?'

The Angel's agreement pierced his heart completely and filled him with joy. 'Yes, yes I can!' Alex said trying not to gasp with the intensity of the sensations.

It will give us a touchstone that we can work from, so this time when I open the book take us to where you are right now on earth..!'

The front cover was then opened up to display a glorious abundance of rainbow details and sensory uploads.

'Oh my god...!' Alex exclaimed as his mind that he'd always believed to be fairly sharp was suddenly opened up to new measurements and stretched wide. Focusing on the Angel's instructions as hard as he could he travelled to where he was now, to discover his prone and injured body on a hospital bed with its eyes closed. The sensations he felt on seeing this were so incredible yet beautifully simple, he could feel the rough clean sheets and the pillow supporting his head, hear the beep of the machine that monitored his vital signs, and in his greed to see more he began to float above his pale comatose body. He invisibly moved around to see the walls and the pictures on them, the floor, the carpet, the window, all the time becoming truly aware that everything large or infinitesimal had its purpose in the universe, that all things were infinitely important and ever changing in equal measure.

Then he felt a heavy punch to his heart on seeing Linda sitting next to his bed, her face, the face he'd expected to love forever. He fought again to stay in that moment and not let the range of emotions he was experiencing illuminate new memories that may try and take him out of the room. If he had his way he would stay in this second forever with her in his view, but then he recognised the large figure at her side, the greying hair of the older man who had stolen her away. The hurt rising up inside him was of a lion roaring, of the child they would never have screaming, of a whole possible future denied by this successful man's decision to steal his wife. Obviously under any normal circumstances he would hate Gary Swann and quite naturally allow a ferocious need for vengeance to consume him, but this was far from normal circumstances, for within the pages of the Angel's book Alex saw and felt everything of the people he

216

observed, and being so in depth he could see that the man he wanted to detest, genuinely loved his wife. He could feel it as the man wrapped Linda up in her coat and it hurt more than ever, because one thing he'd learned so far from his journeys within the book was that everything was truth. Tearing his gaze away to look at himself he saw the tendril like tubes reaching down, penetrating his skin, becoming mesmerised for a few seconds by his own unflickering face, sallow but content, and then he...

'ARGHHHHHHHH...!' Alex screamed out.

The Angel jumped up in surprise and immediately slammed the book closed. '...What is it...?' It asked with Alex breathing heavily.

'Where's my fucking arm gone...?'

Linda accepted Gary's gallant gesture and turned her back to let him place the coat on her, enjoying the reassuring warmth as he took the opportunity to give her a hug.

'Let's go then.' She said and they turned towards the door.

The rapid high pitched bleeping sound that suddenly filled the room was odd and startling, stopping them in their tracks. At first neither of them grasped what it could be, the repetitive tone signalled importance like a warning but if so it was the quietest fire alarm they'd ever heard. It was with a rapid rise in panic that Linda noticed the flashing red light on the machine next to the bed.

Oh my god it's Alex...!' She cried and rushed back to the bedside. '...Get help please...now!'

Gary rushed out into the corridor to find the nurse.

Linda looked down at her husband, the incessant tone meant she was half expecting him to be kicking or lashing his arms around, arm singular, but he was as comatose and still as always. Her initial thought was this must be the end, that he was going to die, because if the repetitive beeps indicated he were waking up then surely his eyes would open and he would see her.

Nurse Juliet burst through the door and shoved a confused Linda forcefully out of the way to get to the machine, a Doctor followed quickly after with another Nurse. It was this new Nurse who told Linda and Gary to leave the room immediately and wait downstairs, her serious tone leaving them with no option but to comply as she hastily shepherded them out.

'What's happening to him...?' Linda cried.

'...Please just go downstairs. I promise we'll come and tell you about his condition as soon as we know...!' And with that she slammed the door.

Gary attempted to take Linda's hand for the slow walk downstairs but she didn't want that now, instead putting both hands deep in her pockets, while he followed two steps behind wondering both what was going on, and what time Valentina's shut in the afternoon.

<u>52</u>

The police radio in his car crackled as he got within range of a signal. 'We are at the zoo now Sir. We don't have a visual yet…!'

Harvey hadn't used his police radio for years for the simple reason he hadn't been out chasing criminals in his car for that long. He guessed at a button but the device instantly whistled loudly as if in pain, wrong one! He then pressed another and the silence it delivered invited him to reply.

'…Erm okay stay vigilant I'm on my way…ETA ten minutes!'

Unsure of the correct protocol he thought for a second before saying 'Over!' He then thought some more, do we even still say that nowadays, he couldn't recall the officer saying it to him. His attention was suddenly taken when around the next bend he had to slow because of a roadblock, strangely it was one he'd ordered to be placed there, so crashing into it would have been awful and embarrassing. Over to his right he could see the large white tent set up next to the barn, the blue tractor sat there just as it had been in the drawing, and he pulled to a stop as a uniformed Officer waved him down.

'Oh it's you Inspector. Have you come to view the scene?'

'…Not right now, I'm checking in on the other unit.' Harvey replied, a little annoyed his chase had been stopped temporarily.

'Very good sir…!' The Officer nodded then moved the cones aside to let him through. The road had been closed to civilian traffic ever since the grisly discovery. Harvey was hoping it might make their job a little easier. The last thing he needed was crowds of zoo visitors milling around when he got there, and he thought with trepidation, witnessing what could possibly follow. Contented in knowing the road was closed in both directions he allowed himself to break the law, committing a crime by opening up the drawing of the zoo scene on the passenger seat while driving one handed. He didn't even know why he was doing it for certain, maybe there was still an unseen clue that could prove pivotal, anything to make Oscar's outrageous legal defence that he'd been controlled by a mysterious force more genuine.

Jay Cleaver was concealed sitting down with his back to the roadside hedge. The hunger pangs were growing ridiculous now and he listened to them churn and bubble as he rested and watched for the police. Apart from the car that passed him earlier they hadn't even got close to catching him. This was giving him the confidence to wonder if they'd given up on him or maybe he was just too damn good at this game. In the distance those chattering and whooping sounds let him know he was getting close, now if he could just find something to eat, anything at all, it would give him the energy he needed to finish the game.

<u>53</u>

In the Edinburgh hospital where Alex Webb's life hung in the balance Gary Swann was pacing the reception area like an expectant father. Half an hour he'd been striding about because nobody had told them a damn thing, which meant that Linda was also stressed to hell and as he'd already learned, only twenty four hours ago, a stressed to hell Linda was no fun at all.

Of course that was only his ignorant viewpoint because she wouldn't call it stress, what Linda felt was deeper than that; she was torn asunder once more with guilt and worry. Alex was her husband and though a few days ago she was rude to people who dared to suggest it, they were still wed. Now her thoughts were only about her husband and how she would feel if he died, or maybe worse still, survived and needed her help with only having one arm.

'Mrs Webb...? A Doctor asked who had somehow sneaked up on her. Linda stood at his presence and when he didn't tell her to sit back down, like they often do on the telly, she took it as a positive.

Instantly Gary appeared at her side like the proverbial china shop bull. '...Doctor! What the hell is going on...?'He demanded to know as if it were a matter of life and death to him, but Linda knew that wasn't the truth; he just wanted to get an answer so he could leave.

'Well I'm about to explain...' The Doctor said and focused on Linda. '...We have managed to reduce his heart rate back to acceptable levels, he appears calm again, but we will have a nurse with him constantly for the next twenty four hours in case of another episode...'

'...So he's okay then...?' Gary crashed into the conversation again.

'...Well he's still in a coma if that's what you mean by okay!' The Doctor had answered sharply before flashing a look at Linda, who liked this guy because it was almost as if he understood this situation, the situation being that sometimes her new boyfriend was a bit of a self-important prick.

Gary took the pointed remark on the chin and then one step back before putting his concerned 'I'm listening' face back on.

'What happened to him Doctor?' Linda asked.

'It appears he may have suffered from an extremely distressing nightmare.' The Doctor flicked his gaze from one to the other seeing which one would ask the question first.

Unsurprisingly it was Gary. 'Do people in comas have dreams?'

The Doctor continued. 'It's a bit of a grey area scientifically speaking, there are some neurologists who claim there isn't enough brain activity to have dreams in a comatose patient, due to there being no sleep cycle. By that I mean awake, asleep, awake, asleep, as healthy people do, but on the other side of the fence there are patients who have awoken and reported of being in a constant dream state, which sometimes involved nightmares. I would have to presume something like this happened here because his readings suggest a sudden spike in brain activity.'

'It had nothing to do with his amputation then?' She asked.

'I wouldn't have thought so. We'll let you know if there's any change. Good day to you both.'

The Doctor's manner had soothed Linda to the point where she exited the hospital doors holding hands with Gary.

In the white world Alex regained some control to find his soul, his conscience or collection of stupid particles, whatever the hell his existence could be called now; it was crying tangible looking tears onto the desk.

'I've lost my arm...!'

He proclaimed loudly while looking down at his left arm which still existed in this place, and that was an immensely strange incongruity for anyone to handle, one armed or not.

'It is an unfortunate turn...' The Angel began to say.

'...Oh really you think! You think it's unfortunate? I don't want to live with one arm...!' Alex was running out of tears as he tried to understand his trauma. He finally took in a deep shaky breath. 'That's just...I mean...how will I open things?'

'...Many people have an arm missing and they manage.' The Angel proffered as some kind of assurance.

'You know what I'm not 'many people! It was hard enough before.'

'What was hard enough before?'

'My life, my life was hard enough before!' Alex gave the Angel a stern look. 'I committed suicide remember? From that simple fact alone we can presume my life had not been going swimmingly...and now if I go back...then...well swimming for one...will be really difficult!'

'Perhaps, but please remember it may not happen at all!' The Angel spoke with a cryptic attempt at reassurance.

'It has happened, I've just seen it, it's down there, it's happened and you can't change the past, isn't that what you said...?' Alex was moving from an upset stage into a fury of loss stage. '...This is becoming a total joke!'

'Nothing about this is funny!' The Angel said with a curious look.

'I know I'm being sarcastic! I'm stuck up here with you in some cosmic frigging classroom with two arms, while I'm also stuck down there in a coma with one arm, and this is all happening at the same time you know...!'

'...No, it isn't...it is simply one of many possible futures for you.'

Alex looked away into the land of white nothingness utterly convinced that his bizarre health condition, where he was both in a coma yet wide awake and one armed, yet not, was perhaps utterly unique in the history of the human condition, and he presumed there wasn't even an obscure or rare medical term for it.

The Angel looked down at the book which for a few painful moments had been forgotten about, and it wasn't long before Alex was also drawn back to the small red hardback that resembled a bible, only he knew that instead of scriptures it contained every answer to every question he or anyone else could ever imagine to ask.

'Okay the futures not set; I get it, but tell me what am I supposed to be looking for?' Alex asked.

'I don't know exactly'. The Angel answered unhelpfully

'Oh my God, kill me now!' Alex was losing it again and the frustration rose into an angry query. '...Actually don't, just answer me something that you do know. What would happen if I attacked you?'

'Why would you attack me?' The Angel asked.

'Oh believe me I could find reasons! Tell me... what would happen?'

'I suggest the most likely outcome would be that I disappeared and returned later.'

'Later...when?'

'Well later...when you weren't attacking me.'

Alex fought the urge to jump at the Angel right now, but however bad things were getting, however outlandish and exasperating his time in the white world was becoming, he had to keep reminding himself that this bird guy was all he had in this universe or any other.

'Alright then, what would have happened if you hadn't made the dinosaur disappear? It would have bitten me and I would have died...yeah?'

'No...you wouldn't have died...'

'That's good to know.'

'...However you would have experienced all the agony and searing pain of being eaten alive and then swallowed by a ferocious Jurassic predator, before bumping back to this place again.'

Alex was having real trouble understanding the 'bump' thing, but he believed it existed after his earlier exploits, and especially since the Angel had told him so. It was certainly enough evidence to give up on the idea of dying in this place as a way out, the facts of his plight were becoming unbearably clear; he was stuck here unless they could find an answer in the book.

<u>54</u>

Rebecca Jones may have allowed a demonic killing machine to hide in her head but right now she was in a hospital dreaming, her subconscious mind inside the type of building designed for nightmares, an old crumbling stone building filled with leaves and debris in which she was being offered a choice. It was a horrifyingly simple one, to stay in the house which offered her some level of safety, or to walk out into the dense dark forest that surrounded this lonely haven. In an instant that decision was snatched away when suddenly she was fighting her way through thickets and brambles that were dragging her deeper into the woods. Thick blackened trees closed in tight as the ground became unyielding and heavy, she wanted to scream but snakelike roots and rotten tendrils grabbed her face until she couldn't move at all and a horrifying realisation sank in, she could actually die here, in her dreams. Her panic rose to breaking point but then the forest disappeared, in a blink she found herself in a damp cold room, a cellar perhaps, or a dungeon, where rotting wallpaper scraps hung down. Behind her a key squeaked as it turned in its lock and a door opened. Was that someone coming in to save her...or was it all too late...?

'Rebecca...Rebecca?' A ladies soft voice was breaking her nightmare into pieces. 'I've got your dinner for you. Lamb chops and onion gravy like you requested...' Then the nurse placed the tray on the bedside table. '...Here sit up I'll adjust your pillows.'

Rebecca lifted her confused but surprisingly pain free body up. 'That smells lovely.' She said as the warm aroma entered her senses.

'I'm glad, so shall we call it the last supper?' The nurse said happily.

'What? Why would we do that...?' For a moment she panicked believing she may have fallen into another level of the dream.

'...Because you're being allowed to go home tomorrow, I bet that's the good news you wanted to hear isn't it?'

'Yes...yes it is...that's wonderful news...' And Rebecca meant every word; she wanted to leave this place and try to find some normality, while in the darkest recess of her mind the voice listened in, grinning wildly as it crawled towards the light.

55

Harvey Cooper pulled his car up abruptly on the gravel of the zoo car park. Two of his four man unit greeted him with disappointing news.

'He's not here Sir. We've searched all the pathways, checked all the enclosures within reason, and we've watched the CCTV back for the whole afternoon. He hasn't been here.'

'Where are the other two officers?' Harvey enquired.

'They're patrolling the inside of the zoo, Sir...!' The younger looking policeman replied enthusiastically. '...they're doing the first three hours and then we're going to swap. If he turns up here we'll find him.' Harvey nodded his agreement as the officer noticed the crayon drawing on the passenger seat and indicated towards it. 'One of your grandkids did that picture for you Sir...?'

'...What? Oh this...yes, err yes they did.' Harvey chose to go with the safe option of total deceitfulness, after all he didn't even have any children, so grandchildren were a totally impossible conception, and he was pretty sure the officer wouldn't know that.

'Grandchildren hey Sir...you can't beat them!' The officer said heartily even though Harvey was quite sure this man was a little young to fully appreciate such things.

'...Not legally you can't.' The Inspector replied by way of a joke.

A couple of blank seconds passed before the penny dropped for the officer, and even then he seemed to force a smile, with Harvey realising once again that his rarely used black humour was still struggling for an audience.

The officer briskly changed the subject thinking quite correctly that this wasn't the time for frivolity and it felt a little awkward socialising while hunting a murderer. 'Shall we stay here or do you have another plan of action Sir?'

'I think perhaps...that err yourself...'

'...Chambers sir. Officer Rob Chambers.'

'...Yes!' The Inspector smiled wryly because over his long career he'd always suffered from the same blind spot. His often brilliant logical mind was comfortably able to recall details of every suspect he'd arrested, and most of the witnesses he'd ever spoken to, but when it came to junior rank officers he had a huge problem remembering their names.

'And...?' Harvey waved a finger towards the other man.

'Foster...Officer Lee Foster. We're both four years in now Sir.'

As he thought about that Harvey had what he recognised as an obvious realisation; Cleaver was still on his way here!

'...Okay you two take a drive down as far as the farm then come back again. This time I want you to check hedges, gullies, anywhere you think a boy could be hiding just off road!'

'What about the other two officers...do you want them to carry on here?'

He considered his options before playing the safe hand again. 'Yes for now we'll keep them here on the ground. Hopefully we'll have all our bases covered then and we can get him found quickly and be home this evening!'

Harvey nodded at the officer, who nodded back before walking away, and then he sighed inwardly because for the life of him he couldn't remember the young man's name. Watching the two nameless officers leave he looked out of his car at the late afternoon sky, truly hoping it could be all done and dusted before dark. Surely Oscar's picture was proof that Jay Cleaver was coming to this zoo, the boy had no doubt committed the farmer's murder less than two miles away this morning, so he had to be heading in this direction.

His phone rang, after looking at the caller ID; he answered it with a feeling of blessed relief. 'Hello you' Harvey said happily.

'Hello yourself' Flo's sweet and familiar voice replied.

'I presume you're calling me on a matter of impending importance pertaining to the sharing of my company for dinner this evening?'

'Damn you're good at your job Inspector Cooper!' She laughed and that beautiful sound made his world feel right again.

'I really hope so but I'll have to let you know my ETA ASAP!' He knew what was coming back; they both enjoyed the word dance of their private funny conversations.

'Well that's all AOK. Hopefully C U later. Take care. Love you...' She then blew a kiss and he heard it clearly.

'...I love you too.'

With that truthful sentiment he ended the call and got back to work. Looking around the slowly emptying car park he was still considering the option of closing the zoo, he probably had the authority to do it as well, especially if a suspected double murderer was on his way but of course that was the problem, he didn't know for certain he was coming and couldn't really justify a full closure based solely on a crayon drawing. The zoo management were most probably already pissed off that he'd stopped any latecomers by closing off the road. He didn't need any interference at the minute so adjusted his seat back to more a comfortable position, and waited patiently, like only an experienced policeman can do. Always using any down time productively he reached inside his coat pocket to look at the last drawing, the one he hadn't seen yet and who knew how significant it could be. Unfolding the piece of A4 he held his breath, studied the image, before exhaling with a massive disappointment. It was a red box, and that was all, a deep red wax line around the border of the paper, four straight lines meeting at their ends with a blank space in the middle. It appeared to be a frame for a non-existent picture.

'That's it Oscar...?' Harvey asked the piece of paper. Obviously he'd expected more after the miraculous revelations of the man's previous artwork, all of them incredible and tantalising, but this piece, well it had to be said was a definite downturn in quality. Refolding it along with the zoo picture he put them back inside his jacket pocket. They would be close to his heart and never far from his thoughts but a long way from being fully understood. On the passenger seat the radio crackled and one of the officers sent down the road spoke.

'Inspector Cooper...?' The disembodied voice requested.

He grabbed up the radio. 'Come in...receiving you loud and clear....' Feeling even as the words left his mouth that he was sounding more and more like a prehistoric fossil in this modern world of radio communications. Just talk normally he scolded himself.

'Err...yes Sir...we're about half a mile down the road and we've found something...' The policeman clicked off to receive.

'Well what is it...?'

'Difficult to explain...It's probably best if you come down and take a look yourself.'

'For God's sake Officer...' Nope the name was gone. '...Can't you just tell me what you've found?'

'I could Sir but its unexpected...we could really do with your opinion.'

'Very well I'm on my way down...Over!'

Harvey had quickly assessed he didn't really have anything better to do than sit here waiting for Jay Cleaver to walk through the front gates so he reversed the car and turned to head off down the lane. 'Unexpected' was what the officer had said, well Harvey was certainly intrigued by that description, and certainly after the bloody drawings, twinned with Oscar's tales of demonic possession, he was more than ready to follow more trails of the unexpected.

56

Alex's addictive fervour was rushing with exhilarating anticipation as he waited.

'Just so we are clear and reading from the same page, repeat back to me where you are going.' The Angel asked as its long slender finger softly tapped the red book.

'I'm going back to the exact moment I should have died. When I fell from the ledge and hit the cobbled road. It seems obvious now, because that is definitely the point when things started getting weird for me!' Alex felt with something near total conviction that those words could be regarded as easily his greatest ever understatement.

'Are you ready…?' Its finger slid under the edge of the cover.

'…I'm so ready!' Alex replied with breathless joy.

The book opened and once more his human eyes became conduits for all the infinite moments of reality that had occurred, were occurring or may ever occur, and he was trying to centre in on just one. Focusing his mind onto the last seconds of actual life he could remember made the cobbles of Dalmeny Street appear instantly, they were flying towards his face at breakneck velocity, and he could feel the sting of hopelessness as gravity threw him down. He was witnessing this terrible moment from every conceivable angle. The boy in the window watched his descent, except in the books version of events he could comprehend exactly what the boy had been feeling during those fateful seconds, and it wasn't pleasing. Sadly and quite disgustingly he discovered the boy had felt nothing; absolutely no concern in the mind of Jay Cleaver as he witnessed Alex's body fall. He simply watched it happen, waiting for the sound of the impact, for his chance to steal a wallet and make a killing.

As his body reached the cobbles Alex was close enough to see the stones in intimate geological detail and then…a flash of light…as he glimpsed beyond the curtains of his known perception.

Now he returned to Jay as the boy looked down from the window, at the body down on the cobbles, twisted and silent, and Alex was sharing this view as he descended down the stairs onto the street to see the bundle on the road which he knew was his own. Then he watched his hand, the boys hand to be accurate, take the wallet from his pocket, and he felt it taken away by that shared hand and he couldn't handle the two way imagery and feelings. He was fighting hard to block out these confusingly painful imaginings because he didn't want this view, he wanted the other one, the strange one that he'd perceived. It was just a sliver of light, a place he shouldn't have seen, and with all his new learning he closed his eyes and forced the image to change. Only when he opened them up he was back in the white cell.

Alex lay on the white bunk watching the death of the fly, even considering the spider to be a fortunate soul, able to live its life in a web of its own design with no interruptions but for feeding. Nobody ever questioned its reasons for being; it didn't have to care for anything else, and as it returned to its corner with the corpse Alex presumed it also didn't have a memory so couldn't suffer from the past.

'Nooooo...!' He screamed out in some form of agonising defeat when finding himself at the beginning, back in the white room to witness the spider devouring the fly once more.

The Angel resisted closing the book, even though it could see the man was in trouble. This time it wanted to see if Alex could manage the problem without its help.

Within the book and inside his mortal mind the images were still of him in the cell watching the spider but with a flick of a thought Alex was back to falling towards the cobbles. It was new lesson learned, he'd found the skills to replay a precise moment. Do it again he demanded of his fading fracturing resolve, do it again, and through sheer strength of will he did, then again and on repeat each time tweaking this new found ability to locate the miniscule flash he'd stumbled upon. There was no doubt he'd witnessed something else there, a glint of light between him hitting the road and 'bumping' back to the white cell, and instinctively he knew it was the reason for the warping in the natural order of molecules and ions, because he should be dead but he wasn't. A hidden twist in the methodical ways of the universe's movements had occurred and he was the only soul who could find it. Alex repeated his thought pattern, focusing in tightly on the exact moment of impact that should be his death, but over and over it just became a bump back into the white walled cell. As he concentrated even harder, the Angel noticed the man's veins expand and engorge on his temple; it was a second away from slamming the book closed when the man slowly raised his hand in a gesture that was clearly requesting more time.

Alex was finally through...he'd made it...he was backstage...inside the glitch...in a whole different reality between the memory and the moment, and what he found here was almost impossible to comprehend.

In a snow peaked mountainous place Alex could see the Angel in the distance walking towards him. However this scene was happening within the book and that made no sense because the Angel existed outside of it. So it was with trepidation he watched the Angel appear to him like he'd never seen before. He was confused but knew it couldn't be the future, his instincts telling him this scenario must have happened already, and had most certainly transpired at the exact moment between the impact on the cobbles and his first appearance in the white world.

The sensation Alex felt as this Angel approached was poles apart from their first meeting and disturbingly so because this one, although seemingly identical to the other outside the book, expelled a totally different aura. It approached slowly and seemingly unaware of Alex's presence at first, as if he were somehow transparent, but then smirked when it finally registered the man's existence. Quite naturally Alex wanted to speak, to ask, to discover the explanation of how the Angel was doing this, how could it be both inside and outside the book at the same moment, but a deep survival instinct told him to refrain from making a sound. The wisdom of this decision became abundantly clear when the Angel held its head high and began sniffing the air in an attempt to locate the intruder, this strange action causing Alex to hold himself as still as possible while it scanned the area. It was during this standoff that he began to sense its inhumanity, an icy sensation that felt to him of age and cruelty, and showing him this Angel was pure to the core but its layers only told of slaughter and carnage.

Suddenly this Angel opened its wings then ascended into the winter sky. It soared high into the firmament and as it did so all the colours in this world began to darken. Alex dared not move but watched as it swooped round; he stared with intent on seeing those wings become sharper and more defined, until unnervingly with a roll of its head the Angel looked down to where he stood. The rapidly greying sky became heavy with gathering storm clouds and within them the Angel was changing, its form altering as it flew down, picking up speed with every flap of its now gigantic leathery wings and screaming in fury as black flames began to trail from it hands. The sky turned rapidly into a savage red storm as the winged messenger came shrieking towards him, closer and closer; Alex could see the face distorted in rage with bloodied fangs bared but he was unable to move, his body locked up as fear overtook thought and all the firmament became a hell of blackened smoke. The 'Angel' thundered towards him with ripping talons displayed, its raging green eyes set wide on a cracked open skull, screeching its message as the world went black. Yet the word remained as loud as thunder, clear as a clanging bell ringing through time, and the word was vengeance!

Alex pulled his head up and away at the very last second before impact, slamming the book shut himself, as his mind and body collapsed to the white floor with tears of exhaustion and defeat.

57

The voice had learned many things during its time on earth and now as it waited for the woman Rebecca, and therefore itself, to be taken home from the hospital it pondered this wisdom; It had discovered there were no answers in the past, that onwards is the only path it's possible to tread, and all life travels in a single direction no matter what forces may try to push us aside or hold us down. The future is our hopeful, helpful companion, always there to heave the heart through to the end of the line, and therefore our only true faith. Yes, a being can exist out of the acknowledged parameters of time and not be wound up on a mortal coil but the rules still apply, that all consciousness will have a beginning that will march on blindly until its finale, to be conveyed through 'life' as all things must, its journey not always pleasant or smooth; yet in the darkest moments there will always be a light waiting to be found. When it is discovered you must use its illumination to seek your purpose, your reason for being as to commit to any other action is futile, utterly pointless, and the one who tries this will weep with shame and regret for eternity.

It was beginning to believe itself something of a prophet having already found its light in the darkness, knowing it would never weep because it had always known its true purpose, and now it inhabited a new vessel it could once more be wise and vicious in nature while concealing its very presence, because if no one knew it existed it could never be in danger, always free to roam from desperate soul to desperate soul forcing them to do its bidding. The light the voice had found today was the car journey taking Rebecca home. It sat upfront in her mind studying what she saw, watching the fresh killing fields open up before them, the streets and houses full of people waiting to die making it feel both illuminated and hungry. It sat silently in the small family car when they prepared to leave the hospital, as its human conveyor Rebecca leaned in to hug her mother.

'Hey sweetheart, look at you…!' Mum said on gratefully receiving the cuddle. '…Are you okay, ready to go?'

Rebecca had always loved these hugs. '…Yeah I'm okay, I still get a bit dizzy when I'm walking but I'm so ready to go home.'

Her Mum, Eileen Jones, had rushed to be at her bedside on first hearing Rebecca had been found alive. Then to save money she could ill afford to spend had refused the option of staying in a nearby hotel, choosing to secretly sleep in her car on a side street. Her daughter didn't need to know about that part.

The heavy bandage wrapped around her only child's head made Eileen weep inside but outwardly she displayed a motherly resilience to the disturbing sight. She'd grown tough to such things now after the last two years which had been the worst of her life. Firstly her work friend Kerry Stanton had gone missing for a month until her remains were discovered in a barrel hidden in a dirty lock up only two streets away from her home. This was followed by the unfathomable horror that her own daughter had been taken, spirited away by that same murderer, and she feared the end of both their worlds had come. When the call came that Rebecca had been found, Eileen's heart had almost stopped dead before the policewoman told her she was alive, oh thank god she was alive! The officer on the phone described how she'd received a serious injury where Oscar had struck her and was being taken to the local A&E department, yet it was at that moment Eileen had fallen to her knees with gratitude, because that bastard had failed in his second attempt at breaking her spirit, and he was behind bars again while she had her little girl back.

Eileen had often wondered why the hell that man had become such a significant part of her life, she didn't know him, had never met him, and even when she threw rocks at his van she'd never actually seen him in the flesh. The police had cautioned her that day for the rock throwing incident, but she'd been one of hundreds baying for his blood, and the only thing she was guilty of was trying to make sure her pain was heard loud and clear by the bastard. Now with the nightmare of the last few days behind them, and driving her Angel back home, she only wanted to speak of nice things. To let her know how happy she was to have her back after the hours and hours of sitting at her side, and the uncomfortable nights on the reclined passenger seat, yes nice things only, not a breath about Oscar bloody Downes

'It's so good to have you back!' She reached over and squeezed her daughter's knee through the dress she'd brought along for the journey home. The clothes she'd been wearing when they found her could go rot in hell, they had been contaminated by him, and Eileen didn't want any part of that monster in her home.

'Is Biscuit okay...?' Rebecca enquired.

'Biscuits fine, he's with Jess. I called her last night and she told me he's very excited and can't wait to have you back.'

Rebecca smiled, pleased in the knowledge her puppy was happy, although he was getting a little big to be classed a puppy he would always be one to her.

The voice behind her eyes watched the painted white lines rush by, smiling when it realised they were going to meet a dog, a dog named Biscuit no less, and most likely one it would have to dispose of quickly. In its growing experience it had also learned that some canine varieties could sense its presence meaning appropriate action would have to be taken.

<u>58</u>

Harvey drove slowly down the road before spotting the patrol car a hundred yards ahead on his left. There was no sign of either officer, both of whom he couldn't remember the name of, and he thought once more of exactly what had been reported. 'Unexpected' that was it. Harvey tried to imagine what such a description could entail as he came to a stop on the verge, exiting his car he took a wary walk towards theirs; nothing seemed out of place as he checked all around, even sneaking a look underneath. Trying the door he found it was locked, no surprises there it was standard police procedure, before peering through the window and noticing the outline of a figure reflected in the glass walking towards him. Harvey turned sharply to see the officer he'd spoken to earlier, only now he was stood on the grass with his sleeves rolled up, deep red blood covering his arms from the elbows down.

'Officer what on earth is that…?'

'…Blood Sir!'

'I gathered…Who's?'

'They're over here. Come this way.'

The officer turned to walk back along the road then scrambled down a shallow bank into the field. Harvey followed but stopped short of scrambling after, because from here on the roadside looking down he could see exactly what had been most accurately described as 'unexpected'. Chunks of flesh were strewn around this corner of the field, half a body here, various limbs over there, it was difficult to tell what parts came from which individual in the blood stained soil that covered around ten square feet. There had clearly been a massacre.

Harvey noticed the other officer taking pictures on his phone as the young men did now, recording the slaughter that had occurred, the devastation which could only have been committed by Jay and a large knife.

'I think there's four Sir…that's as many heads as I've found…' He pointed over to the fence where they'd been collected; each one with its glassy eyes on show looking up at the world around them. '…Why do you think he did it Sir?'

Harvey struggled to make any sense of the scene at first, before turning to the professional and logical part of his mind, follow the rules, first of all… motive? Let's see, these poor souls certainly couldn't have threatened the boy in anyway so self-defence goes out the window; they definitely wouldn't have grassed him up or been a risk to his freedom, meaning self-preservation goes out, so what does that leave? Well, if you throw out the highly unlikely scenarios that he had a deep seated fear of them or he just went to this much trouble for the fun of it, then it left just one disturbing reason.

'Food...!' Harvey said. The word came out loud and macabre because there was no other clear motive. To fit all the evidence on display he could only assume Jay Cleaver had been hungry, insanely hungry, when he'd stumbled across the lambs, then began butchering their bodies to consume them raw.

'You really believe that's what happened here Sir...who the hell kills and eats a lamb like this?'

'An animal does...a desperate starving animal!' Harvey felt a slight chill, most likely caused by the late afternoon breeze, and of course the knowledge that very soon he would have to face the monster that could do this.

Jay found himself at the final hurdle, the one surrounding the last level of the game, but right now he was feeling worse than ever. His stomach he thought would be fixed by the food was hurting so bad he sat down; resting his back against the chain link fence in an attempt to catch his breath, but it was of no use as his body twisted to the right and vomited a heavy expulsion containing chunks of black meat covered in splatters of blood and tendon. Thinking it was done he attempted to stand but lost control of his movements as another load retched its way up, these ferocious stomach spasms making him feel delirious, and caused by this body rejecting uncooked raw meat. Every piece he'd gnawed away from the bone, at the time for some desperate reason believing it would all be okay, had been denied entrance to his digestive system. Falling down he turned to the left, his head lolling forward and a cold sweat taking over, he closed his eyes unable to look at what he'd done, because vomiting blood whether it's your own or from a lamb was never the moment visual evidence was appreciated. Finally, with no idea how long it had taken to regain the strength to move, but still panting and weak, he made his way along the fence to find an entry point.

'I've called it in sir and informed the rest of the unit the suspect is close by, their security will be watching the closed circuit for any visual, and if he's in the zoo someone will see him.' As the officer pushed the phone back in his pocket Harvey noted the screen was covered in lamb's blood.

'We have to get back...' Harvey said as he got in his car.

'Yes sir.' They both scrambled up the hill not looking their best.

'...But As soon as you get there go find the bathroom and get yourself cleaned up. I don't believe blood drenched policemen running around a zoo could ever be a positive image for the city!'

Harvey set off driving with the strongest feeling that what lay ahead was the final showdown of an irritating and deadly pursuit. All he'd seen of Jay Cleaver since the day the boy ran off in Dalmeny Street, and absurdly when he'd been within an arm's length of capture, was a trail of blood.

Bringing his car to a sharp stop on the gravel for a second time he walked purposely to the security office flashing his Inspectors badge at anyone stood in his way. He was relieved to see that many punters were leaving as the clock ticked over towards closing time; another twenty minutes and the place should be empty, hoped Harvey.

A groggy but determined Jay Cleaver found an old hole in the fence, one fixed without much care, a shoddy job by any standards; where all someone had done was pull the thick chain link back together with what looked like lengths of fuse wire. Of course their efforts would have been sufficient to hold up a general member of the public who may have wanted to sneak in, but Jay was hardly one of those; No sir he was a sick kid stuck in a mental fantasy game with a cleaver.

With one hefty swipe of the blade the thin wires snapped, reopening the breach, before his thin shaking tattooed fingers pulled it wider, he wasn't in any condition to slither through unnecessarily small holes. However the after effects of throwing up uncontrollably and the nagging neck condition meant he ended up falling through the hole regardless. Laying on his back and looking up at the slowly darkening sky he could smell how close he was.

This battling legend of a player had reached his goal and soon that final boss fight would begin. After struggling at first he determinedly raised his skinny frame up and walked forward, but two shaky steps later the red stained cleaver slipped from his sweaty hands into the dirt. He fastidiously wiped his fingers dry on the blood clotted cloth of Gary's sweatshirt, before snatching the blade back with a strong deathlike grip...Game on!

<u>59</u>

Alex was flat on the ground when he opened his eyes up to the bright white world.

'I need you to tell me what you saw.' Spoke the Angel who was sitting next to him with the book closed on its lap.

That wouldn't be a problem, those images and feelings weren't going anywhere for a while, he could picture it all. 'I saw you!'

'...I seriously doubt that.'

'I...saw...you...!'

That is simply not possible. I exist outside of the book you know that. I've told you...!' The Angel offered its hand to help him back to his feet.

Alex rejected its offer instead shuffling away backwards to a safer distance. '...You've told me a lot of things since I've been here. I'm beginning to think they weren't all truthful.

'Alex, Alex, Alex do you seriously doubt the integrity of an Angel...?'

'...Uhuh!' Alex wanted to run what was the point, he couldn't hide in a world of white, in fact when he thought about it only something wearing the perfect disguise, such as an Angel could achieve such camouflage. This left Alex with little choice but to use this moment of clarity to get some answers.

'Why do you need me...?'

The Angel didn't respond but its eyes were a hardened green.

'...You could have looked in the book and saw everything for yourself...' Then a tiny smile crossed his lips as he ventured his next guess. '...unless of course you can't do that. Is that what this is? You need me to go in there because you can't see things in the book...you can't read it?'

The Angel floated slowly over to tower over him as it spoke. '...That is correct...I cannot see within its covers. I've already told you I don't exist in the book. For someone to be able to see how it works they must be a part of it, to have the universal connection from a shared existence...'

'I knew it!' Alex said with a confident nod. He didn't really know but it couldn't hurt to pretend now.

'So whatever you saw in there could not have been me. Now quickly I need you to tell me exactly what you witnessed...!' The Angel demanded to know while floating over the prone Alex, which worryingly reminded it that this man's mortal body was an extremely fragile tool for such intricate and powerful work.

Alex lay cowering under the inspection of the Angel but he had to fight back somehow as he remained unconvinced by its excuses. Try some truth, he thought, hit it where it hurts.

'I saw behind your mask... All of this is an act of deception, this white stuff and the beach and the dinosaur, this...this is you drip feeding me what you think I want...but in the end it's just to get what you want. You're playing me, using me because I have the one thing you don't...a connection into the machine...' Alex climbed to his knees unsteadily then reaching out he grabbed at its gown for support.

The Angel reached a slender hand down still willing to help its accuser to his feet. '...Clearly this plan of mine has done nothing more than swiftly transform itself into a grave error. I should never have let you look inside the covers. It was always, inevitably, going to end like this. I admit I was mistaken to put all of my faith in you.'

'What are you talking about...?' Alex jabbed his finger into the Angel's chest repeatedly. '...I did everything you asked.'

'Really...?' The Angel grabbed the man's poking digit.

'...Yes I did and it wasn't easy. You're just upset because I saw something I shouldn't have. A moment you didn't want me to see...' Alex tried to yank his finger free but the Angel kept a strong grip, and only after their eyes met did it release.

'This is the very reason why Angels and Mortals could never coexist? We have tried in the past but there is always manipulation and distrust to drive a wedge between us...thus it ever was and thus ever shall be.'

'...But you're not an Angel...' Alex was making a stand. '...you told me that on day one...but what you didn't tell me was that you were a demon. To be fair it's not surprising you didn't tell me that, after all it was much more useful for you to tell me what you're not. Therefore it wasn't a lie...ha, ha...!' Alex staggered forward as he laughed but held his balance. He coughed five times and this exertion was close to dropping him back to his knees. Not now he begged and kept himself upright with sheer willpower. '...I've seen the creature hiding behind that pretty Angel disguise. I'm not helping you anymore.' He turned to walk away but after three steps he faltered again.

'So where do you think you're going?' The Angel asked from behind before instantaneously appearing in front so Alex found his path blocked.

'Leave me alone...I don't know!'

'Oh but I do...back into the book, before it's too late...'

'Too late…! But you said time doesn't exist here so that doesn't matter does it?' Alex yelled at the heavenly faced version and spittle left his mouth to rest on the white gown.

'No, time does not exist here but it does exist in the machine, inside the book, so unless we find out why you are here then the glitch…'

'…What fucking glitch…?' Alex screamed louder but the Angel continued unabated.

'…The glitch that is growing as countless atoms of the machines parts come up against a stationary obstruction, causing them to be held at a standstill, and the longer we delay the more the forces will build until the pressure becomes too great to be stopped and…what happens then Alex?' The Angel asked him like he had even the slightest clue.

'I don't know and I really don't care!'

'So you don't know or care what happens when an unstoppable force meets an immovable object? Didn't they teach you of that in your science based belief system? Tell me another thing Alex, if I were a demon as you suggest…would I care about any of this? Would I want to fix the machine? I'd just let it continue its unnatural course surely, waiting for the big bang that will undoubtedly happen?'

Alex paused for a second trying to find the right words. '…I don't know why you would do anything. You're a demon…the bad guy!'

Once again the Angel didn't react to the slur, perhaps predicting what was about to happen, when for all his will and determined intentions Alex fell to his knees, and with the white light fading he fought, but failed, to remain conscious.

<u>60</u>

Spotting its owner climbing carefully out of the car Biscuit the dog began barking riotously at the window, its tail wagging wildly at the sight of its love returned. Of course this dog couldn't understand time, why it had been forced to live in another house, but knew perfectly the overpowering emotions of loyalty and protection. That human walking up the path was its mother, best friend and protector and now she'd returned. It ran and skidded into the front door then began performing a centuries old dog dance, bounding in circles with scrambling claws on hallway carpet, and with its wild dervish choreography only increasing in fervour until the door opened and she was there.

The bandage on Rebecca's head was a mystery to Biscuit as she allowed him to jump into her arms, pure electricity tingling in its small bones as her fingers ruffled and stroked his fur and they kissed with her lips pouted and his excited tongue licking new flavours from her face. They were mainly sweat and salt but there were many tastes he didn't recognise because she'd been gone away. The hundreds of scents it collected and identified in that moment were the reason its species had survived and thrived for hundreds of thousands of years, constantly evolving a most wonderful gift, the deep sense of taste and smell that allowed it to see the whole pallet of emotion, from joy to fear, from love to hate.

'Come on in you, welcome back Beccy!' Their next door neighbour Jess whooped as she excitedly welcomed them into their own home.

Eileen had given Jess a key because that's the kind of trust a good neighbour is allowed, a show of faith nowadays all too rare an occurrence in the outskirts, but Eileen Jones had made sure she was surrounded by good people after her experiences with the bad.

It had started during her pre-teen developing years with an abusive smacking father to her, who then went on to become an absent grandfather to Rebecca, but hey thankfully he was dead now, and even though common sense would insist she avoid people like that man, she seemed to follow a life where somehow she always ended up with varying examples of debauched selfish bastards just like him. Eventually the penny dropped and ten years ago she decided to get her own house and happily embrace the life of a single mum. It made perfect sense if that was all the luck she was going to get in the dating game. Anyway Eileen didn't need a man now she had Jess, who wasn't just her trusted neighbour; she was also her best friend and crutch, and over the last decade it was as if they'd raised Rebecca together, as a team. In the end she supposed, almost inevitably, that her life had still managed to be ruined by a man, when the looming murderous presence of Oscar Downes had thrown his dark shadow over her world.

As she went to the kitchen to grab the cup of coffee Jess had made, and with her bandaged daughter back home safe and sound, Eileen smiled over at her friend, believing this was all for the best, a true turning point, from now on there would be no more fear of murdering monsters and their evil acts in her home.

Dear little Biscuit just loved being carried upstairs, one more exciting joy in the spaniel's life, nothing better than being taken to the big soft sleeping place with no need to climb up the steep carpeted steps.

'I'm going to lie down for a bit Mum!' Rebecca called out as she reached the landing.

'Okay sweetheart let me know if you need anything.' Jess replied on Eileen's behalf. The two women shared a smile clicking their mugs together. 'I'm so happy she's home safe and well....' Jess said.

'...It's a miracle really but she seems fine. I mean we haven't talked about anything yet, exactly what happened. I'm sure we'll do that when she's ready, not going to put any pressure on her.' Eileen said and sipped her sweet coffee.

'I think you're doing the right thing. Let her get settled and find her feet...' Jess agreed adding '...How long does she keep that bandage on...?'

'...The Doctor said a couple of days. Then she'll still have to wear a hat or something because they shaved her hair off at the back.'

Eileen pulled a funny scared face and Jess gave her own sillier version back. They chuckled lightly because here were two women who had faced the wickedness of Oscar Downes and lived to tell the tale. They were fighters refusing to be bowed by his recurring presence in their world, and together as a family they would move forward as one, out of his nightmare.

Biscuit was happily bouncing around on the bed as Rebecca slipped her jumper carefully up over the bandages and sat next to him. The spaniel hadn't had a good sniff of the strange white dressing yet, not up close where it could try and understand why it was there. It hadn't been there the last time he'd seen her and being a dog he was helplessly curious. Rebecca raised her legs carefully and lay on her left side as not to put pressure on the back of her head. Biscuit snuffled her face then began to investigate the bandage round the back, but within seconds it stopped sniffing, backing away to the other side of the bed with a low confused growl.

'Come here you silly Biscuit...!' She said and reached a hand behind her to calm him, but Biscuit was confused and moving away from each grasp she made. It didn't want to be held by her until it could it understand what it was sensing. This was a year old Cocker Spaniel that had never known true fear. There had been times of course it had been scared and confused, usually when loud noises had taken it by surprise, or other dogs barked, but this was a new sensation and its canine mind didn't like it, not one bit. Her hand stretched round further, seeking her pet, and she was making that noise with her mouth that this dog could never have resisted before. It was the noise that told it to come to her for fur rubbing and fuss, but Biscuit had no urge to move closer. Its ears were flattened down and hackles raised a little, head tilted to the right as it stared at the bandages, not knowing what was wrong, but what it could sense through the colours and smells was that something else was here.

'Biscuit come on...!' She laughingly shouted and at that moment the forgotten voice in her head awoke.

Get rid of it!

She reacted with a gasp before recognising it.

Hello?

Get rid of it Rebecca it offends me.

It's you, you're still here.

As requested so I remember.

I thought you'd gone.

Not at all, we are one and we are going to have exciting adventures together aren't we Rebecca?

I don't know. I can't do anything yet I'm still in pain from where you...split my head open.

It will pass. Until then you will do whatever I need. Do you understand or shall I help you to understand?

I understand but please can I rest for now? I just want to cuddle my dog. He's acting strange. I will let you know when I'm ready...

...SHUT UP YOU BITCH!

Biscuit reacted as its owner did when the hard and sinister words came from her mouth. The dog jumped away then ran to the closed door, whimpering and barking to be let out as its owner, its love and its life, climbed off the bed and stepped in close to pick him up.

'What's going on Rebecca are you okay?' Eileen shouted up the stairs on hearing the commotion.

'I'm fine Mum I'm just playing with Biscuit! He's all dizzy and excited that we're home I think...' Rebecca lied. '...Ouch, bad Biscuit...!'

...'Okay then, but calm it down a bit, you need to rest!' Eileen returned to the kitchen and looked to Jess. 'She'll probably have that dog up there all the time now. I don't like him sleeping in her room but if it help...'

The unmistakeable sound of breaking glass was swiftly followed by Jess spotting something out of the corner of her eye spinning downwards into the back garden. In panic Eileen raced up the stairs three at a time and forced open the bedroom door where she found Rebecca standing at the end of the empty bed, before noticing her daughter's shocked pale expression, which was in complete contrast to the blood that covered her hands.

'He started biting me really hard...' Rebecca cried and held her hands up to show the indented teeth marks and scratches. '...I don't know what happened.'

'Where is he...? Eileen looked around then noticed the hole smashed through the top pane. '...did he jump through the window...?'

Rebecca didn't answer at first and moved over to her mother to be held. '...He was biting me so hard. It was as if he wasn't my dog. I really thought he was going to attack my face...so I threw him.' The rest of the sentence was lost within racking sobs and Eileen held her close before persuading her to go downstairs.

'...It will be alright.' She watched her daughter leave the room before going to the window to see Jess in the garden standing over the barely panting body of Biscuit.

61

The two young police officers had cleaned themselves up as well as they could in a public bathroom, even explaining their sartorial predicament to a curious zoo visitor who had clearly noticed the mess they were in. 'No need to worry Sir, we hit a large sheep on our way up the lane!' The officer stated then followed this with a look that conveyed strongly he wasn't willing to say anymore on the subject. The man in the bathroom hadn't actually enquired about what happened, he'd just given them a quizzical stare, but he wasn't completely convinced by the policeman's story. For a start there was a lot of blood on two different uniforms, and when loading his wife and twins into the people carrier he noticed their patrol car didn't have a mark on it, either way it didn't matter he was just happy to be going home.

Harvey meanwhile was sitting in the temporary control room which was part of a new extension adjoining the visitors centre. He was busily requesting the young video operator to zoom in, freeze, roll on and pan to give him every possible view they had of the grounds. They had been doing this for a good ten minutes without success.

'He's got to be here somewhere...' Harvey was talking to himself and completely at a loss to explain their failure to spot the boy. As he stared closely at the different areas and enclosures split into squares on the screen he thought it quite amusing how any creature caught on CCTV immediately looked like it was up to no good. An African bull elephant that would be beautifully majestic in the Serengeti suddenly looked as if it were concealing someone behind it on purpose; a cheetah quickly turned its back end towards the camera as if to say 'What? I ain't seen nuffin!' and even the giraffes seemed to look from side to side fearful of being arrested for stealing the juiciest leaves.

The two washed policemen entered the control room. 'Sir we've cleaned ourselves up after we hit that sheep!' Officer thingy said with a truly awfully delivered lie.

'That's good but I don't need you here do I...?' The Inspector replied. '...Get out there and find him. Taser deployment is authorised...Go!'

Harvey had deepened his voice for greater authority; after all there were zoo workers in here looking at the policemen with confused concern, and these civilians needed to know who was in charge and they were in safe hands. He began tapping his pen on the desk. 'Pan that one round again. Doesn't it go up any higher...?'

'...If you don't mind me saying hofficer...' The voice belonged to the skinny lad with a ginger afro who apparently spoke with a fake Jamaican lilt.

Harvey hadn't expected that accent to come from this young cameraman and instantly found it irritating. '...For future reference I'm an Inspector. You're point is...?' The big red hair was almost hitting him in the face every time the young man turned his head but Harvey remained calm and professional.

'...How ju you know he even here...? Ya boy could have eyeballed the Babylon and carried on towards the hairport...' He sucked his teeth before continuing. '...Or he could have jumped them passenger buses dat just left...?' The afro man/boy lifted his eyes from the screen waiting for a decent answer.

'How do I know he's here...?' Harvey repeated, stalling for time because he didn't feel he could tell anyone the absolute truth. '...Let's just say I have it on very good authority.'

'Who's authority?' Afro kid asked tenaciously but Harvey didn't answer the question, instead preferring to ask his own.

'Do you have a name son?' He asked in an attempt to move the goalposts using all his years of experience.

'Of course...me name is Clarence.'

'Clarence what...?'

'Clarence Ferguson...'

'...Well Clarence Ferguson...this is the situation. I need your assistance to locate a young man who's wanted in connection with at least two murders in the last three days. I strongly suspect he's in your place of work so let me ask you a question...do you believe you've looked and checked everywhere on all of your cameras to be able to tell me categorically that he's not here...?' Harvey was fully expecting his more sinister tone to shut the man up. It failed.

'Yes I can.'

'What?'

'Yeah me can state catagor...I have checked everywhere. I know dis place inside out and he not here!'

Harvey had a strong urge to explain to Clarence the situation using the drawings, he even touched them in his pocket, but he couldn't do it. It would have been embarrassing, and he wasn't going to let fuzz-top Clarence have the pleasure of laughing in his face, so instead he turned to the three other members of zoo staff that were stood around.

'Do you have any other animals, specifically orange ones with short legs anywhere else…?' He asked this in all seriousness but was self-conscious.

The faces in the room were perfectly set in anticipation of a punchline from the Inspector, only it never came because Harvey had gone as far as he could, he'd shown his hand and felt a bit of an idiot. '…Of course I'm not being totally serious…but if I were…do you?'

A bored looking prematurely balding employee slowly raised his hand, and then glanced round at his colleagues before answering the question. 'There's the holding area…' He said in a broad Scottish accent.

'What's the holding area?' Harvey asked.

'It's where newly transferred animals come in and are held. To acclimatise and find their wee feet.'

On hearing this news Harvey jumped up to his own wee feet. '…And where is this holding area?' He wanted answers quickly, already reaching for his radio.

'About half mile further on up the road…you know before you get to the wee airport!'

'Okay another question that could be a joke…any orange animals there?'

'Aye well lions at the moment…but I'd say they're more sandy coloured than orange.'

Harvey immediately liked this guy and pointed his finger directly at him. '…Right! You come with me. Rest of you stay here and lock the doors.'

As they left the building he was already on the radio ordering the other officers to get their arses back to the cars and follow him.

'Okay then, what's your name…?' Harvey asked in hope he wouldn't forget it this time because the man wasn't a young policeman, not even close, this was a bald middle aged zoo employee who worked with lions and so therefore may come in useful.

'James.' He answered while putting his seatbelt on.

'Well James, I'm Inspector Harvey Cooper, and while we wait for our back up I'm going to take this moment to thank you for your assistance. Firstly I'd like you to direct us to the location and afterwards stay close by following my orders. Is that clear…?'

'Aye it's clear!'

The other four officers came running full pelt out of the zoo gates and jumped in their respective vehicles, and after a thumb's up to Harvey the three cars pulled out in convoy.

'So it's just straight along this road?' Harvey double checked.

'Aye, just up beyond those trees.' James assured him.

'Right then James I have to let you in on the big story here. We have a strong belief the man we are going to apprehend may try to enter a lion's enclosure.'

'That would be a stupid thing to do!'

'Agreed, so when we get there we are going to need you to be our eyes and ears on these lions so to speak, keep us informed on what you think of their behaviour, if you suspect they're going to attack, you know lion habits that we might miss. Can you do that James?'

'I can try but there's no guarantee of success.'

'Because they're unpredictable...?' Harvey guessed.

'...Aye there's that...and the fact I don't know anything about lions...'

That news took Harvey by surprise. '...What!'

'I dunna even know why you asked me to come. I do the fish department.' James looked sheepishly across at Harvey, there was a veritable cloud of disbelief in the air, but then turned away when he saw the chain link fence. 'There just there...stop, stop...!' he shouted.

'...Yes I'm stopping thank you James.' All of Harvey's professional courtesy had disappeared as quickly as the man's credentials for this job.

The other two police cars pulled in on either side. Then the Inspector, his four officers, and fish man James looked over at the hole in the fence.

'Does that lead straight in to the Lions enclosure...?' Harvey asked.

'...No, this'll just get you into the main yard. That building over there is where they keep the food. The one beyond that's a quarantine block for sick animals...'

Harvey was relieved to find James at least knew some stuff. '...What's that building at the end with the smoke coming out the chimney?' He asked while climbing through the hole in the fence.

'I'd rather not say.' James said.

The other policemen were following warily, constantly observant, while listening very closely for approaching murderers or lions. When they came to the end of a long shed like structure James turned back to them and urgently whispered.

'Oh my god...I think your man's here!'

'Where...?'

Harvey moved himself carefully to the edge of the building before peering round the wall, James was right, and with a knowing smile he saw Oscar's drawing had also been correct. There he was, the elusive Jay

Cleaver, bold as brass in the lion's enclosure. He was standing atop a circular dirt mound about six feet high and designed for bored lions to climb and play on. Now in Harvey's limited experience on the subject he'd rarely seen a captive lion do much else than sleep, but of course he could now counter that opinion, by accepting he'd never seen a sleeping lion woken up to find a teenage boy standing on its play area.

In a world of his own making Jay Cleaver was ready for battle while blissfully unaware of the police presence. Not that it would have mattered much anyway because he could see the final Big Boss watching him from its enclosure. He was trying to sense its movement and motives, predict its actions, because there was no room for error now, not if he was going to beat the game and attain legendary status in this world.

All this alternate reality in Jays mind was fuelled by a desire to avoid simply being caught and imprisoned. For sure he didn't believe he deserved to be jailed for the old man's stabbing which had been a terrible mistake, a tragic misunderstanding, and only occurring because he'd misread a situation. The farmer had been almost exactly the same sort of problem. Sure on paper it looked as if he'd savagely tried to decapitate an innocent man, but there'd been extenuating circumstances, the guy told Jay he was calling the police so how the hell was he supposed to know he was kidding.

This complete lack of logic that had caused him to become a double murderer didn't make sense to his addled brain, and it had left him with only two options; to make it a game where he could be the hero, or to be arrested and become just another crime statistic. Well finding himself faced with those alternatives there was really no choice to be made because all Jay Cleaver had ever wished for was to be known for something, anything, and this imagined adventure was the perfect end to the confusingly shit life he'd been thrown into. A game that had begun when he went to a window for a cigarette only to find a complete stranger trying to commit suicide and was the moment his entire future had been altered.

Deep down he wasn't too worried about that future right now as his main desire, the one he was crazily excited for, was happening here on top of this tiny hill. Jay surveyed his surroundings with immense pride before raising his stained weapon to the darkening skies, and proclaiming to anyone who would listen...'I'm here...and I'm gonna kill a fucking lion!'

<u>62</u>

The Angel lay Alex down on the white ground, comforted in seeing the man's gently breathing chest, before reseating itself and spinning slowly and patiently around while it waited for the man to wake up, as they needed to speak as soon as possible, there was work to be done. It had to convince this mortal that the life machine was grinding to a halt, or to put it in a more accurate and worrying depiction, the whole universe was going to end in a shudderingly violent big bang. Alex had to understand that the Angel couldn't fix the problem without knowing precisely where it was failing, and to do that it needed more information from a book it couldn't enter. Without the location there was no way it could predict how long they had, but if pushed for such a prophecy it would have to say most probably sooner rather than later. It was becoming frighteningly clear that the glitch, or anomaly, or whatever you wanted to call it was evolving somewhere between their two worlds.

Although it felt there had been no other option it wasn't convinced that allowing Alex to experience the inner workings of the book was its best move. Those meticulous pages were showing this mortal man moments and realities that should remain hidden. Before his last collapse Alex had returned from the book and spoke of the existence of another Angel within the universe. That was an unexpected piece of news and one that would open new dangerous lines of questioning, questions that would need some very careful answering, because regardless of what Alex thought he could not have seen another of its kind. In fact this Angel would wager its rather lengthy life upon the indisputable fact there were no other Angels, not anymore, as those days were long gone.

Alex started to stir so it quickly took the book from his chest and placed it back on the desk.

'Alex...?' The Angel asked as the man's eyes slowly opened.

'...If you say anything along the lines of what are we to do with you I will throw a punch.' He mumbled.

'Have you forgotten? If you threw a punch I would disappear then reappear, I told you.'

'Maybe...if you saw it coming, watch your back is my advice.' Alex displayed a confused smile while climbing to his feet, but he was feeling somehow rejuvenated by his rest, almost as if that downtime had allowed his brain to compartmentalise all it had learned. He took a few paces to stretch his legs before speaking. 'Okay I'll admit...I don't know who you are.'

'In all truth you have never known who I am...' The Angel replied then with a raised eyebrow indicated for Alex to return to the desk. '...But I have been thinking on what you observed in the book and I may have an answer...'

'...Oh I see...you've worked it out while I've been resting again huh? That's convenient isn't it, how you always come up with answers when I'm not in the room so to speak, or is it simply more lies..?'

'...I have told you I cannot lie.'

'Whatever...!' Alex replied but still listened intently as the Angel told him of a universal yin and yang being played out, explaining once more the concept that all things in existence are perpetually balanced, how under certain conditions another entity could actually exist, and how in all probability it must also be the cause of the glitch.

'So basically you're telling me you have an evil twin...that's a bit amateur dramatics isn't it?' Alex furrowed his brow.

'I would suggest more biblical.' The Angel replied.

'Or that...' He agreed. '...Okay let's say your theory makes some kind of sense and I accept it as gospel. What can we do about it?'

'Well evidently we would have to stop it...!' The Angel ruffled its wings.

'But we can't do that.' Alex noted.

'Why can't we...?' It asked and Alex jumped at the opportunity to answer.

'...I'll tell you what, you relax and let me explain this. You see I understand a lot more stuff now. That book is an amazing workout for the old grey matter and my exercised brain surmises that if you kill the other Angel, then you yourself would have to cease existing, because the universe would be unbalanced wouldn't it?' Alex felt some smugness in twisting its idea.

The Angel shrugged. 'Very well...I will have to cease existing.'

'Oh right...and that doesn't concern you...?'

'Of course not...the machine is breaking down. It has a glitch, a blockage, a state of stagnancy that will rapidly spread. Undoubtedly I would give up my own existence to cure that. Tell me Alex would you not give up your life to save all other matter...?'

'Well if you remember I was trying to kill myself so err...I'm probably the wrong person to ask.'

'Of course...' The Angel half smiled. '...But the least you can do is help. You have to go back in.'

As Alex was drawn to the book once more his mind prickled at the thought of just one more hit, one last trip into those pages of perfect clarity, although he did remember saying never again. It was far too tempting because he was learning so much about himself, for instance even now he was beginning to understand a great deal about the slippery pole of pure addiction, of which a key strategy is the deceptive declaration to fool oneself daily, to insist that everything is under control, that you are going to change, and this last time will definitely be the never again.

The Angel stroked its fingers slowly across the leather cover waiting.

'Now that we have a touchstone, the exact moment you fell from the building, we can go back in and...'

It stopped speaking at the sight of Alex's raised hand. '...I don't need a touchstone or a guide. I understand how it works...just tell me what you want and I'll go in and get it!'

A concerned look fell over the Angels face. 'Be careful Alex, respect what the book represents, it contains all of existence within its pages... '

'...I know it does but clearly you weren't listening...! 'Alex was interrupting freely now, confident in his new abilities. '...I went so deep into the book last time, into a life that I already knew, and worked out all by myself what I could really do in there and I broke through what it was showing me into another realm...a different dimension...deep into the spine where the demon hides.'

The Angel pursed its perfect lips. 'Very well...then we need a plan. What do we know of our glitch problem?'

Alex had a small unformed theory but was assured enough now to air it anyway. '...We know that I'm part of it somehow and if your summary's right then the other Angel is also linked with it...' Some pride was growing as Alex felt he was starting to get these fantastical questions correct.

'True...' The Angel was tapping its forefingers gently on the book. '...we also know where the stagnancy began; somewhere in the place you call home, Edinburgh. Within that area is where the glitch between the realities lies. The other Angel could have entered at some fractured point in the same way that you exited to arrive here?'

Alex listened and understood perfectly before attempting to improve the Angel's thought. 'If you don't mind I'd like to simplify that, just for myself. So there's a tiny hole or fracture, a split even, between our realities that the other entity caused and then by sheer chance I fell straight through it as well, but in the opposite direction...?'

The Angel allowed this impudence to slide before speaking. '...That is what I said.'

'I know, but I said it better...' Alex added a wink.

As gracious as it tried to be it couldn't let that insolence go unmentioned. '...This is not a game!' The Angel said slamming its hand on the desk before regaining some composure. 'You have to concentrate and be ready for what lies ahead. Every second you spend inside those pages will change you.'

'It's already changing me...and it's wonderful.' He needed to experience the book again whatever the cost. 'So what do I have to do?'

'Quite obviously you have to kill it!' The Angel stroked the book subconsciously.

'...Are you fucking serious...killing a demon?'

'Yes! However you have to find it first.'

'I know where it is!'

'No...you know where it was!

'So it's moving?'

'Wouldn't you if you had just been discovered...?

Alex thought about that and found he couldn't disagree with its point, the Demon had detected his presence, aimed itself directly towards him. '...So how do I find it again?'

'Logically of course...It's in Edinburgh somewhere although I'm quite sure it won't resemble me as that would surely stand out in your world, so if it has managed to remain hidden, in for what all we know could be millennia, then we must presume it is concealed completely, and based on those facts I believe like all good hunters we should start by looking for its tracks.'

'How do I do that...?'

'You need to look around in your life, in the past of course never trust the future that can be changed with a single word, but your life Alex, is all we have to work with, so using it we need to find a pattern, a trail if you will, then we can identify and confront it.'

'You still mean kill it?'

'Of course...'

'Could I even do that? You of all entities must appreciate I have no physical presence inside the book, all I can do is observe. I'm barely even particles when I'm in there. The actual me in that world, the physical me that could possibly do something about this…he's a one armed man in a coma…!'

To allay any self-doubts that were thinking of taking root, and to avoid the question, the Angel opened the book.

Alex fell silent, then fell in.

63

The large male lion slowly gathered itself to stand on enormous paws; it shook its thick mane before fixing an unblinking gaze on the intruder then padded forward from its enclosure, where it now stood defiantly and its sheer bulk drew the teenager's full attention.

'Fuck!' Jay whispered while gripping the knife tightly in his skinny fingers ready to face his final challenge. All the craziness of the past few days had been building up to this event but he was ready, he wanted this, win or lose he wanted this. The huge lion was around fifteen paces away but Jay wasn't giving up his advantage of the high ground, no way, that big old cat was just going to have to come up and get him.

The lion paced to its left then turned right, it was moving slowly, its focus fixed on the boy because this was new. With its entire life spent in captivity it had no knowledge of the wild, since being a cub it had been handled and was well used to the sight of humans being around. It had none of the experiences a wild lion would learn but in the blink of its eye, rising up from deep inside, an instinct raw and untamed took over its powerful body. The reason for this was primeval and perfectly natural. It was because it perceived the boy as a threat, and the lion could not allow any threats to be here at this time. So it held its ground swaying slowly from side to side, watching the boy become entranced, and that was just perfect for its next move.

Harvey Cooper, his four man unit and fish guy James, stepped carefully towards the enclosure witnessing the standoff between boy and considerable beast. As they approached it became clear how Jay had managed to get inside; by climbing on a low wall and using a cable, probably electrical, that was slung across the water. This was of course no use to lions but perfect for a skinny boy to grab and shimmy across.

'Jay...!' Harvey tried quietly but the boy remained silent, impassively watching the lion, which to be fair was exactly what Harvey was doing. '...Jay, its Inspector Cooper we met back in Dalmeny Street...do you remember?

Stupid question, of course Jay remembered the Inspector but he hadn't wanted to talk to him back then and certainly didn't want to talk to him now.

Harvey knew he had to cobble a plan together and quickly. 'Spread out around the enclosure...get as close as you can to him...safely...Tasers ready!'

The unit obediently moved into position surrounding the boy. The closest officer to Jay was about fifteen feet away and Harvey reckoned that may just be sufficient for successful Taser deployment, and he also knew his next call would be extremely important, even though at the moment he had absolutely no idea what it would be.

The lion continued its slow pacing and swaying clearly interested in the skinny interloper.

Harvey looked back over his shoulder to find James stood back, smoking a cigarette. 'What are you doing...is that absolutely necessary...?' He asked with disdain.

'...Well aye, I'm finding this a very stressful situation.' James replied before blowing out a grey cloud.

'...Put it out now and get over here!'

James obeyed Harvey's request but not without an insubordinate huff.

'Do you know anything at all about lions?' Harvey was becoming desperate.

'Not really, I've a wee cat at home...but that's not the same is it?'

Harvey thought probably not, but he'd never been much of an animal person. His wife kept two goldfish in the kitchen but he didn't want to get into that with James right now.

'So what kind of things does your cat do...?'

Harvey felt he was walking a fine line between making a plan and having a polite conversation.

'It just sleeps and eats...that's it.'

'That's it, of course...!' Harvey said.

'Aye...!' James nodded.

'...No I mean that's it! Go and get me something that lion will eat...and do it fast...'

Thinking on his feet, James didn't move fast until he was out of sight of the lion, then he ran full pelt to the food stores, frantically raiding the first fridge he found before running back to the Inspector.

'Will this do?'

Harvey eyed the rugby ball sized piece of meat. 'I would have thought so yes. Now take it down to the other end of the enclosure. Try and get the lion to come towards you. I'm thinking if we can get a little time, and a lion with a full stomach, we just might be able to get him out.'

257

'Excuse me…' James looked at Harvey. '…you want me to just go and tempt a lion…?'

'…No, I want you to help save that boy's life!'

'Aye okay, but I tell you now if I get hurt I will put in a claim…'

Suddenly the lion snarled, and pounced forward to within eight feet of Jay before turning to amble back, a full on bluff charge. The big cat was toying with the boy and fair play to Jay Cleaver he hadn't taken a backward step thought Harvey, who surprisingly found himself gritting his teeth. He relaxed his jaw slowly while he looked across to his unit's four standing positions. If they could just get the lion far enough away they could Taser deploy on Cleaver, but of course that would raise the obvious problem of getting the incapacitated boy out safely and smoothly, and as this Inspector was beginning to understand, nothing moved safely or smoothly in a lion's world.

Harvey could see Fish guy James hanging over the wall waving the big hunk of meat and making the same noise he probably used on his own cat. A sort of CHH CHH CHH, now whether the lion was picking up the scent of the meat, or that sound was actually irresistible to all cats he couldn't say, but this beast was certainly showing a distinct interest. For the first time its full attention wasn't on the boy, and even if Harvey didn't have a full strategy yet, maybe just maybe there was a small chance he could bring this to a safe ending.

The boy stood atop his tower of dirt and watched the lion disengage its attention, it turned and began to warily slink away, heading for a bald man offering it some meat at the other end of the enclosure. Jay's eyes darted around to see officers on all sides looking at him, and then he stared down straight into the gaze of Harvey Cooper, the policeman who just wouldn't stop messing up his fucking days.

For Jay this was another moment where his life began to change, it was out of his control, as incrementally the video game fantasy started to fall apart. He was realising who he was but more importantly where he was, no longer a battling player on the cusp of victory, but a boy on a hill in a lions enclosure with policemen watching. This cold reality was starting to dilute the fantasy and nothing felt as exciting as it should, he began to tremble as one does when adrenaline runs dry to decrease the blood flow, and all of this simply meant that Jay was now completely aware of his surroundings and seriously beginning to question his reasons for being here. He doubted all the motivation he'd been following so strictly because fact was killing fiction, he was in trouble, hearing every pound of his shaking heart as he began to feel stupid and scared.

'Jay can you hear me...?' Harvey tried again as he noticed the boy's body language alter. '...Jay...?' He was whispering loudly because he was pretty sure shouting wouldn't help anything.

'...What?' Jay responded with a frightened forced whisper.

'We're going to get you out of there okay. First of all I need you to drop that knife.' Harvey was smoothly transitioning into police negotiator mode, a skill he'd trained in for years, although he had to admit this wasn't a common practice scenario. He looked to his left and the lion had almost reached the unexpected treat the bald man was offering.

'Drop the knife, throw it away, then we can sort this.' Harvey asked again.

'But there's a fucking lion!' He answered through gritted teeth.

'I know there is Jay, but let's be honest, I don't think that knife would do you much good. You'd have to be pretty lucky to win that fight and then we would still have to get you out of there afterwards...so throw down the knife...away from you...!'

Harvey was already thinking fast about what to do next if Jay complied.

'Okay.' Jay said and tossed the bloodied cleaver down into the moat where it splashed heavily.

Alright then, that's gone, thought Harvey, quickly piecing together another few seconds of his unfinished symphony of a plan. He looked again towards the lion that now had its meat; it was holding it down with one giant paw to tear at it with its many giant teeth. Okay we can do this, of course we can.

'Okay Jay, that's really good son. Now I need you to move carefully but quickly...okay...grab that cable and get out the same way you got in.'

After a brief considering pause Jay began to move slowly, staring at the lion all the time, as he shuffled slowly down the hill towards the cable. At this rate it could be thirty seconds before he got there so he considered running, of throwing caution to the wind to leap on the cable like Spiderman, scramble across so that big lion wouldn't be able to get near him.

Harvey was watching Jays progress intently and wishing it was over with already, but each step the boy made and every bite the lion took of its now half eaten meal seemed to be in some uncomfortable measured sync.

'...Sir...SIRRR...!' A male voice disturbed the suspense.

The officer on the other side of the enclosure behind Jay was shouting. Harvey looked over immediately to rebuke the man but when he saw the new problem arising he wholeheartedly agreed this new situation deserved such a hearty call.

Jay turned to look as well, then immediately wished he hadn't.

The sleeping lioness had awoken to the smell of meat. Most probably the sounds wouldn't have woken her, she was used to that after living in various crowded zoos, but the smell of a hunk of flesh always triggered a response. As she stalked out of the shadows she couldn't see her mate, or where he was feeding, all she could see was the boy, and all she could feel was hunger.

Jay panicked and started to run the final ten feet to the cable.

The lioness started to run the fifteen feet to the boy.

Jay was leading the race and ready to leap, he put his full weight down on his right leg to get the lift, but never got off the ground. The faster lioness had pounced forward to catch his trailing left leg with a heavy swipe that knocked him over and into the dirt. Now her prey was on the ground and whimpering she moved in closer to see more clearly what she'd brought down.

Jay could feel the heat on his leg as blood began to pour out of the severed wound, looking across at Harvey he raised his hand, begging through teared filled eyes for help. The helpless Inspector mentally punched himself because he should have known; there had clearly been two orange blob animals with stick legs in Oscar's drawing, but it was too late now. Harvey didn't want to watch as the lioness padded towards the stricken boy and sniffed at his leg. She could taste the warm blood on her nose and began pacing round the struggling boy looking for the killer bite. Jays face told Harvey it was all over, as the Inspector looked over to see the male lion leaving the last chunk of its treat, it began to move towards the new action, but the lioness noticed this and growled at the lion, he backed off a little way as she pushed her snout towards the back of Jay's scrawny neck and opened her jaws.

All of a sudden the lioness stiffened before falling in a heap next to the boy. Harvey could see her legs twitch before she urinated, and then he noted the thin wires leading to two silver points sticking out from her fur. The officer stood closest to the boy had tasered the lioness. With the whole moment reaching a terrible juncture he hadn't known what else to do. The lioness was prone, her body quivering at the bottom of the mound, while the large male was clearly confused, and having just eaten it headed for the safety of its enclosure.

'James?' Harvey shouted as the big lion disappeared into the shadows.

'Aye...?' the bald man lumbered over.

'So help me god, you'd better be able to get us in there?'

'It's just a big latch...on the door...down there.' James set off to the gate situated back down where he had just been. Harvey followed him.

Six long and unbelievably tense minutes later, and with the air ambulance en route, Jay Cleaver was carried out of the enclosure. One of the officers immediately began tightening a tourniquet on his leg to keep him alive, while the other officers lowered their weapons. Thankfully the large male lion had played along, keeping out of the way, and hadn't needed shocking. The lioness was still on its side, stunned, panting heavily but alive, as the door was locked.

Harvey looked around at his team, the two officers he didn't know by name were talking about the tasered lioness now gingerly climbing back to its feet, muddled but otherwise unharmed. The other two officers whose names he knew but had forgotten were on their radios guiding various ambulance and service crews in. This had been an unprecedented situation and he was proud of all five of them. James the fish guy deserved a medal he thought, and the other officers were worthy of commendations because this had been a job to never forget. As he walked round the group he gave each of them a pat on the back before finding himself face to face with the bald man.'...Thank you James, we couldn't have done it without you! I'll be sure to mention you glowingly in all of my reports.'

'Aye...it was an honour serving under you.' James replied and lit a cigarette.

Harvey couldn't tell if he was being sincere or not, but at that precise moment he also couldn't care less, they had got Jay Cleaver out alive, and once more his job was the best one in the world.

64

Rebecca Jones had slept solidly since the horrible events with Biscuit earlier in the day, thanks to the aid of a mild sedative, but had now awoken frantically trying to recall why the puppy wasn't in the bed with her, the whole thing a blurred space in her memory. The clock told her it was midnight as she groggily found her way to the bathroom. Pulling the cord she flinched at the light entering her eyes and sat down, on the floor in front of her was an empty space where Biscuit should have been, and knew her decision back in that layby had caused this. She was getting upset and wanted a word with the thing that was causing her to feel this way. After making her way silently downstairs she stepped into the kitchen and found her mums emergency pack of cigarettes, they were, as always, pointlessly hidden in the back of the canned food cupboard. Then Rebecca located the lighter behind the toaster and went out into the moonlit garden where sat on a wooden bench she inhaled her first nicotine in close to three years, it made her head spin wildly for a moment, before she inhaled some more and drew up the courage.

Can I ask you some questions?

You can ask me anything but I don't have to answer.

Rebecca was still having trouble believing she was talking to a voice in her head. Knowing this wasn't a different part of her personality pretending to come through in an imaginary fashion, and it wasn't as if she was going crazy, this was quite simply another being, an overly aggressive being that was occupying her brain. It had been in total desperation that she'd allowed its inception, because there was no way she was going to die behind a hedgerow in a layby, point-blank refusing to be just another helpless young woman caught by Oscar Downes the serial killer. Only he wasn't a serial killer, he was just a physical murder weapon that the voice inside her now had wielded.

Do you have any questions, Rebecca?

Yes, For starters what do you call me?

Rebecca.

I know that, I mean, what am I to you, am I a host or a vessel, a weapon or...could I be a friend?

I can tell you one thing Rebecca...one thing that is very true. You are my first female.

Right well great, I don't know if I should be honoured that it's me or disappointed because I know you had no choice really. *(Silence)* So is it any different that I'm a female?

There are certainly a lot more questions.

Is that a joke? *(Silence)* So men never asked you things?

Men do as I order without question.

Yeah I bet. Listen I need to ask you something important because I have to understand it, if this is going to work.

HA, ha, ha. It will work. It always works.

Why did you kill my dog?

Me…? You threw it out of the window.

I didn't. I would never do that.

I believe little Biscuit may dispute that point

Are you going to make me kill people and stuff them in barrels, that's what you made Oscar do wasn't it?

Go to bed Rebecca!

I don't want to and you can't make me.

Rebecca! I don't usually give warnings but this is your last chance…go to bed.

Petulantly she sat holding on to the bench and waited to see what it would do, how it would manifest itself in controlling her, because there was not a chance she was going to move by herself.

Go to bed! (Silence) *Very well…let's go and kill your mother.*

What? Don't say that!

Rebecca found herself walking briskly back to the kitchen and there wasn't a damn thing she could do about it. Her fists were balled tight and already she knew these hands were going to beat her sleeping mother to death where she lay. Without hesitation her feet climbed the stairs and she watched her hand move to the bedroom door, as it opened slowly she could see her mother's sleeping head on the pillow, illuminated by the streetlight through the crack in the curtains.

'NOOOOO…!' Rebecca screamed inside of her head while standing framed in the doorway petrified and still. This confident young woman was shown to be just a little girl in disguise, with all self-control taken from her, and at the mercy of a monsters will. A tear fell down her cheek which she tried to wipe but couldn't move a muscle.

Go to bed Rebecca.

Yes

Now thank me for the only mercy I will ever give you!

Thank you!

The voice fell silent leaving this daughter and her sleeping mother in peace. Rebecca was suddenly able to move freely and quickly returned to her room. The tear was finally wiped when she lay back down, and all was quiet but for the gentle night sounds breezing in through a broken window pane.

65

Alex raised his head to take in the sight of the Angel's beautifully flawless skin. Moments ago he'd exited the book after hundreds of attempts at finding a demon in his own world. There had been intensely detailed searches from his first memories until his last, depending on your point of view, to find some identifiable track the demon may have left behind. 'This is so difficult…!' Alex complained to the Angel, only to find himself challenging one of his own previous announcements, and now believing those four words could easily qualify as the biggest understatement of his life.

'Rest again, Alex!' The Angel requested.

Together they were seeking some pattern in a universe of memories that dragged Alex in deeper every time he looked, because this whole experience wasn't like seeing pictures in a normal book; it was an all-consuming cacophony of joy, intrigue, love and pain hitting him like a tidal wave would on a grain of sand. Also as a team they weren't the perfect pairing when one couldn't see the pages while the other didn't know what to look for, but some progress was being made. As Alex became better skilled in the ways of controlling his memory searches he found he could move on quickly from scene to scene and wasn't getting himself so entangled. In the beginning these journeys had seemed impossible to control, where every moment of his past existence became a trap to pull him further in as he followed all the beauteous breadcrumbs of his every emotion and reality replayed. There were times spent with family, friends and special places, all experienced through again, only this time he knew how they ended. One of the hardest memories relived had been the unadulterated joy of feeling a hug from his Grandma, before it became a broken heart doubled as he once more experienced the devastation of her passing.

It was all within this book and although quite naturally most chapters ended in some level of sorrow there was so much love on the journey, so much love in his world, and he was seeing all of it in an overwhelming cascade of depth and lucidity to the point where knew he would never be the same again. The mortal man Alex Webb was gone forever, and whoever lay in that hospital bed unconscious, unknowing and with one arm missing, would never be who he was becoming now.

'We need to try something else...' The Angel stated and ruffled his wings in a feathered form of frustration. '...There has to be another way to find it!'

'What if there's not?' Alex was tired but recovering fast. He reckoned he could go another couple of rounds.

'If there's not...?' The Angel looked up once more to the white sky. '...Well if there's not then this universe will end a lot sooner that it should, of course before all of that happens the demon shall continue its killing, causing pain and destruction to everyone it meets while you and I remain here helpless, and spending the time we have left knowing just one thing, that we have failed because of our ineptitude!'

Alex was pretty sure he knew what ineptitude meant but didn't want to show any weakness by asking the Angel for conformation. He didn't feel it would be appropriate when they were getting on so well, so instead he chose to go on with what he was really thinking, although it was neither cheery nor helpful. 'I'm going out on a limb here but people die every second of every day, this book is proving that fact to me over and over...so if this demon is killing a few more then...I don't see how it makes much difference!'

The Angel gave Alex a quite curious look. '...Really, so you don't believe every soul is unique, equally important and deserves to live it's allotted time?'

'No of course I do...that's not what I'm saying.' Alex was trying to articulate and justify his clearly fatalistic comment.

'Then what are you saying...?' The Angel really wanted to hear this.

'...I'm trying to get my head around it, that even if we found this thing and stopped it...people are going to carry on dying in other ways.' For all his new found confidence Alex was struggling to explain himself clearly so the Angel took the opportunity to help him understand.

'Yes of course they will but this is what the machine has always given us, balance, and a natural scale where a person dies so a new one is born. Even if, or to be more accurate when, the last human dies there would still be balance in the natural order of the universe, this is how the life machine works. The monster we seek is within that machine now and it has weight and enough solidity to shift the equilibrium and it should not be there. It is also the cause of the glitch that is slowing the machine down so our troubles are two fold, but we can fix all of it if we can stop the demon existing.' The Angel's green eyes had sparkled when it spoke.

'Okay...then what you're saying is that all of this, well everything bound up in the fabric of our universe, is dependent on me?' Alex asked because he wanted to hear the Angel say it out loud.

'No, not at all, it depends on us...working together!'

'Right so we will be the heroes then?'

'In our own minds yes, but only briefly, because almost undoubtedly we will both die in the process.'

Well the Angel had finished that conversation on an extremely bum note, Alex thought. He sighed deeply and looked at the book sat under its resting hand and desired its gifts again. That little six by four inch red leather hardback was rapidly becoming his only wish, after all it was his, theirs, and everyone else's apparently, only hope. Without him going in again they could never find the Demon, but of course if he went in and found it that would still only be half the job. After that they would be stuck again because how do you stop a murderous Demon when you have no physical presence...?

'Then we must gain a physical presence.' The Angel said.

'Stop reading my mind!'

'I'm trying not to...' The Angel touched Alex gently on the back of his hand. '...I want you to go back to the window ledge when you fell.'

'Not again, I've done that a thousand times already and it isn't exactly a highlight of my life!'

'We need to know more about the boy who was there...'

'...Why? He was just a cruel kid that didn't help me!' Alex railed against the Angel's idea and it responded in kind.

'He was there when everything changed for you and when that happened, everything changed for me as well, also to be honest, as I always am...I haven't got any better ideas.'

'Obviously...!' Alex replied under his breath.

The Angel resisted the temptation to bite back. 'Just find that moment then follow him!'

'Follow him, who the boy in the window...where to?'

'To the demon...obviously...!' The Angel said returning the comment with a hint of sarcasm.

'...Why...you reckon that kid knows the demon?'

'No Alex...because I've got nothing else...!'

So a mortal man journeyed into an Angel's book again but when he came back out he slammed his hand on the desk in an act of frustration. He'd gone back to Dalmeny Street, good old memory number one, and he'd seen the boy but couldn't follow him. Not when a total and utter overriding natural instinct made him stay within his own body, even when the boy stole his wallet, Alex just followed his own life and ended up bumping back to the white world. How in hell are you supposed to fight that urge, you can't follow someone else's life when you are umbilically attached to your own...are you reading my mind now Mr Angel?

'I got something about *'umbilically'* but that was all. It just looked like you were complaining...' The Angel wore the slightest hint of a smile.

'How can I follow someone else's life when I'm inside my own memories? Do you see why that won't work...?'

'Yes of course I do, in the memories of your own life you can't follow him because you didn't see where he went, you have no recollection, because you were flat on the road and you have to stay with yourself because this is all about you...'

'...Exactly and that's the fault in your reasoning!' Alex felt embarrassed for even having tried to do it.

The Angel unfurled its wings so the man knew there was something big on the way. 'Not as clever as you think are you?' It said.

'I'm getting there...'

'...Not really, if you are failing to understand the basics of the book...you aren't in a world of your memories Alex, you are in a world that contains your memories, and also everyone else's. So in fact all you have learned is how to look at your own life, and like any conscious organism looking at your self is primarily the most rewarding interest. However having searched through your memories we found nothing to help us, therefore we need to follow the only other person who might be of use, and to do that you need to advance your skills.'

'Really and how do I do that?' Alex asked.

'I wouldn't know...but I can assure you of one certainty Alex. You have to start thinking in a different way, in a new direction I would best describe as more universal and less self-centred, this isn't just about you anymore.'

'Fine...I'll do that then. Open the bloody book...!' Alex demanded acerbically and was instantly on his way back to the cobbled street to follow the boy in the blue tracksuit.

66

A week had passed since the arrest of Jay Cleaver and the authorities had more than enough evidence to push forward with his case. A court hearing about his double murder charge had been arranged for exactly three weeks but until then he'd recover from his mauled leg injury at Longmarsh prison.

It's where all the bad ones end up thought Harvey, although for once Jay Cleaver wasn't his main concern today, he had new interviews to conduct involving the case of Oscar Downes. Ironically the Superintendent had put him back on the serial killers case almost as a reward for catching the teenager, and yes Harvey found it quite funny that it had taken risking his life in a lion's den to get what he wanted, but quite a few things had changed since the events at the zoo. For instance Oscar's pictures were now in his second drawer down; a week ago they'd been in his jacket pocket before their relegation to the top desk drawer, proof they were slowly falling down the pecking order, and being put out to pasture, for those who can handle their metaphors mixed.

Harvey's first interview was booked for 10 AM; it was now 9.26 so he decided to fish them out and have another look, hoping they would get him into the correct frame of mind for discussions about the man who'd drawn the childish scribbles. Of course Harvey still couldn't fathom just how Oscar had done them, unless the whole story of an evil entity in his head were true, but over a week had passed since their last meeting and his initially strong acceptance of the supernatural was beginning to fade, although opening up the pictures and seeing the images again was certainly tipping the scales back towards...well maybe.

He scanned over them, while in his head he gave short critical appraisals, first up was the park scene with a UFO shooting daggers down, this image remained a mystery and one he really didn't hold much hope of ever actually happening, so Harvey classed it as useless, yet strangely he also thought it was by far the artists most complete and detailed work. This was followed by Oscar's modern classic entitled 'MAN FALLS FROM WINDOW OBSERVED BY BLUE BOY AND ANGEL' which Harvey thought to be his most profound work, but also the one he'd spent hours studying already so he moved on. Picking up the next, it was the most personal piece for this critic as he studied once more a moody abstract that Harvey titled, COMA ROOM.

Moving onwards through a most productive period for the artist, he'd then produced an as yet untitled work depicting an unrecognisable male having his head bitten by a large green dinosaur. There was no observable blood on show so maybe the man moved out the way just in time, but those teeth looked pretty damn close to his skull, but what did it matter anyway as blatantly this was another picture of a non-event, mainly due to a mass extinction sixty six million years ago. Harvey was sure it could be discarded but then, oh what do we have here Mr Downes, an oversight by the Inspector on his first viewing but there it was, over to the left standing in a white gap between the green trees, the Angel again with white on white aiding its excellent concealment, Harvey considered that perhaps he hadn't noticed the figure the first time because of its unimportance to the problem at the zoo, and to be fair he'd also been looking through them quite sharply at the time as his whole career had been at risk.

So Harvey went totally logical on the recurring Angel theme, but not before checking the time, 9.37 okay, time was on his side. Now think Inspector think, what could it mean that there are two Angels in two different pictures, the one where a man is falling and the one with a dinosaur. He thought on it but couldn't find any great epiphany, so his brief summary followed that perhaps Oscar is quietly religious and/or enjoys drawing Angels occasionally. He placed the drawing down having nothing more to add on it then threw a light on the next piece in this Oscar Downes retrospective. Now Harvey considered himself to be a good man, while accepting his humour could be a little dark, and he was proving that description to be accurate after he'd unconsciously titled the next picture, FARMER AT REST. His keen eyes explored the blue tractor and the brown shed and the farmer with his head missing, of course on closer inspection the head wasn't actually missing it was hanging back against the shoulder blades, all the red crayon blood Oscar had rubbed on being unhelpful with details, and this piece he honestly thought, needed no more words.

Now to the wonderful picture that saved a man's life and this policeman his pension, which Harvey simply called 'THE LIONS DEN', Jay Cleaver on a hill shouting 'completed', which now struck Harvey as a little odd because he'd been there and Jay had shouted nothing of the sort. Of course Harvey was becoming aware that trying to take these pictures too literally was a minefield, for instance in his first hand opinion the two orange blob animals with stick legs in the drawing had been a lot bloody scarier in real life. A less forgiving critique than his may even suggest that perhaps the artist had missed a little of their power and majesty…and their massive bloody teeth.

This brought him down to the final piece of work, which was difficult to comment on because there wasn't a great deal to it, being nothing more than an abstract red border around a blank middle, in reality a framed nothing. Harvey placed it on top of the rest and checked the clock, 9.50, the perfect time to go get a coffee before entertaining his first interview. Hopefully these witnesses would be of some use in tying up the loose ends of Oscar's case. Flipping his notebook open he saw the first name scribbled down next to ten o'clock. It was a forty seven year old man who had spent a lot of time with the accused over the last few months, one Allan Kosminsky. He'd been the senior guard in the facility. Okay let's get this over with thought Harvey as he stood, straightened his tie, and left for the interview room.

'Now then Mr Kosminsky, are you okay, do you need a drink…?' The female officer asked as she popped the large man down on the interview room chair. He shook his head in response and she left thinking he seemed nice enough but wasn't convinced he was all there mentally.

Kosminsky thought the police lady was very pleasant as she left the room but all thoughts of her disappeared when she was immediately replaced by a bright and breezy Harvey Cooper.

'Good morning, I'm Inspector Cooper, Mr…sorry is it Kosmink…?'

'…Kosminsky!' The man stated in an almost weary tone.

'Of course well thank you for your time.'

'It's Polish' Kosminsky stated.

'Good, good…so you know why you're here today and you're aware there are cameras and other recording tech around. Please don't feel pressured by it all, we're not trying to catch you out, we just have to keep evidence for our prosecution procedures you understand. So please if you could be as straight and truthful as possible in answering my questions…okay?'

'…Yes.'

Kosminsky took in a large breath which Harvey noticed, and he didn't need any of his skills in body language 'tells' to see he was either uncomfortable or troubled by having to go through with this. Harvey wasn't totally surprised by this revelation, he'd read the initial report of how this man had spent a whole night locked in a small room with the partially scalped female corpse of one Doctor Katherine Kelly. The

Inspector thought it might be wise to not open with questions about that, so instead he proffered. 'Right then, you were the guard on duty during Oscars escape yes?'

'Well I wasn't exactly on duty at the time. I was locked in my guard room with a mutilated doctor when he escaped.'

'...Yes you were, very good...' Harvey took it all back about starting the interview gently and noted his body language reading skills maybe needed a little refreshing. '...So could we perhaps clear up one grey area we have in your initial statement. It says here that you have no recollection of how you ended up being locked in that room. Does that still stand?'

Harvey watched Kosminsky's head rock on its neck muscles which was a sure sign of someone trying to release tension. Harvey could only hope it was for the truth.

'...I do remember now...what happened.'

'You do, that's excellent news! So from the beginning could you tell me exactly how it all went...?'

'...He took over my mind.' Kosminsky stared straight at Harvey during this admission with a look that screamed please understand I'm not crazy.

'Took over your...I'm sorry, in what way precisely?'

'I don't know...like mind control I suppose...I remember going to his cell because he was trying to eat crayons.'

Harvey had nothing to add to that statement so he didn't.

Kosminsky continued. 'I got there in time to stop him and made sure his airways were clear then I confiscated his crayons. It was all perfectly procedural.'

'Of course...!' Harvey spoke because he felt he should say something.

'Then I locked him in and I was walking down the corridor...that was when he screamed. I was shocked...he'd never made a sound before!'

'What type of scream, was it one of pain, shock, fear?'

The guard paused as he considered the best word to use. 'Desperation...!'

'Desperation...?' Harvey repeated as a question.

'...Yeah, the kind that you can't ignore...so I returned to see what happened and he was just standing there...looking at me.'

'He didn't attack you or threaten you?'

'No...don't recall anything like that. I didn't feel anything...but the next time I was sure I was awake I was...locked in my room.' The man was visibly trembling as Harvey realised this was the part of the story the guard was uncomfortable with and not so much the dead doctor.

'...Can you recall anything in between, were you asleep, or drugged perhaps. I'm just trying to get a picture....'

Kosminsky stood up and pushed his chair away gently, choosing to walk around the room as he related his story, and although it wasn't the Inspectors normal procedure to let an interviewee do this Harvey was reluctant to stop the big mans flow.

'...I was in a maze, in my head, looking for Oscar and he...he was in the middle of it.'

'Okay and you believe you were being manipulated in some way by the prisoner to see this...maze?' Harvey's fascination was increasing at the tricks Oscar could do, not only prophetic art but now hypnosis as well, impressive stuff, although Harvey wasn't prepared to believe in demons yet. Big Allan Kosminsky was clearly agitated and becoming more so, but Harvey knew the watching officers behind the one way glass would be ready if he turned too unruly.

Suddenly the man slammed his large hands on the wall then turned to face him. 'He was hiding in the maze....inside his head not mine. There was...it's really hard to explain...''...It's alright. Just take your time.'

'He was trapped and scared...calling out for me to find him.'

'How did you feel when you woke up from the maze...?'

'...I was pissed off with him. When I realised he'd locked me in and broke all my computer stuff...if I'd got my hands on him then...but this last week it's all come back and I think I understand it now.'

'What do you understand Mr Kosminsky...?'

'That Oscar...has got somebody else in his head!'

At that moment Harvey felt a rush through his body he couldn't fully explain, it conveyed both shock and excitement mixed in with a light headed disbelief, as his thoughts were once more dragged towards a truth he'd been trying to deny.

'Did you witness that somebody else...?'

'...No.'

'Then how could you be sure...?'

'...Because I was there...!' The big man snapped back.

Harvey stood up calmly. '...If you don't mind Mr Kosminsky I'd just like to take a few minutes. I'll get a drink sent in for you and I'll return shortly. Excuse me...!' He then left the room which was extremely unusual, so when the female officer locked the door she asked him if everything was okay. '...Oh yes I'm fine. I'm just feeling a little err...I've got a bit of a...get Mr Kosminsky whatever he needs...I'll be back shortly.'

67

Rebecca had chosen to discard that offending bandage a few days early, her entry wound now covered with a small piece of white tape, which she felt was ample protection for the remaining stitches which the doctor had said would dissolve away. She also hadn't followed his other piece of advice about wearing a hat; instead she'd rediscovered head scarves. Trying a blue silk one in the mirror she thought back to the Biscuit incident, and the terrifying moment she'd almost murdered her mother. It had been perfectly calm for two days now and it was no coincidence that in that time the voice had been quiet, she liked it that way, being in no rush to try and chat with it again. It did concern her that the dreams she'd been having were deep and worrying, knowing that when they occurred the voice was behind them, but a gentle tap on her bedroom door took her attention to better thoughts.

'Hello...?'

'...Hi Becky, its Jess...'

Rebecca thought it quite telling their conversation was taking place with the door closed.

'...I just wanted to let you know that Biscuit is going to be okay. I took him straight to the vets and they operated on his little legs. It's going to take a few weeks and he's got one of those lamp shades things to stop him biting his stitches, but he should be fine. He's in front of the fire at the moment in a cage. I just thought I'd let you know, I'll keep him round at mine a little longer, you do understand don't you...?'

She said she did, thanked her, and sat on her bed a bit overwhelmed by the news that *she* hadn't killed him. Unfortunately her joy was brutally countered by a heavy feeling of double loss; she had no idea how she could ever see her puppy again, or even have him inside the house, and as Jess told her the good news Rebecca had felt the tension between them, the friendly neighbour act was just that now, and she could tell the relationship with her 'other mother' had been severely dented. Anyway it was no time now for trying to understand her neighbour, Rebecca had to get ready. Trying a white scarf round her head she removed it quickly, with it looking as if she'd just reapplied the bandages, and threw it back in the wardrobe. Finally choosing the blue one she was busy tying it up when the voice spoke suddenly, the sound of it making her jump and initiating a wave of nausea.

What are you doing Rebecca?

I've got an appointment. Where have you been...?

I've been busy...searching.

What for?

For everyone who has ever hurt you. It's my gift of revenge.

What? No I don't want to do any of that!

Are you going to need more lessons in how to behave?

Of course not...but I can't do that. People would work it out. If I went around killing people I didn't like the police would soon know it was me...us!

So you don't want my gift?

No.

You know I can make you do it of course.

Yes but I don't want us to get caught and put in prison.

You will discover it's always more enjoyable when we share the experience.

I'm sure I'll be fine when I get into it but I don't want to be locked away. I need time. Look I don't want to fight with you, we can do this together. I just need you to be nice with me. I'm different to the rest.

You certainly are, however my hunger is beginning to gnaw and we need to satisfy that...don't we?

How soon?

Tonight!

What!

Shhhhhhh

The shush gently faded away and she knew better than to disagree with its direct order, before wondering if the voice had been the same with all the others, talking to them, building their confidence, before making them kill.

Her bedroom door opened. 'Hey sweetheart, come on now we can't be late. I thought we might do a little shopping when you've finished...' Her mother suggested as she whooshed into Rebecca's bedroom with ironed clothes and began putting them in drawers. '...Are you okay...?'

Rebecca looked at her mother's reflection in the wardrobe mirror thinking of how easily she and the voice could have taken her life. The whole idea was abhorrent now but she knew these hands would have done as it asked.

'Sweetheart...Rebecca...?' Eileen put her hands on her daughters shoulder.

'...Sorry I was miles away. Yes I'm fine, let's go and get this done.'

They hugged and the mirror reflected it back to them, Rebecca held on tight trying to conceal her heavy regret for ever inviting the voice into their world.

Ten minutes later in the car travelling to her appointment, Rebecca was sat quietly observing the people on the streets enjoying the sunshine, knowing that whatever was going to happen tonight would change that for someone. It was how it was going to start for her until little by little, day by day; these people would grow wary again, become afraid to walk the streets, the hunted human prey of whatever was inside her head. She thought of Oscar mutilating those five women, who knew if there were more, and imagining how helpless he would have been to resist the voice as he stalked them, before ramming their remains into the barrels where he kept them. Why did he do that? Would she have to do something similar and would she ever begin to accept it the way he had? That damn voice was now connected to her and she would raise her hands and strangle or stab as it demanded, whatever it took to keep it satisfied. Maybe Oscar had tried to fight back at first; perhaps he'd fought with all his might, but in the end caved in under the pressure from a killer that controls you from the inside. Creeping out from the dark where it hides and no one can ever find it because it doesn't exist to them, so this voice in her head was truly the ultimate killing machine, invisible, clever and insatiable, and it was her now and she was it, and there was no chance of help because no one would ever understand.

<u>68</u>

Harvey had returned to the room and was now concluding his interview with the guard. The ten minutes he'd spent in the toilets had been to convince his own mind that he wasn't being played for an idiot, because he was a Policeman trained to hunt the living, not the supernatural.

'So Mr Kosminsky we have your full statement and I'd like to say thank you for your time and honesty. It's been quite eye opening.'

'You don't believe me! You think I'm crazy.'

'I don't think that at all Mr Kosm...' Harvey tried to say but was cut off.

'...Yes you do...no one's going to believe me. I'm telling you about a killer that lives in Oscar's head...that he's innocent of all his crimes and I know for a fact that is true.'

'Very well, let's play the scenario through shall we...hmm will that help...so let's imagine everything you're telling me is true, that inside Oscar Downes there's an evil demon for want of a better word, and we have to deal with it. How would you suggest we do that...?' Harvey was playing up for the cameras of course, he already knew Kosminsky was telling the truth, but he couldn't be seen on the interview recordings to be so readily accepting of an unnatural presence. The thought of the Superintendent seeing such footage was uncomfortable in the extreme. He also didn't want to be viewed as the weird inspector who believes in ghosts. 'Well...?' Harvey asked.

'...You would have to get into his head like I did.'

If what Kosminsky was suggesting were true then Harvey knew such an option was redundant, the damn thing wasn't in Oscars head anymore, the little man had sworn it was gone. Perhaps that meant the horrors were over with, the controlling mind killer had stopped its games so the city could rest peacefully again, but as always Harvey would trust his instinct on that theory, and his gut feeling told him this was far from over.

'Can you explain how I would get into his head...?' Harvey continued playing his part of a cynical investigator.

'...You've got it trapped right now in Longmarsh with Oscar. Go talk to him.'

'I have already spoken to Mr Downes at length.'

'And did he tell you about it...?'

Kosminsky waited patiently as the Inspector paused. Harvey could tell this man would know if he lied. This whole scenario was changing so fast; it was if suddenly Harvey were the one being interviewed and his responses being noted. For the sake of his reputation and Kosminsky's truth he needed to talk to the big man in private where he could open up about it.

'...Did he tell you about the voice in his head?' Kosminsky asked again with genuine passion.

'No...!' Harvey lied. '...He never mentioned that to me.' He then concluded the interview by standing up and turning towards the door. 'You can stop the recording now, we're done here.'

Kosminsky moved closer to stand face to face with the Inspector. 'He's innocent...he hasn't done anything wrong...but you have to keep him locked up...always...you understand that?'

'...I know how to do my job...Mr Kosmosky...sorry!' Harvey was being intentionally flippant in hope the big man would bite and he did. Kosminsky moved in close to Harvey's face wanting to make him listen good and well.

'...You don't know anything Mr Cooper...!'

While the guard was in his face Harvey took the chance to whisper a few words in his ear. Kosminsky stepped back just as two officers burst through the door believing there was a threat of physical violence.

'...Okay gentlemen stand down. Mr Kosminsky can leave. I believe we've sorted everything out...'

Harvey smiled his most passive smile and the big man returned the compliment with the merest of nods and left. The slightly shaken Inspector sat back down in his chair to have a moment with his thoughts only to be immediately disturbed.

'Sir your next interview is waiting!' The female officer informed him.

Harvey was a little surprised to hear this but to be fair the big guard had taken a little more time that he'd reckoned on, now he had to start all over again, going through more details, more bits and pieces of Oscar's escape that he already knew could never be as interesting as talking to Kosminsky some more. He quickly jotted down a few notes on the guard's statement whilst barely giving the parts about the voice any credence, well aware that was his private domain now, one he would investigate off the record until he could offer up some proof. He required some hard facts that weren't based on wax crayon drawings from a serial killer or the testimony of a clearly affected guard.

'Shall I bring up the interviewee...?' She asked.

'...Fine...and could you possibly get me a coffee please, two sugars?'

Harvey relaxed into his chair and pushed his shoulders back after not realising how tense he'd gotten in his time with the guard. Listening to

Kosminsky talk about the voice in Oscars head had changed everything in an instant; it was all bloody true, there really was a monster on the loose. Damn he needed this next interview over quickly so he could start hunting for it, but that would take time, the main problem being how do you find something you can't see, something that never shows itself to you?

'Here is your eleven o clock interview, and your coffee, Inspector...!' She put the cup down on the table hiding all hint of resentment.

Harvey nodded his thanks and looked at his notebook to confirm the name of the eleven o clock interviewee, before pasting on a professional face for the woman.

'Good morning please take a seat. I'm Inspector Cooper and you...'

'...I'm Rebecca...Rebecca Jones.'

Harvey quite liked the blue of her scarf; went very well with her eyes. As always he began to notice the little things that give away so much of a human personality, a skill that comes naturally after years of observing and looking for clues. It had taught him a great many things and his first impressions of Rebecca Jones and her body language were of mixed messages, maybe an indication she was hiding something.

'...Okay Rebecca...I believe you've spoken to our desk sergeant and you understand what this interview is about?'

'Yes...its... it's about that man escaping from the facility. The one who kidnapped me...!' She was blinking a lot, Harvey noticed. '...Well it all started while I was at work in the reception area...all of a sudden...'

The Inspector raised his hand in a quietening gesture. '...If you wouldn't mind just answering the questions as I ask them.' Harvey snatched back control of the interview because although he didn't know why, he wasn't warming to this girl, and also why did she call Oscar 'that man' as if she didn't know who he was? Odd!

'I'm Sorry!'

'That's alright Rebecca don't worry about it. I presume this is your first time in a police interrogation room?'

'...Yes it is!' She answered with nervous pride.

'I thought it must be. Now is there anything you can tell me about your relationship to the patient Oscar Downes?'

'Relationship...?' The girl exclaimed and blinked even more. The voice also heard the question and came forward from the darkness for a better view of this Harvey Cooper.

'My apologies, that was a poor choice of words...I'm simply trying to establish how well you knew him while he was at the facility?'

'I never knew him...he was just a patient...well a subject, that's what they call them...the first time I ever saw him was in the car park...when I thought he was going to kill me.'

Harvey was desperate to find some crumbs to help his monster hunt and actually she might know something, after all this girl had been kidnapped by that monster when it was in Oscar, so might just have a vital bit of evidence in her head to help his search.

'You believed Oscar was trying to kill you...?'

'...Well yes I thought so.' Rebecca answered honestly.

'Why did you only think so...?' He asked.

'...What?'

What does that mean Rebecca?

The voice suddenly spoke from behind her eyes leaving her with no choice but to listen as its words filled her head. She really hadn't wanted this to happen. It was no less than mental and emotional bullying if the two of them were going to be questioning her.

'...It means...I thought he would...but he kidnapped me instead.' Just be cool she told herself and don't mention the voice otherwise he'll think you're a loony and it will be annoyed.

'So why do you think he kidnapped you...?' Harvey was constantly trying to understand the full spectrum of Oscar's inner workings.

'...Because he needed my help to escape. I still believed he was going to kill me.' Rebecca was trying her best to stick to the facts.

If this policeman doesn't stop we may have to kill him!

This was such an exasperating time for the inexperienced Rebecca, she'd only learned of one way to speak to the voice so far and that was by vocally conversing with it. Obviously that line of communication wasn't an option in her current situation so she was forced to listen and hoped to god it wouldn't go all rogue and murderous.

'But that didn't happen...he simply took you on a long car drive...' As Harvey spoke he began tapping his pen on his palm, a subconscious act he did when he was in the groove, and this was certainly one of those moments.

'...Yes.' she replied carefully.

'Until you were found unconscious next to the burned out taxi...?'

'...Yes' She was beginning to feel a little disorientated, exactly as Harvey intended. Police techniques for questioning are many and varied but one of the basics is known as shuffling the pack. It's simple enough to follow if you're the one shuffling, just avoid asking questions about an event in chronological order. Any liar can remember a list of proceedings, the trick is to mix them up, go to the end, back to the start and occasionally throw in one from the middle.

'So did you escape the taxi just in time? Did he release you before he set it alight? How did that bit play out...?'

So many questions Inspector Cooper! Tell him you escaped just in time. That sounds like the exciting option.

She really wanted the voice to shut the hell up. '...Err he took me out of the boot and put me on the floor. I don't remember anything after that until I woke up in the hospital...'

'...Uhuh...So he hit you on the back the head? It caused quite a hole so I'm told. Do you think perhaps he believed you were dead...?' Harvey stopped tapping his pen.

'...I...err I think so...I don't know I was knocked out.'

Liar!

Why are you goading me? It's hard enough to concentrate as it is.

'...So going back to your time spent in the boot of the taxi, did you hear anything or were you unconscious then as well...?' Harvey didn't really have a plan of action, he was just firing off scattergun questions to satisfy anyone listening in, and trying to get this interview done and dusted.

'...I didn't hear anything.'

Well that was a lie, thought Harvey, the way she looked away then down to the ground, everything about her reactions told him she would be rubbish at poker. 'So you didn't hear anything at all...?' He pushed a little harder but not with any great vigour.

'...I heard the engine when he changed gears but that was all.'

'So you don't think he let you go as such, it was more that he made a mistake...' Harvey asked shuffling the pack again.

'...I err...really don't know!'

'What exactly did he say to you?'

'When...?' She found she was already out of synch with the events.

'When he first put you in the boot Rebecca?'

'...Erm he was threatening me but said I could save my life if I called the guard on the gate.'

'Oh so you called the guard and requested he come down to the car park...a request that ultimately cost that man's life.'

'...Yes...but I had no choice.'

'I see!'

Her eyes widened at the Inspectors abruptness. This wasn't her fault.

Keep going Rebecca. Stay calm.

Then she unexpectedly had a tiny impulse, one so small she hoped the voice might miss it, an urge to tell the Inspector what was in her head. Maybe he could do something to help her, even though she couldn't imagine what.

'When he spoke to you in the car park what did he sound like...?' Harvey continued with his gentle grilling.

'He sounded frightening. I was scared of him.'

'Scared why because he sounded like there was a monster inside his head?' Harvey tried to make the question sound like a small private joke to the other policemen listening in. After the interview with Kosminsky he'd nothing left to lose and because her story was matching up with her original from last week.

What the hell did you just say Inspector Cooper?

For the first time their thoughts were in perfect alignment as Rebecca questioned exactly the same thing. 'What does that mean...?' She asked feeling a freezing sensation wash through her.

Please tell.

'Nothing...simply trying to ascertain how scary he was being...'

Harvey did feel a little mindless for asking such a question, finding he was already uncomfortable with how this monster hunt was affecting his normal job. The two investigations had to be kept separate and distinct. He certainly didn't want to lose his career and reputation based on some ghostly discovery that in turn may never be understood.

Rebecca sat in silence, still struggling to believe what she'd heard. Why on earth had he mentioned a monster inside Oscar's head? Did the Inspector know about the monster? How could he know? It took a prodigious deal of willpower for her not to scream out and tell him everything, admit it was real, and that what he was looking for was right here in this room.

'...I apologise it was a stupid question....' Harvey smiled softly. '...I'm afraid it's been rather a stressful time just lately. Anyway you'll be happy to know we're all done here Rebecca.'

Not if I kill you before we leave the room!

'I can leave then?'

'Absolutely Rebecca, We may need to talk to you again but I think we've everything we need for now. You have a nice day...its lovely out there.'

<u>69</u>

The Angel was pacing around the desk which Alex still found strange when it could always hover or flit around with it wings. After all the *time* they'd been together he was starting to conclude the Angel was maybe more similar to a mortal than it cared to believe.

'That is a most incredible tale!' It said.

'I know...I've just watched it happen and it was...yeah incredible.'

The Angel stopped pacing for a moment while it digested the information Alex had brought back from the book. It had listened keenly to the man's tale of murder, threat and deceit, then more murder, followed by a slaughter of lambs before ending with an attack by a lion.

'And you're quite sure the demon isn't in this teenage boy?' It asked.

'Positive. I've just spent a long time with Jay, in depth from every angle, and all I saw was a kid who's made some horrible decisions. Don't get me wrong he is a sociopath in every definition, he's deceitful, reckless, has no regard for other people's feelings and also, clearly, can be overly aggressive.'

'Overly aggressive...he hacked an innocent man's head off!' The Angel responded.

'Yes I know I was there, sharing what they both felt and I don't want to do it again. Trust me, I'm not implying he's forgivable or somehow misunderstood, but what I am saying is he doesn't want to be that way. The poor kid is without any shadow of a doubt a victim of his environment; ironically he was getting by just fine in life...until he met me.' Alex couldn't help but feel some guilt that all of Jay's problems were directly linked to his own suicide attempt, and experiencing the poor kid's misadventures first-hand only made it worse. 'Mister Angel...?'

'Don't call me that!' It replied sharply.

'What should I call you then...?'

'...How about by my actual name...'

'Well wow! We've been together for ages now and you never once mentioned you had a name.'

'You never asked...'

'...You never offered.'

'...And to be honest Alex I didn't believe the situation would escalate so rapidly. In the beginning I was quite sure we would get you out of here with as little interaction as possible.'

'Yeah good luck with that...So what is it...your name...?'

It looked into the distance as it spoke. '...I am Metatron!'

The Angel's revelation caused Alex to hold back a smirk that could so easily become an incredulous laugh.

'Meta...tron? Huh I'll be honest I wasn't expecting that.'

'Have you heard of me...?' The Angel Metatron asked proudly. '...You will find my name recalled in many scriptures.'

'Sorry, religion...' Alex shrugged.

'Yes I'm constantly reminded of your lack of faith.'

Alex glanced across at the book and urgently wanted to be back inside, anything to be away from this heavenly awkward situation, he felt the Angel's, sorry Metatron's, last comment may have been weighted with some deeper meaning. He paused a moment before attempting to bring things forward and out of the boggy name issue. '...So what's the next plan of action? I mean Jay Cleavers not your demon so that was a dead end. Do I just go back and follow any random person, see if they're the one? I mean seriously, even disregarding time as I know it, that method could take a while.' He laughed gently.

Behind its green eyes the Angel Metatron was finding all of Alex's new found familiarity hugely irritating, clearly those experiences and learnings from the book were changing the man, and not necessarily for the best. This mortal was becoming cocky and disrespectful and would no doubt soon start believing he was perhaps an equal. Obviously this situation was of no great surprise to the Angel; the sudden increase in mental and emotional knowledge at such a heightened rate of learning will make a small brain think it's a large one very quickly. The downside of such a leap is the subject becomes to believe their intelligence is growing limitlessly, that their knowledge will become infinite, but for now the Angel would have to accommodate Alex's expanding ego because it needed him to enter the book and uncover the demon. Afterwards though, well things would be different.

'Where is the boy now?' It enquired.

'He's in a place called Longmarsh Prison, it's where they send all the murderers.' Alex was clearly simplifying his explanation to help Metatron understand better, but this meant the Angel had a colossal desire to slap the man down. Instead it calmed itself, it was an Angel after all, and displaying any deficiency in its serenity was naturally unbecoming.

'I'm well aware of that...but what is a sixteen year old boy doing in an adult male prison? That doesn't seem right.'

'It's local and maximum security. They had to put him somewhere while they wait for his court date. He's in a separate wing, kept on his own away from the main body of the prison.'

Alex was again over simplifying to try and help his partner.

'We are not partners...!' The Angel cut in.

'...You're doing it again!' Alex strongly objecting once more to the mind reading but the Angel ignored him and carried on with its teachings.

'...We are two totally separate life forms. However we have been forced together due to an exceptional set of circumstances and are now stuck with what appears to be the responsibility, as the only ones who can do anything, to save the machine and therefore the whole of the universe's past present and future.'

'Yeah alright Metatron...!'

The Angel laughed at this comment and Alex laughed with it, believing his humour had been appreciated at such a significant time, and thinking it a lovely moment they'd shared. However the truth was significantly different, the Angel's laugh was being caused by its own private thought, the one where it pictured exactly what it would do with Alex when all this was over.

'I need you to go back in...' The Angel said.

'...Obviously!' Alex pulled a funny face as he said this, enjoying their new level of understanding, feeling that due to the book journeys he was attaining equality with the Angel's intellect.

'I need you to follow the policeman.'

'The Inspector Cooper guy...?' Alex was surprised by this choice because he seriously doubted the cop was a demon serial killer. '...Can I ask our reasoning for this...?'

The Angel ruffled its feathers and looked straight at Alex with pure contempt but disguised it as a look of deep concentration. '...The Inspector is investigating your case, and although you are clearly only a small part of it because you didn't die, all the same he will have information pertaining to your accident. I considered following Scott Hutchinson but I feel he wouldn't be as useful. Perhaps he should be next on our list though. So now if you wouldn't mind doing as I ask...'

'...No problem, I'll go see what Cooper knows and we'll go from there. It's great this isn't it...?' Alex said.

'...What is?'

'Me and you working together, we're like Holmes and Watson chasing the Hound of the Baskervilles.'

The Angel considered letting the man's comment go but was far too irritated to do that right now. '...No we are nothing like that because there are two anomalies with your analogy, firstly Holmes and Watson are fictional characters which we aren't, but if you still wish to follow that reasoning then you must also note the hound in the story was fake, and what we are chasing is most definitely not.'

'...Wow you even sound like him!' Of course Alex didn't want to be the 'Watson' in the partnership forever but nonetheless he was accepting of the position for now.

'Shall I open the book...?' The Angel asked and wanting him gone though he knew it wouldn't be for long enough.

'...Let's do it. I'll be back in a minute...whatever that means...!'

The front cover was lifted and Alex entranced again, his mind flew inside, flying fast and free in a world of everything, until the Inspectors story was revealed.

Meanwhile the Angel looked around at the world of white surrounding them and sighed heavily.

70

Kosminsky had taken a seat in the furthest corner of The Lifeboat public house, the rickety wooden chair creaking under him as he took a sip of his lager.

'Thank you for agreeing to meet me...err...can I call you Allan?' Harvey asked as he sat and joined the big man.

Yeah of course, Kosminsky is a bit of a mouthful.' The guard was still genuinely nervous but the feeling was underpinned with excitement that he had someone to talk to, another soul that may understand, and it was so much better than being saddled with it alone.

'I'm happy you want to talk about it...' Harvey said with a grin.

'Not as pleased as me...! I thought I was going to have to shake you to make you listen. Then you whispered you wanted to meet me...well for the last two hours I've been...ah...argh!' Suddenly Allan Kosminsky began to cry but it wasn't a sad affair, just the gentle sound of tearful relief.

Harvey put his hand on the man's considerable shoulder. 'It's okay Allan, you let it out. Do you want me to go get a tissue or something...?'

Kosminsky drew his shirt sleeve sloppily across his nose then rubbed his eyes with a massive paw. '...No I'm fine. It's just been driving me mad...' He took a swig of his beer this time and released a huge sigh. '...So where do you want to start, Inspector?'

'...Inspector? I don't think so. You can definitely call me Harvey on this one. I'm sure we can both agree this is not official police work. So what else can you tell me about the thing inside Oscar?'

'It was torturing him...that's what I got from it. Like I said before I was in a maze with thousands of identical corridors and there wasn't a roof...you could see the stars but they were moving. I tried to use them to find a way to the centre because I knew that's where Oscar was...but they didn't help at all.'

'Hmm...so what made you believe it was torturing him...?' Harvey asked because he had to start somewhere.

'...It was the sound Oscar was making, he was trying to help me find him but he was desperate and afraid, like I was his only hope. He never said that directly but I knew he needed someone to help, to help him fight it. It was all so real, it felt like days I was in there searching and I was getting closer. Every junction he was just one more turn away. I believed I could find him and together we would kick it out and free him.'

'There's something you need to know Allan...' Harvey sipped his water. '...The voice isn't inside his head anymore. I spoke to him under similar subterfuge to this and he assured me it was gone. It disappeared soon after he escaped the facility. Oscar is free of it now...'

'...I don't understand...you believed him?'

'Yes...!' Harvey let the news absorb into the guards mind before continuing. '...During our meeting he told me everything, of course I didn't just blindly accept it as true, that would be madness right? Then you came along and confirmed it, and of course there are the drawings.'

'Oscar's pictures...?'

'...Yes, they aren't just mindless crayon scribbles...pretty much all of them have been representations of real events, mostly deaths, but moments that he could not have physically seen.' Harvey took another sip waiting patiently until Kosminsky broke the silence.

'So you think the drawings were from the voice...?'

'I don't know but he said it took him away in his dreams and they saw these things together.'

'Jesus Christ what the hell is going on here?' Kosminsky asked.

'Whatever it is, it appears we're the only ones who have any chance of finding that out.'

Kosminsky suddenly remembered a telling moment and now seemed the perfect time to put it all out on the table. 'He tried to kill himself with those crayons!'

Although Harvey knew this wasn't official police work he had to treat it in the same way. All the clues were lining themselves up and it was time to start making some educated guesses. It was simple enough; all he had to do was find a way to make a perfectly logical theory, using purely illogical evidence.

'Trying to commit suicide by swallowing crayons...' Harvey said and his puzzled face looked across at Kosminsky '...Does that hang right with you..?'

'None of it hangs right, Inspector, sorry I mean Harvey.'

'Agreed, but it's that particular part that's troubling me.'

'Well you're the Detective.'

'Again agreed, but you're the man who was there, surely between us we should be able to scratch this itch.'

'I've told you what happened...I saw him on the CCTV acting weirdly so I went in to the cell and he was ramming all the crayons into his mouth. I physically had to grab him and force them out.' Kosminsky then shrugged to indicate that was all.

'How did you do that?' Harvey asked.

'I put my fingers in his mouth and pulled them out.'

'Right...how far did you put your fingers in his mouth?' Harvey was chasing something gossamer now, a suspicion he couldn't explain, and almost certainly another bone he couldn't chew.

'...Right into his throat, I mean I had to pull some out that he was in the act of swallowing.'

Harvey went for a long shot hoping it would hit some kind of target. 'Do you think that's how you got in?'

'Got in...where...?' Kosminsky looked puzzled.

'Oscar wanted you in his head. We know that.'

'Okay, I see where you're going, but I walked away and locked the door. It was only when he screamed that I went back and was taken over.'

'Yes but who took control over you...?' Harvey was piecing together his most peculiar theory. '...From what you're telling me that was the only unusual occurrence up to that point. Apart from that, the day had been normal enough...' Kosminsky nodded. '....Right so let's say he knew the voice was going to control you, I mean they were pretty closely connected, so what if he created a moment where he could take a piece for himself, to physically get you into his head...' Kosminsky was listening intently as Harvey continued. '...Look I don't know how it works obviously, but from what you've described to me, the voice was controlling you physically....but what if Oscar used whatever unusual contact you had with him, such as your fingers in his throat to somehow make his own connection, to sneak you in to his mind, to get you where he wanted you to be.'

'Don't you think that's a little too crazy...?'

'...For this particular case Allan...nowhere near...!' Harvey said.

Kosminsky knew he'd no good reason to slap down any of the Inspector's theories. After all he'd been trapped for hours in an imaginary maze only to wake up locked in his office with a mutilated doctor. It still troubled him greatly that she had been savagely attacked only a few feet from where he'd been sitting and yet he remembered nothing. He finished his beer then looked down at the table and spoke.

'It's a weird notion and it fits the situation perfectly but it doesn't help anything Harvey. I don't want to tell you your job but we have to deal with the facts. That voice has disappeared now we both know an innocent man is going to spend the rest of his life in prison...'

It was then Harvey realised, to the big man's credit, that Allan was much more concerned about Oscar being found guilty than whether the voice was still out there waiting to kill again. He couldn't help but find this an endearing trait in the guard, like big old Lenny looking after his little George, Harvey warmed inside as he remembered his favourite book growing up, but the guard was right of course, it was just a useless theory unless they could find out where the voice was hiding now, and that would mean waiting for it to show itself in the only way it knew...by killing again.

Harvey stood. 'I have to get back to the station.'

Kosminsky remained seated and replied earnestly. 'No problem, thanks for the drink and for...well just thanks.'

<u>71</u>

Alex tore himself free from the kaleidoscope images and slammed the book closed trembling and breathless then he refocused to tell what he'd just witnessed. '...We've got help!' He said excitedly.

'What kind of help?'

The Angel picked up the book and slipped it back in its robe. He didn't want Alex distracted if they were finally getting somewhere.

'The Inspector, you asked me to follow him and bang straight away he knows about the Demon, except he's calling it the voice but it sounds like the demon to me. It used to be inside a serial killer called Oscar Downes; he committed murders and put women in barrels, anyway they caught him and put him in a secure hospital but he escaped when the voice took over a guard. So that guard knows about it as well and he's helping the Inspector...'

'...Calm down Alex you're rambling...'

'...Anyway the voice has disappeared and they've lost track of it, but it's been exposed to the light, these two men know about it, we can hunt it together. We're a four man unit now, well three men and an Angel called Metatron. What do you think of that...?'

'They've lost track of it...?' The Angel coldly asked.

'...Oh what really, you pick out the only bad point in my whole discovery and you're going to focus on that?'

'I understand you're thrilled by following a trail that's finally given us results but let's not forget I suggested it. Can we also remember that finding mortals who believe in the Demon was not really our goal, as a matter fact all you have actually found are two men who are even further behind in the hunt than we are.'

'But we're closing in on both sides...a pincer movement...we know its close by.' Alex offered his words as some kind of defence.

'And how do we know that...?'

'Stop making this worse?'

'No Alex you're misunderstanding me...we know that it's close because it's not travelling. It's still in close proximity to the place where it entered...' The Angel clapped its hands once in a genuine gesture of excitement, quite unlike its naturally sombre personality, and even its voice seemed an octave higher as it continued its idea. '...I find it hard to believe that a demon who could go anywhere on the planet to kill is still right next to the place it came through. This tells us something very important, it can't move very far...'

'...A little bit like you up here...' Alex ventured.

The Angel returned to its normal emotional level while ignoring Alex's glib comment. 'Did you see anything else on your journey...?

'I really didn't think I'd need to see anything else. I went straight to the Inspector and the Guard and they were talking about it. I've was sat in a pub for twenty minutes. Do you want me to go back further? See what else the Inspector knows? It seems pointless but...'

The Angel was annoyed again with Alex's overbearing familiarity, a mortal believing it was on equal footing was distasteful to its spirit, but still it had to bear the load and pretend. 'Excellent work Alex. You're doing a wonderful job.' Its insincerity remaining cloaked within a heavenly smile as it brought the book back to the table.

Those words made Alex feel like a child again for one beautiful moment, the one who'd had his hair ruffled by his father, and he glowed from that magical memory of receiving parental pride.

Now this fake fatherly figure had a decision to make, it was willing to risk Alex going back in once more, too many more times and it was concerned things could become challenging, so it had to make the right choice in whom to follow. Where in all this chaos was the Demon hiding? It had searched Alex's life and Jays and now the Inspectors, who was there left to look at, who would have had the opportunity, who was hanging around the periphery down there appearing all innocent and perfectly camouflaged?

Alex suddenly disturbed its moment of contemplation. 'Err I need to ask you a question, Holmes!'

'...Don't...!'

'...I'm joking. I just need to know something...this evil twin of yours...do you share the same skills...?'

The Angel queried this question with a curious glance.

'...I'm just interested you know. I think if I...we...we knew what it was capable of we could catch it quicker.' Alex looked over at the Angel and saw the light reflect softly on its divine face. It stood in silence and he took this as permission to ask some more. '...For instance...can you control someone's mind like it does?'

'And why would you ask me that, Alex, are you worried I'm controlling you?'

'I was earlier maybe...but not anymore.' Alex replied confidently.

There was that cockiness again, causing the usually serene Angel to burn up on the inside, but still it was better to let the man have this moment than ruin the plan so outwardly it remained calm. 'The Demon has clearly had to learn new skills to survive in a world of mortals.'

'...Not really a world though is it...just a city, he's stuck remember. Pretty rubbish demon if you ask me, more of a tethered guard dog, toothless unless you get too close. I reckon we can take him.' Alex laughed at his own nervous bravado.

'Let us hope so. Anyway I have made my decision on whom to follow next....'

'...Oh right go on then...whom?' Alex grinned broadly.

As the Angel slowly lifted the cover it gave no answer, wanting to surprise the man by revealing its choice at the last second, good luck mortal!

<u>72</u>

'Are you sure about this Rebecca? I'll come with you if you like…'

'…I'm okay mom, I'll be fine. I just need to get out of the house for a while. We had enough of this the other year during that stupid lockdown. I'm feeling institutionalised, stir crazy isn't it? That's what they call it…I'm just going to go out for a couple of hours, clear my head.'

'But I'm worried. What if you faint or something…?'

'…I'm not going to faint mother. I've got my phone. I'll call you if I need picking up…' Rebecca then put on the coat that closely matched her headscarf. It was a dark green ensemble for the evening. '…I'm just going for a walk.' She spoke the words softly while warmly hugging her nervous mother. On the inside however there was no doubt she completely agreed with her mother's concern; as going out alone was a risky thing to do only a week after a serious head injury, but then again she wouldn't be totally alone, because this was what the voice wanted, and as she'd already learned and understood, what it wanted, it got.

Walk out now, Rebecca…leave!

Releasing herself from the safety of the hug she stepped through the front door. Walking confidently down the path she then took a right towards the City and looking back saw her Mum watching from the gate. Rebecca shooed her back in urgently because that was, and always would be, embarrassing.

Keep walking. Take me to where the people are.

I will.

(*Silence*)

Now that I'm doing this for you could we maybe walk and talk?

If we must

I want to know something that nobody else knows.

Do you now Rebecca…and what would that be?

Why did you make Oscar put those bodies in the barrels?

(Long Silence)

Okay if that's the way it is.

It is!

Why did you keep the bodies?

If I tell you then you have to make me a promise.

Okay anything. What's the promise?

Kill the dog next time.

Stop it! Why are you like this?

A taxi pulled over ten yards ahead of them.

Get in the taxi!

Where are we going?

The City of course!

Rebecca jogged slowly but made the cab easily as a fat man struggled out, when he turned to reach back for his briefcase he saw a young woman in green was already sitting down and handing it to him.

'You shouldn't just jump in like that Miss. I have another pick up I need to go to!' The Taxi driver rebuked her.

'Is it in the City?' Rebecca asked coyly.

'Matter of fact it is.'

'That's just perfect then...' She smiled tilting her head slightly in a full on charm offensive. 'Take us there...!'

'...Us?' The driver asked and held her stare to see what she meant.

'Well me and you obviously. Do you see anyone else...?' She jokingly patted the empty seats on either side of her.

'...Right you are love...and whereabouts in the City am I dropping us all?' Nige the cab driver made his joke and laughed because he already quite liked this lady, she was quirky and friendly, and he always needed more of that from his punters, most female fares still seemed worried that all taxi drivers were murderers because of that psycho Downes. Nigel Isaacs hated the fact the papers had reported how much Oscar loved his job, well he certainly had a funny way of showing it, there were quite a few cab companies who'd gone out of business because of his murderous antics.

In his mirror he saw the young lady straightening her headscarf. Unusual fashion choice for a girl her age but she carries off quite well, he thought, a touch of the Audrey Hepburn about her. 'Anywhere in particular...?' He asked.

'Oh I don't know, surprise us...!' She flashed him her most attractive smile. Rebecca was going along with the voices demands and trying her best to comply, and yet unbeknownst to her through the simple act of that smile, she and the voice had made one taxi drivers life a little bit better. Ironically what Oscar and the voice had almost destroyed, Rebecca and the voice were now fixing, maybe not quite balancing things up in the great scheme of things, but definitely inadvertently helping.

The voice fell silent as the cab pulled away; after all it had spent years doing this very thing, while Rebecca sat back and together through her eyes they watched the lights go by. There was no denying she was nervously excited in the most part by this new beginning, this life within a life that she was experiencing, a reinforced understanding of her reality she could only have dreamed of before the kidnapping, and she also couldn't deny the gift the voice had offered earlier had been very tempting. Who in all honesty wouldn't enjoy a little revenge on past wrongdoers? So yes there had been a few times she'd wished passionately to be a merciless justice serving bitch, especially on the boyfriends who'd ripped her feelings apart, all those selfish bastards who'd used and abused, the liars and the tricksters who had wasted her time, broken her heart, and even stolen her money. Then there were all those two faced female friends, bitch sisters from different misters who didn't give a shit, the sneaky women who were worse than the men on occasions.

Rebecca knew where her pain festered, it came from the longest relationship she'd ever had, being just over two years before Duncan had finally lost interest, and after she'd done everything he wanted, even though she'd never enjoyed it. Then one day, boom, with one text he finished it, and in a gangster style during the reddest of her tears she discovered their joint bank account had been emptied of its fifteen hundred pounds. This had been their wedding fund, and then she discovered the arsehole licker had moved to Spain with it, so yes she would love to meet his disgusting face again. There were a few others as well, especially now she had this inside her, this anger and strength to kill, her wild and untamed superpower.

The voice was an entity in itself, a part of her that she couldn't control, and humanising it appeared to be impossible. Rebecca however was a friendly soul who could charm her way into most people's good books; her looks were her gifts, not too beautiful that she would be judged by them but attractive in an appreciable way. Averaged sized Rebecca who would drink with you, joke with you and trust you, the last one always being her biggest weakness, but the voice was now an extra layer of protection, because she knew only too well that this savage monster didn't trust anyone.

The taxi driver Nigel whistled quietly to himself as he stopped and sped, turned and weaved, ever onwards towards a City where the people weren't scared anymore. They'd watched and read their newsfeeds about how the mad lion kid Jay Cleaver had been captured, the psycho Oscar Downes was an imprisoned fading memory, so the streets of Edinburgh were safe again, full of people, full of life, waiting to die.

73

As Alex's mind was engulfed by the book he began to feel both humbled and fearful. The Angel had given him its chosen destination just as he entered. So here he was as instructed, living the life of another soul, and what a beautiful and familiar soul it was. It contained many memories and feelings incredibly rich in their love for him, as if he were achieving a lifetime award with all his personal glories being praised, his humour, charm and lovemaking were the greatest in her world, as his invisible presence stood in awe, lost in the mind of Linda Webb.

Special moments from their shared past flooded through, and he couldn't or wouldn't stem the tide, when she and Alex first began their romance, that wonderful year and the last time it had all been perfect. He relived their first date when they'd walked along those castle walls in an evening bloom of unstoppable curiosity for one another, when every word they spoke was truthful, patient and informative, when each urgent feeling set one upon another began to build a mountain made of hope and anticipation. With every unhurried step along the ancient battlements they edged closer to holding hands, and when that layer of trust was reached they both understood the next physical stage would be a kiss. As their lips locked in passionate contact it shared the hidden information of their hearts and they wanted to unlock it all, until when finally releasing the clinch they stood wrapped together against the cold north breeze as they looked out over Edinburgh City at night. A beautiful beyond words, living breathing metropolis blanketed in twinkling lights and deep shadows reaching down to the sea and up to the mountains, it was their backdrop, their stage, both ready to play their perfectly cast parts. On that first date all of this existed only for them, two tiny specks on a blue dot held in the arms of a spiral galaxy. It was where it began and Alex wept tears in his heart watching those tiny specks, feeling the love coming from her, because he saw clearly now it had been just as strong as his own.

With that first date relived he mourned for it momentarily but the scenes in the book moved on until they were sharing their first intimate passions, and this was a feeling unequalled, to experience their love making from the others point of view. All the pre performance nerves and worries he thought had been only on his behalf, well now he knew for sure she'd been just as apprehensive.

Alex could see and understand that every beautiful detail in the first moments of a relationship were finely balanced, it could go either way and, it was all part of the tilting scales of the universe, and he found that love was no exception; this strongest of emotions had also to rise and fall as it fought bravely to keep itself relevant and smooth. Through her eyes he watched the stability of their relationship begin to teeter then slump as the months went by, although their wedding day seemed to briefly slot everything back into equilibrium, it was only now he could see how it was forced and demanded of them by family and friends. So many cards, so many hugs, all those best wishes and drunken words telling them it would all be okay now they were betrothed, but a painful fact remained, that every word he'd been told on that ridiculously expensive day had been wrong.

This journey with Linda was relentless and hurtful, as the arguments when they'd fought tooth and nail were rebooted and replayed through the book. Alex felt sick to the stomach as he saw clearly what a total prick he'd been at times, but on the other hand and for the sake of parity, he also saw how ridiculous her thought processes could be, how sometimes she'd just wanted a fight. Considering it all over again it was clear there had been no specific point when those building blocks had begun to teeter then tumble, no particular comment or action in a singularity that started the demise; it was simply the progression of one more sadly doomed relationship.

This visualised chapter of what was supposed to be a demon hunt was becoming agony for Alex, he couldn't fathom why the Angel had sent him to see this, and he so desperately wanted to close the book. Even that simple choice however really wasn't on the table because it was all too important, too visceral and too personal to stop watching. Knowing he was almost certainly the first human in all of history to experience a loving relationship from both standpoints start to die, to watch a purity of love with its millions of variations of light and shade begin to crumble from within, as trusts became less and less. So it inevitably followed that he witnessed her first meeting with Gary Swann, at that job interview, and he felt what she'd experienced. How a handsome successful man with confidence piqued her interest, a single man who offered her a decent job in his accounts department and a new flirty and fun relationship in her failing life. Alex lived through it all, agonisingly seeing himself ruin whatever chance they had of making it work with his recurring selfish petulance and suspicious questions. He remembered feeling she would be his forever simply because of the ring she wore, that somehow the power of that wedding band meant she would come round to his way of thinking, but he'd been so wrong, and now the stupidity of that philosophy was scorching lines into his soul as he was forced to observe her new romance.

It wasn't the same as how their relationship had started, with Gary it was purely physical at first, but Linda's love grew from within that intimacy. Alex was stuck in his own personal hell as their couplings were shown to him, and he wanted to leave the book now more than ever, trapped in her joy, and with fresh expectations formed through excitement and risk.

Alex listened again as she lied to him about her plans, watching those plans come to fruition and then came the worst part, the pain that punched him down over and over again because he saw, almost unforgivably, that not once did he try and change himself to win her back. He simply let her go, let it happen, then selfishly attempted to make her feel guilty even though none of his words and actions contained or displayed any love on Alex's behalf. It was all pure spite, a textbook victim mentality kicking in and he was repulsed to see himself that way. Yes of course it was entirely his fault when the evidence was presented like this, through a magical three hundred and sixty degree viewpoint, and what he saw now in Linda's heart was the final nail. She loved him, not Gary, she loved Alex and she always would. All of these impossibly detailed visions were allowing him to swim in her feelings, see through her decisions, to understand just how it had happened.

People are different, genders are different, but any hateful experience will always shape a loves reactions. Alex plainly saw how he'd forced Linda away, in an analogy he likened to pushing her sled down a steep snowy hill; at first she would always clamber back up because it was their sled and she was his girl, but soon his pushing away became stronger, and inevitably when you push someone away so far and so often, they get to see other things, things they would never have seen if you'd have just held them close.

In a blink the book moved him to the side of his hospital bed, listening to the machine beep and seeing the space where his arm used to be, and even now he felt the love she had for him, wishing more than anything she could take the pain away and make them both whole again.

On this mission Alex had revealed a lesson refused or misunderstood by most, a confusing truth, but one as pure as the fresh snow you can sled down; in a competition between men, man versus man, which is often how the male mind works, she loved him more than Gary because Alex was the first, the original, and she'd seen all of his faces, the good and bad. Linda hadn't forgotten how it had been for them, she'd simply put it all away in a secret place but she would keep it forever. This coupling with Gary was for different reasons, monetary, physically and emotionally of course, she could love him and stay with him for the rest of her days if that's what the future held, but at the centre of her very being, in a hidden heart shaped box there was, and always would be…her Alex. He would have never been able to understand that without entering the book to discover the layers and levels, the intricacies of every distinct human thought, so after the grandest of all tours he now grasped a new rule of consciousness, feeling both delighted and overwhelmed that he'd never need to ask 'why' again.

Another blink and the invisible untouchable Alex was sat across from them at the restaurant table, listening to her speak to Gary.

'I really like this place, lovely atmosphere and this food's to die for.'

'I've always thought so.' Gary replied.

'This is delicious.' She was chewing gently to savour the taste.

'Well it is our anniversary.' He smiled.

'What…which anniversary…?' She asked surprised.

'…Six months…'

Linda waited for some elaboration but he was playing hard to get. '…Okay I'm trying to work that out…what, since we met…?' She ventured.

'Yeah I suppose, since you first walked through the door of Swann Financial Services for your interview. I'm a little OCD when it comes to things like that. Usually it's the woman who does that kind of thing…'

'…Well clearly you're a better woman than me.' Linda said putting her hand across the table to touch his.

He responded in kind. 'It's been a rocky road just lately…with Alex and that Jay kid but we're getting through it. I just wanted to let you know that I love you…no matter what.'

Linda was genuinely moved and squeezed his hand tight. This Gary was a genuine guy, even if sometimes he was a little cocksure of himself; there was a nice soul underneath that flashy exterior. In fact she was sure if you took away the business success and the trappings it acquired he would still be a man she could spend the rest of her life with, and realising that most of their problems arose because a lot of the time he had to be two men, a boss and a boyfriend, and he changed to fit the circumstances, so it wasn't always easy for her to understand which one was in the room at any given time.

'It's been pretty rocky from the start. I was in a marriage, still am officially, and I didn't know if I was doing the right thing. You know office romances and all that, sleeping with the boss...'

'...Shitting where you eat?' He suggested, being accidently gross.

'No...I wouldn't have put it that way, especially while we're eating.'

'Sorry, would you believe I was trying to help...I'm such a moron sometimes. So what would you like to do after this...?' Gary sat back in his chair patting his stomach to indicate he was done.

'That's no pudding for you then chunky...!' Linda raised her eyebrows in a look of comedy surprise, showing she could also be wholly inappropriate at times, before she savoured her last two mouthfuls and placed the cutlery in a cross on her plate.

'You can have one if you like...' Gary offered but Linda wasn't falling for that trap.

'...I don't think so. I'm not leaving myself open to more critique from the bloody housekeeper. I told you the other day what she said, well hinted, that I'd put on a little weight since I moved in.' Linda was being brutally honest because it had brutally hurt at the time

'You just want me to sack her...!' He said half-jokingly.

'...I do and I don't.'

'What does that mean...?'

'...I think it means I do want you to sack her...but I don't want to be there when you do it.'

This relaxed happy couple sitting by the window laughed together, the other diners nearby enjoying the sound, then the waiter noticed and took it as his signal to go and collect their plates, and all the while Alex watched from somewhere deep behind her eyes. There was no doubting she was happy now, he could never make her feel this way again, that ship had long sailed and hit every iceberg on its fateful voyage, but it was fine because he could still make her proud by waking up from this coma and telling her how he felt. He could hold her hand with his one hand and wish her all the happiness in the world before moving on with his life. Give her the perfect end to what had been their perfect start, and to show her he wasn't that suicidal prick anymore, he was her Alex, and he would love her forever.

74

The taxi pulled up outside the train station in the centre of the City. Nige the cabbie glanced in the rear view mirror at the young lady in the middle of his back seat. He hoped all his fares this night were as calm and relaxed. 'Will this do for you, Love…?' He asked turning to look at her over his left shoulder.

Rebecca looked at him as if coming out of a trance before noticing where they were. '…Oh yes this is perfect.' She reached across and tried the door to get out but it was still locked because taxi's had to wait for payment before they could release it nowadays, and a thick toughened screen separating driver from fare was now also a common sight leaving just enough room to slip the cash or card through.

Suddenly she began yanking hard on the plastic handle.

Let us out!

Her voice seemed different and the sound of it unsettled Nige. '…Woah, whoa, it's locked. You have to pay me first. That's twelve pounds love!'

'Oh we've got to pay as well…!' She said resuming her earlier tone and continuing the joke from the start of the journey.

'I'm afraid *we* have…' He forced a smile hoping this was as innocent as it seemed, he would swear her eyes and features were harder somehow, crueller.

'…Hang on I've got it here' She began searching in a pocket.

'No rush.' Nigel replied although he was lying because the sooner she got out the better. There was something about the girl didn't feel right. He would have sworn the whole atmosphere in the cab had changed from light to dark hearted, and at this moment he fully appreciated that thick plastic screen as she placed a twenty pound note through it with two fingers only.

'There you go. Don't spend it all at once…' Rebecca smiled sweetly but he wasn't convinced by her congeniality anymore.

'One minute I'll get your change…!' His voice calm but it was the only part of him that could say that. He wanted this woman out of his cab as quickly as possible.

'…Oh don't worry about it. You can keep it.'

'Are you sure, that's a big tip for that journey?' He said holding his change bag open.

Rebecca nodded playfully so Nigel pressed the release and she got out while repeating it wasn't a problem. As she closed the door he put the bag down between his feet then jumped out of his skin when she knocked on his door.

'Shi...are you okay?' He asked from behind the safety of the closed window but she indicated she couldn't hear and for him open it. Tentatively he placed his finger on the window button and lowered it no more than an inch as he repeated his question.

'Are you okay...?'

'...Believe me we are better than okay. We just wanted to say thank you...!' Then with a final knowing smile Rebecca turned away and Nigel watched her green coat and scarf disappear into the bustling streets. With her gone his heart slowly returned to normal, and even to this day he couldn't explain exactly what he'd just experienced.

Rebecca wandered down the main thoroughfare wanting to speak to the voice, but thinking it may be best to not be seen talking to herself. Then again to be honest she probably could speak out loud to herself in this city and no one would bat an eyelid. There were always plenty of desperate people doing it every day in every city and they were all easily ignored, however they were more than likely not speaking to a real voice that carried itself with murderous intent.

You can speak with your thoughts Rebecca. I'll understand.

Really! Okay so what do we do?

Well who do you want to kill?

I don't know. I've never done this before.

Can you hear the noise from all those beating hearts?

You don't like that sound?

Pick one!

Hang on this isn't easy.

I can always choose if you prefer.

No! If it's up to me then I'm choosing my first one. Shall we look around some more...I don't want to rush it. It has to be perfect...for both of us. So the young lady in green roamed the grey streets watching all the pretty colours go by. She had a choice that began as almost impossible, but as she got into the mind set found she could create a justifiable reason for killing almost anyone. That man's shoes were awful and with that jacket what was he thinking, how did that woman get by in this world with a face as bitchy looking as that? Then a policewoman walked by, looked at her and nodded a friendly smile.

Rebecca?

'No...!' She reckoned that would be far too big a target for a first hit and besides they would be safer doing it indoors. Rebecca looked to her left and saw a narrow corridor leading to a public house. Above the archway a wooden sign swinging in the evening breeze read The Hole in the Wall. I think that could be the one.

Yes take us in there.

It wasn't too busy, the music was quite loud, and that was perfect she thought as she approached the bar.

'Can I help you...?' The young barman with a heavily tattooed neck asked.

Rebecca usually wasn't crazy about tattoos but she didn't find his angular face unappealing. '...Chance would be a fine thing!' She replied, trying a little sass to suit her current mood.

'What...?' He replied with a bored puzzlement.

'...Nothing...I'll have a small glass of Pinot please...!' Obviously he wasn't the sharpest knife in the drawer.

As the barman went about doing the job he clearly hated, Rebecca Jones slowly threw her gaze around the low roofed space, at the bar to her left an old man was looking at his newspaper for tomorrow's winning horse no doubt, over in the corner a couple not speaking but they seemed comfortable in each other's company and to her right another couple deep in conversation and clearly in love.

Adding up the pros and cons was actually becoming a fun part of the exhilaration, it could be a problem if she chose one of a couple, surely the body would be discovered sooner meaning she would need to make her get away quicker, so perhaps someone singular would be the way to go tonight.

'Five pounds eighty please!' The barman said.

Rebecca was in the killing zone, all her feelings were sharp and keen on the task ahead, but that suddenly stopped for one shocked moment. 'Five pounds eighty...!' She exclaimed looking at the small glass which would be emptied in four sips at best. '...Isn't that a bit much?'

'Probably...but that's the price.'

The barman didn't even have the wherewithal to be cheeky or concerned about it, he just came across as a robot, a pretty young buck but for god's sake don't ask him to think on anything requiring creativity. She handed over a ten pound note then watched him press his fingers on the greasy computer screen. Rebecca noticed he still had to look at it to confirm the change, so perhaps killing him would be of some small advantage to the world, and she was strongly considering it while walking over to an empty table.

Five minutes passed in silence during which she found two tiny swigs equalled four sips and the wine was gone, with no effect felt, or expected.

You were thinking about the barman.

Yes I was.

Think again, he's working. We would be caught in minutes.

I'm going to the bathroom.

Rebecca entered the ladies to find the two cubicles on her right both taken. One had a broken door but there was an occupant in there all the same so she waited and washed her hands. The other cubicle door then unlocked and a shockingly colourful little floozy came out.

KILL HER!!!!

No!

KILL HER!!!!

No not her. I'll kill the other one.

Rebecca was going rogue on the voice and ignoring the growing screams in her head. The painful cacophony began piercing her eardrums from the inside out, making her face wince, as the demons actions were displayed physically to the outside world.

The young girl in the luminous pink, skin tight mini dress glanced at the lady holding her head '...You alright...?' She asked.

'...I'm fine, leave me alone.' Rebecca ordered tight-lipped.

As those wedge heels clopped away Rebecca removed the silk scarf and tightened it in her hands. She then stood in the empty cubicle and waited as the lady flushed and pushed open the broken squeaky door.

Do it now!!!

To Rebecca's surprise it was remarkably swift and straightforward for both parties. As her victim stepped out she flashed the scarf around the ladies throat crossing her hands tightly to pull upwards. The lady staggered back into the cubicle but Rebecca somehow naturally allowed for that and sat down on the seat allowing the women's torso to fall onto her lap. With her left leg she pushed the broken door closed then snaked it around the ladies shins to stop her kicking out and making a sound. Rebecca hadn't wanted a loud commotion on her debut, some leggy woman spoiling her fun with thumps and bangs or cries for help, so this position was perfect for a silent almost effortless execution, and in less than a minute the lady lay choked and dead in her arms.

75

Alex was helplessly addicted to watching his ex-wife living her new life with Gary Swann. He was enjoying watching her smile and glow as she hung sweetly on his arm, the way she once did on his. They left the restaurant and glided down the street together as the happiest of couples. Alex should have left the book then and returned to the Angels questioning but found he couldn't, perhaps scared of losing some vital clue or because he missed her so much he couldn't be without her anymore. It helped greatly that no matter how much it hurt he could take the pain, now, the messy riddles of his relationship breakdown with Linda had been solved; all the questions he'd ever raised were now answered, meaning he could simply observe and enjoy the woman she was becoming. Floating alongside the two of them he watched as they disappeared into the shadows, he followed them through to the light at the end, sitting with them as they engaged in a comfortable confident silence and started their drinks. The pub was dingy and almost empty but his wife was truly happy as she excused herself to go to the bathroom.

Alex chose not to follow because even in this metaphysical state he was a gentleman. However four minutes later even this polite invisible observer could feel the sudden change in Linda's condition. Alex's attention stormed into the bathroom to see her being propped up straight, seated on the toilet, and the young lady in the green coat closing the cubical door to conceal her body. It made Linda look like a drunken woman who just hadn't bothered to lock it properly. Alex then moved round to watch the lady in green place the scarf back on her head, she didn't appear upset at all as she neatened it, and he got the perfect view of the woman who'd just murdered his wife. Ex-wife! The young woman's eyes were large and brown, kindly even, but nothing made sense to Alex, she had killed Linda in cold blood before calmly leaving the bathroom and heading back onto the streets. Shocked and confused he did the only thing he could and began to follow her to find out why, who was she to do this and what could he do about it? Moving in for a closer look at her emotional state, he tried one his new tricks to enter her feelings, but was met instantly and savagely with the full fury of the demon.

The Angel was astonished to see how his head snapped back in recoil as it slammed the covers shut.

'Alex, talk to me...calm down...what happened...?' It held onto him tightly in an attempt to bring him under control but only with a massive effort did it begin to still his struggles.

Alex was crashing around in a blackened world, falling in all directions until the Angel's voice began to penetrate that panic, and slowly he came round as the world became white again. He looked up at the Angel cradling him and whimpered a single word 'No...!'

It could have been a lifetime, but just as easily no time at all, before Alex felt composed enough to tell the Angel of his dreadful mission. Even then it was with a clenched jaw that he related the story of a love lost and demon found.

'Rebecca Jones! That's her name and the demon is inside her. It saw me, I don't know how but it knew I was there and it reacted!' Alex looked to his partner for help.

'Of course it reacted. You surprised it!'

'It killed Linda...why?' He cried out.

The Angel was remaining calm and thoughtful while trying to make sense of Alex's emotions 'I don't believe we can make a definite presumption on how it chooses its victims...'

'...What? So you don't think there's a connection, it's just a coincidence that I'm the one hunting it and it kills the woman I love...?' Alex stormed away into the white world only to end up back at the desk no matter how fast or far he travelled.

The Angel's words reached him wherever he went, its reasoning stretched but never deniable, reciting a message he didn't want to hear. '...What may appear as a billion to one coincidence to you would be no more than chance when you have your wife and the demon out in the same city. This Rebecca had to start somewhere so perhaps chose that woman for ease.' When Alex didn't respond, just stood unmoving with his head down, it was able to confirm the positive message of its reasoning. '...but I believe we can safely say we've found its tracks now. We know where it is...!'

The words washed over his soul, Alex was still implacable though he didn't have the strength to fight right now, he needed time to recover, then he could get the job done with his partner hopefully prepared to pull its weight this time.

'Oh I have been pulling my weight...!' The Angel protested sternly.

'...I hate you...!' Alex screamed at the top of his voice but with nothing for the words to echo off they quickly faded away.

'You have to calm down and work with me...' It demanded.

'...I have done nothing else but work with you on this. I've seen and felt every splintered second of four different lives which have broken my heart wider every time. You're an Angel existing here in your ivory world, you have no idea what it feels like to lose someone, the person you love...so let me die...let me die now...!'

The Angel began to stretch out its wings then realised this could be seen as inappropriate so eased them back down smoothly. It remembered how the mortal used to be impressed by them, his worries eased by knowing he was with an Angel, but this Alex had grown so much, attained insights higher than any man should ever see. Undoubtedly the great book had presented him with the deepest truths he sought but was now extracting its full price for such privileges.

'...I can't let you die, Alex, that decision is not in these hands, my only purpose is to maintain the machine, to keep it working, which means I'm afraid your life, or death, is of secondary importance to what I have to do.'

Alex sat back down and rubbed his never ageing hands through his same length hair, still finding it impossible to fully comprehend Linda's death, and finding the pain he felt wouldn't sit in a grieving slot. Only one thing would allow him that tiny mercy, they must finish their task and be the heroes who killed the demon. The slaying of that murdering beast the only action that could open his heart to understanding, allowing him to move on, wherever such moving on would lead.

'We have to go and get it...' Alex said reaching out for the book but the Angel pulled it away.

'...I agree Alex...only we need some form of plan. We know where it is now but we also know you can't do anything about it in your current form.'

'So what the hell can we do?' Alex asked demandingly.

'I'm working on it...pulling my weight so to speak.' The Angel half smiled but the man wasn't playing along anymore.

'Can't I let those other men know, the Inspector and the Guard? They could make a difference surely, couldn't they? I mean they're so close.'

'You have no presence in their world you can only observe...scream and stamp as much as you want they won't hear you.'

Alex knew the rules but knowing them only made the whole of his adventure more frustrating. What had it all been for, to have endured so much pain for answers, then to have no one to share them with? It meant his only hope, as was ever thus, the Angel stood before him.

'Okay so what exactly are you working on, if we can't make a difference to it from here?' Alex asked.

'I'm working on a concept that may be able to briefly give you some physical form.'

'What, to my one armed comatose self...?' Alex perked up although the thought of the months it may take to get fully mobile again concerned him.

'...No...this you...but another's body!'

Alex jumped past perky to full intrigue. 'I can do that?'

'There could be a way I just haven't found it yet. You will have to go back inside the book and find out how the demon passed from Oscar to Rebecca...that information is key to my theory.'

The Angel then pushed the book back towards the man.

'But won't the demon know I'm around again. It didn't appreciate my intrusion last time.' Alex asked warily.

'As I said before I believe you surprised it. It could be different now that element is lost, of course it could also be waiting for you to appear so be careful, watch her closely but not too close, Do you still want to go?'

'I've got to do something...so yeah I want to go.'

They both looked down at the closed book concerned by what it could reveal this time.

Harvey Cooper lay in his bed taking a sip of warm coffee but he wasn't enjoying the taste with only one spoon added. This ongoing fifty percent sugar reduction was Flo's idea. It was after she'd told him with a concerned grin he was getting a little podgy, an observation he couldn't argue with because the last hole on his belt was beginning to strain. So the answer as always was to follow her advice or buy a bigger belt, and hell would freeze over before he went shopping for one of those.

They had been happily married for what felt like forever and he still loved her more than life itself, although that didn't mean he just lay down when a disagreement occurred, no not this Harvey, he believed it was the secret to what worked for them. If there was a problem talk it out, don't bottle anything up, always be straight and let the dice fall where they may.

An hour later Flo kissed him on the lips as she did every morning when he left for work. It was one of life's exceptional feelings that set him up for the day, he thought of it as an extra layer of armour against the horrors he could face. Being an Inspector in a major City was never without its stresses, and although Harvey was winning in the real world, those other worldly problems were causing major issues in his work schedule.

Arriving at the office he received the morning reports from this sleepless City, finding out in only nine hours away that things had been busy. A forty three year old man had lost most of his penis in some domestic violence issue, a nineteen year old boy had taken a jump from a renowned railway bridge onto the tracks, the third one this year he mused, and there was more, a thirty year old woman was found choked to death in some public house toilets, while a particularly vicious gang of known youths had confronted a rival member outside a kebab shop. Some verbal disagreement ensued, before they sent the lone boy to hospital fighting for his life from multiple stab wounds.

Bloody hell Harvey thought looking at his workload, it's only Wednesday! This was the recurring problem he was facing daily now, knowing he should be looking at each case on its own intrinsic merits, but he couldn't stop scanning over each new crime for a clue or pattern in helping him find the voice. It was a preoccupation causing him to keep glancing back over reports because details weren't going in the first time, and although he believed he was covering his distraction quite well, he fully recognized it could prove costly one day.

Meanwhile some ten miles away in gloomy concrete complex a little man was being allowed some morning exercise. This accompanied walk in the prison square was as good as it got for Oscar Downes, but it was so much better than the Blackford facility where he'd been treated like a lab rat.

The main issue with Oscar was that he didn't fit anyone's ideal of a serial killer; the whole country startled at first when he was caught and shown on TV, even he agreed that the authorities themselves would have preferred a meaner beast to show the world. There had been genuine disbelief in some quarters that this sad little man could have killed five women and kept their bodies to rot in barrels, and then that doubtful reputation wasn't helped by his decision to keep silent. In the end he became a great disappointment both inside and outside the prison walls, even his latest escape with the Doctors murder and the young father barely registered. Sometimes he thought the voice chose him for that very reason, because he would never appear as a threat to anyone, because he didn't matter to anyone.

It was going to be a long stormy day he guessed looking across the square. He noticed the face of a young man staring out from a barred window. Oscar held his gaze for a few seconds before resuming his forced new life of putting one foot in front of the other.

The young man couldn't believe he was looking straight at the notorious murderer in his midst, there had been definite eye contact as well, and he was excited by this shared moment because to him that man out there was a true legend. He was the real deal and Jay knew he could have been as infamous as Oscar Downes if he'd used his head a bit more, not done everything in such a rush. After all he'd killed two people and had a hand in another if that guy Alex never woke up, yeah maybe not the greatest numbers when put up against the five women Downes had killed, but he'd clearly been heading in the right direction. What most annoyed Jay was the simple fact that Oscar's killings must have taken some planning; the guy executing his murders with a pattern and style, while he'd just gone running around like a scared kid with a big knife! He partially remembered a saying, something about never getting second chances to make a first impression, and yeah his shot at the title was gone now.

Jay's cell door was suddenly unlocked and a surly looking prison officer entered. 'Cleaver, stand in the centre of your cell...!' His deep voice demanded. Such a simple instruction but standing wasn't that easy for Jay still carrying the injury caused by the lioness. Although in the end it had turned out to be just a deep flesh wound it was still sore.

'I said centre of your cell!' The guard repeated as he entered.

The boy struggled to his feet determined to do exactly as he was told, mainly because two days ago he'd stupidly tried to find out just how much he could get away with by telling this same officer to fuck off. He'd been having a bad day which had soon got considerably worse after the guard slashed his baton across the back of the boys legs. That single whack from the billy club had dropped him to the floor screaming, as he painfully learned his position in the pecking order of the prison, and exactly where his respect level stood, rock bottom and falling. Those injured legs were trembling now as the guard came closer.

'Hands on your head you piece of shit!'

Jay complied immediately as the cuffs were locked into position. He felt helpless and they were tighter than ever, and he wanted to complain but his mouth stayed shut for fear of the stick again.

'You have a visitor Cleaver. It will be behind glass and recorded so be very careful what you say....' The guard raised the baton slowly waving it in front of Jays face. '...understand?'

'Yes...' Jay agreed wholeheartedly.

'Yes what...?'

'Yes Sir I understand.'

'That's better. Now walk in front of me, hide that limp boy, and when I say stop you fucking stop, otherwise I will see it as an act of insubordination, and if I see it that way I'll be legally allowed to crack you hard around your person, legs again, across your back, perhaps even smack you really hard in the bollocks. So are we going to behave ourselves...?'

'...Yes...I mean yes Sir I'm going to behave myself!'

Jay hated this guard more than anyone he'd ever met, an evil bastard with a legal job, the worst kind of mongrel to be faced with. He followed the guard's instructions to the letter and sat down in the visiting room looking through the reinforced window at an empty chair. The guard sat behind him only five feet away with his hand resting on the ribbed handle of the stick. The tension was growing unbearable until finally a familiar face was ushered in and took a seat on the other side of the glass.

'Hey man...' Scott Hutchinson said then smiled broadly because he thought it might be what was needed.

Fuck! On seeing his friend tears were close by but Jay fought them back. Oh yeah that bastard of a guard would love to see him cry because his buddy had turned up. 'Hey bruv, you come to visit me. That's really fucking great!' He said in non-discerning way.

'Yeah…I err…just wanted to see you were doing okay.'

'Me, yeah I'm good.'

'Are they treating you alright…?' Scott asked then actually smiled at the guard who didn't respond.

Jay found himself being tested for the first time on his ability to adapt to his lowly respect level, frighteningly aware the guard was listening intently to everything they said. 'Yeah definitely…it's all good man…you know its prison innit.'

'It's my first time in a prison.' Scott said looking around him.

'Mine as well!'

Jay half laughed at that ridiculous admission and then his friend joined in a little nervously. Their brief forced joviality immediately followed with an uncomfortable silence as Scott was suddenly stuck for anything else to say, all of a sudden self-aware that he wasn't exactly sure why he'd come in the first place. The only reason he thought was the knowledge that this kid didn't have anyone else who would come visit him. Jay Cleaver had burned all his bridges for the rest of his life in only sixteen years on earth. Given that fact Scott could have stayed away as well, tried to forget about him, but you can't fight your nature. Neither of them could, hence he'd come to visit his friend, and that friend was locked up for double manslaughter.

'So what do you know?' Jay asked.

'Err…I don't know.' Scott replied unhelpfully.

'I mean what's happening with you…?'

'…Oh right yeah course yeah, I think I'm fine. That Inspector Cooper said he doubted they'd try and charge me for anything, as good as said all I did was some driving about and that I didn't have anything to do with anything…' Scott realised with some slight embarrassment how many times he'd just said the word 'anything', and he also realised that the guard was the reason for his non descriptive repetition; the vibes of the man were making him nervous.

'You didn't do anything wrong Scotty, just helped a friend and when I get out I'll pay you back man. Anything you need I'll do it bruv!'

Scott thought perhaps visiting Jay might become something he would regret in the future. He also realised that between the two of them the constant use of the pronoun 'anything' could mean something, everything or nothing.

Jay sat silently with his handcuffed wrists on his lap while Scott tried desperately hard to think of something else to say. Then he remembered.

'Do you need me to bring you anything...?' Scott asked.

The first words that formed in Jays head were 'Yeah...weed' but they didn't come out of his mouth. This short incarceration had already taught him to speak carefully and never impulsively.

'...Like what?' He replied playing the role of good little prisoner.

'I don't know...magazines?' Scott offered.

'Magazines...?' Jay repeated the word back as if it were the first time he'd ever heard it, and to be fair it wasn't one he'd used much in his previous life, reading not being one of his strengths although he thought maybe he could use this time in prison to sort that problem out.

'I've brought one in for you...' Scott said. '...you don't have to have it...if you don't want it. You know what it's probably me just being stupid man. Forget it!'

After a brief moment of confusion Jay sat forward and lowered his voice. 'Show me...'

Scott felt ridiculously self-conscious as he reached inside his jacket, but the guard didn't react to this shady move because he knew the man would have been searched thoroughly before being allowed access to the prisoner, he just sat back watching on as Scott pulled out a glossy video gaming magazine. It was the pricey sort that contained reviews and pictures, all the latest releases and articles written by people who loved gaming as much as his friend did.

Jay looked at the magazine in Scott's hands and truly didn't know what to say, this gift that shouldn't mean anything suddenly meant the world. Scott held it up to the glass so his friend could see the cover better.

'Sorry Scott!' Jay held back the tears by turning them into honest words

'What for...?'

'...For being a total bastard to you, for dragging you into all this...for messing up big style...!'

'...The biggest of styles man...fucking epic Jay!' Scott laughed and it grew louder until Jay had no choice but to join in. They shared this meaningful moment under the dead eyed gaze of the guard. All the bullshit stuff Jay had ever heard when people used the phrase, turn that frown upside down, he now realised it was true because tears of pain or tears of joy are exactly the same tears, only the reasons for them change. They could be altered by a friend when needed and then sometimes, as in this case, by the gift of a simple magazine. Eventually their laughter died down and they were both breathing heavily just to feel normal again.

'Excuse me Sir...?' Scott said to the guard.

The guard stood and strolled up behind Jay who could feel every step. 'Yeah...?' His voice was rough and cold.

'Could you give this to Jay please Sir...?' Scott held up the magazine.

'...Sir? The guard said placing a rough looking hand on to Jays shoulder. 'Do you hear that Cleaver...he called me Sir. I reckon that's why he's out there and you're in here. Do you think that sounds about right...?' He then leaned forward to open a letterbox sized slot next to the window. Jay never looked at the guard by his shoulder but spoke the answer the man wanted. '...Yes...Sir..!'

'Pass it through...' The guard waited as Scott folded it gently in half then pushed it into the slot. Jay could only watch wide eyed as that brightly coloured magazine entered his grey world. His fingertips felt the glossy pages, he could smell the ink, and his heart was in rapture.

'...Thanks man. I'll look at it later!' Still trying so hard to play it cool and keep up a little of the bad boy exterior.

'Time's up!' The guard lied. He knew their time was nowhere near up but they didn't, also he was in charge so he could do what the fuck he wanted. 'Come on Jay let's get you back to your cell.'

'Yes Sir.'

'Okay...I'll come and see you again man...' Scott said then touched the glass with one hand because he'd seen enough movies to know that's what you did to say goodbye in prison.

'Yeah cool Scotty...anytime you want.' Jay nodded a little excessively as he spoke and squeezing the magazine as he stood. He held it up in his manacled hands then gave it a gentle wave in acknowledgement for the gift.

With that tiny gesture in his head Scott Hutchinson left the prison room, a room that in his heart he knew he'd never return to again.

As Jay walked obediently back to his cell the guard would have to admit he'd had no trouble from him at all. Maybe that visit from his cissy boyfriend would be the lesson to teach young Cleaver how to be a model prisoner and not give him anymore shit. As he put Jay back in his cell and removed the cuffs, he took the magazine from him and flicked through the first three pages. 'You like video games then do you Cleaver?'

'Yes I do…Sir.'

'They've never really interested me…' The grinning guard said as he slowly tore it to pieces in front of Jay's widening eyes before whispering '…Fuck you, Cleaver!'

His bottom lip began to tremble as the guard locked the door taking the torn pieces away with him, because grief is such a personal emotion. Mary, the widow of the decapitated farmer was feeling it still, and Goldie the Labrador would never forget its owner stabbed to death on the street, their grief would always be real. Always remaining as a vicious truth almost too much to bear, and now as Jay Cleaver sobbed at his own loss, the universe proved once more that it doesn't care for your beliefs or reasons…because all grief is relative…and it will fucking hurt…every single time.

The lawman who'd helped put Jay into the hands of a sadist guard was sitting at his desk unaware of the young man's heartbreak. Harvey Cooper had problems of his own in deciding who should be detailed to each of the cases delivered to him this morning. He thought perhaps he should take the gangs knife attack at the kebab shop as he already knew a few of the faces involved. The bridge jumper was a little below his pay bracket, which wasn't to say any life was worth less than any other, it was simply the cold fact that a teenage suicide on the train tracks very rarely had a suspect, only a victim, usually in various pieces.

All of a sudden Harvey's breath stopped as he read another brief report through twice; even looking at it a third time, because he couldn't quite believe what it was telling him.

LINDA SARAH WEBB. 30 YEARS OLD
ASPHYXIATION SUSPECTED STRANGULATION.
CITY CENTRE PUBLIC HOUSE, THE HOLE IN THE WALL
BODY FOUND IN TOILET CUBICLE APPROX 21.00.
BOYFRIEND PRESENT - GARY ARCHIBALD SWANN
NO OTHER SUSPECTS REPORTED YET.

Harvey dropped the report on his desk in some vain attempt to assemble his thoughts. It felt like a vase had been smashed inside his head and hundreds of shards large and small were scattered around, so many tiny pieces needing to be put back together, because this made no sense yet somehow it made perfect sense; Linda Webb, Alex's estranged wife was murdered last night.

Harvey stood bemused but slowly, gradually, and with great effort his mind began connecting the dots, although at first they were surrounded by a thousand other dots, eventually he found one connection that he couldn't let go. They were separate cases so at first he couldn't see how the voice could be connected to her...but obviously Alex was connected to her...and Alex was connected to Jay and she...oh my God...of course...she'd appeared in Oscars drawings, the one of the hospital room.

Connection made...but what the hell did it mean?

<u>77</u>

Rebecca had found she'd slept surprisingly soundly following her previous night's murderous debut, no nightmares for this young lady who was currently being called by her mother to come downstairs for breakfast. Flipping the quilt off her to the other side of the bed she sat up carefully then saw the green scarf hanging on the handle of the wardrobe, before it all came back to her. Between her, the voice and that green scarf they'd killed a stranger last night, they'd strangled her before serenely walking away through the city, even calmly phoning her mum to pick her up when she was getting tired halfway home. She also remembered the voice had been screaming loudly as they left the pub but she didn't believe it had made a sound since then.

'Hey...Good morning...!' She whispered in hope of some shared cheery response from it, but there was nothing stirring in the darkness, maybe it was having a lie in this morning she thought and a tiny smile broke on her innocent looking mouth. The radio was playing something jaunty and eighties as she entered the kitchen feeling the best she'd done in years, if not ever, but then her mood dropped rapidly.

'Morning sweetheart...!' Her mother said as she stood next to the oven with a spatula in her hand, but she wasn't the problem. Rebecca's eyes were instead drawn to Jess sitting at the table cradling a freshly poured coffee.

'Good Morning you...!' The friendly neighbour said with a cheery smile that would have fooled most people, but not this recipient.

'Hi!' Rebecca tried to think of a quick plan to hopefully get permission for breakfast in bed this morning, although she didn't hold out much hope of that happening. It was already becoming clear that her mums mollycoddling behaviour was slowly waning, last week that stay in bed treat had been every morning but now she was expected to sit at the table and get back to normal. There were two key components for that change, firstly her Mum was nobody's fool, and the other reason was sitting at the table and about to speak again.

'How are you feeling today, Rebecca...?' Jess asked.

'I've got a bit of a headache.' She replied.

'...Maybe you need another walk. You were really happy when you got back last night.' Her mum interjected and just throwing that information into the conversation was something Rebecca really didn't appreciate.

'Oh you've been out and about?' Jess asked and sipped her coffee.

'Yes I needed a change of environment. I think I might go for another one today...' Then she stood up but her mum reacted instantly.

'...I don't think so Rebecca Jones I've cooked you breakfast. You're not going anywhere until you've had that...coffee or juice?'

Noticing her mum plating up a full English breakfast, minus the tomatoes because she still knew how her little girl liked it, Rebecca sat back down with no help or reinforcement from the voice which was nowhere to be heard.

'Did you go anywhere nice?' Jess enquired.

'I err not really...just went for a walk...juice please!' Rebecca started her breakfast in hope it may stem the questions.

'...All the way to the city centre she went. I picked her up on the way back, didn't I?'

These comments from her mum were not helping the situation, as Rebecca realised she had no choice but to go along with playing the dutiful daughter. 'You did mum...I was getting tired by then.' She followed this with an almost apologetic laugh in hope of easing her growing tension.

'That's a long way for a first trip out. Well done you!' Jess said supportively but Rebecca still didn't trust it.

'I got a taxi into the city then I started to walk back...' Rebecca explained.

'...Oh you didn't say that. I thought you'd walked all the way in.' Eileen said with a little surprise and disappointment.

Why wouldn't her mother just shut up! Rebecca was beginning to stress even more as an extra piece of toast was placed in front of her.

'Get that down you!'

Rebecca continued to play the game for now and buttered it. However uncomfortable this situation was becoming there was no denying the fact she was really hungry after last night's adventures.

'Did you hear what happened to that woman...?' Jess asked Eileen and put her coffee mug down. Rebecca hoped with all her heart it wasn't going to be what she thought. '...The woman in the pub!' Jess exclaimed like some bedevilled town crier, because she was a loyal and caring friend, a social media monster, and a furious gossiper.

'What happened...?' Eileen asked genuinely concerned.

'...They found her body in the toilets at that pub. What's it called, the Hole in the Wall, you know the one...'

'I do know the one. Dead you say...?' She asked for the confirmation because after all was said and done her good old mum was partial to a tasty bit of gossip herself.

Jess became more animated as she retold what she'd heard. 'Someone strangled her!'

'In the pub...?' Eileen was shocked as she'd imagined a fight at the bar.

'Apparently the woman was in there having a drink with her boyfriend, or husband or whatever, anyway she went to the ladies where someone choked her to death and left her there...!' Jess was in her most natural of habitats now, the one of storyteller in someone else's kitchen. '...I don't know any more than that but there's a rumour they've got her fella under suspicion...'

'Well didn't anyone see anything...?' Eileen was asking the question while Rebecca chewed as quietly as she could to listen to the answer.

'...Not as far as I know. I got a phone call this morning from Beth Simpson who used to work there, anyway she's still friends with the Latvian lady who cleans there now and that's what she told her...' Jess was drying up on actual third hand facts now so if pushed would probably start to fill in gaps with speculation and her own imagination.

Rebecca had wolfed her breakfast down to stay out of the conversation and wondered if the voice was listening or even cared.

I hear everything Rebecca.

Picking up her plate she took it to the sink before declaring. 'I'm going to have a bath!' Then she ran up the stairs because the voice appearing like that had almost made her throw up the food that was barely down. Locking the bathroom door she sat on the edge of the bath and started the hot tap running to cover the sound of her conversation.

Where the hell have you been?

Something has found me?

What? How?

Your murder last night was witnessed

Nobody saw me do it. I walked away.

They were in there with us, experiencing it. I don't know who or what but they will come back.

But they can't get you...I mean you're in my head.

I don't know what they can do. I have been hidden for so long and this...this is a new perception, an unpleasant one.

Can't we run? I have a little money we could get away from here. You know I'd quite like that at the moment.

Running is not an option.

'Do you think our Rebecca's okay…?' Jess asked whilst drying a mug with a floral tea towel.

'Yes I think so. It must have been a terrible experience but she's bouncing back…' Eileen looked at Jess. '…Why, what do you think?'

'Well nothing much, I have noticed she doesn't like me anymore, and then there was what happened to Biscuit…!' Jess raised her eyebrows as if proving a point.

'The dog attacked her…' Eileen said. '…You saw the bite marks!'

'Yes I did…and I'll agree that some dogs can be unpredictable but not Biscuit. He misses her, I can tell.'

'I'm sorry, what's your point…?' Eileen asked as she emptied the soapy water down the sink.

'Were you listening, she hasn't even asked about Biscuit. I think that's a bit odd you know…that she doesn't want to try again with him.'

'She just needs a bit more time.' Eileen said hoping that was the end of the conversation about her daughter.

'Well I'm just thinking you should perhaps keep Rebecca from wandering too far.'

'…Why?'

Well she was in the city last night and a woman got murdered.' Jess said.

'…And what do you mean by that?'

'I mean that I don't want Rebecca walking the streets at night if there's a murderer out there strangling women in ladies toilets…!' Jess placed the tea towel to dry on the radiator quite satisfied she'd said her piece.

Eileen took a calming breath. 'Fair enough I appreciate what you're saying and I'll keep a closer eye on her. I can't go through all that again.'

'None of us can…!' Jess replied then hugged her neighbour and best friend. '…I've got to get back now. See what little Biscuit's been up to.'

Rebecca had slipped into her bath in a mutual silence with the voice. Apparently there was nothing more to say, even though she wanted to make a stronger connection, it was becoming clear the voice was only concerned for its own survival and she could go rot in hell. This was the way it was and she understood that now as she soaped her legs and took the razor from the shelf. Suddenly the slightest flicker of an idea appeared but was instantly killed.

Don't waste time thinking about suicide Rebecca. I would stop you, although not until you had hurt yourself a great deal, then you would still be with me, but in a terrible condition.

I wasn't thinking of killing myself.

Liar!

<u>78</u>

Harvey was replaying everything he knew so far though his analytical mind. All the drawings were opened up before him covering the desk, then after scrabbling in his drawer for pins he went old school and reached for his long retired corkboard. It was kept behind the back of the large filing cabinet and took a bit of effort to pull out, but damn it had its uses. For the next hour he mixed up all the stuff he had on Oscar and the voice with everything to do with Jay Cleaver since the time of Alex's fall. He wrote on post-it notes and in his notebook, he printed off reports, cross referenced dates and times before realising quite soon he was going to need a bigger board. There wasn't time for stationery shopping or subtlety so he walked into his secretary's office and started unpinning everything on hers; it was twice the size of the one he'd already filled, and she could only watch in a stunned silence as he angled it through his doorway and disappeared. This newly appropriated board was perfect because he could rearrange the drawings properly now and place them in some form of chronological order, pinning names along the top he drew lines in pencil connecting people to places in and out of the real world, and by this process found the one linear participant in this whole mess of information...a person in a hospital, in a coma, with an amputated arm.

It was going to take some working out but that's what he loved to do. Step one, there was no direct connection between Oscar and Alex apart from two of the drawings, one of the falling man and the other of the hospital bed, unless of course Alex had at some time been attacked by a giant dinosaur, but even this newly open minded Inspector doubted that had occurred. Harvey placed his spinney chair in the middle of the room and got to work, so Jay Cleaver had no connection to Oscar apart from again appearing in two, no three drawings, the falling man, the farmers decapitation and of course the zoo scene, and obviously Jay had been directly involved with Alex's suicide attempt. Linda was in the hospital picture because she was estranged from Alex who'd tried to kill himself because of their split and now she'd been murdered. No matter how he cut it Alex Webb was at the centre of it all, yet Oscar had no idea of who Alex was, which meant something...but what...ha...it could only mean one thing...of course...the voice had a connection to Alex!

Oscar had said the drawings were of where the voice took him in his dreams, suggesting he was nothing more than a conduit, a way for the voice to be heard. Harvey was burning through connections in his logical cortex on this one, attempting to play serious detective with crayon drawings and voices, trying to link them to real murders in the world where humans had actually died. In the end he sat back in his chair and tried to look at the bigger picture as it appeared on his wall. A frustration grew and then hung like a coat of lead weight on his shoulders, and worse of all he had no one he could talk to about it. This was just before he smacked an open palm on his forehead as the penny dropped and he realised he was wrong on that thought.

Twenty six minutes later the large man trudged into the station and Harvey greeted him warmly.

'Thank you for coming Allan...' The two men shook hands warmly. '...hoping you can help me!'

'I'll try. Have you got something new?' Kosminsky asked and followed the Inspector to his office.

'You could say that. I've got everything in one place, I just can't...ah you'll see...' Harvey closed the office door behind them and revealed the double corkboard mess to the guard.

'Who the hell are all these people...?' Kosminsky asked genuinely confused.

'...Every one of them is linked to the voice either by direct contact or they appear in the drawings. I've put Alex Webb at the centre because that's the only way I can see it.'

'You'll have to fill me in.' Kosminsky asked, then over the next half an hour and a coffee each it was all explained, and the big guard couldn't deny, or understand completely, the glaring fact that this damn voice appeared in every strand they studied.

'So what do you think...?' Harvey asked tapping his pen.

Kosminsky turned slowly towards him. '...That Alex is the voice and he's controlling all the rest of them from his hospital bed!'

'...What...? No!' Harvey exclaimed then explained his disbelief. '...Oscar had the voice inside him way before Alex ended up in a hospital, and even then if Alex was the voice why wouldn't he have just done the murders himself without using Oscar?'

'I have no idea!' Kosminsky replied, accepting his guess was wrong, and looked back over the board again.

'Bloody hell, we're missing something...!' Harvey stretched his arms up while listing out the problems he faced in his head, and came up with a vague solution. '...I'm going to Longmarsh to speak to Oscar again and while I'm there I might as well give Jay Cleaver a visit. Now I can justify

324

talking to those two because of the ongoing investigations, but the other two people I'd like to talk to may be a problem. It could get questioned by my Superintendent, wanting to know why I'm interviewing people who I've already seen...' Harvey rubbed the back of his stiff neck then looked across at the guard because he knew it was the only option he had left.

'I need you to go and speak to them Allan. You're not working at the minute you'll have time to do that...won't you?'

'...What? You want me to go and do your job...I'm not a detective...'

Harvey was grasping at what he knew were the thinnest straws he'd ever tried to hold. 'Just go visit them and ask a few questions, I'll write the questions down if you want, then we can meet back here and see if we can't narrow this down any further.'

'Who do you want me to talk to?' Kosminsky asked hiding just a hint of excitement at the thought of being a pretend detective.

'Scott Hutchinson for one...he's Jay Cleavers friend and knows him the best. There might just be something that Jay did or said that could open this all up.'

'Okay...who else...?'

'...An old friend of yours...Rebecca Jones.' Harvey smiled but Kosminsky looked blank.

'Rebecca who...?'

'...Seriously? You worked together at the same place...' Harvey said exasperated.

'Oh, Rebecca the secretary...yeah I didn't really know her, we might have said good morning once or twice.'

'Then that's perfect, go see her first, find out if she knows anything else.' Harvey placed his pen back on the desk and waited for more questions from his accidental, but desperately needed, sidekick.

'So I'm working for you now...? Kosminsky asked.

'No...you're simply helping me with my enquiries.'

'I see...do I get paid for that?'

'Again no, but if you get some answer's I'll take you out for a beer.' Harvey smiled because it was actually the best he had to offer.

'...Deal...more than one though.'

Kosminsky and Harvey shook hands and their new partnership now sealed with a firm grip. The Inspector began searching through the scraps of paper for the addresses of Scott and Rebecca, they'd never been of much importance before so it was no surprise they weren't to hand, but flicking through his notebook he retrieved one of them.

'Okay right here we go...!' He gave the guard Rebecca Jones address while still skimming through for Scott's details, but the young man's address wasn't in here and to be totally fair he didn't remember ever having it. More than likely the officers who'd done the surveillance on him while Jay was a fugitive had taken it. '...It doesn't matter for now just go and see the Jones girl. I'll send you Scott's address when I find it...'

'And who shall I say I'm working for? She knows I'm not a policeman!' Kosminsky asked quite sensibly.

'Well you're not working for anyone are you? Tell her, I don't know, that you were concerned for her, being an old colleague.'

'Do I look like the concerned colleague type? Look at me!'

Harvey conceded that Kosminsky had a point; he was a lump of a man with a thousand yard stare who didn't appear as if thoughtfulness or compassion would ever be high on his list of natural attributes.

'Just do what feels natural, take her out for a drink or something. I'm going to Longmarsh, so just work it out. Okay?'

'...Okay!' Kosminsky paused. 'You want me to go now?'

'The sooner the better don't you think, call me when you're done and don't worry you'll be fine...'

Kosminsky stood to leave before asking one final question. 'Do I at least get a little petrol money...?'

Harvey took his wallet out. '...Keep the receipts!'

<u>79</u>

The Angel was sat deep in thought. It hadn't yet responded to the news from Alex's latest journey, the one where he'd followed Rebecca back in time to the kidnapping, the one where he'd been there in the layby to watch the journey of the beast from Oscar to Rebecca and he understood even more.

Alex knew he was becoming a god in his own lifetime, all that empty unused space in his brain was being filled now, new connections were being formed, and all of them leading to fresh virginal fields of storage to keep his new understandings. These beautiful unexplored pathways were giving him the confidence to question all things, while having no doubt he was an important part of the machine now, integral even, because it had shown him how it worked. The Angel had taught him some basics, how all things reacted and became entwined with everything else, that all substance no matter how unimaginably vast could never work without the ridiculously infinitesimal and vice versa ad infinitum, but seriously all that was A for Apple in comparison to what he was learning now. By witnessing the machine in motion he was divine in comparison to the man who'd fallen from a building so many lives ago, and he was ready to believe he could better this Angel sat before him.

Finally it spoke. 'So you saw the demon again?'

'I didn't need to.' replied Alex.

'So you haven't seen it since you split the atoms back at the cobbles?'

'...That's true but I know where it is, and soon I'll know what to do about it, and then we can bring this to a close.' Alex was straight faced as he informed the Angel. 'It knows I'm after it. I could feel its concern.'

'That's very confident of you Alex, but it appears to me that you don't even know what it is yet, or what it's capable of...' The Angel suspected this moment was the turning point in their relationship, journey, and it was now entering a battle of wills with the mortal.

'You lied to me!' Alex said coldly and though the Angel didn't appear concerned he could see the tiniest feathered tips of its wings tense up a little tighter.

'How could I have ever lied to you?' The Angel stood to its full height and glory in what was clearly a futile attempt at dominance.

'You said I could go back in another form but it isn't true.

'...I said I was looking at a theory of how that may work but yes you are right, you cannot go back in another's form...only your own broken one...'

As the Angel spoke Alex picked up on the merest whisper of a sneer, and when the Angel picked up on that the gauntlet, wasn't so much thrown down, as placed gently at its feet. '...You are aware Alex that there will be only one winner if you choose to challenge me?'

'I'm not challenging you...Metatron. Huh...why would I do that, you're an Angel, an entity that maintains the universe and everything within it...?' Alex felt the confidence and powerful duplicity in his words, he only spoke them to see what the Angel would do, and if it did what he suspected then he would gain the upper hand.

The Angel felt the pressure start to build, most of it emanating from within the man's spirit, as he began to question the Angel's worthiness to be called a superior being. So the mortal was beginning to care less about the Demon and more about his new persona, therefore his new perceived rank in the natural order of things, and this was of no surprise to the Angel, it knew exactly what trick Alex was playing, it had played this one itself many times before.

'...I have warned you Alex that the book is dangerous to a mind the size of yours. Such rapid expansion will give you delusions of grandeur, but I knew the risk when I told you to enter...' The Angel was gently shifting the topic, directly in reaction to Alex's new demeanour, the equivalent of a defensive pawn strategy.

'Don't you find it strange Metatron, that an Angel who has the power and responsibility to look after whole the machine...is unable to read the instruction manual...?'

'...I don't need to be able to read it. I understand everything within it because that is all part of my domain. I put the information in there...' The Angel said dismissively.

'Yes, I know you do. I just think it's interesting that only a mortal can read the Angels book. Don't you find that fascinating? It must mean something...' Alex was stood tall facing the Angel on a level footing. '...So I'm going to use my time here to work out why that is. After all isn't that the real issue...?'

'No...the issue is to find the Demon and stop it!'

Alex stared past the Angel into the infinite whiteness of this world, appearing as if his expanding mind was elsewhere, but still taking it all in.

'Are you listening to me Alex?'

'Of course I am. So where do you want me to go next?'

'Hmm surely if you are so enlightened you can work that out yourself...!' The Angel's annoyance showing because more than anything it wanted to snatch up the book and disappear, leave this mortal man in limbo alone for eternity, but it was out of such hateful options, the machine needed saving.

<u>80</u>

Kosminsky had hard bargained with the Inspector and managed to secure a shiny twenty pound note for petrol, a small gesture for his time, but one that did not appease his other main worry. As he rode his motorbike out of the city centre he was struggling to think of any possible way for this not to be weird for him or Rebecca, yes he knew her from work but they'd never casually chatted, not once. She'd been administerial whereas he'd been much more front line; it was a rare day when those two faculties met, although she most probably knew more about him than he knew of her.

Reining his motorbike in from what it was actually capable of doing, there being no need to draw attention to his quest; he trawled the streets to find her house. Harvey had messaged some information to his phone and he'd had a quick read of the kidnapping report, the interview Rebecca had given, and a few personal safety notes informing him he was under strict orders to not push too hard. If she or her mother filed any complaints then eventually enough questions would be asked to uncover their sneaky game of hunt the ghost, and that would be bad for both men.,

The big guard pulled his bike over, the sound of the engine probably disturbing everyone in the street let alone the barking dog in the house next door. He removed his leathers and helmet and placed them in his the top box before walking casually toward the front door. All he to do now was act like a concerned colleague, and not a man trying to locate a demon...how difficult could it be?

Eileen walked warily to the door in response to the knock, years spent as a single mum, and the small fact of a serial killer periodically invading her life, meant she didn't open it straight away. 'Hello who is it...?' She asked through the letterbox because she wasn't even going to risk using the chain. Also a hefty walking stick sat by the coat rack, it had never once been used to aid a limp, and she eyed up the thick chestnut weapon so it could be in reach if called upon.

'Hi there, is that Rebecca?' A man's deep voice enquired and she moved her hand closer to the weapon, ready to wield the stick.

'No it's her mother who are you...?'

'..Oh...yeah hello...my name is Allan...erm Kosminsky...me and Rebecca work together at the facility. I was just wondering how she was...?' He'd consciously softened his voice but even now it refused to sound either warm or friendly.

'...She's fine, why are you asking?' Eileen was remaining suspicious.

'...Well I was there on the day it happened, I'm the guard that Oscar Downes locked in the room when he escaped. Do you know about that...?'

Eileen certainly did know about it because the newspapers had been full of the horrible details. Some versions said Oscar cleverly deceived the guard and forced him into the room under life threatening circumstances, but others focused on the hours he'd endured locked in there with the bloodied remains of a murdered doctor. So it was that if anyone else had come to the door like this she would have sent them packing, but two things in particular curbed her flight instincts, first of all she had an obvious affinity with anyone who was also an enemy of Oscar Downes, and this poor man on the doorstep had certainly suffered the evil of him, almost paying with his life. Also If Eileen had an opportunity to talk to someone who could make her hate that murderer even more then she would listen. Then a third thing that suddenly convinced her was the appearance of the ever vigilant Jess coming out of her own front door carrying Biscuit. The dog was barking at first but happily accepted the offer of the man's giant salty hand, enjoying the fuss it was being given.

'Who are you...?' Jess asked from her side of the small fence.

'...A workmate of Rebecca's.'

Eileen opened her front door and got her first look up at the man standing on her threshold. The sight of the dog accepting the large man's presence assured her a little more that opening the door had been the right thing to do. Jess had upset her this morning so she thought it might be about time to make a line in the sand when it came to hers and more importantly her daughter's independence. There was no question Eileen truly appreciated all the help that Jess had given her and Rebecca throughout the years, but there was also a time, like right now, when she could just shut the hell up and leave them alone. After all if this male caller was deceiving her then his choice of disguise was perfect, he looked like a security guard, a protector of the good, and because of that and nothing more she invited him in, before closing the door with a small wave and sideways glance towards Jess and Biscuit.

'Mr Kosmo...I'm sorry...?' Eileen said as they walked him into the living room.

'...Call me Allan that's fine.'

She gestured with an open palm so he placed his sizeable behind on the sofa. His nerves were palpable.

'My names Eileen it's nice to meet you Allan.'

331

Up in the bedroom Rebecca was laying clothes on the bed, trying to pick the perfect one for the evening's adventures to come.

Eileen knocked the door but then walked straight in because that's what this Mum did. Rebecca turned abruptly to look at this parental intrusion.

'There's someone here to see you...' Her Mum said enthusiastically.

Rebecca at first panicked then calmed down, then felt nervous before puzzlement took over, and all of it within one second. It couldn't be anyone bad like the police otherwise her mum wouldn't be this calm while checking how she looked in the mirror, and the preening narrowed it down for Rebecca, because it was either someone very unthreatening, or George Clooney.

'Who is it...?' Rebecca was curious. The voice stayed silent.

'...It's Allan...the guard from the facility, the one who looked after Oscar.' Eileen smiled as she said this as if Rebecca would just bounce up in excitement, but bouncing anywhere is never the natural act when you have no idea what's going on, until in a flash of inspiration she remembered his last name.

'Allan Kosminsky...?'

'...Yes that's it Kosminsky!' Her mum replied still smiling and playing with her hair.

'Why would he come visit me? That's just odd.'

'If I had to read between the lines darling I would think he wants someone to talk to...you know about what happened...'

'...Can't he come back another time?'

'Well he's sitting on the sofa now and I'm about to make him a drink so probably best you come talk to him. I think it will do you both the world of good.' Eileen then left the room pushing the bedroom wide door open and leaving it like that, before almost skipping downstairs to inform big Allan she was putting the kettle on, and that Rebecca was on her way.

'Thanks mum!' Her disgruntled daughter said under her breath.

We have a visitor, an old friend of mine, this should be fun.

Rebecca stupidly hadn't connected the voice to Kosminsky straight away, but of course it knew who he was, and suddenly a million pennies dropped but it didn't feel like a big win.

What shall I do?

Go talk to your visitor.

The nervous young woman made her way slowly downstairs before reluctantly entering the living room where she saw him, and unsurprisingly, there was no warm recognition at all, the only time their paths had crossed he'd been in uniform or the odd time when she'd seen him ride off on his motorbike. It just was so strange seeing him in her family home, like a giant in a dolls house, and dressed in normal clothes as well, blue jeans and a black shirt.

'Hello...?' It was the best she could muster.

'Hi there, Rebecca...!' He offered by way of equally uncomfortable response but then he ploughed on. '...I understand this is probably a bit strange but I err...I just wanted to see that you were okay after erm...everything...see how you are, were, are.'

Rebecca wasn't wearing the scarf in the house so the wound on the back of her head was small but visible. The new hairstyle had helped to take the focus from it but Kosminsky still noticed as she turned to see where her mum was, and it immediately gave him his next question.

'Is your head healing okay...?' No surprise that subtlety wasn't one of his strengths either.

'Yes... it's nearly done with now...stitches are going to dissolve soon then the doctor says I'll be right as rain.'

Eileen came tinkling in with a pot of tea and three of her best cups on a tray. When her mother spoke Rebecca noticed a definite change to her usual voice, softer and more welcoming. 'I thought we'd have some tea. Is that okay with everyone...?' Oh no, this is really happening thought Rebecca, her mum fancies the guy.

'Mum...?'

'...Yes dear?' Eileen replied quite jauntily while placing the tray down on the coffee table.

'I don't know whether Allan might want to talk to me in private...err do you Allan...?'

Suddenly Kosminsky was thrown into an awkward situation, because Rebecca's mum was being very nice, but the truth was yes, he would prefer a one on one. His silent pause, rather than answering quickly, was picked up loud and clear by Eileen who took it with grace and a slighter posher voice.

'Oh of course how rude of me, you don't want me fussing about. I'll be in the kitchen if you need anything dear!' Then she poured her own tea and left, pushing the door to but not clicking it shut, her vigilance was lowered, but never forgotten.

Another silent pause slowly grew uncomfortable before falling heavily pregnant. 'How are you doing with it all...?' It was Rebecca who broke the stalemate as she poured out the tea, allowing him to rediscover his power of speech.

'...Oh you know it was...pretty traumatic event what we went through. I've been talking to a friend and he's helped me a lot. I suppose that's why I've popped round you know...because I've realised it's good to talk about stuff. You don't want to be keeping things inside.'

Rebecca half smiled at the rather belated advice, she then handed him his cup and indicated the sugar if he wanted some. It looks like a baby cup in his hands, she thought.

'Thank you.' He said declining the sugar.

How does he know where you live?

Rebecca listened then spoke in total agreement with the suspicious voice. 'How did you get my address?'

'I err...' Shit! He had to think quickly and was only half lying when he replied. '...I asked the police for it!'

'The police...?' She tilted her head.

'Yes...I was interviewed. They told me you'd been to...and I err... I took the opportunity to ask that Inspector Cooper for it.' Kosminsky took a sip of his scalding hot tea for a moments respite, a stupid move as it burnt his tongue savagely but he showed no pain.

'Is the Inspector allowed to give out peoples addresses...?'

Now he had to trust his instincts and not mess this up. '...No, no he's not. That bit was my fault...I really badgered him for it...just wanted to know that you were okay, sorry I know it was wrong of me...' His head was beginning to spin already from the pressure of acting.

'It's okay.' She said, however her eyes and appearance didn't convince him that anything about this was okay.

'I told him that if we had a chat, you know, something new might come up that we'd perhaps both forgotten about.'

'Oh I see...I thought you were checking on my health?'

Fuck thought Kosminsky. '...I was. I mean I am...I was just telling him a white lie...look this is all getting a bit awkward for me!'

'Why...?'

Her one word question was brutally causing his head spin to turn into a full nosedive; he had to rescue himself and the conversation before he crashed and burned. '...Why...because...I blamed myself for what happened to you...' He said with no good reason to.

'...Why?' Rebecca with her damn one word questions!

'Well because he was my prisoner...so clearly if I'd done my job better, properly even, you wouldn't have had to go through this...and...'

'...And.?' She asked.

Kosminsky wanted to punch his own face for adding such a totally unnecessary 'and', allowing her to keep the pressure on. Her large brown eyes were looking at him innocently after asking a simple question, and were now quite naturally expecting an answer, although it was one he was struggling to come up with, but he had to say something, anything.

'...Err I saw you at work every day and...I think...me...I...I...may have developed a soft spot for you.' Even as those words tumbled out, his stomach flipped knowing he was entering a strange new world of trouble now, and he was proving in style that he wasn't cut out to be a detective. Let's face it under the first hint of pressure he'd panicked and told her he fancied her, and what made it worse was that it wasn't even true, he was twice her age...and size.

Rebecca looked away and out through the window trying to carefully select an appropriate response.

You have a fan Rebecca. How pathetic. I think we should kill him.

'No...!' She answered the voice but it came out loud.

'...What?' A puzzled Kosminsky asked.

'I mean no...you can't have a soft spot for me...seriously no offence but I don't have any feelings like that for you.' Rebecca thought that about covered it and hopefully killed two calling birds with one stone.

Kosminsky was relieved to hear that answer but of course he was still in trouble, accepting he was about as far away from his objective as he could possibly get. He couldn't even remember why the hell he'd thought he could do something like this in the first place. He supposed in his head he imagined they would have a little chat, then he'd bring it round to the kidnap and she would tell him what the voice sounded like, and he might get a nice cup of tea. Instead all he'd done was savagely burn his tongue and announce an unrequited and untrue admission of his feelings for her. Go hard or go home Allan, he thought, don't mess this up any worse than it is, come on save the conversation.

'When I say soft spot...I mean more brotherly...fatherly even. I just wanted to see you and to try and help...as a friend.' He wasn't sure if he'd backtracked a little too far now and was coming across as a massive weirdo, literally.

'I see I'm sorry I thought you were...' Rebecca started to say.

'...No, no, no not like that. Gosh that would be creepy wouldn't it...?' Come on Allan you're lifting the nose of the conversation up, this plane may fly again. '...I'm sorry if I upset or confused you I'm just a big clumsy oaf...actually that's what my mum used to call me...all the time!' He laughed softly because he was fighting back hard with all his best ammunition; friendliness, self-deprecation and family values, he could only hope it was enough to end this freefall and that she wouldn't just ask him to leave.

'It was my fault. I jumped to the wrong conclusion...' She said.

'...Not a problem Rebecca it was the way it came out...' Kosminsky was convinced he'd levelled the plane and all he had to do now was land it safely by concentrating on the job. '...I'm not a weirdo honestly, I just thought that we'd shared a terrible experience and if we talked about it then we may both benefit...'

This man is an idiot! Inwardly Rebecca requested the voice to be quiet while outwardly she spoke to the BFG on her sofa. 'Is there something about what happened that you're struggling with...?'

'...Err...' Think Allan think! '...Yes there is a little something...it's not your fault but I spent a long time with Oscar, he never spoke to me but he spoke to you. It's probably silly but I find that frustrating...' Kosminsky was keeping the plane on a steady course and looking for a landing strip.

'...It wasn't really a conversation Allan. He was threatening me, saying that he was going to kill me if I didn't do what he said. It wasn't very pleasant and I don't know what else to say...' Rebecca sipped her cooling tea.

'I don't suppose it could have been no. Look I'm just being curious but... what did he sound like to you?' Kosminsky asked.

'...Like I said he was angry...threatened to strangle me if I didn't call the guard on the gate.'

'Brunt...!'

'...I'm sorry...?'

'...Phil Brunt, that was the name of the guard he killed. He was a good man, only twenty six...he didn't deserve that.' Kosminsky found he was trying to personalise things, he'd watched a few cop shows where they'd emphasised it was important to do that when negotiating, although to be fair the only thing he was negotiating for was more time to think of better questions.

'Oscar didn't give me a choice!' Rebecca on the other hand was more than ready to wrap this up now.

Kosminsky could sense he was losing her so changed tack and went into story teller mode as he related his experiences from that event. Obviously he left out the mind control part but he did hint there was something about Oscar that scared him more than it should have. As the big guard's rather slow paced version of events was related back to her the voice suddenly jumped up.

He'll tell you about the crayons next. Ha! I'd forgotten about the crayons.

'What crayons...?' Rebecca said out loud, again accidently blurting it out in response to the voice, and knew she had to stop doing things like that, but trying to have two conversations at the same time was very confusing.

Kosminsky didn't react immediately to her outburst, instead he fell quiet while he replayed the story in his head, and thought that unless he was going crazy he hadn't mentioned anything the crayons. All he'd said was that he believed Oscar had been trying a suicide attempt, and was pretty certain she couldn't have known what part the crayons had played in that. Kosminsky also seriously doubted Oscar had told her about it during the kidnap, why would he when she was locked in the boot of a taxi? Instinctively he felt this was split second decision time, heads or tails, raise or fold, time to go all in.

'Err...yeah, those crayons...that was just outrageous. Who would try and kill themselves with crayons...?' Kosminsky proclaimed then watched her poker face for a small tell while keeping his own curiosity cards close to his chest.

That guard is an idiot. Oscar wasn't trying to kill himself. I wouldn't have let him.

'...I really don't want to carry on this conversation Mr Kosminsky. It's upsetting and I've got some pain in my head.' Rebecca's words rang loud and true in an unmistakeable tone of closure.

'That's alright I understand...I probably should be making tracks now, probably shouldn't have come in the first place...' The guard said and meant it.

Less than a minute later Kosminsky had said his goodbyes to Rebecca and Eileen, who he noticed had put on a lipstick she hadn't been wearing earlier. He then ducked through the front door before waving to the neighbour who failed to conceal herself quickly enough behind the curtain she was peeking around. Jess gave a small and slightly embarrassed wave back.

Setting off towards the city he pulled his bike over when he was out of sight, at the first corner and took out his phone. He needed to report this to Harvey, tell him of the strange crayon conversation, but disappointingly he found the Inspectors' phone was busy...or turned off.

81

The reason for the Inspectors muted mobile was it sitting on a shelf in the reception of Longmarsh prison, while Harvey was following a tough looking prison officer down a corridor, the one leading him to Jay Cleavers interview room. As he was shown to his seat he found Jay already in position, and although it hadn't been more than a week since Harvey arrested him he appeared a different looking boy altogether, his hair was longer for a start. From a shaved head to a full head of hair hadn't taken long at all, and Harvey couldn't help but wish he still had those adolescent genes for hair growth; the best he could manage in the hirsute department nowadays was only nasal or auricular. The most surprising change in Jay appearance thought Harvey, was how he wore the look of a prisoner who'd already served ten years, his bright blue eyes were sunken and dull, his skin pale leaving him with a look of anaemia. There had definitely been something taken out of his previous personality or, as he strongly suspected, something brutally added.

The guard took his seat directly behind Jay and waited with interest for this chat to begin. He was looking forward to watching the little bitch struggle. It turned him on.

'It's okay you can leave us now officer...' Harvey said in an official tone.

'...I don't think so. I was told I have to stay with him at all times he is out of his cell.' The guard replied solidly with no recognisable acceptance of rank or acknowledgement of file.

'Very well Officer...?'

'...Keates!' The guard answered with a suggestion of venom.

Harvey stood and made his way to the door; Keates immediately asked him what he was doing and the Inspector gladly replied.

'...Well Officer Keates if you would like to accompany me back to the reception area I'm sure we can straighten this all out with Warden Knill. You see I requested a private interview with Mr Cleaver here to discuss issues concerning his upcoming trial, and as far as I know the last time I checked, you have nothing to do with that...' Harvey was sounding deliberately officious to cover the fact he'd requested no such thing from any such warden.

'...I'm just doing my job, doing what I was told.' Officer Keates replied calmly, trying to hide his desperation to stay, to make sure the little twat didn't say anything out of turn.

'...Very well, we all have our jobs to do, I suppose...' Harvey remained standing. '...Now I'm going to speak candidly to you Keates. Please listen to what I have to say carefully, I've requested that you leave us and you have ignored that request, I have then asked you to come with me to clear this up with the warden but yet again you are unmoving in what you mistakenly believe is best, so this is how it's going to play through now. I am an Inspector from this City's Metropolitan Police Force and young Mr Cleaver here is under investigation in a double murder case, a case that I'm leading. Even his current attendance at this prison is only temporary while evidence is gathered for his upcoming trial, therefore he's technically not one of your prisoners, meaning this young man is a detainee still under my supervision and care as the law of this country states, and because of those legal reasons alone you cannot be allowed to stay while I interview my suspect.'

'I don't care...' Keates attempted to say but Harvey wasn't finished.

'...Of course if that simply sounds like a load of official claptrap then may I remind you in the strongest terms possible that the psychological bullying and or physical abuse of any prisoner, including young Mr Cleaver here, is an extremely serious offence. Do I make myself clear or shall I go on...?'

'...I haven't touched him and if he says different then he's a bloody liar...' Keates had butted in with this comment so Harvey raised his own voice.

'...Officer Keates! I have been in this job for a good many years and I know when an inmate is being broken. I haven't spoken a word to him yet, and even allowing for the injury caused by a full grown lioness which I witnessed first-hand, I can already see some marked differences. For instance by the way he's sitting with his weight on his left leg tells me I would certainly find some severe bruising on the right one. His complexion and pallor tell me he hasn't been able to sleep peacefully for quite a few nights now, and those eyes of his are telling me a great deal more...'

'...That's bullshit!'

Harvey ignored the profanity. '...I strongly suggest you leave this room Keates or I guarantee you will be sacked before the end of this shift, after which you will be arrested and charged with actual bodily harm.' Harvey sat back down.

'...You've got five minutes...!' Keates said as he stood. Yes he was giving ground but he wasn't giving in.

'...I will have as long as I wish Keates, and I'll whistle when I need you, as anyone would to get the attention of a cowardly dog. Now get out!'

Keates left in a raging disbelief that the pompous prick had made him look weak in front of the prisoner. Well fuck him that was fine, because now he would really teach the Cleaver boy a lesson, extra helpings later to make sure he still knew who the boss was in this prison. He slammed the door shut as he left, locked it, and took a seat in the silent hallway.

'Hello Jay!' The Inspector could see the fear in the boy making it abundantly clear this wasn't the same Jay Cleaver who'd had the grandiose plan of killing a lion. 'You can speak to me...I strongly suspect I may be the only friend you have in here.'

'...Friend?' Jay questioned quietly.

'Yes a friend, I'm wearing two hats today you see. Not only your arresting officer but I am also the only person who can get you transferred out of here. Would you like me to do that?'

The boy didn't reply but he nodded strongly and his pale blue eyes filled up. Harvey strongly suspecting this accepting mime was because the boy believed Keates was listening in just outside the door.

'Before tonight...?' Jay's voice carried a candid desperation and he stared at Harvey for confirmation. He couldn't take anymore darkness under the watch of that bastard, the disgusting predator that would come and have an hour with him whenever he liked, physical, sexual and brutal. '...Please Mr Cooper!'

'Of course Jay, I'll make sure you are transferred immediately into my custody and I will keep you at the station. Does that sound better...?' Harvey thought he could actually feel the joy and relief from the boy pass through the glass screen and warm his own face.

Oh my god, thank you...!'

'It's okay but first of all I have a few questions...'

'...Ask me anything. I'll tell you everything.'

'They may not be the questions you were expecting.'

'I couldn't give a fu...sorry...I'm not bothered...' Jay's hands were trembling with an excitable relief.

'...The man on the window ledge.' Harvey said then removed his pencil and began tapping it lightly on his thigh.

'Alex yeah...?'

'Yes. Alex Webb. Did you know him before that day?'

'No, I'd never seen him before.'

'And you only knew his name because you stole his wallet...?'

'...Yeah.'

'...So where's the wallet now...?'

'...I gave it to Linda.'

'His ex-wife, Linda...?' Harvey's eyes widened with curiosity. '...you met her?'

'Afterwards I did...' Jay was obviously telling the truth but strongly suspected from the Inspectors face they were on different pages with this one.

Harvey moved quickly taking out his notebook to join the tapping pencil. In his mind he drew a piece of string across a corkboard between the names, Jay and Linda. Everything was becoming connected.

'...I found her photo in his wallet. It had an address on the back. So I went to the house.'

'Why...?'

'...To rape her.' He was all in on telling the truth now.

Harvey let those three little words sink in and then chose not to write them down. '...Again why...if that's not too stupid a question...?'

'Because I thought it was another part of the game.'

'The game...?' Harvey asked.

'Yeah...I went crazy for a while. It all happened when Alex fell off the ledge. Sometimes I think if I'd helped him things would have been a lot different, because after that it all went to shit. Everything I did was like being in a video game in my head. I thought I was playing as a character you know, none of it was real. All I knew was I had to get to the zoo and kill a lion...'

'...I was going to ask about that.'

'You wouldn't understand.'

'Try me...'

'I don't know...a couple of years ago I kind of got obsessed with a game called Shonan Knights, you played as a samurai. I spent fucking...sorry...I played it for weeks. When I got to the end you had to defeat the final boss and I tried so many times but I couldn't...it was too strong and quick. In the end I smashed the console to pieces because that game was a cheat...it wouldn't let you win.

'Now this really isn't my field of expertise but would I be right in presuming the final boss was a lion...?' Harvey asked.

'Yeah sort of...a massive lion warrior, fucking cheating piece of shit...!' Jay was trembling with rage, frustration, regret and fear. '...After Alex fell I didn't know what was happening to me. I do now though. I can tell what's real again. I know exactly what I did!'

Harvey couldn't help but feel some pity for this mess of a boy who was openly admitting to his wrongdoings. 'Yet you didn't rape Linda...?'

'...No, no chance, she was really nice to me, let me have a bath and fed me, even gave me some of her boyfriend's clothes and you know what...what made her really special...she didn't judge me or try and tell me what was right. Of all the bad crazy things that happened to me during those few days...she was the only good part. If you see her will you tell her that?'

Instantly this new dilemma began to tear Harvey apart. Should he tell Jay what happened to Linda or let it lie? Unfortunately his decision had already been made because their whole conversation today was rooted in truth, meaning he'd no choice but to hurt the boy some more, and even though it saddened his own heart to do so. 'I'm afraid Linda Webb died yesterday, she was murdered.'

Jay's face became a grotesque mask of pain. His breath clipped. 'But...that doesn't make...any sense.'

'Believe me Jay I know it doesn't.' Harvey let the boy fight his tears awhile before feeling he had to change the subject for both their sakes. 'Do you know Oscar Downes...?'

The boy looked up gulping in air. '...I don't know him no. I know he's here. I've seen him walking around the yard. Why...?'

'It doesn't really matter...one final question then I'll get you out of here. It may even put a smile on your face because it's kind of silly.'

'What is it?'

'Do you believe in demon voices that can force people to commit murders...?'

Jay slowly raised his tear smeared confused face and half smiled. 'Err...no!'

'...I didn't think so, right okay let's get you out of here....' Harvey reached for his phone to make arrangements then remembered it was back at the reception office. Oh well he'd just have to take Jay back into his custody using the old school methods if required. Harvey kicked the door and demanded it be opened until he heard the keys turn. Unsurprisingly Keates was loitering in the hallway looking even more like a hired thug from a classic gangster movie. Without asking they both walked straight past the guard to the next locked door. 'Unlock this and be aware the detainee is in my full custody from now on...!'

Keates didn't move a muscle at that request having spent his time waiting for their meeting to end, and preparing himself for another battle with this cocky policeman, so at this latest demand he looked around the corridor in a horrible mock fashion. '...Oh I don't think so Inspector Cooper, I don't have any paperwork for that. I need paperwork for all movement of prisoners. There are rules I have to follow...'

Harvey motioned for Jay to stay where he was, then calmly walked over to Keates to stare up at him. The Inspector was quickly evaluating his situation and surroundings, noting that if things got out of hand and the officer decided to attack then that baton was quite a nasty looking advantage. He also saw the savage look in the guard's eyes, implying that he wouldn't mind having a go at him, to teach this old cop a few new lessons, off the record so to speak. With all that information put into Harvey's computing mind, this freshly evaluated situation and surroundings search gave only one result so he actioned it, by suddenly reaching down he unclipped the baton from the clasp on the guards belt and forced it up under the mans surprised chin in one swift smooth movement. '...Here are your new rules. Listen carefully I don't want there to be any grey areas. Open the door for us now, or for every three seconds that door isn't opened I will remind you...with this stick...about your new rules. One, two...' Keates was standing his ground either through confusion or stubbornness.'...three!' So Harvey cracked the guard sharply across the ribs undoubtedly breaking at least one. This initial blow and the explosive pain that followed took his breath away as Harvey knew it would, and caused Keates to bend over as he supported himself against the wall.

'...Open the door...' Harvey repeated. '...One...two...'

'Okay...Jesus Christ...I'm going to report you for this....' Keates words were spat out in gasps as he painfully unlocked the door.

Jay moved around behind Harvey using him as a barrier from the guard who was breathing heavily now while holding his side.

'...Thank you...' Harvey moved to the door before stopping. '...Oh sorry one other thing Officer Keates...you said something about how you were going to report me?'

'Yeah you bet I am...you've broken one of my ribs!'

'I don't think I did break one of your ribs. I'm quite certain you'll find its two ribs, and also you're elbow has taken a severe beating...'

'...What...?'

Harvey raised the baton before bringing it down with his full force onto the back of the guards arm, who first squealed then squeaked as he slid to the floor, as having the elbow broken with a sudden heavy accurate blow is a truly eye watering experience. The Inspector then dropped the baton onto his crumpled form.

'Now I strongly advise we keep this between ourselves Officer Keates. Clumsy you must have fallen down the stairs, which is exactly what your injuries will correspond to, and if that's how you choose to remember this moment you can keep your job and your career…if not then we have a major problem and I'll see you in court. Do we understand your position?'

Harvey waited for a response but he didn't wait long.

'Yeah, that's what happened….' Keates spluttered the words out with his elbow in blinding agony caused by a humerus in at least three separate parts.

'Come on Jay…' Harvey said but the boy slipped back past him. '…What are you doing…?'

Jay didn't answer or waver as he marched over and kicked the guard as hard as he could in the groin, the sight and sound of it causing Harvey to wince and turn away, it was a justice well served in the most primitive of fashions, but still an incredibly effective one.

'Are we going…?' The happy boy asked.

'Probably best…!' Harvey replied picking up the guards keys. '…Do you feel better now?'

'…I only kicked him in the bollocks because you can hurt those falling down stairs can't you? I was just trying to make it more believable…' Jay said with a smirk.

Harvey didn't respond as they made their way back to the reception, after leaving Officer Keates to writhe in breathless agony, but there was a hint of sprite in the Inspectors step. Once there he reclaimed his phone to call for a unit to transport Jay back to the station. When he was done he noticed two missed calls from Kosminsky, and he was pretty sure they'd be requests for Scott Hutchinson's address which he still didn't have. Hang on a second, yes he did, it was stood right next to him 'What's Scott Hutchinson's address…?'

'Forty six Marlborough Drive…!'

Harvey Cooper had been all ready to text but on hearing Jays answer his fingers froze.

82

After no luck with his calls Kosminsky had decided to go home and try the Inspector again later, however the conversation with Rebecca was playing over and over in his mind so he'd held off on the idea and found the nearest pub. Her unprovoked mention of the crayons had thrown him but he was trying not to jump to any big clumsy oaf conclusions, maybe she'd found out about the crayons during her interview with Harvey, which was also a good reason for wanting to talk to him. On the surface there wasn't much to suspect Rebecca was harbouring the voice apart from two bits of flimsy evidence, firstly she'd been kidnapped by Oscar when it was pretty certain he still had the voice inside him, and then she'd mentioned a crayon suicide attempt which he was surprised she knew about, not exactly an open and shut case so he took a sip of his beer before trying Harvey again.

'Hello.' Harvey answered.

'Bloody hell you're a hard man to get in touch with...!'

'...When I'm in a maximum security prison, yes I am. You're lucky you caught me now, I've got to hand my phone back again in a minute...off to see our old friend Oscar. I have some new strange information...'

'...Well I'll see your strange information and raise it with some of my own.'

They both paused waiting for the other to speak.

'Tell me then!' The Inspector insisted, he was trying not to get aggravated but this day already felt like a week and he still had to go and see Oscar.

'It's more of a question that I need answering.' Kosminsky said.

'...Okay...what...?' Harvey really was trying to move this along.

'Is there any chance that Rebecca Jones could have known about Oscar ramming the crayons down his throat...?'

'Not from me...!'

'Are you absolutely positive about that...?'

'Yes...!' Harvey confirmed the fact.

'Okay. Well she knew about it.'

'Maybe Oscar told her, he did have her kidnapped for a whole night.'

'I thought that but it seems unlikely...she never mentioned it in her statement, only that he threatened her.'

'...Yes I see what you mean. I suppose if she just came out the blue and mentioned the crayons then it's questionable but...' Harvey paused to reassess. '...How do you fancy a bit of surveillance work Allan?'

'...What, spy on her?'

'No...not spy...just to see what she does...stay out of sight obviously and if she goes somewhere keep an eye on her and report back.' Harvey knew he was asking a lot of Kosminsky but this man was the only support he had.

'That's called spying Harvey..!'

'...Is it?'

'I'll do a couple of hours but I'm not staying out all night.'

'I wouldn't expect you to.' Harvey said with a smile to himself.

'So what's your strange news...?' Kosminsky asked.

'...Oh right of course. Well there's a reason I don't want you to go round to see Scott Hutchinson, well certainly not alone...his address is 46 Marlborough Drive.'

'Why does that sound familiar?' Kosminsky asked.

'Because it was all over my corkboards earlier, it's the same house where Oscar said the voice entered his head...'

Kosminsky fell silent as he took the information on board, it seemed to him that once more they were being handed a vital piece of an amazingly large puzzle, only it came dressed up as coincidence, but his questioning thoughts were scattered when the Inspector asked him for another favour.

'...So I thought perhaps you and I could go round there tomorrow. Give the place a proper look over. Would you be up for that?' Harvey knew he'd agree because he could tell deep down Kosminsky was enjoying their new partnership.

'...Yeah okay...I'll go keep an eye on Rebecca and call you later.'

'You do that, partner. I think we're getting somewhere!' Harvey clicked end call and switched his phone off. Across the reception area Jay stood up still handcuffed and nodded his thanks as two policemen led him to the van for transfer to the station. Harvey subtly acknowledged the young man before making his way to the other much larger wing to see Oscar Downes. As he walked down the concrete corridor he couldn't help but wonder if that was it for the surprises today.

<u>83</u>

Kosminsky had left the pub and his pint, parked his motorbike two streets away from Rebecca's house, before walking to the top of her road to find a decently unsuspicious hiding place. Aware that physically he wasn't really designed for blending in surveillance work so he chose to stay a good two hundred yards away in a small overgrown park. This old play area had seen better days, only containing a couple of benches now and both drowned in graffiti, sitting next to the vandalised remnants of a roundabout. He thought of how popular this place would have been to him growing up, spinning faster and faster until he was drunk with dizziness, but nowadays kids round here rarely went to play in a park, which he believed was a tragedy.

Unimaginatively his plan was to sit here and wait, determined to last an hour at least, and if nothing happened then he might have a little walk around before calling it day. As it turned out he became bored after only ten minutes of trying to casually glance down the road as if he were just a man resting on a bench.

'Hello again...!' A woman's voice behind him said.

Kosminsky swung his head round in shock and looked the woman up and down; upwards to see the nosey neighbour from earlier and down to see the dog in her arms straining to reach his hands again. 'Oh fff...hey yes hello...!' His stuttered reply while berating himself for once more proving he was the worst detective ever born; ten minutes of covert surveillance and he'd already been rumbled.

'...You're Rebecca's friend from work...?' She said knowingly then sat down next to him bold as brass leaving him with no choice but to accept the love of the dog she was holding.

'It's Allan...!' He said trying his best to act naturally. '...We weren't introduced...'

'...I'm Jess, Jess Sweeney, and this is Biscuit, he's lovely isn't he?'

'He certainly is. Do you always have to carry him...?' Kosminsky only asked to make some form of conversation that would perhaps avoid the inevitable question of why the hell he was sitting here.

'...Well I do at the moment. He had an accident last week but he's getting better. I just bring him out for some fresh air. Well me and him both...' Jess had started the chat but now she wasn't really sure why. '...He's not my dog!'

'Really...you're just looking after him?'

'I am yes...he's Rebecca's dog.' Jess was wondering whether to tell him the whole story or not, but of course that decision didn't take long to be resolved because she did so love to tell people things. 'Look I don't like to gossip but there was an accident when Rebecca came home from hospital last week. We think Biscuit got confused by the bandage on her head...apparently he savaged her...!'

'This dog...?' Kosminsky asked while practically having the skin licked from his hands by the allegedly ferocious pup. '...and you think it was because of a head bandage...that's a strange one.'

'I know...don't tell Rebecca I told you this but...she threw this little ball of fluff out of her bedroom window...!' Jess told him while shaking her head and Kosminsky's look was more than a little surprised. '...and when I say threw him out of a window I mean straight through the pane of glass. The poor soul could have died, but I'm nursing him back to health. He'll be fine.'

Jess and Allan were now both fussing the top of Biscuits happy head.

'That's horrific!' He exclaimed.

'I know that's what I thought...between me and you she hasn't been the same since the kidnapping...' Jess was relieved to have someone to tell her story to and this man Kosminsky was all large ears. '...It's like she's not herself. She doesn't seem to like me anymore and we were fine before all of this, and then...I mean I've saved her dog that she really loved...but can you believe she hasn't even asked about him...?' Jess glanced down the street then continued. '...I don't know why I'm telling you this but I feel I can trust you.'

'Of course you can. I only wanted to find out how she was and see if I could help.' He lied while continuing his fuss of Biscuit.

'...Well did you hear about that woman who got murdered last night...?' She asked furtively.

The guard really hadn't been expecting that to be the next sentence out of Jess's mouth, but if she wanted to talk some more then he was still listening. 'The one in the pub...?' He asked playing down his keen interest.

'Yes that one...!'

'Did you know her...? He asked.

'No but that's really not the point...' Jess stopped momentarily because what she was about to suggest was dangerous in the extreme. All the same though a suspicion is a suspicion and she had no one else to talk to.

'So what about her...?' Kosminsky's face was a picture of concern and trust.

'...Well Rebecca went out yesterday evening into the city. She didn't say where she'd been but she phoned her Mum, Eileen, to pick her up. That was about half nine...plenty of time if you see what I mean. I honestly don't want to think these things...I just worry for her and Eileen!' Jess glanced down the road again towards her house then panicked when she saw Rebecca walking up towards them. In alarm she grabbed Kosminsky by the arm and tried pushing him down towards the bushes.

'What the hell are you doing?' He asked with her yanking on his arm.

'...She's walking up the road!'

Kosminsky instantly allowed his huge frame to be manoeuvred into the bushy concealment, and now he was crouched down and hiding, with a woman he barely knew, and a slightly disabled but still overly enthusiastic, dog. The three of them watched through the leaves as Rebecca walked by wearing a black coat and a brown patterned scarf around her head. As she rounded the corner and walked out of sight Jess took her hand from the dog's snout, pretty certain they hadn't been spotted, while Kosminsky jumped up to follow his target.

'Where are you going...?' Jess asked as they stood up. To any casual observer they looked a fine pair straightening themselves up as they pulled themselves out of the bushes.

'...I've got to follow her and see where she goes. Thank you for all your help...erm Jess!' He then awkwardly nodded his appreciation and walked after the girl.

'...But I thought you were just a concerned workmate...?'

'...I am. That's exactly what I am. Don't tell Eileen anything about this...do you promise...?' Kosminsky requested while hoping to god she wouldn't.

'...Of course I won't. I'd look a bigger idiot than you....' She grinned and felt genuine relief when he beamed back.

'I'll be in touch.' He said enjoying her smile.

'I hope so!' Jess replied and using her hand she waved Biscuits paw in farewell.

Kosminsky had to agree that was a cute gesture; he would also agree that Jess was a lovely lady, so maybe he would get in touch. There was no time for that now though; he had a monster to follow. He called Harvey as he set off but as expected there was no answer, so he left a voice message stating what he categorically believed to be true, that Rebecca Jones had the voice inside her and could be going out to kill again.

Losing sight of her for a minute when she rounded a corner he jogged in the gathering dusk to spot her again. She was heading up towards the city, and he considered going back for his bike but that would risk losing her altogether, so was there an option to call the police? Then he remembered Harvey saying how this was an unofficial inquiry and anyway what could he actually accuse her of. At best it was a theory he'd pieced together in his untrained detective head, and although all his lights were flashing he didn't have a definite reason for anything, so he just calmly lumbered on, trying to stay as small and hidden as he could.

84

Meanwhile Harvey was being allowed into Oscar's cell by pulling rank over the whole prison by the look of it. He'd already accepted that his Superintendent would find out about this visit and look unfavourably on his actions, but if he wanted answers then this was his only plan of attack. He walked in to find Oscar sat at a table under a small window, unlike Jay he didn't seem altered by his time in Longmarsh, and looked no different to Harvey eyes. The man's small unassuming face, lit from above by a cage covered light, appeared melancholy, almost as if the Inspector had interrupted some form of soulful meditation.

'Are you okay Oscar...?' Harvey sat down on the end of the bunk; he wasn't playing status games with the man today, because this chat was to be on an equal footing, about a shared problem.

'I'm fine Inspector, how are you...?' Oscar asked politely.

'Oh you know...I'm chasing an invisible murderer in the dark that nobody on the force would believe in and now I'm locked in a cell with a serial killer again...same old, same old...!' Harvey was only half joking but as he spoke he felt this was about to become more surreal than ever. 'I need your help Oscar.'

'What can I do for you?'

'I need to know more about the voice...' Harvey took his notebook and pencil out.

'...You can put those away. I don't know any more than what I've already told you.'

'So you never spoke to find out what it is, where it came from?'

'It doesn't tell you things like that. I asked of course I did...but it never gives a straight answer, goes silent for days, weeks, before taking over again.' Oscar subconsciously rubbed an itch on the back of his head.

'Okay why did it want to keep the bodies of the women?'

'Huh?' Oscar smiled even though he hadn't wanted to.

'Those five bodies in the barrels...why did it keep them...?' Harvey was fishing again hoping something may tug on the line.

'If I told you that Inspector it may change your opinion of me.'

'I just want to know if it is likely to do it again!'

The little man laughed lightly to himself. 'I doubt it...'

'How can you be certain?' Harvey asked seriously.

Oscar then turned to fully face the Inspector and sighed deeply. '...Because it was my idea to keep the bodies!'

Harvey suddenly grew wildly uncomfortable, feeling perhaps he'd been a bit too accepting of Oscar as an unwilling participant in the whole affair, maybe even a touch hasty in putting all the blame on the ethereal voice. This admission made him a bigger player in this and therefore not an all sweetness and light victim. As Harvey thought on this he once more became aware of his unsafe surroundings and just how trapped he was. '...So why did *you* choose to keep the bodies?' Harvey wanted to know the answer even if Oscar's reply risked his own life.

'I wasn't given any choice Inspector in what happened concerning the ladies lives, but I did have some in what to do with them afterwards. The voice and I were together for a long time and we spoke of many things, some of those came to fruition, most did not. However one particularly horrible day I forwarded the idea that if we kept them we may be able to use them again in the future...' Oscar stood up and walked the length of his before continuing. '...I convinced it that if we kept the bodies then we wouldn't be discovered, we'd be able to move around more freely, with the police looking for missing persons rather than studying a serial killers victims.'

'And just how would you have used them again in the future...?' Harvey asked.

'That was the clever part...the clincher if you will...if and when we got caught they would be a bargaining tool for us to wield, only giving up the location of the bodies in exchange for leniency.'

'...But that would never have happened. It's not how we work!' Harvey said with some intent.

'I know that...but I convinced the voice otherwise. The only victory I ever had...' Oscar smiled down as Harvey looked up for clarity. '...I agree it was an intricate and cold hearted plan but I needed the bodies to be found for us to be stopped. You see Inspector it's extremely difficult to get anything by the voice. It can see and anticipate actions, sometimes even read your mind, and it takes control whenever it chooses. If it orders a murder to be done then the murder is done, meaning all I could do was leave a clue somewhere.'

'Those corpses were a hell of a grisly clue!' Harvey stated.

'But because of them you caught me and stopped any more murders.'

'So that was your plan...to be caught?' Harvey didn't like the way Oscar was moving around the cell.

'…Of course…' He was now standing over the sitting Inspector. '…but I need to ask you a question Harvey. Your answer could be very detrimental to me and my case.

'Before I do would you mind sitting down Oscar.'

'No Harvey I won't…answer me this, how many unsolved murders were there in this city in the last five years…?' To help the Inspector relax a little, and answer the question, the small man walked back to the window.

'Over the past five years…?' He thought hard about the numbers. '…I don't know for certain…there are around seventy to eighty murders each year and perhaps three of those become unsolved ongoing investigations. So using that criteria let's say fifteen. I'm not counting your five obviously.' Harvey decided to stand up in a casual fashion because he didn't want to be under Oscars gaze again on such a serious subject.

'Wrong Inspector…! You may need someone to take a look at those facts.'

'…Why's that?'

'Because the voice and I killed thirty three people over the past five years, and please don't even think of questioning my total, I know what we did. I may not always be able to accurately recall all the whys and wherefores because of its noise, but I had to take care of the bodies afterwards.'

Harvey couldn't fully comprehend what Oscar was telling him, in truth he didn't want to believe him, it was surely unfeasible this man could have done that much killing, but even more unbelievable he was making it up. 'So where are all these bodies…?'

'…Oh various sites…ten were weighted down and dumped in the river. That was my first solution to the problem, but of course I risked being discovered that way because those bodies do have an irritating habit of floating after a while, although you have to believe I did a very thorough job in keeping them down. Six of them were buried up in the woods on the hills as a change of tack, but that was pain staking work because when I dug those holes…they were deep. The other twelves remains were left in various building works around the city, dropped into the foundations that are very deep Inspector and obligingly already dug, so those bodies are now helping to support quite a few of this governments new builds…' Oscar had said this while facing the window. He turned now. '…and the last five were the ones at the lock up!'

'That's impossible, Oscar!' Harvey was close to sitting down again under the weight of this information. 'No one could get away with that…!'

'No one...really...? Believe it or not Inspector but I won't gain anything by this admission, so listen on and try to understand. I was a taxi driver Harvey, randomly killing people, then storing them in secret places like the lock up or the boot of my car. I could go wherever I needed at whatever time I wanted and I had no one at home to question those comings and goings. That lock up housed ten barrels at one time, all filled with formaldehyde which helped preserve the bodies and reduce the decomposition. Of course they were never there too long, a day or two at the most, and then with my knowledge of the city, of what was going on or being built, I could get rid.'

Harvey sat down. His legs were shaking as his heart thumped the blood to his extremities. 'Get rid! Why are you telling me this?'

'Contemplation, time, it's all leading me to an inner peace.'

'What the hell are you talking about?'

'Me Harvey...I'm talking about me! For the first time in over five years I'm free inside my own head. I'm allowed to think and imagine, to consider all of my possible futures, and I can assure you in my current position most of them are desperately bleak. Because of this entrapment in my own mind I feel it's crucial to point out the flaws in your investigation. I can't have history believing you did a great job catching me, when I wanted to be caught. Do you really believe that I had that voice inside me for more than five years and only killed five women...one a year?'

'Maybe I convinced myself you'd fought against it, only in the end you had to give in and that's when you started...' Harvey linked his trembling fingers.

'...You can't fight this thing when it's in your head. I did my first murder within a week of leaving the hospital. There were some fallow periods when it wasn't hungry but generally we found victims and disposed of them on a monthly basis. I could sometimes distract or delay it, but eventually we would continue working our way through the population...men, women, children...!'

'You killed children?' Harvey shouted in surprise and Oscar turned to face him.

'Why yes, two children from the same school, they were walking home in broad daylight. We offered them a lift and then...'

'...I don't want to know the details Oscar!' Harvey snapped because he perfectly recalled the missing children. The search had gone on for two months for the Newton girls. Katie and Jane were sisters aged seven and nine who'd disappeared without a trace three years ago.

'...Hmm that was during the height of it...' Oscar calmly continued. '...We killed four in total that week then rested for something like three months. I was actually starting to believe it could be over, but it wanted more, so we drove round the streets and continued, it was all extremely random. It wanted me to extinguish life...that was its only need...' The small man sat back down as if exhausted, allowing Harvey to deal with it all.

'Hey Oscar...?'

'Yes inspector.'

'You were right about one thing, this will change everything for sure but there's still a problem. No one will believe you, even an admission like this won't hold up in court without proof. Can you offer me any of that? Not to doubt you too quickly but did you know at the end of the nineteenth century at least five condemned murderers when stood on the gallows claimed to be Jack the Ripper, just as the noose was being put round their necks. Nothing but bravado of course, but they tried, in a desperate attempt to shine a brighter light on of their sad existence...' Harvey knew he was tip toeing though his life right now.

'Ha-ha you want proof Harvey, want me tell you exactly where they are..?'

'I think that's the least you could do!' Harvey slowly moved away from the bunk so he had a little more room if things got ugly.

Oscar walked forward and stood before him. 'I have told you everything Inspector and this is how you treat my confession? I'm saddened by that, here I've told you when, how and why, even given you the mystery of the barrels which wasn't such a mystery after all. It was never for necrophilia or devil worship or cannibalism as some hacks believed, it was simply storage that I hoped would be found to finally end it all...and it did...for me!'

'Okay tell me where just one body is, if it's there I'll believe you!'

'How about the two children Harvey, do you want to see them?'

'Yes Oscar I do. Tell me where they are.'

'Oh if only life were so easy...I can show you where they are...I'll take you there...we could dig them up together.' The little man grinned,

'We can't do that Oscar...'

'...Yes we can!'

'Why don't you just tell me where they are...?'

'...Because I want something Harvey! I want to go outside and stand in the centre of that city, watch it go by for a little while...just me...without the voice. If you do that Harvey...I'll show you where they all are.'

Oscar's demand caused Harvey to naturally start adding up the pros and cons of such a dangerous manoeuvre. Who would need to know and how could it even be logistically done? He'd asked for the centre of the city but taking Oscar to the centre of anywhere, especially after his latest admission, would be extremely difficult. So no matter how Harvey shaped this one it was a non-starter. It was totally immoral in Harvey's head, but in his heart he wanted the little man to be telling the truth, there was so much to be gained, maybe five years of unsolved murders laid to rest. Those poor families who were still lost in their grief and confusion could finally be given some awful but final closure, and now all of this rested on the biggest and most dangerous decision of Harvey's life.

Kosminsky was breathing heavily as he continued his sneaky pursuit of the far sprightlier Rebecca Jones towards the City centre. Now that he wasn't into physical fitness anymore, he suffered from knee strain if he walked any kind of long distance, and the worst part was he couldn't even hazard a guess of where she was going. He was really wishing he hadn't chosen to follow on foot until suddenly, and to the great relief of his worn cartilage, he saw her turn into the cinema doorway. It was a place he knew well, where he went to see films on the rare occasion he did that sort of thing. It was housed in a small innocuous building and housed only one screen, privately run, and he used it because he hated the large overpriced multiplexes. He thought of it as the connoisseur's picture house, for those who respected the film they were going to see and the other paying cinemagoers, somewhere you didn't get strangers feet on the back of your chair, and where mobile devices were always dutifully turned off. It was how things used to be in his rose tinted past and he much preferred it this way.

By the time he reached the entrance Rebecca must have already gone in to take her seat because the small foyer was empty. The elderly man in the kiosk recognised Kosminsky by sight, which wasn't an unusual occurrence for this gentle giant, and after a couple of minutes bantering of how are you and isn't the weather changeable he purchased a ticket. Before entering the already darkened cinema he looked over at the pink poster advertising the main attraction, a female lead comedy which held no interest for him but he wasn't here for watching, he was here for working, and let there be no doubt he'd be keeping the ticket stub to claim his money back from Harvey.

Walking carefully into the dark he already knew he was going to take a seat on the back row. It made sense both professionally and personally as it would give him the best vantage point of all the other seats, and because he always sat there otherwise people complained they couldn't see around him. He apologised to the young couple on the end of the row as he shuffled past them to get to the seat with the clearest view, but already the rude lighting from the scenes flicking harshly between light and dark, meant he was struggling to locate the outline of Rebecca sat somewhere down the front. He counted twenty heads in the twelve rows of seats but couldn't find her anywhere. Half an hour of the film had passed without a single decent gag, so Kosminsky wasn't enjoying it or the fact he couldn't locate her. Perhaps she was one of those types that slouched down low in their chair to look up at the screen, something he certainly wasn't, even if he'd wanted to be. Looking around there was no one on his row to the left and only the young couple to his right. Where the bloody hell is she?

Kosminsky was stuck there for another hour until the pointless film ended, but he didn't move as the credits rolled, he just sat there wondering how so many "talented" people could take credit for creating such a shallow pile of shit. Eventually the house lights came up and he spotted her a few rows down, still sat in her seat, watching the very end of those end credits as the cinema emptied. He knew the wise move now would be to leave before she got up, he could follow her again when she exited, but Kosminsky hesitated for a second too long, time enough for Rebecca to stand and immediately recognise him.

'Allan…?' She said quizzically from six rows away.

Kosminsky pretended to be surprised then stood to greet her as she walked up the steps. 'Hi Rebecca…what a coincidence…Did you enjoy that?' He asked.

'Not one of her best. Are you a fan…?'

'…Me err no, no erm I was just looking for something to do and…err I thought I'd go to the cinema…wasn't really bothered what film was showing to be honest.' He was fidgeting in his pockets and looking down at his feet more than he should.

'Alright then, well I'm heading home now…you take care!' Rebecca said tilting her head in acknowledgement. Kosminsky couldn't help but try and sneak a peek behind the mask. 'Are you okay…?' She asked.

'…Yes thank you…why?'

'You're staring at me…'

'Am I? I am yes, it's my eyes…just getting used to the light again. Sorry…' He found himself feeling a little trapped with Rebecca blocking his way out, although to be honest he wasn't sure now if his earlier assumptions had been correct, she undoubtedly looked and sounded perfectly normal and in no way possessed by an evil demon voice.

'…Okay, bye Allan…' She smiled almost apologetically then continued up the shallow stairs to the exit where the door swished behind her.

Kosminsky could feel his heart beating but felt a reassuring sense of calm when she'd left. It was definitive proof she wasn't some bloodthirsty monster who would kill him in a darkened cinema. Still he took a deep breath to steel himself for the upcoming pursuit as he struggled to understand why he should be scared of a girl half his size anyway, whether she had a murdering spirit in her or not he'd be able to defend himself against her, but just to be safe Kosminsky decided to wait a couple of minutes before leaving.

The thin blade entered the top of his spine and slid clean through to exit his throat via the windpipe, Rebecca's hand twisting it gently from side to side severing arteries and tendons, it was a simple and effortless move for someone who knew what they were doing and rest assured the voice knew exactly what it was doing. Kosminsky fell back across two seats as the knife was pulled out, unable to move or scream as his airways filled with blood, and with the instant paralysis only allowing him to lay there twitching as he stared up into her eyes. So with her victim silenced but for a small gurgling sound she pushed his huge frame down on to the floor between the rows, with a bit more effort she rolled and kicked his body under the back seats. It was only as she started to walk down to the emergency exit to discreetly leave, that her own thoughts came back in to full focus, and the voice released her from its grip.

Well done. Clean and precise and you barely needed my help at all.

Of course Rebecca knew that wasn't true because all she remembered was saying goodbye to Kosminsky and walking out. It was then the voice had taken over, leading her round to re-enter through the adjacent door, and find herself behind the man with the back of his neck at their mercy. The knife had also been the voices idea, personally selected from the back of the kitchen drawer, one of the unused ones kept for sentimental value if anything, and because her mother would surely have noticed if one had been taken from the wooden block. It also knew what blade worked best; around eight inches, serrated with a comfortable handle, the same type Oscar had wielded on occasion, and now with it secured safely back in the torn lining of her coat she slunk out of the cinema with not one drop of blood on show. As she strolled calmly home this innocent looking young lady thought it strange that Allan would be there watching that movie.

You are too trusting Rebecca. There are events going on in your world and mine. But we'll be ready won't we?

<u>86</u>

Harvey had returned to the prison reception area to reclaim his phone before requesting another police van for the transport of Oscar Downes to the police cells. This second request was greeted on the other end of the line with some gentle barbed banter; was he going to be transferring all the prisoners at Longmarsh back to the station tonight, and should they perhaps send a coach instead to save on time and fuel? The Inspector's response had been strident, to the point, and perfectly dishonest, a contrived suggestive tale that Oscar had offered some new pertinent information so would have to be interviewed a second time. Obviously this type of evidence needs to be officially recorded which wasn't possible at the prison...So just send the bloody van! After a little more toing and froing he managed to secure the vehicle to return and collect Oscar. He'd also found out the Superintendent had gone home for the day so in truth Harvey was the senior officer on duty, of course that wouldn't be the case tomorrow morning when a furious Jeff Shilling came back in to find out what he'd been up to, but by then Harvey hoped to have uncovered the crime of the century.

With his call finished he then watched with interest as Officer Keates was conveyed out to a waiting ambulance, the whimpering guard was laid flat out on a stretcher with two medics wheeling him.

'What happened here then...?' Harvey innocently asked another officer standing nearby.

'Clumsy bastard said he fell down the stairs. He might have broken his arm, maybe a rib as well.'

'Or two...' Harvey offered.

'Maybe...We don't need this we're short staffed as it is...'

'...What was he thinking?' Tutted Harvey.

As the door closed to signal Keates departure, Harvey suddenly remembered he had the guard's keys in his pocket still, thinking quickly he walked over to the exit and pretended to pick them up.

'I think that guard just dropped these...' He said offering them to the officer on reception.

'...Thank you Inspector.'

'Here to help!'

With that itch well and truly scratched he made his farewells then looked at his phone again. There was a voicemail message from his favourite one man surveillance team and as he walked to his car he listened to Kosminsky's heavily breathing whisper explain what he'd found concerning Rebecca Jones. Harvey hadn't been expecting a lot, perhaps just a few words telling him nothing much had happened and he was on his way home. He certainly wasn't prepared for Allan's communication.

'...Hi Harvey I have just spoken to Rebecca's neighbour. Her name is Jess Sweeney and she's told me some things that point to us being correct. I really think Rebecca is carrying the voice and I think she killed Linda last night. I'm following her now but I don't know where she's going. She threw her dog out of the window when she first got out of hospital. I'm sorry if this is a garbled mess but we need to talk. Call me as soon as you can okay...?'

Harvey hit call back to hear the tone telling him Kosminsky was busy or his mobile was switched off. Either way it was a frustrating time to not be picking up, but if he was still trailing Rebecca there could be any number of reasons he wasn't able to answer. Harvey decided not worry about it right now, he knew Kosminsky would see he'd a missed call and they could sort this out later, hopefully before Rebecca killed anyone else. As he was about to put his keys in the ignition a thought began bugging him, a nagging feeling, he chose to try Kosminsky again but unsurprisingly got the same result. This time he left a voicemail for the big man with an instruction, one that he hoped Allan would follow to the letter. '...Allan...I've got your voicemail. Just be careful. I know I told you to follow her but make sure you don't get seen. Do not make contact with her. We don't know exactly what we're dealing with...I repeat mate...do not make contact. Speak to you soon...'

Harvey wasn't sure he could have been much clearer and anyway he had his own problems to sort out. Oscar Downes was about to be transported to the station meaning Harvey had to be there waiting for him. He drove through the gates and headed back with his phone on the passenger seat showing full signal, and with every mile that passed he waited on Kosminsky's call, even trying to call the big man one more time but it was futile. Then just as he approached the motorway section his phone rang and he snatched it up.

'Finally for crying out...!' He barked.

'Ooh hello you.' Flo said in her lovely soft voice that he could listen to for eternity. Just not right now though.

'I'm sorry darling I thought you were someone else.'

'Clearly...' She said.

He took a deep calming breath so not to worry her. '...Can I help...?'

She unnecessarily paused before saying the obvious. '...Nothing special I just wanted to know you were okay...what time you'd be home...but its fine I can tell you're busy so I'll leave it...I don't want to bother you...!'

Harvey snapped back into his old self just in time to stop her putting the phone down. '...I'm here darling I'm fine...sorry, I'm just driving back to the station. It's all a bit hectic at the moment.'

'It sounds it...so you won't be back for dinner then...?' Her voice was solid, giving nothing away of her feelings of disappointment, she'd endured decades of it already and knew to a professional level what loneliness at mealtimes felt like. When Harvey hadn't confirmed what he was going to be doing when he got back to the station or the night ahead, it obviously meant he couldn't tell her, and so he wasn't coming back early.

'...I'm afraid it's going to be a late one tonight. I've got a big interview to do...bloody Oscar Downes again...I'll try and be as quick as I can.' But Harvey was lying because often in this job the truth could cause more problems than it solved, and yes he hated himself for doing it but it was only because he didn't want her to worry.

'Okay then...you stay safe and wake me up when you get back... love you!'

'I love you..!' Harvey clicked off this call feeling a lump in his throat. He checked the phone again and there were no missed calls or voicemails.

'...Come on Allan let me know what the hell is going on!' But still that phone remained silent as he pulled into the station. After he got up to his office he called for the ETA on Oscar, he was told twenty minutes and that they would bring him in through the back gates. The Inspector agreed heartily with their decision then steeled himself for what lay ahead; acutely aware it was an act his Superintendent would fire him for if unsuccessful, meaning quite simply no job, no pension, no future, but what else could he sensibly expect for taking an unauthorised trip into the city at night...to find the remains of two murdered schoolgirls...alongside the serial killer who'd put them there?

<u>87</u>

Alex was inside the book and back at Dalmeny Street, once again stood on the narrow ledge looking down at the cobbles. He carefully turned his head to see Jay Cleaver in the window but nothing changed the outcome no matter how he tried. He'd gone as far as explaining everything to the boy in the brief moment they were locked in their war of words, trying to change his mind, even telling Jay that this decision to let him fall would mean he'd go on to commit murders and be caught at the zoo, and then jailed for the rest of his life. On another occasion he told him about the Angel and the Demon on earth and of Oscar Downes and how he would meet his estranged wife and how she would also die but none of it made any difference! This boy just wasn't for turning, every time Alex tried to relate what would happen if he didn't help him Jay would laugh his vicious cackle, then over and over watch him fall, no matter how he changed the scenario there was nothing he could do to save himself or the boy.

So he now moved it on a fraction and replayed the moment when he'd split the atoms to witness the demon in its true form. The disgustingly hideous beast aflame and furious with hate as it flew towards him, and Alex expected to die every time it came close to making contact, but instead he bumped back and appeared back in the white world, where the Angel watched and waited to see if the man had found an answer.

'What are you doing exactly...?' It asked with a concentrated look after observing how the man was increasing his universal intellect, the answers he came back with now were becoming progressively more interesting, which both pleased and concerned the Angel.

'I'm attempting to understand why it can't touch me and I can't touch it...' Alex raised his eyes to look at the Angel. '...I don't understand why that should be.'

'Because you are on different planes of existence...' It said with a heavy exhale.

'You know I thought that to begin with but...but somethings not right. I can touch you while we're here, and if that demon found me on earth it could touch me....true?'

'Yes using someone else's form it could kill you...!'

'No...I said touch!' Alex corrected the Angel.

'Let us accept those two things probably mean the same to the Demon. It doesn't walk around touching mortals does it...it kills them. This is all very disappointing. I truly believed you were beginning to understand how it worked but clearly not...' The Angel said holding the book to its chest.

Alex straightened himself up in his chair. '...No, no, no that's far too simple now. I'm way beyond thinking of it in those terms.'

'Are you now...?' The Angel replied with interest and the merest flash of apprehension.

'Yes I am Metatron, way beyond it, you need to try and keep up. This isn't about Demons and Angels and Mortals and what plane we might exist on, rather it's about the fabric of space and time and the intelligence which existed to start the machine in the first place...' Alex had spoken his thoughts and waited for a reply which wasn't forthcoming so he continued. '...You've said to me already, almost mocked me, that letting my tiny mind loose in the book was a risk you were having to take. So eventually I needed to ask why would you take such a risk, for what reason?

'Someone has been busy. So what is this answer you think you've found?'

'...Well like I said I'm working on the problem that I can't touch the demon and vice versa. I totally understand we're on different planes but when I broke through at first we saw each other, it flew directly at me, but whatever forces are at work in the fabric of time and space they wouldn't allow us to touch. Why? Why? Why? Mister Metatron? Then just now as we spoke I worked it out.'

The Angel decided to stand for this particular moment because it could be vital, either this mortal had worked it all out, or he was still miles away and it could relax, contented the mystery would continue. '...Tell me Alex, share with me everything you have and I will act impressed...but of course you understand that whatever it is...I already know it...'

'I don't doubt you want to believe that, but I'll tell you anyway. Would you like it from the top...?' Alex asked then raised his eyebrows.

'From the very top...'

So Angel and Man faced each other once more and Alex began. '...Then listen carefully, when I arrived here the first question you ever asked me was why? Nowadays that is the easy part to answer; I fell through a time space rip, slash, tear whatever you wish to call it, made by the Demon when it came through to my world originally. So simply put I'm stuck here unless we can reverse the process and send me back through, however we can't reverse anything at the moment because the demon is still earthbound. This is giving us not only a simple stalemate, but also a cataclysmic dilemma , one which is causing the life machine to break down, and if it remains unsolved this dilemma will bring the whole universe to an alarming shuddering standstill!'

The Angel listened on, unmoving and unmoved, allowing the mortal to carry on.

'Now focus because I'm getting to the good part, and you know what...I'm concealing it from you at the same time, aren't I becoming a very clever mortal? That's how much I understand now you see; it's truly incredible what the book has done for me, after seeing how it all works. Okay before I upset you...and I will upset you, I want to say thank you for letting me be here to witness all of this...' The Angel remained impassive but emphatically engrossed as Alex went on. '...Now the problem we have, and I think we can both agree on this is that we didn't understand the big question...why? Okay here goes...you told me right back when we first met, as if it wasn't important or didn't matter anymore, that Angels and Mortals cannot exist together, that they end up distrusting and trying to cancel each other out...God damn Metatron that was clever on you part...such a vital bit of information that you dressed up as some kind of threat. So with that realisation all I had to do was to make that a certainty in my new equations and it all began to make sense. The reason the Demon and I cannot make physical contact in that place where it flew at me is because that place...is here. The Demon was coming from here to go there and because I already exist here and the only other entity that does so is you, well I'm left with the only deduction possible. You and the demon are the same; it isn't an evil twin to balance out the universe, and to be fair you never said it definitely was, I just naively assumed it must be a separate being...but it is not. You made that rip in the fabric and you sent a part of yourself to earth to continue your good fight...to kill mortals.' Alex paused for a response.

'Fascinating...!' The Angel said softly then nothing more.

'Now this raised another question in my ever expanding mind, why are you killing us so slowly, why not become some Hitler type tyrant that can execute millions, billions even...and do you want to know what I think the answer is to that?'

'Please do...!' The Angel left the table.

'...You've never done this before, mistakes and surprises have occurred in your workings out, which meant that frustratingly your demon couldn't travel anywhere. Your revengeful beast is stuck in the place where it entered, a few miles round here and there but it can't go any further. I'm guessing it would bounce back if it tried, that seems to be the way things work around here. So there it is down on earth tied to an invisible leash, no wonder it's so angry...' Alex gave his broadest smile as his mind continued to solve all problems. '...It would be polite of me to ask you if I'm correct in my assumptions, but I already know that I am, because you messed up with the pictures!'

'...Pictures...Oscar's pointless drawings...?'

'...Oh no far from pointless, they were the key to bringing it all together, because if you and the Demon were the same then while Oscar had the Demon inside his head he also had a connection directly to you. Those drawings that he did, they weren't from the voice as such; those were images from inside your mind.'

'Irrelevant then, to a mortal...!'

'...To a mortal yes, but to someone like me, extremely relevant...I even got to study them through the eyes of an extremely gifted policeman, but where he was unable to decipher them fully, I saw the answer, and it's how I know for a stone cold fact that you and the Demon are one!'

'So you got your fanciful answer from inside my mind...?'

'From your subconscious in fact, who knew, every brain has one even an Angel's apparently, that capricious expanse where chaos rules and plays its games while you sleep. It's a fair point to note that Oscar never drew any of his pictures while the voice was awake, only when it, and therefore you were dreaming. Blissfully unaware you were giving them away, and to be fair of course so was he, but he drew them anyway and by doing so revealed your secret...'

'...What...that I can have dreams?' The Angel laughed.

'A little more than that...those images portrayed moments from my life, to be more accurate things that could happen due to my falling to the street...perilous moments which would affect others around me. People such as Jay Cleaver, or my wife, or even you because you appeared in some of those drawings...in fact you were in the one that gave me the proof, hiding in the background as usual. Have you worked it out yet Metatron...?'

'Enlighten me!'

'You're an Angel...how more enlightened do you need to be...?'

'Tell me!'

'Oscar drew a jungle and a man being attacked by a dinosaur!'

'So...?'

'...Well that moment didn't happen on earth did it, it only happened here; in this white world with you, and it was a direct connection. Only we two could have known about that particular moment yet Oscar drew it as if he was there...which in a way he was...checkmate!'

The Angel wanted a few moments to absorb this barbed gloat but Alex continued regardless.

'Isn't this incredible, here we are just the two of us, an Angel and a Mortal, sworn enemies, although you may find when questioned most humans would say they've forgotten all the differences we may have had, most couldn't give a shit about Angels!'

'Then they are feeble and unworthy animals!'

'...Hum...perhaps, but err...well we aren't the race sneaking around your world picking you off one by one while hiding inside other Angels heads and forcing them to do our bidding. In this war we aren't the sneaky cowardly assassins, and also we haven't messed things up so badly that we have to go begging to the other side for help...' Alex stood tall now with his mind an exploding star of knowledge.

The Angels wings spread wide while its green eyes darkened. 'You have no idea what you're doing!' it thought.

'...Wrong again Metatron because I know exactly what I'm doing and precisely who and what you are...!'

Its breath was momentarily taken by the man's ability to read its thoughts.

'Ha don't worry about that...it's only the obvious ones near the front of your mind ha-ha.! Well I've been busy reading up on the Angel Metatron, you were polite enough to tell me your name so I did a bit of digging. You see when I'm in the book I can go anywhere and do anything, so guess what, I popped into a library...ha-ha! It's too funny. Now bear with me because my research is based on ancient scriptures and hey, we all know how unreliable they can be. Anyhow it turns out you may have oversold your role because I don't believe you maintain the machine like you said, no from what I read you simply keep records of how it performs, and that's why you don't know how to fix what you have broken. In fact I'd go as far as to suggest all you can actually do is write things down, or however you record this stuff. So please don't misunderstand me, I'm not belittling you, if you are indeed the Metatron angel...'

'...I am Metatron!' The Angel's voice boomed.

'...In which case I'm happy to admit the scriptures paint you in a very positive light. There's no official Angel hierarchy recorded but from what I've seen...you're quite a special one, given great responsibility.'

'Well done Alex...you can read.'

'...It gets better though because you're quite a unique specimen in the history of the universe...as you used to be a mortal yourself...I'm sure you remember that, back before you swapped sides. Now I'm not sure of exactly how that happened or what kind of deal you cut, but either way you ascended to the heavens and in anyone's book that is a horrible act of desertion. To not just simply swap allegiance...but you utterly transformed and began to kill your own species. Wow...so which do you prefer to be called nowadays...turncoat or traitor?' Alex stood face to face with the towering Angel.

'I could kill you now for this insubordination?' The Angel's voice bellowed forth but Alex stood firm.

'Oh you're making this too easy Metatron. Two things to point out from that last threat alone; by definition insubordination is a refusal to follow orders from a higher authority and I do not recognise you as one of those, also, and this is the one that really makes you mad, you couldn't kill me even if you wanted to. It's too late for that now, because I'm the only one who can stop this and fix the damage you've done. Do you know for an Angel with such great responsibility, and for one who also used to be a human, so surely must uniquely appreciate both sides of this story...well you have really fucked this up...!'

The Angel marched forward and placed its hand on Alex's throat, it was nothing like the warming touch he'd felt previously. 'I could kill you easily...'

'...Yes, I know you physically could but the problem is...in reality you can't...I really don't think so, your killing side is down on earth skulking around in the dark, picking off innocent civilians in the name of a conflict that ended a long time ago, you're a bit like that Vietnamese soldier they discovered hiding in the jungle years after the war had finished...'

Alex took hold of the Angels' wrist and gently pushed it away from his neck.

'...Also you're on your own up here Metatron and you've been that way for millennia. I suppose that loneliness and desolation drove you to do this. To try to continue this war even though you knew it could end disastrously, until with some screaming madness you could no longer resist you lied to the book. You wrote yourself, well your hatred at least, into its pages to see what would happen, to find out what you could do, and now we're all reaping the cost of that morbid curiosity...'

'...The war will never be over between Angels and mor...'

369

'…In your deluded head I accept that as true, but one thing you have to listen to and please listen well…the first question you asked of me was why I am here and the answer I gave earlier was how I got here…but now I will finally answer that most important of questions…why! Well I'm here because you prayed for help, after losing control you didn't know what else to do, and as a direct result of your prayers help came from earth. It may have happened by accident because in a billion to one chance I found the space in the book where you placed your lie, but all the same I'm here and willing to help, so never forget that Metatron, because at this exact same moment during every second on earth someone prays for help from the heavens and your kind never came…not once! Far too wrapped up in your ancient and unrequited hatred, leaving us to fend for ourselves, and we haven't done a great job I'm well aware of that. We've fought and bred inequality between race and species. Even now we face killing our own planet, but through all of it, and this is what I'm most proud of, we survived, and I believe we will find a way to survive much longer without any help from you!'

'Such a wonderful story Alex but this war, our war, is the balance of the universe.' The Angel removed the book from its gown in an attempt at some calm defiance.

'No, no it isn't Metatron. Damn this is so frustrating for me! You're thinking too small…it is far, far bigger than that.' Alex reached across, placed the book on the table and squared it up between them. '…The balance of the Universe that you hold so dear is right under your beautifully angelic nose…' Alex pointed to the table and the Angel followed his thought. '…That book my desperate winged friend is the balance. Don't you see? Your purpose is to comprehend and fill its pages yet you cannot read it. At the same time it is the same book that a human can never fully comprehend yet they can read it, and within those spaces in between, rests our commonality. Here is where the books existence ensures we will always need each other, the proof that we must both understand for it is the only thing we have that binds us, the only object that exists in heaven as it does on earth…is this book!'

'Are you talking of bibles now Alex. I thought you weren't religious…?'

'…That book is no bible! A bible is a collection of texts and scriptures based on fragments of the last time our species existed together, and that some still hold up as sacred. This is not a bible…this is an encyclopaedia, a book that contains all information on every subject, a literary tome that literally has all the answers. Only this is a truly exceptional encyclopaedia because it also contains every thought, every feeling, positive, negative, useful and useless, that has ever occurred. Only by looking at this can one understand the power of all that knowledge and therefore finally comprehend who and what we truly are...!'

The man stared at the Angel and the Angel stared back.

'Remarkable...truly Alex you have managed to come up with one unique unifying theory and I am impressed. Alas even with our knowing all of this we still have a problem to solve.'

'I'm coming to that...'

'...Oh you have more?' The Angel sat back down.

'Oh yes Metatron...I have much more...!'

<u>88</u>

Harvey Cooper was sat in his office looking over the corkboard crimes and their connections while watching the clock tick slowly by. It was 11.30pm now and in another hour he planned on going down to Oscar in his cell. Mostly everyone in the station would be gone by then, the late patrols would still be out on the streets and in the cell block there would hopefully only be Bob Jenkins. Harvey was sure they could reach some new understanding about his plans for the night ahead.

He was still concerned about Kosminsky as there had been no contact but he alleviated his worry with some logical thinking; the big man had probably lost Rebecca because to be fair he wasn't trained in tailing people, but to put his mind at rest he called the number again, there was still no answer. Harvey reverted to his original reasoning that Kosminsky was fine, just having technical issues, or at this late hour he was at home asleep. To appease his anxieties the Inspector decided to bring his own plans forward. Picking up his coat and keys he made his way down under the station.

Officer Bob Jenkins clearly heard the footsteps coming down the corridor this time. Ironically, and dutifully, his phone was safely put away in a drawer while he sat quietly filling out his worksheets. He was wide awake and fully alert in case of an emergency situation, and decided to prove it to whoever was coming down the corridor by being stood to attention with his hat on. He actually felt beautifully vindicated and a little smug when the Inspector himself appeared at his door.

'Good evening Sir.' This perfect little policeman said.

'...Good evening to you Officer Jenkins, hope I haven't caused you any undue stress by ordering Cleaver and Downes to be brought back here...?' Harvey noted the professionalism of the cell guard and thought perhaps he may have played a small part in improving the standards within the force. The situation quite simply two sides of the same coin.

'No Sir, no stress at all, just doing my job...' Thankfully Bob stopped just short of clicking his heels Gestapo fashion.

'...Good man, is Cleaver okay?'

'Yes sir quiet as a lamb...!' Bob replied with no hint of a reference to Jay's adventures concerning bovidae mammals.

'Excellent! Could you keep a close eye on him please, he went through a rough time at Longmarsh. Regardless of his crimes we can't allow any form of abuse to prisoners under our accountability.'

'No of course not sir, I won't let anything happen to him...'

'...I know you won't Bob. Now I need to ask you a favour, it's rather a large one, but it's vitally important concerning the case of Oscar Downes. If you do this favour for me without question, I will do everything in my power to help you rise quickly and seamlessly up the ranks. Would you like to be given an opportunity to rise up the ranks...?' Harvey smiled confidently as if he'd some magic wand up his sleeve.

'...Yes sir I would very much like to do that.'

'Very good...any position or role in particular...?'

'...I have always wanted be mobile sir, motorbikes!' Bob nodded while still standing to attention.

Harvey didn't think it would be too difficult to get Jenkins signed up for the training courses. However he needed an extra edge, a bigger carrot to dangle, something to entice this guard to agree to his unusual demand. He pursed his lips before offering a considered and tantalising vegetable. '...Obviously you could look up that sort of thing on your own Jenkins, but I'm just saying, just putting it out there, that I could get you to the top of that list for the next training school. Would you like that Bob...?'

'Yes sir, I would very much.

'Then allow me to do that for you...' Harvey paused and took a deep breath. '...Obviously in exchange I would like you to open Oscar Downes cell and allow me access...'

'...That's not a problem Sir. I would have done that anyway. It's not as if it's the first time!' Bob laughed conspiratorially then found Harvey wasn't finished with him yet.

'...However that's not all. After you have opened the cell you will stand aside while Oscar and I leave the station...'

'...Fucking leave...!' Bob shockingly exclaimed in pure disbelief.

'Yes...you will then return here where you can play on your phone the rest of the night for all I care, but you will not return to Oscar's cell until five AM. By that time I will have returned with the prisoner and you can lock him back up. Do we have an understanding...?' Harvey watched the guard closely as he struggled to find a response to this outrageous, highly irregular, and totally illegal request. Bob was actually stuck for words and filling up with serious doubts.

'...Sir, with all due respect you are asking me to allow you to sneak out a known serial killer. You know I could refuse your offer and take my chances on getting a police bike license by myself...' The guard was still trying to understand the situation. Was this a test or was the Inspector actually losing his mind?

'It's what has to be done I'm afraid...!' Jenkins reaction now meant Harvey was left with no choice but to come clean. '...I should have known it would come to this and perhaps it would have been more prudent to have been straight with you from the start.'

'Please Sir, what's going on?'

'Oscar Downes admitted to me earlier this evening that there are more bodies, numerous more, and he's willing to take me to one of the burial sites to prove it. If I don't do this we may never know if he's the telling the truth. I certainly don't believe he would offer this to anyone else.'

'And you believe him...?' Bob asked because he'd heard the rumours, like all the officers had, about Oscars peculiar mind games.

'...I don't know if I believe him. All I know for certain is that he won't be out of my sight for a second...and I have this.' Harvey pulled his coat open to reveal the shoulder holster that held his police issue Glock 17 pistol. A firearm he was legally allowed to carry but had never needed or wanted to before. However this evening it was loaded and lay heavy under his jacket.

'Inspector please, you have to understand my position here...'

'...I do understand Bob! Do you think for one minute I'd risk my life and career if I suspected he was lying. All I need is the proof and we will have nailed the biggest serial killer this city has ever known. If I don't do it, we will have let all of that go; dozens of unsolved murders will stay as just that. The families of those victims will never have closure and it will all be because we didn't have the guts to check it out. So Bob please, all you have to do is let us out of here, we'll be back before dawn and Oscar will be safely back in that cell. Nobody will ever need to know, and given a month or two you could be revving up for your first day on a police bike.' Harvey finished his unofficial covert beg hoping it would be enough because he had nothing else left to offer.

Bob looked at Harvey while flipping a key off the silver ring on his belt. 'Sir you know I can't give you this key. It's more than my jobs worth...' He placed the key on the desk. '...All I can say to you with any guarantee is this, there is every chance I am going to be facing that way for the next twenty minutes and I'm not going to be turning back around. So if that's all then I will see you at five AM. Goodnight sir!' With that Bob Jenkins sat in his chair, spun round to face the wall, and became only a tiny part of the conspiracy.

'Thank you, Bob...'

On reaching Oscars cell he calmed himself outside the door for a minute, contemplating a hundred times over whether this was a sensible course of action. Sprinkled on top of that doubt were a thousand other things that could go wrong, and finally there was the massive question, one he'd never had to worry about before in his whole career, should he tell Oscar Downes that he was carrying a gun?

Ten minutes later the Inspectors car pulled quietly out of the station gates with both occupants apprehensive as to how this was going to play out. Harvey Cooper was driving while sat next to one of the most dangerous men on the planet with or without a murderous voice in his head, while the physically unrestrained Oscar Downes was sat next to an Inspector who'd just told him he was carrying a gun, a loaded weapon that would be used if he tried to escape. Something akin to a universal balance lay concentrated in the car as it drove towards the city centre.

'So whereabouts are we going?' Harvey asked in a professional tone.

'Go to the North Bridge and pull into the car park underneath it on the west side...' Oscar spoke quietly and confidently.

Of course Harvey wasn't completely unprepared for this bizarre outing, he'd been busy this evening, as well as cleaning and loading the gun he'd thought ahead to put a shovel and two head torches in the boot. Even the crayon drawings were in the passenger door pocket in case Oscar wanted them. He'd also filled a flask of coffee before he left and now as they drove he asked Oscar to pour himself a cup. Again he believed himself to be ahead of the game as Harvey hadn't boiled the kettle fully, because a steaming beverage could be dangerous in criminal hands. So Oscar poured out a lukewarm coffee and finished it in two swigs before pouring another one for Harvey and placing it in the cup holder underneath the radio.

'There's no need to worry Harvey I'm going to show you where I buried them.'

'I know you are Oscar. I'm not worried. I just wouldn't like anything unusual to happen.'

'Unusual, what like me trying to make an escape? I mean look at us, I have no restraints and we'll be in the dark under a bridge, fair enough you have a gun but I'll be holding a shovel...' Oscar laughed a gentle chuckle as he stared through his side window.

'What is this Oscar? Harvey hadn't seen this version of the man before.

'Nothing...I'm just trying to add some brevity to an extremely tense situation. You could have turned left there, cut off the corner, couple of minutes quicker!' Oscar was displaying that he still retained the knowledge.

'I'll go the way I know if that's okay.'

'Absolutely, but don't you dare try and charge me extra for that.'

Harvey watched the bridge appear up ahead. 'You're in a good mood tonight.'

'I am Harvey. I see you've brought along the drawings, a nice thing to have done but I don't need them, they're for you to keep and use. No, we don't need drawings because tonight we're simply two men trading wishes, which I believe to be a good and rare thing in this world. Ay? You wish to know the truth of what happened and I...well I wished for this, to be driving through this city at night one last time. You see I recognise that I'll never be released from prison for what happened and I don't care about that anymore...I only care about this, this moment, look can't you see I'm savouring every yellow lamp that glows on me, every street name, and every person still out and about in the place that I loved for so long.

'Very poetic, Oscar...'

'...I thought so.'

Harvey dipped down into the car park, fortunately the barriers were still up for entry, and they were always open for exit so the men knew they had some time. As he pulled the car to a halt he thought of Oscar being here three years ago, the bodies of two children in his boot, and how he must have dragged them out onto the gravel...

...He quickly forced his focus back to the job in hand. 'Right Oscar this is how it's going to work. We're going to the boot now to get the torches and shovel. We wear a head torch each, you can carry the shovel to where we need to go, but I will have the gun primed and ready to shoot just in case. You understand why, don't you?'

'Of course, but wouldn't it be just perfect if we didn't do that.'

'It would but this is clearly far from a perfect situation.'

Then with a calm assuredness the two men played their parts and walked down to the base of the bridge towards the largest column. It was pitch black in the shadows and Harvey was already struggling to keep Oscar under full coverage of the head beam. As they walked over the rough ground he would be able to see all of the man, then just his torso, and sometimes only his legs and the shovel would disappear into the blackness completely. Harvey placed his hand in his jacket and unclipped the Glock, knowing he would be able to draw and fire in less than a second as long as he could see the attack coming, but that really wasn't guaranteed under these conditions.

'You certainly chose the darkest corner Oscar.'

'The darker the better for this kind of work wouldn't you agree?'

Harvey chose not to respond.

'...Well here we are. This is the place. Three feet underneath here, most probably in petrified shreds of a black plastic bin bag are the two schoolgirl's remains.' Oscar was kneeling at the foot of a large brick support column as if he were ready to lay flowers rather than dig up bodies.

'Are you positive this is the place, Oscar?'

'Really Harvey...?'

'...It's been three years that's all I'm saying.' Harvey looked at Oscars small head and then realised that if the man looked directly at him he would be temporarily blinded by the beam of his head torch.

'Look I'm going to give you an amazing gift tonight Harvey. A thank you no less...because through all of this you've trusted me.'

Oscar stood up and facing Harvey he raised the shovel a foot off the ground. Harvey felt for the gun and clicked the safety off. Oscar stabbed the shovel blade down into the undergrowth so it stood up on its own.

'What are you doing? You know this is a loaded...'

'...Of course I do.'

Harvey noticed the man's head torch was being deliberately shone away from his eyes. If he didn't know better he would have sworn Oscar was aware the beam could cause a problem for the Inspector and was avoiding it.

'So what's this gift?' Harvey asked.

'Well for that you'll have to come closer...' The small man was standing dead still.

'Err yeah...I don't think I want to do that Oscar.' Harvey could feel the sweat of his palms slippery on the grip of the gun.

'Oh but you'll love it I promise. Just one last bit of trust is all I ask, and I'll give all of it to you, every single body in every location.'

Harvey moved forward through the darkness, slowly and carefully, fully alert, ready for the slightest twitch of Oscar's torso. He stepped into the thicker grass hating the fact that by getting closer he reduced his beams scope. Oscar's feet and the ground around him disappeared into black, and then the man's legs went out of view as Harvey moved to about a shovel swings length away, and as the half lit serial killer beckoned him forward.

'Just a bit closer and you will be able to see clearly…'

'…Oscar I swear I don't want to…but if forced to I will shoot…' Harvey threatened almost apologetically.

'You wouldn't shoot me…not if you thought about it first…after all I might have led you on a wild goose chase…then all you would have actually done is illegally brought a known serial killer out of the station and executed him under a bridge. I suppose you do have the shovel so you could always bury my body, then return to the station and come up with some elaborate scenario where I escaped my cell but you don't know where I am…' Oscar was assuredly calm as Harvey gripped the handle of the gun tighter still.

…Oscar, don't do this…!' Harvey looked into the man's blue eyes, never bluer than in the light of this torch, and never as clear.

'…I'm just telling you what could happen if you choose not to trust me anymore. You see I've told you before all of this I was a good man. Only after the attack at 46 Marlborough Drive did I become…well you know…but now I'm finally free to choose what I am. It's my decision to be good or evil, and you have always believed what I told you no matter how crazy it sounded…that I had a voice in my head, you opened yourself up to the possibility, when I told you the voice had left me you accepted it as true, complete blind faith… and for those little things I am eternally grateful.'

'Are you trying to get yourself shot?'

'Just two more steps so we're side by side and I'll show you what you want and what all of this has been for.'

'Oscar you know I can't do that!'

'But you have to now…otherwise you'll spoil it…!'

Harvey considered the two options that were left as he prepared to step towards the place where his beam would only illuminate Oscar's face, a horrible place, where he would be vulnerable to attack or shooting a man at close range.

'…Fine we'll do it your way Oscar.' Harvey whispered moving forward to stand next to him.

Oscar indicated with his eyes towards the brickwork of the footing. 'Down there…'

Harvey felt like a helpless fly trapped in the web of a clever spider, aware that when he looked down the lamps beam would render Oscar completely invisible in the dark. One more moment of trust the man had asked for, so he pointed the gun in the direction of where he believed Oscar was standing and lowered his beam to the wall behind the tallest heads of the grass.

'What is that…?' He asked puzzled. In the white circle of light he could see the gouged brickwork, the scratched lines forming the shape of a car about four inches square.

'…That's my mark…' Oscar said. '…It's my taxi. I scratched it in all the places where I buried bodies, now you'll be able to find them all if I tell you where…and that's my gift to you Inspector because you trusted me completely, then and now, when you had no reason to.' His voice was coming from the pitch black above Harvey's right shoulder; he couldn't be stuck in a more vulnerable position if he tried. The Inspector stood back up and turned his head to illuminate Oscars face when he heard the shovel being sharply pulled from the soil.

'Now if you'll give me some more light I'll dig these two up…'

Oscar plunged the shovel blade into the dirt as Harvey backed away to what he considered a safe distance, and illuminating the scene as Oscar began digging deep, but just as he removed the first shovelful of grass and soil Harvey walked forward and placed his hand on the small man's shoulder. 'It's okay Oscar. I believe you. You don't have to do this.'

The small man laid the shovel down. 'Well thank you again Harvey. To be honest I really didn't fancy doing it. Certainly won't be a pleasant job for whoever does.' Oscar sounded somehow ashamed by the conversation, maybe even a little embarrassed by it all.

Surprisingly though Harvey felt a little deflated and was trying to understand why; didn't he have everything he'd been looking for? In the end he guessed his mood could only be explained by the knowledge that Oscar would now be imprisoned for life. Harvey paused for a moment. 'I was thinking I'll call this in later. They'll send a forensics team out then to take care of exhuming the bodies, much easier to work in daylight.'

'So that's it then we go back to the station now…?' Oscar asked removing his head torch as they returned to the car.

'That would be for the best…' Harvey stopped by the driver's door. '…But seeing as it's only two o clock and I have you booked out until at least four. Would you like to…see the streets for a little longer…?'

'And I thought I was the crazy one Inspector? You can drive us back right now and not risk anything else for me…'

'…I know I could… but I thought we were exchanging gifts?'

Oscar walked up to Harvey, the Inspector standing rigid as the grateful man tapped him on the shoulder in a tribute to his trust. A bizarre and touching moment shared between the two, and one that convinced Harvey to bestow the ultimate accolade. '…You can drive if you want….' He said. '…My gift in return for yours, all's fair in the world then.'

Harvey threw the keys over to Oscar who in any great movie scene would have caught them one handed with his pose and timing perfect, however his reflexes weren't so sharp nowadays, and his attempt to catch them only deflected them from his outstretched hand into his own face.

'Ouch…!'

'…Are you alright?' Harvey asked spotting the small cut on Oscars lip.

'I'm okay…' He replied dabbing his hand to his mouth. '…A little bit of blood never hurt anyone…'

Oscar's humour was blacker than the shadows as he took his seat behind the steering wheel, adjusting the height before putting his hands forward to hold it tight, feeling the leather under his palms.

The Inspector poured another tepid coffee before buckling in for the ride. He knew that what he was doing would most likely appear ridiculous to anyone else, but to Harvey it felt right. Giving a small helpless man a tiny reward for a job well done, and when something feels right you have to follow your gut, it's the only way you ever learn lessons that truly last.

With a final look across to check that his passenger was safe and comfortable Oscar pulled out of the car park and back onto his city streets.

89

Standing silently on the landing she could clearly hear her mother snoring. Rebecca had sneaked out of the house a few times back in her adolescent past, usually to meet friends or boys, and her mother had always been upset at such deceit. This latest night excursion however had a far more sinister reason, but still the same problems faced her as way back when, keeping those floorboards quiet still the most difficult thing to achieve as she put on her coat and shoes at the front door. It was two o'clock in the morning and she would always be amazed how every little thing could make such an unnecessary squeak or creak at this ungodly hour. So slowly and carefully she clicked the front door closed behind her and walked silently to the gate, past experience causing her to turn and check the curtains of that nosey neighbour that so loved to twitch. Nothing stirred, not even a Jess, so soundlessly through the gate Rebecca headed back up the road towards the city. It was after only a brief internet search that she'd located the address of tonight's target, and now she'd finally escaped Housewitz, a name coined back when she was a moody teenager, she planned to find a taxi on the otherwise empty streets. It would take them to 7 Wilkes Avenue, the house where she and the voice believed Inspector Harvey Cooper would be quietly sleeping and with the knife concealed inside the tear of the coat again they began to speak as the big city lights came nearer.

When we get there you must leave it to me.

So I can't do it myself?

No. This one must go smoothly.

I did the first one smoothly.

No! We may be caught.

Rebecca had just rounded a corner when she stopped herself from walking any further. She wanted to clear up a small point, the one about the chance of imminent capture.

Why would we get caught?

Three murders in twenty four hours of people who can be connected! Surely even your feeble mind can see questions will be asked.

But with Inspector Cooper gone it should be easier.

It will never be easier.

Have you any ideas about the other problem. The unexpected events you were concerned about?

Be quiet Rebecca!

Oscar had unexpectedly applied the brakes causing surprised Harvey to shoot forward spilling the last of the coffee from his cup, the tepid liquid falling onto his left leg and over the drawings in the passenger door pocket.

'Bloody hell Oscar...!' Harvey looked across into a pair of widened eyes.

'There was a rabbit. It just ran out in the road. I missed it, look it's there. That was close...' Oscar smiled as he watched all of those lucky rabbits feet hop off into a hedge.

'Great news for the bunny I'm sure but I'm a little damp here, it's gone all over your pictures and my door.' Harvey pulled the soggy papers out and shook them as one to release any trapped coffee.

'Don't worry about those Harvey, they don't matter anymore. It was the voices work, not mine. Throw them away if you want...'

'...I certainly won't be doing that Oscar. Are you happy to keep driving?'

'Yes...I would like to drive a little more. There's a place I want to go.' Oscar took a left and headed out of the city down towards the docks.

'Fine but look, I think we've reached a lovely balance in our trust so don't mess it up, I still have the gun!' Harvey had hoped he wouldn't have to remind the little man about that threat; but they were both once more in unchartered waters, so some reliance and understanding were becoming increasingly vital, and it wouldn't hurt to know they were still on the same coffee stained page.

'I'm never going to throw these pictures away. If you don't want them then I will keep them in my own private black museum. To remind me of the first time I ever believed in err...another realm of understanding.' Harvey was doing all the talking as they drove down Leith Walk and past Dalmeny Street, the street Oscar had visited in his dreams, the place where the first drawing to be deciphered had been copied from, the falling man, Alex Webb. That mystery seemed a million miles away now. 'Do you know that street back there Oscar...?' Harvey was still curious in every facet of the case so couldn't resist asking.

'Dalmeny Street, yes of course I know it, I know all the streets, every single one for a twenty five mile radius. They're the tools of my trade...were the tools of my trade.' Oscar appeared content enough as he drove on with steady ease.

'So you know what happened there...?' Harvey enquired.

'No...' Oscar replied blankly.

'...You're not aware that's the street you drew in that picture, the one where the man was falling from the window...?'

'No because they weren't my drawings. Yes I drew them but I don't know where they were or who was in them. I've told you that before.'

'You did tell me that.' Harvey said and relaxed back in his seat.

Oscar turned left at the bottom of the hill heading away from the docks. After a roundabout he came to a stop at the temporary traffic lights that were still messing up everyone's daily commute. He pulled the car to halt in front of their crimson glow.

'I think you can probably just drive through Oscar, there's no one around, and we can both see it's clear ahead. Also I'm a policeman and I'm not going to issue my own car with a ticket.' Harvey was wafting the drawings to help them dry before putting them in his jacket pocket.

'On this auspicious occasion I'd rather obey the law of the land Inspector.'

Harvey struggled to resist the incongruity involved when Oscar Downes mentioned obeying any laws of any land, then he noticed him glance across and give a knowing playful smile.

'Where are we going exactly?' The Inspector asked beginning to struggle a little with the gift he was giving to Oscar. Time wasn't a major problem yet if everyone stayed in their beds and no one noticed the empty cell at the station, but on the other hand the uncomfortable truth was that Harvey was still risking his career with every second he was gifting the man.

'Haven't you deduced where we're going yet Inspector?' Oscar turned another right.

'I wouldn't have asked if I knew.' Harvey looked over his shoulder to read the street sign but it was already lost in the darkness that followed them.

'Here we are...' Oscar pulled the car into the kerb and switched off the engine. '...the last place on earth I was really me.'

Harvey looked past Oscar to see the house number and then understood all too clearly. 'This is where it happened isn't it, this exact spot...?'

'Yes.' Oscar replied.

'46 Marlborough Drive.' The Inspector said while nodding gently.

'Hmm innocent, hardworking Oscar sat here one night before being attacked by two drunken women who accused him of being evil. They hospitalised me and when I woke up and recovered from my injuries...I discovered I was…' The little man seemed to pause at that thought. '…It was in that house waiting Harvey…the voice was in there and it came out to find me. In a bizarre way you've never met the real Oscar Downes, he died here that night in every sense of the word, stopped existing as he was…everything I'd ever done or said or wished for was just… wiped away.'

As he spoke the tears fell but he wasn't sobbing, he wasn't breaking down, Oscar was sitting perfectly still staring ahead, thinking on a life lost and each and every life that he'd been forced to take.

'Scott Hutchinson lives there now…' Harvey said in an attempt to alleviate some of the gravity in the car.

'Who…?'

'…Oh you will love this. It's all connected in some bizarre way. Scott is the best friend of the guy you drew chopping off the farmers head and the one standing in the lion's cage…' Harvey reached inside his jacket for the drawings but Oscar grabbed his arm firmly and held it as he shouted in his face.

'Leave them alone! They're not mine…how many times!'

'…Woah Oscar okay…calm down let go…!' Harvey was having his right arm pinned down to his side by the surprisingly strong wiry man, meaning there was no way he could reach the gun from this position which concerned him, as he'd be needing his right hand to reach the left sided holster. Staying as calm as he could while his thoughts were racing he faced more of Oscars sudden fury.

'Those drawings are not mine. I didn't kill anyone…none of this is my fault and you know that so shut up…!' Some of Oscar's warm spittle flecked over the Inspector's cheek.

Harvey was attempting to reach the gun with his left hand. The small man noticed this and decided to help him out by reaching in and grabbing it from its holster. The Inspector stopped his struggle as Oscar held the Glock in his small right hand and disengaged the safety.

'Oscar, what the hell are you doing…?' Harvey even managed to sound remarkably composed considering his position.

'You know what Harvey I don't know what I'm doing…the last time I knew that was five and a half years ago!' He was still holding Harvey's right arm and the gun but at least he'd stopped shouting.

'Why did you want to come back here…?' Harvey asked trying hard to rebuild their connection and convince himself it wasn't going to end like this.

'...I'm visiting my grave, Inspector! Isn't that what good people do? Go and pay their respects to their dead, to the person they lost...let them know they're still thinking about them...that they miss them every day...and it hurts...and it always will...'

'...Oscar!' The Inspector tried to stop that train in its tracks.

'With all due respect Harvey if I were you...I'd be very quiet right now, as a mouse in fact, because I have something to say and I also have your loaded gun, and if that's not persuasive enough then you really aren't grasping the uncertainty of my situation. Strange isn't it...I remember a time not so long ago when the only thing you wanted was for me to talk. You even used salacious lies and insulting smears about my parents to make that happen. I did tell you back then I would never forget what you did.'

Harvey felt himself go cold while trying to think his way out of this. His options being severely limited, there was nothing he could do physically right now, and Oscar was threatening him to remain quiet, so the little man had the upper hand in every way.

'...You know I'm a firm believer that a bad thing one day can become a positive the next...now look at what's happened...we've swapped roles. I have always trusted that principal, that everything balances itself out in the end, but who would've thought I was right all along?'

Harvey had no option but to give in completely when Oscar raised the gun and pointed it towards to his listening face.

'Inspector, Harvey, trusted friend...I really don't know what to call you right now. All I do know is that I'm finally holding the reins of my life again, and because of this loaded gun I'm also holding yours...' He tapped the barrel on Harvey's forehead. '...It's just so powerful what goes on inside there, deep in the mind, where you have dreams and knowledge and all the answers but this gun, this simple piece of engineering, can end all of that right now. In a flash of carbine there would be nothing left of you, all the things you'd ever imagined, all the rules you followed, all the lessons you've learned would be gone, wiped away...if I chose to move my finger less than one half inch. Do you understand now...you can speak?'

Harvey had never been asked to converse with a gun tapping gently on his head before. It felt like a strange twist on the old Chinese water torture, the one where the repetitive drops of water would stop you from sleeping, forcing you to stay awake until your mind broke, and after which you would tell your captors anything they wanted to know. '...What do you want me to understand Oscar...that you're going to kill me?' Harvey then thought he would be terribly disappointed if those were to be his last words.

'I want you to respect me...nothing over the top or fake, just tell me that you understand why I'm like I am...'

'...Of course I understand...I doubt anyone understands more!'

'Prove it!' The little man snapped sharply. 'Show me you know what's going on in my head. For instance what do I want...right now...what do I want?'

Harvey was only sure about one thing at this moment, the threat that he couldn't be blasé with his response, trotting out some nicely worded calming answer would almost certainly result in his death. This was no time for trained police negotiations, or psychological tricks, to help control a situation until back up arrived. His only option was to work it out, then answer as honestly as possible, and if his last words were exactly how he truthfully felt, he could live and die with that. '...You want me to let you go!'

'Correct..!' Oscar smiled though it appeared as a ghastly grimace to Harvey. '...You do understand...but I'm concerned about something else, I'm concerned that if you let me go you would you try and hunt me down again, even though you know I'm innocent. Would you do that Inspector?'

'Yes I would.' Harvey was going all in with honesty and hoping Oscar was still of sane enough mind to understand that.

'So quick with your answer, it must be true. So Harvey tell me...why would you chase a man who you know is innocent...?' Oscar was clearly enjoying this exchange.

'...Just because I know you're innocent doesn't change anything about the case. I doubt anyone else would believe it, so when it comes to that I'm afraid...majority rules in this instance, you would still have to have your day in court.' Harvey could feel a cold bead of sweat running down his back.

'But I couldn't prove a god damn thing Inspector. I would stand up in front of that judge and blame a voice in my head...'

'...But I would vouch for you. It may damage my career but...'

'...Damage your career!' Oscar said and began laughing. 'You need to wake up Harvey; your career at this moment is just as damaged as my future, because I'm not going back to that cell tonight, and take my apologies if that inconveniences you, but let's call it a little karma for all those insults you bestowed on my parent's memory. Does that seem fair to you?'

'...Do you know what Oscar, in another situation with another gunman...I would believe, because of the time you're taking, that you aren't going to shoot me. So if I follow that logic with your current emotional state I can take a good guess that you haven't actually made up your mind about what you're going to do.'

Oscar looked puzzled before replying 'That is really not the answer to my question, however it is true...I am a little undecided...but please without further distraction do you agree that losing your career is a fair price to pay for what you said about my parents?'

Harvey took a deep breath before attempting to explain himself using only the truth. 'Well ultimately that's your decision. I don't care what you think and I care even less about your opinion on what I think. Is that clear enough for you? I will say one thing Oscar before you do whatever it is you're going to do. I gave that disgusting description of your parents for exactly this reaction, to make you talk, and to find out what you really were, so to that end I consider my original decision to be a valid and complete success. That's the only answer I can give...' He waited for the blinding flash from the muzzle, accepting of this fate, his only wish that his wife would understand how much he loved her.

Oscar pressed the gun firmly onto Harvey's skull.

91

Rebecca had successfully located a taxi, a different driver altogether, and after an uneventful journey she'd been dropped off at the end of Wilkes Avenue. Inspector Cooper's house, number seven, was quite unsurprisingly in complete darkness as she approached the front door.

Are you ready to have some fun?

I so am.

92

'I know how to end this.' Alex announced to the Angel.

'So you have it all worked out in your tiny mortal mind?' It asked.

'Yes I do, and as you well know it's not so tiny anymore.' He tapped his forefinger on his temple.

'Then choose your path and prepare to fail.'

'I don't think so, Metatron. All of this is your doing. You tampered with the book, you wrote yourself into it so a part of you, the warmongering hateful part of you, could slip through the tiniest gap you created and appear on earth. The opposite end of that tiny split came out at 46 Marlborough Drive and once it was there, your mighty Demon sent to purge the world, well it found out it was useless, inept. Exactly the same as when I go into the book. I can't change anything or physically move an object, all I can do, and all it could do, was observe then ghost around invisible and pointless.'

'But you didn't come here from that address.' The Angel said.

'That's really not the point, your gateway or glitch is moving, exploring, it's becoming a living entity in itself now. You created it and I fell through, but what you desired was pointless to begin with because your Demon was unable to act on your hate. '

'It was preparing for my vengeance…!' The Angel said proudly.

'…That's a lie or at best a ridiculous overstretching of the truth, unless of course you consider preparation to be a silent haunting full of frustration and anguish. Your Demon was stuck in total desolation until by sheer fluke it found a way to enter a mortal mind, through the back of a man's split skull. I suppose I shouldn't be surprised, it's typical really that the mighty Angel Metatron would use such a disgusting form of introduction.'

'I'd call it adapting to the circumstances.'

'Well I'd call it a virus, and that is quite literally an insult to viruses. When it found a way in it then discovered it could control its host through mental torture and physical manipulation. Oh the mighty Angels in Heaven above shall seek the men of earth and smite them!' Alex held the Angels stare.

'Are you mocking us…?'

'…No…because there is no us, you're the last of your kind and you have no recourse but to continue doing your job.'

Alex was ready to take his place upon the throne of ascendency. He was becoming the greater power. 'Where did they go Metatron, your armies, your higher authority, your friends...why did they leave you here all alone in the world of white? Were you abandoned...or perhaps you were sentenced to this solitary existence...?'

The Angel stood and turned its back but Alex didn't care about the snub.

'...You know when I first arrived here I believed I was in a prison cell. Some place I was condemned to be stuck in for eternity...only now I know I was half right, this is a prison, only one not designed for me...this jail is just for you. It's obvious you're serving a penance, a sentence for whatever it was that you did. Do you want to tell me about it or would you prefer I surmised some more...?'

Alex watched the Angel figuratively fall from its pedestal high up in its own conscience and felt it land in a crumpled heap, its head dropping slowly to its chest, and those once magnificent wings now appeared ragged as the cloth of the Angel's gown begin to fade, from astonishing white silk to worn grey linen.

'Alex, Alex, Alex, what is to be done with you? I could answer your question but there would be no point, it will not help our plight.' The suddenly ordinary looking Angel said.

'Hey we all need someone to talk to.' Alex said to the man in dirty robes, with greying hair and liver spotted hands and the one who spoke back to him with an aged voice.

'...I knew when I let you in to see the book you would have an increased capacity in knowledge, that inevitably you may even begin to believe you could ascend to my heights of spiritual awakening. However, you have superseded those estimations me and are still improving, refining your abilities, however it should not have been this way.'

'Well when you mess with things you don't understand, you get burned. So tell me what happened here, why you're condemned to be alone...?' Alex still had some spaces in his knowledge to fill, but not many.

'Very well...' The crumpled Angel began. '...You are correct in your assumption that this is a prison for me...but it wasn't always like this. At one time there were unknowable numbers occupying this realm, and we gave of ourselves. We gifted all of our love and hope, creativity and perfection to mortals everywhere. We watched and guided lost souls and asked for nothing in return...'

Alex raised his hand to interrupt the Angel. '…Please stop…you keep on lying. There's no point in twisting the truth with me…'

'…I know what we did!' The Angel screamed but that voice no longer carried or boomed. It was just the desperate whimper of an old man.

The book had shown Alex this Angel's true nature and he believed it was time to share, to clip its flighty fantasies, and bring it down to earth for good. '…You gave us nothing for free…you demanded everything in return. You expected all the mortal souls to praise you and remain spiritually indebted to you for the gifts you were giving…but all of those things existed anyway, and we would have found them by ourselves eventually. Technically speaking all you did was get involved in the middle of our evolution and tried to take the glory. When humankind slowly grew with or without your help and learned of nature and science and the building blocks of our own existence you were finished. Our giant leap of knowledge over faith meant those Angels were no longer required, all their false claims and deities, their threats of hell and damnation were slowly and rightly found out. Leaving them with no option but to move on and out into the vast unexplored emptiness of a billion other universes, to find ones still at that infant stage containing young planets green and learning, and where their help would be accepted and of some use. They all left, evolved if you will, except you. The Angel condemned, staying here because you still believed in the ancient injustices of a long forgotten time.'

'Truly impressive my mortal friend…'

'…Friend? I thought we were partners trying to solve a problem, Holmes and Watson I recall, except I'm blatantly the one wearing the deerstalker now.'

'Hmm perhaps, but you still haven't grasped a most important element…!' The old Angel smirked then began to laugh. It was a cold hearted sound full of goading.

'…What…what don't I know…?' Alex didn't have much headspace left but worryingly he it was right. He was missing something.

'…What is the most important question of all…?' It asked proudly.

Alex slipped smoothly through the vast vaults of his beautifully organised mind and quickly found what he sought. 'Why…!' He answered doubtfully.

'…Correct. Why! Of course it's why…' Incited the Angel '…After all who, what, when and where are just details, mere details. The question 'Why' is the reason behind everything that has happened. It is the question all fledglings ask more than any other, any young parent will confirm that statement, and right now you are the ultimate fledgling!'

Alex began unconsciously biting his bottom lip as the solution to his sudden concern began to slowly form, the puzzle pieces starting to slot into place. 'Of course...all of this...yes, oh my god...why...I stopped asking it too soon...why would you do this...it's bigger again isn't it...?' He said with the gravest concern.

'...It most certainly is Alex. You will never understand...I could allow you access to all the knowledge and experiences of a trillion human lifetimes but you will never ascend to my heights...for I am the Angel.'

Alex's mind began to see quite clearly how he'd been played from the beginning. His heart pumping fast and his knees buckling now that Metatron was cutting his puppet strings. Oh no.no.no...!'

'...Yes Alex. Have you unscrambled it?'

'You want all of this to end...of course you do. You're stuck here while this universe continues. When everything collapses you can make your escape, move on like the others, your job would be over with because...well what would there be to record. This isn't your universe is it? It's mine...' He fell to his knees in the shallow white mist.

'...Ahhhhhh and so the penny drops with a resounding clang. Can you hear that? It's very similar to the sound of a machine breaking down.' The Angel shone brightly as it laughed and while resuming its former glory

'...No...I can still stop it from happening!' Alex countered though he had no idea how as his brain flicker booked through all of its new knowledge for answers.

'...Oh if only that were true Alex but I'm afraid it's not possible. All you can do is stay here with me, safe in the knowledge that my Demon is making mortals pay in the last years of their existence. I invite you sit here at my side until I make my escape. Soon enough this book and everything in it will be gone. With no evidence remaining I will have won and you will be extinct...as I planned from the start.'

'...No...I can go back and kill the demon!' Alex slammed his hand on the book as the Angel gave its reply.

'Oh for certain that would be perfect...but as we've discussed you can't do anything down there. You are nothing but a one armed comatose patient in a hospital. A desperate situation is growing by the way, questions are already being asked about turning off your life support, and it is also why you were the perfect subject for this experiment.'

'I'm an experiment...?'

'...Of course you were. I needed to know that my...what did you call it again... oh yes my warmongering hateful side, was doing as I hoped. From the very start Alex you have been nothing more than my little errand boy. Thank you for your service in a job excellently done...' The Angel began to glow even brighter as its perfect wings spread wide and full, taking its eyes from the book.

Alex took his chance to grab it, tearing the covers open his mind entered while his body fell to the floor while his mortal hands gripped it tightly to his chest. The Angel responded knowing it must remove it from that grasp. 'Come back Alex give me the book...!' It screamed and once again its voice carried, and its voice boomed.

Alex instantly appeared on Wilkes Avenue standing invisibly in front of the woman who'd just exited a taxi.

93

The barrel of the gun was leaving a distinct imprint on the Inspector's forehead. Oscar was staring at the tiny circle with some interest but couldn't understand why anymore. All that remained inside his head was the wreckage left behind from the voices tenure, any moments of lucidity in recognition of his former self appeared as blowing clouds that disappeared with a perpetual movement. Every passing minute he was sane, then not, then he was empty, then he was crazy, and he was lost in a cold desert of doubt without the voice.

Since it left his world Oscar had tried to tidy up the debris scattered in his head. To walk calmly back into his previous life by picking up his original step from where he left off, but five years is far too long a time to be away. Everything he'd known so well and took for granted, including his original soul, was now malformed and unrecognisable. For sure the basics were still there, the geography of his personality, familiar thoughts and pathways but they were old and used, weathered and worn, and didn't identify to him anymore. Oscar found he was stuck in an abandoned city of a mind where all the rules had been changed, all broken so badly he couldn't make sense of it anymore.

'…Harvey, you have a map of the city in your car…?' Oscar asked grasping at a tendril of calm thought.

'Of course…it's in the glove box. It's old though!'

Oscar removed the book with its torn cover and placed it on the dashboard with the gun still pressed against the Inspectors head '…Do you have a pen…?'

Harvey resisted his initial instinct to move and spoke instead. 'There's a pencil in my inside pocket, left hand side.'

Oscar slid his hand inside and removed it. '…Right, I'm going to cover your face now with this book but don't worry, understand though if you move or try anything unexpected…ha-ha…I will fire this gun into your head. Trust me when I tell you the scales of your survival are tilting up and down faster and faster all the time and I have no preference for which way they fall…' He placed the book across the Inspectors face and began scribbling tiny x's on pages that showed the city centre, the woodlands in the hills, and the pathway down to the river. '…Now that is approximately where they all are Harvey. I'm sure your men could find them with my car engravings also marking the spot. There…I have given you everything wicked that I have ever done and my price is for nothing more than a kind judgement. You're a good man Harvey and I don't want to shoot you, but thoughts are telling me different, because my survivalist side really wants to pull the trigger...' He lowered the book and placed it on the Inspectors lap. '...I need you to know one more thing...before I make my escape, that all of this; all of your time and trust you have given me will stay in my heart for as long as I walk this earth. Now look at me. I want you to see I'm telling the truth...'

Harvey opened his eyes and saw in the yellow halogen glow of the streetlamp a tiny smile on Oscar's mouth, the glistening of a tear, as he turned the gun to point at his own face, and fired.

It was almost a minute before the Inspector managed to take a healthy breath; his ears still ringing from the sound of the confined blast. Oscar's body lay slumped forward on the steering wheel with a hole blown out the back of his head, and Harvey found himself strangely paralysed with a mourning sadness and an agonising frustration. He could see the gun still in Oscar's hand, and the blood dripping down to pool under the pedals his feet were still resting on. The small man had died as he'd lived, at the wheel, and that may never seem much to anyone else, but to Harvey it was the most poignant of visions.

Scott Hutchinson had been playing a samurai video game when he heard the gunshot. From his front room he could see the blood sprayed over the inside of the driver's window, and after everything he'd been through lately he was terrified. He was still trying to talk to the call operator, who had asked him to hold the line, when he saw Harvey Cooper get slowly out of the car and walk, almost stumble, towards the house.

'Inspector, are you okay...?' Scott was already asking as he opened the front door of 46 Marlborough Drive.

'...Yes Scott I'm fine.' Harvey said but he sounded far from it as he looked down at his blood splattered jacket. 'I had a prisoner in the car he's just shot himself. Can you call the police...?'

'...They're already on their way. Do you want to wait inside, get cleaned up a bit? It's all over your face...' Scott was trying not to ask but the words came out regardless. '...Is that Jay?'

'What...?' Harvey replied then realised. '...No it's...not Jay!'

Sirens began to wail in the distance as the front doors on the road started to open and carefully the curious and concerned came to see. Harvey couldn't deal with any of that now, he needed time to think,

Looking down he found the A to Z map book, relatively untouched by Oscar's brain matter, gripped in his hand.

'Where's the bathroom...?' He asked and Scott pointed.

Once inside Harvey locked the door behind him and threw up a brown liquid bile which was mainly coffee, and unsurprisingly warmer than when it had been swallowed. After washing his blood spattered face he looked up at the cracked plaster on the ceiling. This was the house where the voice had first come from, the place it had started, and for Oscar at least, had now ended.

Back at the front door Scott was talking to a uniformed officer while the other was looking into the car with a torch.

'The Inspector Cooper...?' The officer asked quizzically.

'Yes he's in the...' Scott stopped talking when he saw Harvey walking towards them.

'Inspector...?' the Officer said.

'...Chambers...!' Harvey said, remembering for the first time in his life an officer's name. He looked across at the other officer stood by the car waiting for an ambulance and backup. '...No I've forgotten his.' Then their awkward moment was disturbed as Harvey's phone rang and he grabbed it up quickly in hope that Kosminsky was finally reporting in, but unexpectedly it was his wife again. Perhaps he shouldn't be surprised, it was four in the morning, he hadn't come home and she loved him. A fact proven daily and he loved her back, otherwise he would have considered this moment as a trifle too serious to be taking personal calls.

'Hi there darling, I'm sorry I've been...'

'Shut up and listen...!' A vicious female voice whispered. It certainly wasn't Flo. '...You need to come home. We want to see you.'

'Who is this...?' The colour disappearing from his freshly washed face.

'...You know very well that I don't have a name here. Come back home now...alone!'

'Where's my wife?'

'Lying right next to me, so do not hesitate in your actions Inspector, because I can assure you...I certainly won't!' The line went dead.

Harvey looked at the scene in front of him which appeared to be moving in flashes and bursts of colour. He had to keep his thoughts together just to force a single step forward, but he had to make a move to get home, this wasn't done yet. It was waiting for him.

'Scott, give me your car keys now...!' Harvey shouted and Scott ran inside to get them.

'Inspector I must strongly suggest you stay here until this is cleared up.' Chambers implored.

'I don't have a choice. You stay here, sort it out best you can...'

Chambers had one final question as Harvey grabbed the keys from Scott and headed towards the small black Golf. 'Sir who is that in your car...?'

'It's err, its Oscar Downes...!'

'...What?' Chambers voice came out unnaturally high as Harvey jumped in the black VW Golf; and where he immediately picked up on two uncomfortable facts, the fuel gauge was touching red, and the whole thing stunk of cannabis.

Rebecca and the voice sauntered around the bedroom picking up objects and studying them before turning back to the lady on the bed. 'And what is your name...?' They asked.

'Florence.' Harvey's wife answered with the freshly opened four inch slash on her cheek moving as she did so.

'Florence...pretty name...do you know what it means...?'

Flo chose not to answer; instead she continued watching closely the young woman who'd invaded her home.

'...It means to flourish or to prosper, of course looking at your dwelling and your current situation that description is either plain wrong or a sick joke. What do you say to that Florence...?'

Again the lady didn't answer and they didn't blame her. Florence was of no relevance other than bait, and she was only going to be breathing until the Inspector got there.

Flo's cheek was stinging from the gash but she wouldn't give the bitch the pleasure of seeing her cry or beg. Instead she did the only thing she could, and something she had picked up off Harvey over the years; if in doubt, study the problem. So with that in mind Florence just laid there quietly, watching the woman, looking for an opportunity, a moment of weakness, anything she or her soon to be home husband could use. It didn't take long for her to notice the woman was talking under her breath.

We must kill the Inspector quickly. He may have a gun. This is why we are keeping his wife alive. I want to know he is unarmed before I kill them both.

I understand.

Excellent! Shall we cut this woman some more? She hasn't squealed yet.

No there's no need. I'll kill for you but please don't make me torture.

Listen to you now...a murderess with morals.

Unbeknown to either woman or demon there was someone else in the bedroom watching this all play out. Alex's attempts to thwart the Demon's actions or to make it aware of his presence on his arrival had failed and he knew time was running out. In another dimension the Angel and his other self were grappling for control of the book. As he had entered he'd gripped it to his chest as tight as he could, hoping it would give him enough time to find a way of ending it, but even now he could feel himself weakening, the

Angel's desperation growing stronger to take the book from his hands and force him back.

Harvey dragged the car around the corner of the street and braked hard outside his house, the petrol gauge still showing red so maybe there was someone helping him from up above. As he got out he looked up to his bedroom window where he could see the feint silhouette of Rebecca Jones against the thin curtains. Sickeningly he then realised in the turmoil he'd forgotten the Glock still in Oscar's dead right hand. Perfect he thought, so here he was unarmed and extremely fatigued, because he was finding out that even adrenaline has limits.

He opened his front door with no fear of being heard and stood at the bottom of the stairs. 'Leave my wife alone. Come down and face me!' He shouted up to Rebecca.

'No! You will come up here or I will kill her right now.'

'How do I know you haven't already...?'

'...Shall we kill you Florence? ANSWER ME!' The voice roared.

'No...!'

Hearing his wife's frightened voice and her name spoken by the monster chilled him to the bone and his adrenaline fired again. The bedroom door was ajar as he reached the top of the stairs so he could see Rebecca standing at the bedside looming over his wife.

'Please leave her alone...!' Harvey spoke through gritted teeth as he stepped carefully into the room with no plan and little hope.

'...Why would we do that...?' Rebecca placed her hand on Florence's hair and pulled her head back, exposing her throat.

'Okay, okay you clearly have the upper hand and I can't stop you from doing anything...I know that...all I want is...'

'...Don't dare stall for time Harvey, trying some pathetic small talk until help arrives, you people of law sicken me more than the rest.' Rebecca's mouth was moving but Harvey knew it wasn't her speaking.

'I'm not doing that...!' He said desperately. '...There's something I need to tell you. You might be interested.'

Rebecca drew the knife with the flat edge down so it didn't quite pierce the skin of Florence's other cheek. 'I have no interest in anything you have to say mortal!'

'But I know all about you, Oscar told me everything, how to kill you and send you back to hell...' Harvey was lying but knew he'd earned another ten seconds at best as a repulsive laugh came back in response.

'...Ha Oscar was an old suit I once wore and discarded. I'm surprised the coward isn't dead yet without me. He knows nothing because I don't come from hell...far from it!' Rebecca lowered the knife this time to rest on Florence's throat. 'Do you have a gun Harvey?'

'No I came unarmed...I wanted to talk with you.'

'I don't want to talk to you...I have enough with this one...' Rebecca's finger pointed to herself.

'Then at least kill me first...!'

'Hmmm decisions. Surely watching your wife die would be more painful!'

'Why does it matter to you? You're going to kill us both anyway...'

'...Oh it matters to us...!' Rebecca began to slowly cut across his wife's throat, her murderous eyes never leaving Harvey, and adoring the result it wreaked upon the man.

'NO! You bastard...!' Harvey screamed, he rushed forward to stop the nightmare but with blinding speed Rebecca sidestepped his ugly lunge then with knife in hand she pushed him to his knees.

'Know your place...!' The voice spoke. '...under my mercy!'

'No...' Harvey whimpered with defeat.

'...Oh I almost forgot...I killed your friend by the way, did you know...?' The blade with his wife's warm blood on it was playfully tapping under Harvey's chin with the voice enjoying every second. '...Your friend, Oscar's old guard, I could never pronounce his name...yes he's dead, where I left him, under the back seat of a cinema to be found with all the other rubbish when they clean up...' They angled the blade round to slice. 'Good bye Harvey!'

'Leave him alone Metatron...!' A female voice suddenly spoke.

Rebecca's head turned slowly round to witness Florence getting up from the bed, with her throat bleeding although the knife hadn't cut it through completely. That was to be the final act, another level of sadistic cruelty; it had wanted to finish the job while the dying Inspector watched.

'...I said leave him and face me!'

Rebecca's grip loosened on the Inspector, grave puzzlement painting her expression, and the voice itself was struck dumb for a moment as Florence gradually dragged herself up to stand before it.

Harvey, still down on his knees was unable to move as his brave wife stared Rebecca and the beast down.

'I know all about you Metatron and I do know your weaknesses. I can send you back to heaven anytime I want...' Florence was stood perfectly still as she spoke.

'What...is this?' The voice asked.

'...I know all about the machine and the book, the war between men and Angels...and I'm here to send you home so bring the knife this way, if you can defeat me you'll be free to do as you want!'

As she spoke the blood seeping from Florence's cheek and throat made a glittering red scarf around her neck.

Alex watched the demon from within her human form and knew he had no time to waste; he had to learn how to operate Florence's injured body quickly. So far his plan had worked; he'd entered through the gash on the woman's cheek and was now in her mind, seeing through her eyes, speaking through her mouth, as he finally had some physical form within the book.

Harvey found he couldn't speak as Rebecca lunged forward, helplessly he watched on as Florence respond to the attack, catching the younger woman's arm and using her own momentum to turn her in the air so they both crashed onto the bed. He was struggling to focus on the wrestling pair as the brawl became a blur of red with flashes of knife blade in a whirlwind of primal ferocity. Then as quickly and viciously as it had started, it stopped, and his desperate hopes were crushed once more as Rebecca rose to her feet while Florence lay prone on the bed. There was blood in the young woman's hair but Harvey only had eyes for the body of his wife on her back, unmoving and silent. 'Florence...Flo..!' He begged with a whispered scream, his desire overwhelming to be next to her when the demon killed him, to hold her close so they would travel onwards together. Harvey struggled to his feet as the young woman towered before him

'Harvey...Harvey?' The voice inside Rebecca spoke.

'Just let me hold her before you kill us...'

Rebecca's voice cut him off. '...Harvey, listen to me! We haven't got much time. Phone for back up, get everyone here. Officers, cars, helicopters, whatever you need. Get them here now...!'

'What ...?'

'...My name's Alex...Alex Webb...we've never met properly but I'm here. I'm inside this woman's mind hunting a monster in a maze. Get help now...!'

Rebecca Jones body stood transfixed as the sounds in her head became stranger. There were two voices now so her true self took the decision to seek cover and conceal her consciousness; a survival instinct to thwart this new invasion that felt like her only resort. She was scared, confused by her own mind as a deadly game of hide and seek ensued, one she was hosting but didn't want to be part of.

'My wife...?' Harvey said.

'...There's still time if you get that help quickly!' Rebecca's voice snapped back then fell silent.

During the struggle on the bed the stitches on Rebecca's wound had opened. Alex had seen the blood, sensed the opportunity, and through sheer force of will had taken it, to put himself inside her mind, but now looking around it he found he was as lost as he'd ever been.

The Demon had sensed his arrival, then instantly constructed and concealed itself within a labyrinth of its own design, meaning if Alex was to succeed he'd have to solve it, hunt it down and kill it before he lost his grip on the book. All the time the Angel in the white world was slowly beginning to turn that tide, gradually working its perfect fingers under the man's locked grip to take it back, to retrieve its life's work and win the war. Meanwhile, standing alone and dwarfed beneath the soaring walls of the maze, Alex was listening for the slightest clue of which way to go but there was nothing. He looked up to see the stars in their firmament, the same ones Kosminsky had mentioned, totally useless for navigation because of their movement. Of no help at all...unless...of course they were moving, Alex thought, they're not stars, they never were.

He was wiser now than he'd ever been and saw them for what they truly were. Those moving stars were neurons passing information in miniscule sparks of electricity within Rebecca's brain. Each twinkling light was a new thought or action currently in conveyance to the appropriate department, because this was the life machine in action, and the answer was up there in the sparkling darkness, if only he could read their patterns. What did it mean? Work it out! Think Alex!

Yes! There it was, the answer making perfect sense to his glorious intellect, if he wasn't using her brain to make those stars move, to create this observable sky then the Demon must be. This new hypothesis caused him to concentrate on the direction the vast majority of the stars were travelling, and he now set off in the opposite direction, through the maze, back to the source. Alex began to jog then run as he grew more confident with his strategy until with a sickening thud he was dragged to the ground. There was no one here and nothing to have tripped over but he knew perfectly well what had felled him; his grip on the book was being loosened by the Angel at the table in the white world. The war was raging on two fronts with only one soldier to defend both borders, but he would not be seen to fail in that duty until his blood ran cold, and heaving his fractured form to its feet he marched on towards the Demon.

Harvey had phoned for the ambulance then decided to call his Superintendent even though it was still five in the morning. He didn't even allow Jeff Shilling to speak as he explained in a desperate outburst the ongoing situation. All Jeff managed to understand was that Harvey and his wife had been attacked and were still in peril, time was of the essence, and the attacker was still in the house. The Superintendent made some calls, pulling rank to get exactly what he needed, and hoped to god Harvey hadn't caused him to look a fool. Meanwhile Harvey was laid next to his wife holding a towel to her bleeding throat, praying no main arteries or airways had been severed, until in the distance he heard sirens and their promptness gave him hope. Their wailing also seemed to cause another direct reaction in the room, as Rebecca suddenly walked forward and out onto the landing.

Those stars were lit up brighter than ever in the minds sky above him. Alex knew the demon was on the move. It must be taking full control of Rebecca because whatever it was doing was generating a lot of neurons to fire across the heavens above. The walls of the maze where aglow under their illumination and Alex could see precisely where they emanated from. Just one more corridor, then one more corner, and as he turned the last one he found the blackened burnt wings of the Demon waiting for him.

The paramedics rushed up the stairs to attend to Florence as Harvey ran downstairs to find Rebecca. An officer stopped him in the hallway.

'Did you see her?' Harvey snarled at the young PC.

'Who sir...?' He asked.

'Woman mid-twenties bleeding from her head, black coat...you must have she's only just gone...!' He noticed he was gripping the officers' lapels and let go.

'There's nobody on the street sir...!'

Harvey looked round to see the door that led to his back garden wide open. He pulled the young officer with him as he bolted towards it.

The Demons black lips snaked into a smile. Its teeth glinting like jagged shards of glass. 'It's you!'

'You'd better believe it.' Alex replied. Trying his best to show no fear, while understanding that for all his new knowledge he had absolutely no idea what to do now...not now he was faced with...this.

The Demon began to walk slowly, dragging its monstrous frame around the maze, circling Alex. 'I saw you...'

'Just a trace of me...we shared the same hole in the fabric of the book. You came through it five years before me but it's a crossing point that still exists, and one I intend to send you back through!' Alex was talking strong but growing weak from fighting two separate battles, and for the first time felt he may be losing both. His energies were fading fast to hold onto the book in the white world, while struggling even harder to work out how he could fight this killing machine a few feet away.

'That's your plan Mortal?' The Demon asked with a grim disdain.

'My names Alex, and yes my plan is to send you back to your lonely existence...then take the book away so you can never do it again...' He thought that sounded strong enough, like a great plan even, but at the same time he was dreadfully aware they were only words, and he doubted words would be enough to challenge this abomination.

'...Such a mighty strategy for such a sickly feeble animal. You understand that to action it you would have to kill me here and now. Look upon me. I am wrath, I am vengeance and I killed your little wife...' The Demons laughter filled the labyrinth, every step it made bringing it closer, with each revolution closing the gap, so soon it would be circling within the distance of a talons slash.

Harvey and the young officer looked around the Inspectors empty garden in desperation. The sun was slowly rising on a new day and in the half light they spotted a bloodied hand print at the top of the fence.

'Time to climb...!' Harvey ordered, so both men struggled but managed with some great effort to scramble over, and there in the dawns light they saw Rebecca with blood glistening on the back of her skull staring at the next fence which was higher still. The two policemen moved slowly towards her while she appeared to be working out her options, and better still didn't seem to be taking any notice of their approach.

'Perfect...' Harvey whispered to himself.

Suddenly a loud honk shattered the silence as the young officer trod on a children's stuffed teddy. Harvey looked over at the man then down to see the overgrown lawn strewn with various brightly coloured toys.

'...Great!' He muttered under his breath with the element of surprise now lost.

Rebecca twisted her head slowly to look at the men, showing them the bloodied knife still gripped in her hand, her face expressionless as the demons thundering roar filled her ears.

'I don't know how you imagined this would end Alex, but I can assure you that whatever it was, you were wrong. I shall tear you apart in this existence and you will die in every other...!'

The Demon was almost close enough to substantiate that threat, to rip him wide open, and Alex had nothing with which to defend or attack. The book was being loosened from his grip in the Angels dimension, in seconds it would all be over, meaning he might as well have died when he hit the cobbles for all the good this extra time had done him.

A Police helicopter came into view over the tenement buildings that backed on to the gardens. Harvey could see the faces of the officers within it and when he looked back at Rebecca she hadn't moved, still looking at the fence as if she were fighting with some inner conflict on what to do next.

'Have you got your Taser to hand officer...?' Harvey asked, confident he could end this right now.

'...No Sir.'

'What...why not...?'

'...My weapon training is next week sir...' He glanced at Harvey who stared back incredulously before giving a deep exhale. At that precise moment Rebecca made her move as she strode forward and grabbed something lying flat in the lush grass. Standing it up she leaned the frame against the fence and climbed the rungs of the children's slide to escape.

The Demon was assured enough to go right up to the mortal, after all this man had no weapons, no surprises and nowhere to run, and also it wanted to look into his eyes as it gutted him slowly. One black calloused hand took hold of Alex by the jaw as the other swung back to slice him through with its talons of weathered bone.

The police marksmen in the helicopter targeted the woman and opened fire, shooting downwards with his sound suppressed rifle. The first shot missed its target while the second tore through her shoulder and she bucked hard to the left, but then incredibly she stood straight back up again. The next bullet ripped firstly through her thigh and followed down through her opposite calf which exploded bloodied sinew, before the final shot followed its course straight and true, a perfect head shot and Rebecca crumpled over with the back of her scalp hanging off. Her body falling forward onto the slide and then with a horrible screeching sound of skin being forced over plastic she slid slowly down to the grass where she lay lifeless.

The Inspector had seen this image before but glancing around knew he was missing an element from Oscar's picture. As the helicopter wheeled away to disappear over the rooftops the officer at his side asked him what he was looking for. Harvey didn't reply, instead he scanned the garden before finally locating the missing piece. It's appearance made him smile outwardly, but in truth his heart was breaking threefold at this moment; at the memory of Oscar and his drawings, for his seriously injured wife, and at the pointless death of Allan Kosminsky...as up there stuck high in the tree to his left was a blue kite, and allowing his eyes to follow the string down he saw no one was holding it.

95

Alex was stood once more on the narrow ledge high above the stone cobbles of Dalmeny Street. This horrible moment forcing him to lose his grip on everything, his footing, his love, his life, and now quite savagely all of his gained wisdom. The incredible learnings amassed from his journeys through the book were disappearing from his mind, even though he was trying so desperately to keep them. Alex didn't want to lose it all, he wanted some of it, please just any of it. For the briefest of times he'd truly understood all things, been capable of formulating answers to the problems we all faced and had no doubt he could have been a benevolent God on earth. He imagined how he would have turned this planet into a better place, perhaps even the beautiful peaceful paradise we all dream of, but the speed and force with which his mind was emptying told him there was no way that gift could be allowed. Clearly there were rules in the universe that can be bent, manipulated, and twisted right out of shape, but they can never be broken, and will always return to their natural state.

The wind hustled suspiciously along the walls of the building as if trying to push him off. Alex was holding desperately on to his life and knowledge as long as he was able. Picturing that wisdom as a sea of white paper post it notes beginning to spiral and flutter around in his head. He tried to catch them, keep them, but inevitably every handful he grasped would have to be released when he tried to grab more. In the end he gave up scrabbling and instead imagined both his arms reaching up to the stars.

Some of the last memories to leave his mind were of the blinding light as Rebecca received the bullet to her head. With the woman killed an immense shift had occurred, and he found himself back at the table with the white world surrounding him but he couldn't understand why, surely he was dead now?

It had to be over?

What else could there be?

These questions began then instantly disappeared when he saw the Angel in the low swirling mist. It lay on the ground with its body twisted and torn; its once beautiful wings now no more than a gnarled weave of chaotic dead leaves on browning twigs, its golden hair falling away in greying tufts from its ageing skull face, and as it reached out to the book with skeletal fingers they crumbled at the joints when it looked into the eyes of man. Some dust covered saliva dribbled from its trembling parched lips, but no words would form in the death rattle it emitted, so Alex allowed this feeble animal to die out of pure mercy, and watched as the Angels arm dropped to the floor before dissipating in the wisps of grey.

What more could he do now?

Then he saw the book sitting pristine on the table, its red leather covers untouched by the carnage it both caused and contained. Alex felt the urge come back and so wanted to open it again, but this was to be his last moment, his final thought of the white world. The Heaven he'd known disappeared from his memory and with it the Angel, the Demon, and the book with all its vast knowledge. With these remembrances departed he could find no answers because he couldn't know the questions anymore. Once again he was just a normal man stood on a high ledge, trembling in the wind, waiting to commit his suicide. Again living the death he'd chosen to take away the hurt, the pain of losing the only one he'd ever truly loved, and knowing nothing could change that.

Then a voice to his left asked. 'What are you doing?'

Alex slowly, carefully, looked across as the wind began to whip by.

'...I said what the fuck are you doing?'

The boy's face looking out from under a baseball cap looked familiar to Alex; he searched for his name fairly sure he knew this boy from someplace, although he couldn't quite remember where. This felt like déjà vu because he knew that boy, he was sure of it, and deep in his emotions, in the darkest shadows of his mind, he understood this boy could change everything.

'Jay...!' Alex suddenly announced the name just as his knees were starting to buckle under the force of gravity and the exertion of remembering.

The boy's blue eyes looked alarmed. 'Do I know you?' He asked.

'You must do...' Alex replied as the tear he remembered fell from his face. He watched it tumbling and turning in the wind until it splashed apart on the cobbles. '...Help me back in...please...I don't want to die like this!' Alex stretched his left hand across the wall, his fingers crawling, insect like for grip, closer and closer towards the curious boy. '...Help me!'

Jay looked over at the man's hand and made his final decision.

DAVE PITT

<u>96</u>

It was the 11th of August in the cloudy city of Edinburgh; the people out on its bustling streets were being blown along by a strong breeze. From high on its castle walls you may command a view all the way down to the docks, or up to the hills towards the zoo. While in between there were a thousand streets, weaving strands that made up tangled grids of hotels and shops, churches and bus stops, houses and hopes, dreams and deaths, and on a good day such as this, you could witness it in its full splendour and watch it breathe…like a living machine. Its trains and trams, coaches and cars came in and the hordes would enter to feed its hunger for life, and later they would leave spreading its energy to other component parts that it nourished. All of this energy is connected and self-sustaining because it all moves and it collides and it is perpetual because matter, and what really matters, cannot ever be destroyed.

Returning from a relaxed and early lunch, Inspector Harvey Cooper pulled into the police station car park. His main concerns today were as always in the present, being logical to the point of obsession, he didn't deal in fantastical musings.

Locking the car door his phone rang, he answered it sharply on seeing it was his secretary Emma, and she related the news just coming in.

'Where…?' He asked, as the cogs of his mind began clicking into place. Then on reaching her office the secretary put down the phone and continued to explain the situation to him face to face.

'Dalmeny Street you said…?' Harvey recognised the name vaguely.

Emma checked her computer screen again for more details. '…Yes the one down Leith Walk…two males have been found seriously injured. An older man appears to have been stabbed and a younger male hit by a vehicle or fallen from a height…it's too early to tell.'

Even with his excitement growing Harvey's first thought was for his wife, as the lovely Florence would have to be called now because this might end up being a late one. A smile danced across his mouth as he entered his office while looking over the initial report. It was another moment to remind him of how much he loved his wife, loved this job, the thrill of the chase. He placed the sheet of paper down and sat back in his chair to think on this new curious case. 'Some things never change!' He said to himself, before deciding to head on over to the hospital and check on the two men.

THE LIFE MACHINE

THE END...

Printed in Great Britain
by Amazon

23103966R10233